THE

"Jodi is a very likable and relatable character, and the novel delivers on its promise to wrap things up satisfactorily, but not without many juicy twists along the way." —*Bookreporter*

Praise for

CUL-DE-SAC

"As perfect a character-based thriller as you can find. . . . Fielding has created some of her strongest, most compelling characters. An outstanding thriller and a perfect beach read."

—*Booklist* (starred review)

"[A] gripping psychological thriller. . . . As Fielding slowly reveals each character's secrets, she nicely upsets readers' perceptions and expectations as they try to figure out who will be the first to snap—and who will die. Suspense fans will be well rewarded." —*Publishers Weekly*

"Set within an upscale neighborhood brimming with dark secrets, this captivating thriller thrums with delicious foreboding on every page. I was entranced by the gifted storytelling and magnetic characters, whose twisted paths converge in a shocking, explosive climax. *Cul-de-sac* proves once again that Joy Fielding is an ingenious master of domestic suspense."

—Samantha M. Bailey, #1 national bestselling author of *Woman on the Edge*

PRAISE FOR JOY FIELDING

"Fielding masterfully manipulates our expectations."
—*The Washington Post*

"Sort of like experiencing the horrific head-on crash between two speeding runaway super-trains before the crash actually takes place, this is what it feels like to get inside a Joy Fielding novel and meet her characters, one thunderous explosion after another until finally the main event is upon us and the loose ends are tied up. Disgruntlement then settles in because you know it will be between eighteen months and two years before you get your next fix of Fielding suspense." —*Toronto Star*

"Fielding is a master of anticipation and knows how to create a labyrinth of tension, never providing an exit until the very last page. To date, I have never been able to guess the surprise ending of a novel by Fielding." —*The Globe and Mail* on *Lost*

"A wild ride with a life all its own, strewn with surprises and consequences for all parties along the way. Fielding's characters and plot are strong and well-developed. The story is gripping, always leaving the reader guessing, and culminates in a deliciously untamed twist of a conclusion."
—*Winnipeg Free Press* on *The Wild Zone*

"If you're in the mood to bury yourself in a book . . . pick up Joy Fielding's latest novel. . . . It's guaranteed to reduce you to tears, and once they've dried, will leave you feeling a little readier to tackle life's challenges."
—*Montreal Gazette* on *Puppet*

By Joy Fielding

THE HOUSEKEEPER

A NOVEL

JOY FIELDING

SEAL BOOKS

SEAL BOOKS, 2023

THE HOUSEKEEPER
Seal Books/published by arrangement with Penguin Random House Canada
Doubleday Canada edition published 2022

Library and Archives Canada Cataloguing in Publication
Title: The housekeeper / Joy Fielding.
Names: Fielding, Joy, author.
Description: Previously published: Toronto: Doubleday Canada, 2022.
Identifiers: Canadiana 20220175691 | ISBN 9781400027026 (softcover)
Classification: LCC PS8561.I52 H68 2023 | DDC C813/.54—dc23

Cover design: Derek Walls
Cover image: © Mark Owen / Trevillion Images
Title-page art: stock.adobe.com/soupstock

Printed in the United States of America

www.penguinrandomhouse.ca

2 4 6 8 9 7 5 3 1

Penguin
Random
House

To Warren,
always

THE HOUSEKEEPER

— ONE —

It's my fault.

I'm the one who first brought up the idea, who championed it, who set the ball rolling, and who ultimately insisted on hiring her. My father was adamantly opposed to the idea, my mother ambivalent at best, my sister as indifferent as always. Only my husband, Harrison, thought it was a good idea, and only because he hoped it would take some of the strain off me.

"You do too much," he was always saying. Followed by "There are things you can control and things you can't. You can't be all things to all people. Concentrate on *our* family. Let the rest go."

He was right, of course. Except it wasn't that easy to just let the rest go. And try as I might, I couldn't help hearing the unstated corollary: *If only you'd put half the effort and energy into our house . . . our children . . . our marriage, as you do into your parents . . . your sister . . . your career . . .*

Forget that it was precisely that career that not only covered our mortgage, but paid all the bills, thus allowing him the luxury of working full-time, and without any noticeable remuneration, on his latest novel.

I say "latest," although it's been almost a decade since his first novel was published. To great acclaim, I might add. But still . . . If I sold only one house every ten years, I think I might be tempted to try my hand at something else.

To this, Harrison would undoubtedly point out that writing is more a calling than a career, rather like the priesthood, and nothing at all like selling real estate in an overheated, overpriced market. This would likely be followed by "It's not easy to create anything of value with two young children underfoot."

This last argument might hold more merit were it not for the fact that our son, Samuel, who is eight, is in school most of the day, and our daughter, Daphne, age three, is in daycare. True, Harrison is sometimes tasked with putting them to bed when I have an evening showing, or entertaining them when I have weekend appointments. Selling real estate isn't exactly a nine-to-five profession. Rather like writing, I'm tempted to say.

But, of course, I don't, because it would likely lead to a confrontation. And I hate confrontations.

"The male ego is a fragile thing," my mother once told me. And she would know. She was married to my father—never the easiest of men—for almost fifty years.

Not that my mother was any shrinking violet. She gave as good as she got, and their loud fights were legendary in their upscale neighborhood of Rosedale. Some of my earliest memories consist of lying in bed with my hands pressed tightly against my ears, in a vain effort to block out the angry accusations and furious denials flying up the stairs, threatening to burst through the door to the room I shared with my sister, who lay sleeping in the twin bed next to mine, as oblivious as always. Even now, when I can't sleep, I hear their raised voices piercing the stillness of the night to shout in my ear.

A therapist would no doubt explain that this would account for my aversion to confrontations. And the therapist would probably be right.

If only the rest of what happened were so easy to explain.

Of course, my mother's voice had all but disappeared in recent years, lost to the unrelenting ravages of Parkinson's disease. In response, my father, having lost his favorite sparring partner, had little choice but to mellow accordingly.

Oh, he could still be difficult—the male ego is a fragile thing, after all—but he could also be solicitous and even tender on occasion. Eight years ago, he resigned his position as head of the real estate company he founded—yes, the same company for which I work—to devote himself full-time to my mother's care.

A noble idea, to be sure.

But the man was in his late seventies, and while he remained healthy and enviably spry—not to mention still rakishly handsome—he was no longer a young man. And caring for a woman with advanced Parkinson's is no easy chore at any age.

Which is why I suggested hiring a live-in housekeeper.

An idea that was promptly, and soundly, rejected. ("We're quite capable of managing on our own, thank you very much!" he bellowed.)

I tried enlisting my sister's help. Tracy, four years my senior, had always been my parents' favorite, a blond, blue-eyed goddess, standing six feet tall and weighing all of one hundred and twenty-five pounds. (For the record, my hair and eyes are matching shades of light brown, my height is a less impressive five feet, seven inches, and the last time I weighed a hundred and twenty-five pounds, I was twenty-one years old, some twenty years ago.)

For as long as I can remember, one of the first things out of my father's mouth whenever I visited was always "Have you put on a little weight?" (Again, for the record, my weight is fine. In fact, I'm considered slim by all my friends.)

At any rate, Tracy declined to get involved, which could be another reason that she'd always been my parents' favorite, despite the fact she rarely visited, and then only when she was short of cash.

So, the idea of hiring live-in help was relegated to the proverbial back burner.

Until the day my mother fell out of bed and my father was unable to lift her back up on his own. He tried phoning me but I was at a showing and had my phone turned off; Harrison was too preoccupied staring at the blank screen of his computer to pick up, and Tracy hovered over her caller ID for maybe half a second before deciding not to answer and returning her cellphone to her pocket. The result was that my mother lay on the cold hardwood floor for the better part of two hours, my father reluctant to summon an ambulance—"We're quite capable of managing on our own! We don't need strangers marching through our house, passing judgment on our belongings!"—before I finally checked my messages and rushed over.

Which is when I put my foot down and insisted that my dad hire a housekeeper. They quite clearly could no longer "manage on their own." And the cleaning lady they employed once a week—actually a succession of cleaning ladies, as no one was ever good enough to satisfy my dad for more than a few months—would no longer suffice. They needed someone who lived in, I argued, someone to assist in my mother's care, as well as cook and keep the house clean. Money wasn't an issue. God knows they had more than enough. It was a matter of their well-being.

Reluctantly, my father gave in, and allowed me to start interviewing candidates. He gave strict instructions: her references had to be impeccable, and while she had to be strong enough to assist in getting my mother in and out of bed, she also had to be slim and attractive. If he had to endure the presence of an outsider living in his house, he insisted, then the least she could be was pleasant to look at.

Enter Elyse Woodley.

A young-looking sixty-two years old, tall, slender but with noticeably muscular upper arms, short blond hair, and an engaging smile that emphasized her equally engaging manner, she seemed almost too good to be true.

And what is it they say about things that seem too good to be true?

So maybe I should have been more suspicious. Or at least paid closer attention. Tracy claims the signs were there from the start, although she never voiced any such concerns at the time. She says that what happened had all the elements of a good mystery novel: the creaky old house, the aging invalid and the duplicitous housekeeper assigned to her care, the subtle clues, the red herrings, the dead body at the foot of the stairs.

But I'm getting ahead of myself. The dead body comes later.

And if there's any mystery as to what transpired, it's how I let it happen.

In the end, I have only myself to blame.

I'm the one who let her in.

− T W O −

"What do you know about Parkinson's disease?"

It was always the first question I asked. I wanted to make sure that whoever I hired knew exactly what they were signing up for.

Elyse Woodley sat across from me in one of two matching ivory-colored tub chairs facing the lime-green velvet sofa in our rarely used living room to the left of the front door. She was wearing a yellow, short-sleeved blouse, navy cotton pants, and open-toed sandals. Small gold-and-pearl earrings peeked out from under the neat waves of her chin-length blond hair, the earrings and a plain gold watch the only jewelry she wore. I noticed the lack of a wedding ring and was grateful. One less complication, I remember thinking.

I'd chosen the living room to conduct my interviews, not because it was the most formal of the downstairs rooms but because it was the least cluttered. All the other rooms—the small dining room with its perpetually smudged glass tabletop, the modern open-concept kitchen with its large granite-topped center island, the adjoining family room overlooking a vertical sliver of backyard—were overrun with my children's toys. It was hard to take a step without tripping over a Super Mario figurine or stray piece of Lego. (And don't get me started on the stubborn and seemingly indestructible globs of Play-Doh that clung to virtually every surface.)

"I know that it's a disorder of the nervous system that primarily affects bodily movement," she replied. "That it gets progressively worse. And that there is no cure," she added softly.

I had to bite my tongue to keep from yelling "You're hired!" right then and there. Most of the women I'd interviewed up to that point—six in total—had simply shaken their heads and uttered variations of "Not much."

"Do you think you could handle looking after someone in its late stages?"

"I think so. My mother suffered from MS for years, and my last employer had cancer and was pretty much bedridden during the final year of his life, so I have a lot of experience dealing with degenerative diseases." She produced a sympathetic smile. Dimples, like large commas, appeared at the sides of her mouth. "Plus, I'm a lot tougher than I look."

I explained my mother's situation in greater, excruciating detail: that she'd been diagnosed approximately ten years earlier, her symptoms following along the normal, prescribed path, starting innocuously enough with the trembling of her baby fingers—what the doctors called "resting tremors"—followed by slowed movement and increasing muscle weakness leading to rigidity, and a change in her once-perfect posture that ultimately resulted in a frozen gait.

My mother had been a dancer all her life, and now it seemed as if her feet were glued to the ground. She lunged instead of walked. What's more, her handwriting had shrunk until it became so small as to be illegible, due to changes in those parts of the brain that affect motor skills, and made it difficult, if not impossible, to control the movement of her fingers and hands.

She had difficulty sleeping, perspired excessively, and suffered from frequent bouts of constipation. "It's a lot to deal with," I was forced to admit, reluctant to leave anything out and risk her quitting when the extent of my mother's illness became too obvious to ignore, "even though my father will insist on being her primary caregiver. So the job would probably involve more housekeeping and cooking," I said hopefully, "and being around in case . . ."

". . . they need me," Elyse said, finishing the sentence for me. "You might want to breathe," she advised, dark eyes widening as the dimples returned to tease the sides of her lips.

I realized I'd been holding my breath, and I laughed, although the sound that emerged was more of someone gasping for air. I pictured an old tree, gnarled and twisted in on itself, and wondered if that's how she saw me. "Do you have any questions?" I asked, bracing myself for queries about salary and vacations, the first questions out of the mouths of all six previous applicants.

"When would you like me to start?" she asked instead, then quickly, "Oh, my goodness. How presumptuous of me! I'm so sorry. I didn't mean to assume. My son warns me about that all the time. He says I make assumptions . . ."

"You have a son?"

"Yes. Andrew. He's about your age. Lives in California. Los Angeles. That's where I'm from originally."

"How long have you lived in Toronto? If you don't mind my asking . . ." I added, having read somewhere that would-be employers aren't permitted to ask too many personal questions of prospective employees, although I wasn't sure if that applied to this type of position. It seemed to me that if you were inviting someone to live in your home, you should be entitled to know at least some basic things about them.

"I don't mind at all," she answered easily. "I came here nine years ago, soon after my mother died. I needed a holiday, so I bought a ticket on one of those train trips across Canada, and just fell in love with both the country and its people. One man in particular, if I'm being honest." She raised a hand to her face to hide her blush. "I met this lovely man soon after arriving in Toronto, and three months later, we were married. Everything was perfect. Until it wasn't." She sighed, one of those giant exhales that involve one's whole body. "We were watching TV one night—it'll be four years this September—and Charlie said he was feeling a little dizzy, and next thing I knew . . . he was dead. A brain aneurysm, the doctors said." She paused, her gaze following her words into the past, lingering. "So I was widowed a second time. My first husband, Andrew's father," she continued, unprompted, "he died as well. Massive heart attack when he was barely older than Andrew is now."

"I'm so sorry," I began, not sure what else to say. What I was thinking was that, in some perverse way, they were lucky. Brain aneurysms and massive heart attacks seemed a preferable way to die than the slow, merciless progression of Parkinson's disease.

"Yes, well. Not much one can do except go on. We'd been living in an apartment near St. Clair and Yonge when Charlie died, and I started helping one of my elderly neighbors with her grocery shopping. Soon I was bringing over homemade cookies—I love to bake—and eventually her family hired me to prepare meals, look after the apartment, and keep her company. My son, of course, was horrified that his mother would stoop to doing such menial work. He's a bit of a snob that way. But the truth is that I enjoy looking after people. I'm used to it. And I'm good at it. Besides, I didn't want to move back to L.A. and be a burden to Andrew. He has his own life to live." She leaned forward conspiratorially. "To be completely honest . . . I'm not overly fond of his wife."

I suppressed a smile. "Do you have grandchildren?"

"No." She shook her head. An obvious sore point.

As if on cue, the house erupted with the sound of loud squabbling from upstairs—"Mom, Daphne's taking my things!" "Mommy, Sam's being mean!"

"Daphne," I called back, "stop taking Sam's things. Sam, stop being mean to your sister."

"She won't give me back my Nintendo Switch!"

"He said I could play with it."

"No, I didn't! Give it back."

"Mommy, he's being mean!"

"What's a Nintendo Switch?" Elyse asked.

"Jodi, for God's sake," a male voice interrupted, his words hurtling down the stairs. "Can you do something, please? I'm trying to work."

"My husband," I explained to Elyse. "He's a writer."

"How lovely. Would I be familiar with any of his work?"

I shrugged. "Possibly. He wrote a book called *Comes the Dreamer.*"

"I don't think I know it."

"Well, it was a while back."

"Mom!" Sam cried.

"Mommy!" Daphne echoed.

"Jodi!"

"Okay, kids, that's enough. Get down here. Now." Within seconds, my children scrambled down the stairs and into view, Sam a skinny flagpole of a boy, Daphne a pudgy little bundle of energy, both with my somewhat unruly brown hair and their father's inquisitive blue eyes.

"Who are you?" Sam asked Elyse, eyeing her suspiciously.

"This is Mrs. Woodley," I said.

"Elyse, please," she corrected. "What beautiful children. Such a handsome young man," she said to Sam. "And you," she said, turning her attention to Daphne. "You're just a little cupcake of cuteness, aren't you?"

Both children beamed.

"When I grow up, I'm going to live in New York," Sam announced, something he'd never mentioned before.

"When *I* grow up," Daphne followed, "*I'm* going to live in New York. I'm going to work in a crayon factory," she added for good measure.

I wasn't sure whether to be amused or appalled. *A crayon factory?* I thought.

"What a lovely idea," Elyse said. "Then you could make your own crayons and color all day long."

Daphne nodded enthusiastically.

"I'm hungry," Sam said.

Elyse promptly rose to her feet. For a second, I thought she was about to go into the kitchen and start preparing dinner. Instead she reached into her purse and brought out a lavender piece of paper. "My references," she said, handing the paper over to me. "Why don't you check them out and get back to me once you've finished your interviews. And, of course, if you have any further questions, feel free to call me anytime."

"But we haven't even discussed salary or vacations," I began, reluctant to let her leave.

"I'm sure that what you have in mind will be more than fair," she said, holding out her hand toward Sam. "So nice meeting you, Sam," she said as he latched onto her fingers. "And you, Daphne. I hope to see you both again very soon. And I'm going to go right out and buy your husband's book," she said as we reached the front door.

I watched her disappear down the tree-lined street, fighting the urge to run after her and tackle her into the nearest clump of spring flowers, tell her that the job was hers, that there was no need to check her references or interview anyone else, and that we would gladly pay her anything she asked, give her as many holidays as she desired.

There had to be a catch, I remember thinking. Nobody was that perfect. But the unpleasant thought was quickly drowned out by my children's voices.

"I'm hungry," Sam wailed behind me.

"I'm a cupcake of cuteness," his sister said.

—THREE—

"What do you mean, you hired her?" my sister demanded. "Without consulting me? Without my even meeting her?"

"I asked you to be present," I reminded her.

"And I told you, I had an exercise class that afternoon."

"You have an exercise class *every* afternoon," I pointed out, noting the black leggings and cropped white T-shirt bearing the Goodlife logo that she was wearing. Discomfort fluttered through my chest like a trapped butterfly. The last thing I wanted was an argument. I'd been feeling more optimistic, less stressed, than I had in weeks, and I'd invited Tracy for dinner—salmon, one of the few things she ate—to celebrate our good fortune in having secured Elyse's services.

Tracy tucked her long blond hair, blow-dried ramrod straight, behind one ear, then shook her head, so that her hair returned to the exact spot it had been initially. She adjusted the silver Tiffany heart around her neck and lifted one shapely leg to rest her bare foot on the purple suede of the sectional sofa in our family room. "Oh, God.

What *is* this?" she asked, surgically straightened nose and Juvéderm-filled lips crinkling with disdain as she extricated a small mass of hot pink Play-Doh from her heel.

"Sorry." I peeled the offending blob from her fingers and pushed myself off the sofa, walking the several steps into our kitchen and throwing the offending Play-Doh into the garbage bin under the sink.

"Could you get me a glass of water while you're there?" Tracy asked. "Ew," she said when I handed it to her. "It's not very cold. You don't have any bottled water in the fridge?"

"Sorry." Two apologies in less than one minute, I thought. Possibly a new record.

She deposited the glass on the end table beside her without taking a sip. "So, tell me all about this Elyse Woodley."

"She's perfect," I said, reclaiming my seat on the other side of the sectional. Immediately, I felt a small plastic superhero dig into my side. "Patient, kind, lots of experience with the elderly and people with medical problems . . ."

"You checked her references?"

"Of course. They couldn't have been more glowing." I'd spoken to both the daughter of Elyse's erstwhile neighbor and the son of the man who'd died from cancer, and both had been nothing short of rapturous in their praise. "Trust me. I interviewed a lot of women. She was far and away the best."

"So, how much is Wonder Woman costing us?" Tracy asked.

"Dad's paying for everything," I reminded her.

"Out of our inheritance."

"Tracy, for God's sake!"

"Oh, don't be such a goody-goody. It's true."

I had no desire to debate the issue, so I said nothing.

Tracy shrugged. "You haven't told me what Dad thinks of her."

My turn to shrug. "He hasn't met her yet."

"You hired her without Dad's approval? Are you kidding me?"

"The offer is obviously conditional on both sides liking what they see. I'm meeting her at Mom and Dad's tomorrow. One o'clock. You're more than welcome to join us."

"Why do you always pick a time when I have something else on?" Tracy asked. "You could check with me first, you know."

"Maybe you could reschedule," I suggested, ignoring the challenge in her voice.

"Maybe."

"You haven't visited them in a while," I ventured, issuing an implied challenge of my own. "I'm sure Mom would be thrilled . . ."

"You know I have a hard time seeing her this way."

"It's not easy for anybody."

"You don't understand. You're better with these things than I am. I'm too sensitive . . ."

"This isn't about you," I said, recognizing the futility of my words even as I spoke them. *Everything* was about Tracy. Oddly enough, it was part of her charm.

Another shrug. Another "Maybe."

Once more I rose from my seat and headed for the kitchen, ostensibly to check on the salmon and vegetables I had marinating in the fridge, although there was no need to do so. But there was only so much I could take of my sister's self-absorption without wanting to hurl something at her head, and the plastic superhero digging into my side was a little too convenient for comfort.

"So, where is everyone?" Tracy asked, looking around, as if noticing for the first time that neither my husband nor my children were anywhere in sight. Which was likely the case. "It's so quiet."

"Harrison is picking Daphne up at daycare. He took Sam with him."

"He's a good dad," she remarked.

"Yes, he is."

"He does a lot with them."

"He's their father," I reminded her.

"Still, not all fathers are so involved," she said, perhaps thinking of our own father. "You're lucky."

"Yes, I am."

"Harrison's lucky, too. You're a really good mom," she added, catching me off guard. I was unused to compliments from my sister. From anyone in my family. We weren't exactly a family given to expressing our more positive feelings, although we seemed to have no trouble highlighting the negative. I couldn't remember the last time any one of us had said, "I love you." Had we ever? I wondered. Was that the reason I made sure to tell my children every day how much I adored them, to make sure they never doubted their worth?

"I like to think I'm a good mom," I said, feeling guilty about my earlier unkind thoughts where Tracy was concerned. "I try."

"Will Harrison be teaching that creative writing course again this summer?"

"Yes. He's looking forward to it."

"Maybe I should sign up for it."

"What?"

"Well, I've had an interesting life, and I have a good imagination. How hard can it be to write a novel?"

There's a little thing called discipline, I thought, but decided not to say. "I don't think it's as easy as you think," I said instead.

"You just don't think I can do it."

"Not so," I protested. "I think you'd be great at whatever you set your mind to." It was true. The problem was that Tracy never set her mind to anything, at least not for any length of time. She was what Harrison called "a dabbler." In the last few years alone, she'd spent a small fortune of our parents' money on training to be a Pilates instructor, a yoga instructor, a teacher of modern dance, an instructor at the Arthur Murray dance studios, a bartender, a runway model, and a nutritionist, only to abandon each course before the first semester was complete. There'd also been lessons in bridge, tennis, and golf, none of which she subsequently pursued.

The same was true with the men in her life, a largely appalling cross-section of suitors who usually disappeared after one or two dates.

"I wish I could be more like you," she was saying, another unexpected compliment that underlined my lack of generosity. "But this whole regular job, marriage-and-kids thing isn't for me. You're so good at it. I'm just too creative, too much of a free spirit."

Now, *this* was the kind of backhanded compliment I was used to, the kind I'd grown up with. My father was a master at it. I smiled. I couldn't fault my sister for learning from the best.

The front door suddenly opened and Sam and Daphne burst through.

"So much for quiet," Tracy said as Harrison closed the door behind him and Sam and Daphne raced down the hall toward us.

"Look who's here," I said as they flew into my arms. "Say hi to Auntie Tracy."

"Hi, Auntie Tracy," Sam obliged.

"Hi, Auntie Tracy," echoed Daphne.

"Hi, Auntie Tracy," Harrison said, leaning against the wall.

"How was school today?" I asked my son.

"Good," he replied.

"And daycare?" I asked my daughter.

"There was a slight problem," Harrison said.

"I don't want to go back there anymore," Daphne said.

"What happened, cupcake?" I'd taken to calling her that ever since Elyse's interview.

"There's this boy. Joshua. He calls me names."

"What kind of names does he call you?" By the look of consternation on her face, I doubted that "cupcake" was one of them.

Daphne straightened her shoulders and puffed out her cheeks. "He calls me a fucker and a sucker," she announced.

I looked at Tracy; she looked at me. We both burst into great whoops of laughter.

"Very nice, ladies," Harrison admonished. "Very grown up."

"Will you come with me to daycare tomorrow and tell him not to call me a fucker and a sucker anymore?" Daphne asked, clearly emboldened by our reaction.

"I think you can handle that all by yourself," I told her when I could find my voice.

"Just tell him to go fuck himself," Tracy said.

"Okay, kids," Harrison said quickly. "Why don't you go upstairs and watch TV in Mommy and Daddy's room until dinner is ready."

"Yay!" they both shouted, disappearing up the stairs.

"Really?" Harrison asked Tracy. " *'Tell him to go fuck himself'?*"

Tracy shrugged. "Come join us." She patted the cushion beside her. "You might want to take the stick out of your ass before you sit down."

I had to bite down on my lower lip to stifle a budding but untimely smile. Too late. Harrison had seen it and I could tell that he was annoyed.

"I think I'll try to get some work in before dinner," he said. "Maybe you could talk to the supervisor at daycare tomorrow, get this straightened out."

We watched him climb the stairs until he was out of sight. "Didn't he used to be a lot more fun?" Tracy asked.

FOUR

The large, three-level house at 223 Scarth Road had been built in 1932 and, from the outside, looked every one of its years. If I were describing it to prospective buyers, I'd advise them to try to look past the dark redbrick exterior and thick, old-fashioned windows that made the place look, in a word—my son's word, actually—"spooky." I'd assure them that the inside of the house was a different story altogether.

And, for the most part, it was.

My parents had remodeled the interior several times since purchasing the house almost half a century ago, installing copper plumbing and wiring, stripping the walls of their heavy brocade wallpaper in favor of a crisp white paint job throughout, repeatedly updating the kitchen and bathrooms to keep up with the latest trends, enlarging the closets, and even creating a home theater and fully equipped exercise room on the lower level, a level that opened onto a fully landscaped back garden with a large, free-form swimming pool.

Yet, despite all the updates, the house has retained a curiously old-fashioned feel. Maybe it's because of the enormous staircase with its ornate mahogany banister that sits in the middle of the huge center hall; maybe it's the wide wooden ceiling beams and dark wainscoting of the cavernous living and dining rooms; maybe it's the fact that there are just so many separate rooms, in contrast to the more open-concept layouts favored by today's home buyers.

Interestingly, despite its more than five thousand square feet, the house is one of the smaller homes on the street and, despite its slowly crumbling, "spooky" façade, would likely sell for a not-so-small fortune in this most desirous of locations within days of being listed.

Except that my father had no interest in selling.

I tried for years to persuade my parents to move to a condo, especially after my mother's diagnosis. Or even a small bungalow, I suggested. Something without stairs. Something easier to manage. My father wouldn't hear of it. This was their home, he insisted. They weren't going anywhere.

Now, of course, it was no longer an option. My mother would likely not survive a move.

My father's one concession was to install a small elevator to the right of the staircase. Initially, it saw a lot of action, but the last year had seen its usage sharply decline, my mother too crippled to venture out, too weak to sit in the garden for any length of time, too proud to enjoy being pushed through the streets of Rosedale in the wheelchair she despised.

I saw Tracy sitting behind the wheel of her sporty red Audi at the end of the street as soon as I turned the corner onto Scarth Road. I pulled my decidedly un-sporty white SUV into our parents' driveway and exited the car, walking down the street to where my sister was parked. "What are you doing all the way down here?" I asked, leaning toward her open window.

"You weren't here yet, and I didn't want to get trapped in the driveway, in case I want to leave early," she explained, swinging long, bare legs out of the car. She was wearing a short pale pink sundress and matching flats, her long hair pulled into a low ponytail.

"You look nice," I told her, hoping she might offer up something in return, but whatever she thought of the beige skirt and flower-print blouse I was wearing, she kept to herself. "Why didn't you go inside?"

She rolled her eyes, as if this was answer enough. "So, where's Mary Poppins?"

I checked my watch. "She should be here any minute."

"Not a good sign, if she's late."

"She still has ten minutes."

Another roll of her eyes as Tracy reached inside her purse for her mirrored pink sunglasses.

"Those are cute," I said as she pushed them over the bridge of her nose. "New?"

"Tom Ford. They cost a fortune."

I wouldn't expect anything less, I thought, but didn't say. "I guess we should probably head in," I said instead.

"Do we have to?" she whined.

"Well, we can't very well stand in the middle of the sidewalk until Elyse gets here."

"Why can't we?"

"Because," I started, then stopped, deciding there was no point in trying to come up with a suitable response. Instead, I turned and started walking back toward the house, leaving Tracy no choice but to follow me.

"Wait."

"What?"

"What if Dad hates her?"

"Then we'll find somebody else."

"*You'll* find somebody else," Tracy corrected. "I'm not going through this again."

Just what exactly have you gone through? I asked silently, another thought I kept to myself.

Tracy followed me down the street and up the concrete path to my parents' front porch. "Wait," she said again, stopping on the bottom of three stairs. "I need a minute."

I was losing patience, about to say something I would probably regret, when the door opened.

Elyse Woodley stood, smiling, on the other side. She was wearing white pants and a lilac-colored T-shirt, the outfit highlighting her slim figure and well-toned arms. "Well, hello there, you two," she said, her smile stretching toward her ears. "We were wondering what you were doing out here. Come in. Come in."

Come in, come in, said the spider to the fly, I think now.

At the time, of course, I was thinking no such thing.

And by the time it occurred to me, it was too late.

-FIVE-

"**Y**ou're late," my father said, entering the large center hall from the back of the house as Tracy closed the front door. He was dressed in black cotton pants and a blue golf shirt, his ample gray hair freshly washed and neatly combed off his forehead.

"Actually, they're right on time," Elyse said, her voice so warm and welcoming that it would have been hard for anyone, even my father, to take offense. "*I* was early," she confided. "I took the bus and I wasn't sure how long that would take, so I gave myself more than enough time. You must be Tracy."

"That I am," my sister acknowledged. "Nice to meet you. Jodi has been singing your praises."

"And your father has been singing yours. He's very proud. Of both of you," Elyse added quickly.

"Is that so?" Tracy raised one beautifully sculpted eyebrow. "How are you doing, Daddy?"

"Very well, thank you," he told her. "Is that a new dress?"

"Victoria Beckham," she said, naming the former

Spice Girl who had become one of the world's top fashion designers, and doing a little twirl in place.

I didn't even want to think how much that dress had cost, although how Tracy spent her money was *her* business, not mine, I reminded myself. I had no right to be judgmental.

Except, of course, it wasn't her money. My father covered all her credit card purchases and living expenses. And while I tried not to let that upset me, regularly telling myself that I was in the fortunate position of not having to ask him for money, it still rankled. "Hi, Dad," I said. "You're looking quite dapper." Once again, a return compliment failed to materialize. "How's Mom today?"

"Same as yesterday and the day before that."

"She seemed in good spirits," Elyse said.

"You've seen her?"

"Your father gave me a tour of the house and he introduced us. Such a beautiful woman, despite everything. Shall we go into the kitchen and chat?" she asked. "I brought over some brownies I made this morning, and I've got a kettle on for some tea."

"Sounds lovely," I said. I glanced back at Tracy. The glance said, *Could she* be *any more fabulous?*

We followed my father and Elyse into the all-white gourmet kitchen overlooking the backyard. The garden was in full bloom, with tiers of flowers and blossoming bushes in vibrant shades of coral, red, and pink.

"Oh, good. You've opened the pool," Tracy said, plopping into one of four wicker chairs at the round table in front of the huge floor-to-ceiling window. "Maybe I'll come for a swim on Saturday."

"Good idea," I said. "I'll bring the kids."

"How *are* those beautiful children?" Elyse asked before my sister could object.

"They're terrific, thank you."

My father looked me up and down, his eyes narrowing. "Have you put on a little weight?" he said.

I forced a laugh. "No, Dad. Same as always." *Same as yesterday. And the day before that.* "Here, Elyse," I offered as she was about to pour the boiling water into a china teapot. "Let me help you with that."

"Absolutely not. You sit down. Everything is ready. We'll just let the tea steep for a few minutes."

I glanced at the plate in the middle of the table, feeling my mouth water. "The brownies look wonderful."

"Let's hope they're as good as they look," Elyse said. "That's a beautiful blouse," she told me. "I love a bold print."

"It's bold, all right," Tracy muttered as I took the seat opposite hers.

"You don't like it?" I asked.

"Well, bold prints aren't exactly my style, but it's very . . . you."

I nodded, deciding it was as close to a compliment as I was likely to get.

"Please, everyone. Help yourself to a brownie." Elyse began pouring the tea into the china cups already laid out.

"No brownie for me, thank you," Tracy said.

"Tracy is very health-conscious," our father explained as I reached for the biggest one.

"I'm lucky," Tracy said. "I've never had much of a sweet tooth."

"Unlike Jodi," our father added, shaking his head. "Audrey and I found her in the pantry one afternoon, having eaten her way through an entire box of chocolate chip cookies."

"I was five at the time," I reminded him.

Elyse laughed. "Sounds just like me. I could honestly eat nothing but desserts all day."

"And yet you manage to stay so slim," my father remarked.

"Good metabolism." Elyse shrugged. "And the luck of the draw. Well?" she asked, looking from me to my father. "What's the verdict?"

"Delicious," my father and I said together.

At last, I thought. *Something we agree on.*

"I'm so glad. There's milk and sugar for the tea." Elyse's long, elegant fingers motioned toward the middle of the table.

"Neither for me," Tracy said as I helped myself to both.

"So," Elyse began. "I'm sure you have questions. Who wants to go first?"

We spent the next half hour discussing my father's requirements and concerns. But it was just for show, really. We all knew it was a done deal. The invisible contract had been signed the minute Elyse waltzed through the front door twenty minutes early, carrying a plate of homemade brownies. Even before Tracy and I arrived, she'd managed to disarm our father with her effortless charm and trim physique.

Although being my father, he wasn't about to let her know that.

"Would you mind letting us talk everything over?" he asked as she was clearing the kitchen table. "Jodi will get back to you this evening."

"Sounds perfectly reasonable," Elyse replied. If she was at all put off by the request, it didn't show. "It was a real pleasure meeting you both," she said to Tracy and my father as she was leaving. "And please say goodbye to Mrs. Dundas for me."

We watched her walk down the front path. Once again, it took all my self-restraint to keep from running after her and tackling her to the ground.

"Are you kidding me?" I asked my father as he was shutting the front door. "What's there to talk about? She's phenomenal!" I looked to Tracy for confirmation.

Tracy shrugged. "It's up to Dad."

"You don't think she's perfect?" I pressed.

"She seems nice enough," Tracy conceded. "But it's not what *I* think that counts."

Our father smiled. "You can call Mrs. Woodley this evening. Tell her we talked it over and we're willing to give it a go."

"I don't understand why you didn't just tell her that before she left."

"Because it's never a good idea to let the help get the upper hand," he said, winking at Tracy, as if it was something I would never understand.

"Okay. Fine. Whatever," I said, silently bristling at his condescending use of the word "help," and thinking we'd be lucky if Elyse stuck around a week before running for the hills.

"I should get going," Tracy said.

"Aren't you going to say hi to Mom?"

"Of course I'm going to say hi to Mom," Tracy said, although the daggers shooting from her eyes indicated she'd had no such intention.

I followed her up the wide staircase. The top floor had four bedrooms, two at the front of the house and two at the back, each with its own en suite bathroom. When we were little, my sister and I had shared the larger room overlooking the street, our father using the room across the hall as his home office.

"Maybe she's asleep," Tracy said as we approached the huge master bedroom overlooking the back garden. "We don't want to disturb her," she added, trying to disguise the hope in her voice as concern.

The door was open and I peeked inside. A king-size four-poster bed sat against one white wall, our mother wan and minuscule inside its voluminous sheets. Her failing body was propped up by three well-stuffed pillows at her back and three more supporting each arm. Two years ago, after her condition made it impossible for her and my father to continue sharing a bed, he'd moved into the smaller bedroom across the hall.

"Hi, Mom," I said, approaching the bed and running my hand over her thinning gray hair, hair that was once thick and dark, hair she used to be so proud of, took such pains with.

She twisted her head slowly in my direction. "Hello, dear," she said, her eyes searching the room. "Is that Tracy?"

"Yes, Mom. It's me," Tracy said from the doorway. "How are you feeling today?"

"Better, now that you're here. Come closer. Let me see you." One arm jerked out to grab at Tracy's hand. "What a beautiful dress."

"It's Victoria Beckham," Tracy said, forgoing the accompanying twirl. "So, what did you think of Elyse Woodley?"

"She seems very nice," our mother whispered, pushing each word out with difficulty, the frozen expression on her face revealing nothing.

"We interviewed a lot of women," Tracy went on. "She was far and away the best."

"You're a sweet thing to go to so much trouble."

If Tracy had any qualms about stealing credit for my work, she did a good job hiding it. She hung around a few more minutes, then excused herself. "I'll come see you this weekend," she said, giving our mother a quick peck on her forehead.

"I can stay awhile," I offered, scooting up on the bed beside her.

I like to think I saw her smile.

— SIX —

"She actually said that *we* interviewed a lot of women," I grumbled to my husband that night at dinner. "She hasn't done a damn thing."

"And you're surprised because . . ?"

"And then she tells my mother that she'll come see her this weekend," I continued, ignoring Harrison's question, which I assumed was rhetorical, "when the only reason she's going over there is to use the pool."

"I want to go swimming," Sam interrupted.

"Me, too," Daphne shouted. "I want to go swimming."

"And you will. Saturday," I told them, knowing I was doing this as much to annoy Tracy, whose tolerance for children—even mine—was limited at best, as for the kids. I felt instantly guilty about my pettiness. "Care to join us?" I asked Harrison.

"I'll pass, thank you," he said. "My course starts in five weeks and I've got lots of work to do to get ready. I really appreciate you taking the kids on Saturday. It'll be a big help."

"Speaking of your course," I began. "Did I tell you that Tracy is thinking of signing up for it?"

"What?" Nothing can adequately describe the look of horror on my husband's face.

"I believe her exact words were '*How hard can it be to write a novel?*'"

"Shit."

Sam gasped. "Daddy said a bad word."

"Shit," Daphne said.

"Shit, shit, shit," Sam repeated, laughing.

"Okay, kids. That's enough," Harrison snapped. "Please," he said to me. "You can't let that happen."

"I don't see what I can do about it."

"She's *your* sister."

"My *older* sister, who doesn't take too kindly to my suggestions," I reminded him. "The more I say 'black,' the more she'll say 'white.' The more I advise against it, the more she'll think it's a great idea."

"Shit," he said again.

"Shit," Sam repeated.

"Shit, shit, shit," Daphne said.

"Kids, I said enough!"

"*You* said it," Sam told him.

"Yes," Harrison admitted. "And I shouldn't have. Sorry," he apologized, forcing a smile onto his handsome face. "Sorry," he said again, this time to me. And then, to no one in particular, "Sorry."

—

"Sorry," he said, yet again, this time in bed, gently removing my hand from his naked torso. "I just don't think it's going to work tonight."

"Are you okay?" I tried not to sound too disappointed. It had been over a week since we'd made love, and I'd been hoping tonight would be different. I'd even put on Harrison's favorite red lace teddy and matching high heels.

I thought of my father's earlier observation, and wondered if I might actually have gained a few pounds. Although my clothes still fit the way they always had, I told myself, trying not to take Harrison's rejection personally. He was just tired and preoccupied, the way he always got when he was preparing for the course he taught each summer. I knew it bothered him that he was teaching what he no longer seemed capable of producing himself.

"I'm fine," he acknowledged. "Just . . . I don't know . . ."

"Preoccupied?"

"I guess. Thinking about your sister taking my course threw me for a bit of a loop."

"Relax. She probably won't follow through."

"I'll call the registrar tomorrow. Hopefully my class is already full."

I nodded, swinging my legs out of bed and kicking off my high heels before snuggling back in beside him. Harrison had been teaching a creative writing course at the University of Toronto for the past four years, part of its continuing education summer program for adults. Among the seven-week courses being offered were classes in writing poetry, screenplays, memoirs, nonfiction, and novels, both literary and popular. The total number of students permitted in each class was twelve, and the program was extremely popular, so there was a good chance it was too late for Tracy to enroll. I certainly hoped so, or this "preoccupation" could last all summer.

"At least the housekeeper situation is taken care of," Harrison offered.

"Yes," I agreed. "She's starting Monday."

"That's great. Now you can stop running over there every two seconds and spend more time at home . . ."

"I spend lots of time at home."

"That's not what I'm saying."

"What *are* you saying?"

"Just that you do too much, and that now that the housekeeper situation has been resolved, you can relax a bit," he concluded, giving me a quick peck on the tip of my nose before flipping onto his right side.

I lay there, still in my red teddy, staring at his bare back, listening to the soft sound of his breathing as he drifted off to sleep, the touch of his lips lingering on my skin.

We no sooner arrived in my parents' backyard than my cellphone rang. I glanced toward my sister, sunning herself in her bright orange bikini on a chaise longue beside the pool, knowing she would have ignored it. Unfortunately, I wasn't built that way.

"It's Linda Francis," the voice said as soon as I answered. "I hope this isn't going to prove too much of an inconvenience, but I was hoping we could change our appointment from tomorrow to today."

"Today?" I repeated as my children raced toward the pool.

"As soon as possible, actually. We've just been invited to a friend's cottage for a few days, and my husband wants to leave this afternoon."

My sister glared her displeasure as Sam jumped into the deep end of the pool, sending a torrent of water toward her. "For God's sake, Sam," she cried out. "Watch it!"

"Watch what?" he asked.

"Mommy," Daphne urged. "Come swim with me."

"Can I call you right back, Mrs. Francis?" I asked. "Let me see what I can do."

"See what you can do about what?" Tracy asked, eyes narrowing.

"It's this new client," I told her, explaining the situation.

"Don't look at me," Tracy said, anticipating my next request.

"I wouldn't be more than an hour, tops."

"No way," Tracy said. "This is my afternoon to relax."

As opposed to any other afternoon? I thought, but didn't say. There was no point arguing. I wasn't about to beg and I was out of options. My father had his hands full with my mother, and Harrison wouldn't appreciate his plans being disrupted. I'd have to call Linda Francis back, tell her I couldn't make it.

I heard the sound of a sliding door and turned to see Elyse Woodley walking up the garden steps to the pool, carrying a tray with a pitcher of lemonade, a plate of cookies, and a stack of plastic glasses. She was wearing white shorts, a sleeveless blue T-shirt, and a big smile.

I'm dreaming, I thought.

"Who wants lemonade and cookies?" she asked.

"Me!" shouted Daphne.

"Me, too," Sam said, quickly scrambling from the pool to grab a glass before his sister.

"Sam! Watch it!" Tracy squealed. "You're getting me all wet." She brushed some errant drops of water from the top of her bikini. I marveled that it was possible for anyone to have such a flat stomach, and made a conscious effort to pull in my own.

"What are you doing here?" I asked Elyse. "I didn't think you were starting till Monday."

"I decided to move some of my things over today," she said. "And when I heard your car pull up, I thought you might like something cold to drink. Is there a problem?" she asked.

"Oh, no. Not with you," I explained quickly. "A client just called and wants to see me this afternoon instead of tomorrow."

"Run along, then," Elyse said easily. "I'll watch the children until you get back."

"No! I can't ask you to do that."

"You didn't. I volunteered."

"But . . ."

"No buts. You don't have to worry. I'm an excellent swimmer. I'll take good care of them."

"You're sure?"

"Better leave before she changes her mind," Tracy advised.

"I'll try not to be long."

"Take as much time as you need."

"Thank you. Thank you so much. I'll be back soon," I told the kids. "Behave and listen to Mrs. Woodley."

"We will," Sam shouted, bits of cookie shooting from his mouth, spraying the air like shrapnel.

"Sam, for God's sake," Tracy said, swatting at the crumbs as if they were flies.

"Bye, Mommy," Daphne called as I hurried toward the back gate.

I turned around to see Elyse Woodley, in her shorts and T-shirt, waist deep in the water, Sam in one arm, Daphne in the other.

SEVEN

Linda and Dean Francis lived in Lawrence Park, another well-to-do area of the city, and a good fifteen-minute drive from Rosedale, especially in Saturday afternoon traffic. I pulled my car to a stop on the sunlit street and took a minute to examine the exterior of the large, two-story Georgian-style home. A friend of mine who was their neighbor had recommended me when she heard the Francises were interested in selling. "They're a little eccentric," she'd warned.

I took a few deep breaths, applied a fresh coat of lipstick, and fluffed out my hair before exiting the car. There was nothing I could do about the shapeless floral shift covering my matching one-piece bathing suit or the hot pink flip-flops on my feet. Linda Francis had emphasized the need for speed, so I'd decided not to waste precious time going home to change. This might have been a mistake, I was thinking as I rang the bell. Just because clients might be "eccentric" didn't mean they appreciated that quality in others.

"Eccentric" turned out to be an understatement.

"Mrs. Francis?" I asked, trying not to stare at the short, pigeon-chested woman who answered the door. She was perhaps a decade older than me and dressed all in black. Her dark hair, interrupted by a wide white streak, had been teased into a tall beehive, a style reminiscent of the Bride of Frankenstein. Bright pink lips were outlined in the same deep shade of red that streaked across her cheekbones, no attempt made to blend anything in, and her eyelids all but drooped with the weight of her heavily applied mascara. Large rhinestone hoops hung from her ears and layers of multicolored crystal beads fell around her neck. There was a ring on every one of her ten pudgy fingers and multiple bracelets surrounded her wrists, like handcuffs.

"Thank you for being so flexible," she said, ushering me inside the foyer, where her husband was waiting. "This is my husband, Dean."

Dean Francis was no less a vision. He stood at least six feet, eight inches tall, and was wearing dark green Bermuda shorts, knee-length black socks, black loafers, and a navy blazer. What remained of his hair had been dyed an unfortunate shade of burgundy and combed across the top of his head from one ear to the other, accentuating the sharp, birdlike features of his face.

"Would you like a tour?" he said instead of hello.

Unfortunately, the house proved even more shocking than its owners. The Francises were collectors. You name it, they collected it, although there didn't seem to be anything of any real value. Stacks of old newspapers and magazines grew up the walls like ivy, creepy old dolls and cheap plastic figurines lined every shelf. Unframed family photographs plastered the walls like wallpaper. The living room was filled with enough old sofas and chairs to furnish several hotel lobbies. The bedrooms were a nightmare of conflicting styles and fabrics.

"Is something wrong?" Linda Francis asked as we settled into the high-backed wooden chairs crowded around the kitchen table at the end of the tour.

I tried not to notice the four sets of salt-and-pepper shakers in the middle of it. "It's a lot," I heard myself say.

"We realize our taste isn't everyone's," Dean Francis began.

"But it just takes one person who loves the house," his wife offered.

"It's not the house," I said, picturing each room with a fresh coat of paint and sleek, minimalist furniture. "The house isn't the problem."

"What is?" they asked together.

I bit my tongue to keep from saying *You! You are the problem!* "There's just too much . . . everything," I said instead. "I'm sure the house is wonderful. But all anyone will see when they walk in here is . . . stuff."

"What do you suggest?" Linda asked, clearly taken aback. "We've already . . . what's the word you agents use? . . . decluttered."

I almost laughed. "You need to do more," I began, trying to be as diplomatic as I could. "Normally, we suggest decluttering twice as much as you think you should. But in your case, you need to be ruthless,"

I continued, warming to my subject. "Get rid of all your old newspapers and magazines, or at least put them away in boxes. Pack up your collections and your family photographs. You might have to rent a storage locker, hire a stager . . ."

"A stager? Surely that's not necessary."

"It's necessary if you're serious about selling your house," I said. "Right now, it's impossible for prospective buyers to imagine themselves turning your home into theirs, and it's impossible for me to try selling it in this condition. Trust me, you'd be getting a fraction of what it's worth. I'd just be wasting everybody's time. Look," I said, rising to my feet after several seconds of excruciating silence, careful not to knock anything over. "You're going to a cottage for a few days. Relax, think about what I've said, talk it over with your friends, and decide what you want to do. You can get back to me anytime."

They won't get back to me, I thought as I was driving back to Rosedale, berating myself for my lost afternoon. I should never have answered the damn phone, I was thinking as I checked the clock on the dashboard, realizing that by the time I got back, I'd have been gone almost two hours. I offered up a silent prayer of thanks to whatever gods might be listening for sending me Elyse Woodley.

"I'm sorry it took me so long," I apologized as soon as I entered the house.

"Nonsense," Elyse said. "I loved every minute."

I noticed she'd changed into dry clothes. "Where is everyone?" I looked toward the back of the house. Surely she hadn't left the kids alone by the pool.

"Well, your sister left soon after you did, your mother is sleeping, your father is resting," she began, "and the kids are in the home theater, watching cartoons. I hope you don't mind. They were quite pooped after our swim, and I thought it would be all right."

"Are you kidding?" I couldn't believe she was apologizing. "You're not even supposed to be working."

She shrugged.

"I'll certainly pay you for your time."

She waved aside my offer. "Totally unnecessary. However, I do have a favor to ask."

"Anything."

"Follow me." She led me down the stairs to the lower level.

"Hi, kids," I said, waving to them as we passed the home theater.

Sam waved back without looking.

"Hi, Mommy! We're watching cartoons!" Daphne shouted.

"I changed them into the clothes you left, and their wet bathing suits are in this bag," Elyse said, handing the plastic bag to me as we reached the room that was soon to be hers.

"Is everything okay with the room?" I asked as she walked toward the nightstand beside the queen-size bed. The door to the small en suite bathroom was open and I could see her toiletries already lining the counter by the sink.

"Couldn't be better. Now, if you wouldn't mind . . ." She walked back toward me, cradling a book in her hands. "It's your husband's novel. I was so lucky to find it. They only had one copy. Do you think he'd mind autographing it for me?"

"He'd be thrilled," I said honestly.

"You're sure? I wouldn't want to bother him."

"Trust me. It's no bother."

She handed me the book. "That would be so wonderful. I'd be so grateful."

"It's the least I can do."

We heard my mother cough from the intercom beside the bed.

"I should check on her," I said.

"Why don't I go with you?" she offered immediately.

Please let her be happy here. Please let her stay, I was wishing as I drove home, the kids chattering happily in the backseat.

Be careful what you wish for, the gods whispered back.

But I was too busy congratulating myself on my good fortune to hear them.

— EIGHT —

Looking back, I'm hard-pressed to pinpoint the exact moment everything changed.

Maybe there wasn't one.

Maybe it was just a gradual progression of events, a shift in nuance here, a change in tone there. The sort of thing you don't pay much attention to when it's happening, the sort of thing that, if you notice it at all, you accept as natural, rationalize out of importance. Until suddenly, everything is different.

Until nothing is as it was.

Those first months Elyse came to work for my parents were pure bliss. She was everything I'd hoped for, and more: a wonderful cook, an excellent housekeeper, a great companion. She was patient and kind and caring. No chore was too big. Nothing was too much to ask. When she wasn't doing the housework or preparing meals, she'd sit with my mother for hours, combing her hair, doing her nails, reading to her, making sure she was eating properly, giving my father a much-needed break.

"Tell me the truth," I whispered to him at dinner about four weeks into Elyse's employ. "She's a gift from God. You don't know what you'd do without her."

"It's working out better than I expected," he admitted, unwilling to concede more.

The invitation to dinner had been a surprise, and I suspected it had come at Elyse's instigation. It was the first time my father had hosted the family for dinner since my mother became too sick to participate. And now here we were—me, my father, Tracy, Harrison, and the children, grouped around the long, skinny, dark oak dining room table; my mother, dressed in a long, quilted pink housecoat, her hair freshly washed and arranged flatteringly around her thin face, hunched over in her wheelchair at the head of the table, next to my father— feasting on fresh pickerel, a kale and berry salad, wild rice, and the best homemade apple pie I'd ever tasted.

It felt as close to a miracle as anything I could imagine.

Not that it was easy. My mother had to be fed, she had noticeable trouble swallowing her food, and her conversation was limited to a series of barely audible words and phrases that trailed into nothingness before her thought was complete. Looking at her blank eyes and frozen expression, I found myself wondering if she even knew who we were. I'd read that dementia was a common marker of late-stage Parkinson's.

"So, Harrison starts teaching next week," I said in an effort to banish such unpleasant thoughts, looking for the slightest flash of animation on my mother's once-beautiful face, receiving nothing but the familiar dull stare.

"Why on earth are you still wasting your time with that?" my father asked Harrison, sliding a tiny morsel of apple pie between my mother's barely parted lips. "How much are they paying you anyway?"

"I don't consider it a waste of time," Harrison said, answering the first question and ignoring the second.

"Have any of your students ever gone on to publish anything?"

"Not yet," Harrison admitted. "But that doesn't necessarily mean they won't. It's not easy to get published these days."

"Well, you would know," said my father, the casual cruelty of his remark wrapped in a smile. "How's that book of yours coming along anyway?"

I watched Harrison offer up a smile of his own, and marveled at his self-control.

"It's coming," Harrison said.

"So's Christmas," came my father's instant retort.

"Did Jodi tell you that I tried to get into your course?" Tracy asked. "They told me it was all filled up."

Thank you, God, I thought, bowing my head.

"So I signed up for one of the other courses instead," she continued.

"Really," Harrison said. "Which one is that?"

"How to Write a Bestseller. Which is probably a better course for me to take anyway. I mean, that's the ultimate goal, isn't it? Why write something that nobody wants to read?"

"I think the goal is to produce something of value," Harrison argued, still smiling, although I could tell from his tone that he was reaching the limits of his patience, "and if it happens to sell well, then that's the icing on the cake."

"Bullshit," Tracy said, laughing.

"You tell him, kiddo," our father said. "Did you hear that, Audrey?" he asked my mother. "Tracy's going to write a bestseller."

My mother opened her mouth to say something, but her words were quickly absorbed into a series of violently escalating coughs, the coughs becoming gasps, the gasps triggering her gag reflex, causing her to start choking.

"What's the matter with Grandma?" Daphne cried, jumping off her chair to bury her head in my lap.

"Is she going to die?" Sam asked.

"For God's sake, Sam," Harrison said. "Don't talk nonsense."

"She's not going to die," I assured my son, although I felt far from assured myself. The truth was that I was terrified, as frozen to my spot as my mother was to hers.

Elyse was instantly at my mother's side, cradling her in her arms and stilling the spasms. "There, there," she whispered, her voice a salve. "You're okay. You're okay."

Whether it was the soothing sound of Elyse's voice or the natural lessening of the attack, my mother soon stopped choking and flailing about, resuming her former, rigidly twisted posture.

"Why don't I take you back upstairs?" Elyse offered to everyone's relief.

"I'll do it," my father said.

"No, Vic," Elyse told him, laying one firm hand on his shoulder to lower him back into his seat. "You stay here and visit with your family. I'll get Audrey settled."

"Can I go with?" Sam asked, already on his feet. "I want to ride in the elevator."

"Me, too," seconded Daphne.

"Sit down right now," Harrison chided.

"There's not really room for all of us in the elevator," Elyse said gently. "But I'll take you for a ride in it before you leave. How's that?"

"Yay!" Sam cheered.

"Yay!" Daphne echoed.

"Dinner was absolutely wonderful," I told Elyse as we were getting ready to depart. Tracy had already left and our father had excused himself to be with our mother.

"It was my pleasure. This is your home. You're always welcome."

"Kids!" Harrison called up the stairs to where Sam and Daphne were exiting the elevator for at least the tenth time. "Get down here. We're leaving."

"Aw . . ."

"Now," Harrison said.

The kids climbed back inside the elevator, which began its slow descent. However, as soon as they reached the main floor, Sam pressed the button and up they went again.

"Samuel!" Harrison fumed, spinning toward me, as if I'd been the one to press the button. "Do something."

"What do you want me to do?"

"This is my fault," Elyse quickly interjected. "I'm the one who showed them how to use the silly thing . . ."

"It's not your fault," Harrison corrected, his frustration with the evening spilling into the open. "They know they can get away with anything where Jodi's concerned, so it falls on me to be the disciplinarian." He raced up the stairs to the landing before I could respond.

Elyse leaned toward me. "It's not easy being married to someone who's so perfect," she said quietly.

I wanted to hug her. "Thank you," I whispered. "Thank you for everything."

"Anytime," she said.

It was only on the drive home that I replayed the evening in my mind: the wonderful home-cooked meal, the presence of my mother at the table, the awful choking fit followed by Elyse's calm demeanor and soothing words, the way she'd effortlessly assumed control. *No, Vic,* she'd told my father. *You stay here and visit with your family. I'll get Audrey settled.*

I wondered absently when they'd gone from being Mr. and Mrs. Dundas to Vic and Audrey, then quickly embraced the change. Why insist on clumsy and unnecessary formalities? I was thrilled that things were going so well, that everyone was so comfortable.

But now I wonder if that was the moment.

The shift in nuance. The change in tone.

The moment that everything changed.

—NINE—

I was sitting on the side of my bed, my body still damp from my late-afternoon shower, my neck bent at an awkward angle toward my chest, my arms limp at my sides, my hands resting on the towel wrapped around my torso, my bare legs as stationary and useless as tree stumps.

Without moving my head, I shifted my eyes toward the clock radio on the nightstand beside the bed, noting that I'd been sitting in this uncomfortable position for the better part of twenty minutes. Every part of me ached. *Ten more minutes,* I told myself. *See if you can hold on another ten minutes.*

"What on earth are you doing?" Harrison asked from the doorway.

I jumped, my arms shooting from my sides as my head snapped toward his voice. My towel became dislodged and fell toward my waist. "You scared me," I said, securing it back around my naked breasts.

"What are you doing?" he asked again.

"Daydreaming," I said with a shrug. A lie. But it was easier—less crazy-sounding—than telling him the truth: that I was trying to imagine what it must be like for my mother, to understand what it felt like to be trapped inside your own body, scrunched up like a piece of papier-mâché, unable to move for hours on end, twenty-four hours a day.

All day. Every day.

Year after endless year.

I hadn't even lasted thirty minutes.

"Well, don't you think you should get ready? They'll be here in less than an hour."

I forced myself to my feet, my wet hair dripping toward my shoulders.

"What are you going to wear?" he surprised me by asking.

"What?"

"What were you thinking of wearing?" he rephrased.

"I hadn't given it much thought," I said honestly. "Maybe that orange-and-white-checkered dress I bought last month?"

Harrison made a face, as if he'd just smelled something bad. "No. Don't wear that. Wear, I don't know, something more . . . current."

"More current than last month?"

"You know what I mean. Something a little hipper, more . . . with it."

With what? I was tempted to ask. Instead, I said, "How about white pants and a top?"

"What top?"

Seriously? "Maybe my vintage Rolling Stones T-shirt, the one with the giant tongue. Is that hip enough?"

"That should work," he said, taking my question at face value. "And maybe you could do something with your hair . . ."

"I just got out of the shower," I reminded him. "It's still wet."

"Yeah. So you don't have a lot of time."

"I'll do my best."

"Did you remember to get the barbecue sauce I asked you to pick up?"

"It's in the cupboard."

"Okay. Good." He turned to leave.

"You're welcome," I said.

He stopped. "Sorry. Thank you."

"You're welcome," I said again, hoping for a smile.

Instead Harrison glanced at his watch. "Tick tock," he said.

Harrison's students arrived promptly at six o'clock, all twelve of them within minutes of each other, as if they'd all come on the same bus. I don't know why this always surprised me, but it did. Every year for the past four, Harrison hosted a barbecue dinner for his new students on the Saturday following the first week of classes, and every year, a dozen eager faces appeared at our front door in unison, some bearing flowers, some chocolates, some nothing but eyes wide with awe and admiration for their handsome instructor.

Generally speaking, the women outnumbered the men, but this year saw a more even split, seven women to five men, ranging in age from eighteen to seventy, the majority falling somewhere in between.

"This is my wife, Jodi," Harrison said, introducing me to each one in turn.

"So nice to meet you," said a middle-aged woman named Sarah.

"Lovely to meet you," said Thomas, a bearded thirty-something with a heavy British accent.

"You have a lovely home." Candace.

"Thanks so much for having us." Zack.

"Something smells good." Lester.

And so on. And so on.

I surveyed the group assembled in my narrow back-yard, glasses of wine or beer in hand, everyone chatting happily, all casually dressed, no one a standout, sartorially speaking, and felt a tad conspicuous in my Rolling Stones T-shirt, as if I were trying too hard to be "with it," and everyone knew it. Who, exactly, I wondered absently, was Harrison trying to impress?

And then, almost as soon as I asked myself the question, the answer appeared before me.

"Love your T-shirt," she said.

"Thank you."

"My mother has one just like it."

So much for being hip, I thought, forcing a smile.

"I'm Wren."

"Wren?"

"Like the songbird."

"Lovely name," I said. "It suits you."

Wren was indeed lovely. Late twenties. Tall. Slender but with large breasts. Long chestnut-colored hair pulled into a high ponytail, deep green eyes. Effortlessly chic in the way only young women can be, wearing jeans and a white V-neck T-shirt, a series of small, alternating loops and studs climbing up the side of each perfect earlobe. Her skin was radiant, glowing without a hint of makeup save for a touch of mascara and the faintest layer of gloss on her lips.

"Your husband's so terrific," she said.

"Well, I know he really enjoys teaching the course," I offered in return.

"He has a real gift. Not only for writing. I mean, *Comes the Dreamer* was the best. Everybody knows that. But you can be a great writer and not be a great teacher. But Harrison, he's just so good."

I tried not to blanch at her easy use of my husband's first name. Had I really expected her to call him "Mr. Bishop"?

"Are you a writer?" she asked.

"Me? No. I'm a real estate agent."

"No kidding," she said with a laugh. "So's my mom."

Just shoot me now, I thought. "Really. Who's she with?"

"Re/Max." Her eyes meandered through the small crowd gathered in my tiny backyard, her interest wavering. "Where are your kids? I was hoping to meet them. Harrison said you have two."

"Harrison is right," I said, forcing another smile, wondering when my husband had become so forthcoming about his personal life. *You're being silly,* I told myself immediately. *Why wouldn't he share such innocuous information?*

I knew that Harrison always began his sessions by asking his students to tell the class a little bit about themselves and why they were taking the course. So it was only natural that he would choose to share a bit of himself as well. *Wasn't it?*

"They're having a sleepover at a friend's."

"Those were the days," Wren said and laughed.

I laughed, too, although what I really wanted to do was shout, *What would you know about days? You've had barely enough days to count.*

One of the older students approached. I tried and failed to remember her name. "Is your husband as good a chef as he is a writer?" she asked.

"If you'll excuse me," Wren said before I could answer.

I watched her disappear into the throng gathered around the barbecue. Harrison was flipping burgers and basking in the admiration of his devoted fans. I smiled, remembering when I was one of their ranks. I waved. But he didn't see me.

"This is crazy," I could hear Tracy say as she stretched her neck to see how many people stood ahead of us in line. Ten years might have passed, but the evening I met Harrison remained fresh in my mind, one of those memories you never tire of reliving, one of those stories you never tire of repeating. "There must be a hundred people, and he's taking forever. I mean, what's he doing? How long does it take to sign your name?"

I shrugged, not bothering to remind her that it was her fault we were at the very back of the line, that if she hadn't taken so long primping and gathering up her things, we might have gotten closer to the front. The truth was that I was determined to wait as long as necessary, even if it meant standing there all night. I was wearing my favorite pink silk shirt, and I'd even had my hair and makeup professionally done at Holt's.

"What are you all dolled up for?" Tracy asked when she saw me. "You really think he's going to notice you?" She tossed her long blond hair from one shoulder to the other, as if issuing a silent challenge.

"Oh, my God. I don't believe this!" she cried now. "He's letting people take pictures! We're going to be here forever."

"You don't have to stay," I said.

"Yeah, right. I didn't buy the book so I could leave without an autograph."

"Then stop complaining."

"I wasn't even that crazy about it. I mean, he takes ten pages to describe how to use a washing machine. I can read a manual, for God's sake."

"It's a metaphor."

"Oh, please. Whatever happened to plot?"

"There's a plot."

"Which he takes forever to get to." She transferred her weight from one foot to the other. "Sort of like this line."

"You don't have to stay," I repeated, actively wishing Tracy would leave. I'd been eagerly anticipating this night for weeks, ever since I'd seen the ad in the paper announcing that new literary sensation, Toronto's own Harrison Bishop, would be speaking and signing books at Indigo, and I didn't want the experience ruined. I'd read *Comes the Dreamer* three times, and had a long list of what I hoped were intelligent questions that I wanted to ask its author. But most of those questions had already been asked and answered by the time the moderator saw my hand, and since the evening had already gone way over schedule, I only muttered something about how grateful I was to him for sharing his talent with us.

"God, that was so lame," my sister said as I resumed my seat.

Lining up for autographs, we were instructed to write the correct spelling of our names on a small piece of paper, so that Mr. Bishop wouldn't have to waste time asking, and to try to be patient, that he wouldn't leave until each and every book had been signed and personalized.

"I don't want my book personalized," Tracy said as I was debating whether to dot the *i* in Jodi with a heart. "I read somewhere that books are more valuable with just an autograph and a date. The minute you personalize them, they aren't worth as much when you go to sell them."

"I'm never selling mine," I said, adding the heart, and then, on impulse, my phone number. *What the hell?* I reasoned. *What do I have to lose?*

It was almost an hour later when we finally reached the front of the line.

Harrison was seated at a long wooden table, looking as handsome and artfully disheveled as the photograph on the back of his book promised, strands of dark hair tumbling toward his deep blue eyes. Beside him sat a dewy-eyed and obviously smitten representative from the publishing house, the manager of the store standing a discreet distance behind.

"Just your autograph," my sister announced as we approached, pushing her copy of the book toward him. "And a picture," she added suddenly, thrusting her cell-phone into my hands as she scurried around the table to scoot down beside him. She threw one arm across his shoulders as she produced her most radiant smile. "One more," she directed. "Just to make sure."

I dutifully snapped another three pictures, fighting the urge to throw the phone at her head.

"I just love the way you write," she told Harrison as he was handing the book back.

"Thank you," he said, smiling in my direction.

"I'll take that," she said, grabbing her phone from my hands as I pushed my name and number across the table toward him. If I thought that Tracy intended to take a picture of me with Harrison, I was quickly disabused of that notion. Instead, I watched her scoot off to one side to check on the photographs I'd just taken.

"Friend of yours?" Harrison asked.

"Sister."

He nodded. "Ah," he said, as if he understood.

"You have a sister?" I ventured.

"Nope. Only child."

"Oh."

"But I have a mother."

"Oh," I said again, mindful of the less-than-flattering depiction of the mother in *Comes the Dreamer*.

"Luckily, she moved to Vancouver a number of years ago, and I no longer have to deal with her."

"My mother's just been diagnosed with Parkinson's," I surprised myself by saying.

I heard a not-too-subtle "Ahem," and glanced over to where Tracy was standing. She made a show of lifting her arm to glance at her watch.

"Subtle," Harrison remarked.

"Always."

"I admire your patience," he said. "And not just for waiting so long in line. To Jodi," he said as he was scribbling my name in the front of my book, "with a heart."

I smiled.

He handed me back the book with one hand, slipping the piece of paper with my phone number into his jacket pocket with the other. "I'll keep this, if you don't mind," he said.

My breath froze in my lungs.

"What were you talking about for so damn long?" Tracy asked as we left the store.

I shrugged.

I'm going to marry that man, I thought.

ELEVEN

"What a charming story," Elyse was saying, cutting me another slice of the chocolate cake she'd baked that morning. We were at my parents' kitchen table, staring out at the backyard where my father and mother were sitting beside the pool, my mother encased in blankets in the wheelchair that had become an extension of her warped body, my father in golf shorts and an open-necked shirt, reading aloud from the Sunday edition of *The New York Times* in the chair beside her.

I'd stopped by for a brief visit between showings, and had been about to leave when Elyse offered me a second piece of her delicious cake. I knew I should go home, that Harrison would likely grumble about having been on his own with the kids for most of the day, but I had a full afternoon ahead of me and was relishing these few minutes of "me" time.

Weekends were always a little hectic, as that was when most prospective buyers were free to go house-hunting. Many of these were repeat visits, the wife having already viewed the house favorably earlier in the week. All that was necessary now was the husband's seal of approval.

Do we ever stop wanting that? I wondered. *Do women ever stop judging themselves through the male eye?*

"You really knew then and there that you were going to marry him?" Elyse probed.

"I did." I shrugged, wondering when I'd lost that sense of certainty.

"I guess it runs in the family," she said. "Your father said almost the same thing about your mother."

"He did?"

"He said that he knew the minute he saw her perform that she would be his wife."

"What else did he say?"

"That she'd turned down offers from several prestigious ballet companies to specialize in modern dance, even though it paid peanuts. That she was a magical dancer, but that she chose to give up performing after you were born."

"It wasn't exactly a choice," I corrected.

"What do you mean?"

"I wasn't the easiest baby," I explained, feeling a familiar stab of guilt. Unlike Tracy, whose birth, by all accounts, had been a snap, I'd been stuck in a breech position that necessitated my mother undergoing a cesarean section, which put a definite crimp in her plans to resume her career quickly. Then I was a colicky baby, never sleeping more than a few hours at a time for months on end, unlike Tracy who, according to family legend, had slept through the night at three months and toilet-trained herself before her first birthday.

My mind suddenly filled with images from my childhood of my mother at the barre in the exercise room, her arms floating gracefully above her head as she twisted her lithe body into a variety of seemingly impossible positions, postures that Tracy, standing a few feet behind her, had no trouble imitating, but I could never get right.

"Watch Tracy," my mother would instruct.

"Watch me," Tracy would echo, two words that followed her into adulthood.

Watch me. Watch me. Watch me.

I watched, but I could never duplicate Tracy's easy mastery of the art. In one of life's little ironies, I had the desire, but not the talent, whereas Tracy had the talent, but lacked the desire.

It was that way with most things. It seemed as if there was nothing Tracy couldn't do. She was filled with natural talent. Everything came to her with such astonishing ease that when it came time to settle down and do the hard work necessary to truly succeed, she simply gave up and went on to something else. And something else again. And again.

She was the same with men. A problem arose; the man disappeared.

Friends came and went. Tracy craved admiration, not loyalty. When she ceased feeling special, she moved on, found new friends to dazzle.

"More coffee?" Elyse asked, unaware of the thoughts swirling through my brain.

I glanced at the time. I had an open house in half an hour, but the property was only minutes away. "Sure. Why not?"

Elyse poured me a second cup, then plopped down into the chair beside me. "So, finish your story. When did he call you?"

It took me a minute to realize that she was talking about Harrison and the story I'd been telling her about how we met. Looking back, I can't recall what had prompted me to confide in her. I suspect it was simply because she'd asked, and it had been such a long time since anyone had expressed an interest in anything I had to say that I found myself eager to share my stories, especially to such a sympathetic and appreciative listener.

"He called around midnight," I told her, enjoying the memory.

"That same night?"

I felt a blush spread from my neck to my cheeks. "He said he knew it was late, but he was kind of hyped up from the evening and couldn't sleep and wondered if I felt like going for a walk, and I said sure. And he showed up at my apartment, and basically never left."

"You made love that first night?"

I shrugged, basking in her obvious delight.

"Such a wonderful love story," she said.

"Yes, it was."

"*Was?*"

"Well, it still is," I demurred. "It's just, you know, different."

"Different?"

"Well, we've been married almost ten years." I forced a laugh. "Things change . . . we have two children . . . Harrison's had a bit of trouble getting his second book off the ground . . ."

"But he's such a good writer."

"Yes, he is."

"It must be so frustrating for him, a man of his genius. Although, what is it they say? 'Genius is a pain to live with at home'?"

I smiled. "He's not a pain. Well, not all the time anyway."

She laughed, and I felt almost embarrassingly grateful.

"I mean, it's not like he isn't trying. It's just, like you said, it's very frustrating for him."

"For you, too, I imagine."

Not for the first time, I wanted to hug her.

"He's very lucky," she went on, "that you're doing so well."

"I'm not sure he feels that way."

"Oh?"

"I know he appreciates the money and everything, but . . ."

". . . you think he resents you being so successful?"

"No. Well, not really," I qualified. "Maybe."

"I'm sure he's very proud of your accomplishments."

"I'm sure he is, too," I agreed.

"Just that it would be nice to hear him say so," Elyse said.

My eyes filled with tears.

"Oh, dear. Please don't cry." A tissue appeared miraculously in her hands. She stretched forward in her chair to dab gently under my eyes. "You don't want to ruin your mascara."

"I'm sorry. I don't know what's gotten into me, going on like that. I certainly didn't mean to give you the wrong idea." I swallowed the last of my tears. "He's normally very supportive. And we're fine. We really are. Every marriage has its ups and downs. Well . . . I'm sure you know."

"I certainly do. There were times in both my marriages that I would have been happy to see my husbands under the wheels of a bus."

My lips quivered into a smile. "It's always a little hard in the summer when he starts teaching. He has all these students looking at him like he's some sort of god." *The way I used to look at him. The way Wren looks at him now.* "And then he has to come home to reality."

"Reality's a bitch," Elyse said.

"Who's a bitch?" my father asked from the doorway.

I jumped. I'd been so preoccupied with our conversation that I hadn't heard him come inside. I quickly checked the garden, saw my mother still slumped in her wheelchair by the pool.

"A second piece?" my father asked, noticing my crumb-filled plate. "You think that's a good idea?"

"Vic, for heaven's sake," Elyse interjected on my behalf. "What are you talking about? Jodi is as slender as a reed."

"Is Mom okay out there on her own?" I asked, trying to mask my annoyance.

"She's fine," my father said, looking toward the coffee machine. "Any left for me?"

"Why don't I make you a fresh cup," Elyse offered, instantly on her feet.

"What if she falls?" I persisted.

"She won't," my father said, pulling up a chair.

"Your daughter is right," Elyse told him. "Why take a chance? You go back outside and I'll bring your coffee out when it's ready."

I waited for him to snap at her, tell her to stick to her job and keep her opinions to herself.

"Fine," my father said instead, pushing his chair back toward the table.

"How did you do that?" I asked when he was gone.

"Oh, your father's not that difficult."

"Really? That's never been my experience."

She gave me a look that was half wink, half smile. "You just have to know how to handle him."

—TWELVE—

It doesn't take a genius to understand the psychology behind what was going on here, the underlying family dynamics that drew me to Elyse, the subconscious reasons I chose to ignore the red flags waving in the distance, and then, increasingly, right in front of my eyes.

Unlike Tracy, I never had a lot of friends. Tracy was outgoing and self-assured, whereas I was shy and full of self-doubt. She was undeniably beautiful; I was, in our father's words, "interesting-looking." She was the proud beneficiary of our mother's ballet-thin physique; I was, again according to my father, "sturdier."

Tracy shone bright; I merely flickered.

That Tracy was our parents' favorite was something I never questioned or even resented, there being no point to either. The fact that she was praised for bringing home mediocre marks in high school while my A's were barely acknowledged is likely what drove me that much harder to succeed. I was the "workhorse"—another of my father's favorite words. Tracy was the "artist."

She was indulged; I was tolerated.

For a while, I suspected that I'd been adopted. Not only did I not resemble my parents or my sister in any significant way—I had my father's brown eyes, but that was about it—but I was their opposite temperamentally as well. While they yearned for center stage, I was content to remain in the background. While they sought out starring roles, I was content to be part of the chorus.

Of course, all my mother had to do was point to the raised scar of her cesarean to disabuse me of the notion that I'd been adopted once and for all. There was no other family, no *real* family, out there somewhere, waiting to embrace my imperfections, to find me worthy, regardless of my faults.

"See this?" my mother asked me one day, when I was about the same age as my son is now, lifting her shirt and pulling her slacks down over her hips to show me the proof. "You did this."

I promptly burst into tears and spent the rest of the day apologizing.

I've been apologizing ever since.

I'd always been a dutiful daughter, calling my mother daily just to say hi and inquire about her day, despite her rarely asking about mine. This pattern only increased after her Parkinson's diagnosis. I was the one who filled her prescriptions, who did the grocery shopping every week, who visited on a regular basis, who called morning and night to check on her condition.

Deprive a child of parental approval, and they'll spend their lives trying to get it. And the sad, undeniable fact is that I spent most of my formative years just trying to get my parents' *attention,* let alone their approval. The more they withheld it, the greater my attempts to attain it. It was obvious that I was never going to become a dancer, like my mother, so I became a Realtor, like my father. The reason I chose to join his agency, why I strove to be one of its top-earning representatives, was to win his respect. To prove to him that I was more than just an "interesting-looking workhorse."

That I was a sleek and beautiful stallion.

Of course, whatever I did, it was never enough.

So, was it really a surprise that I fell so quickly and easily under Elyse's spell?

She was warm, caring, considerate, even solicitous of my feelings. She asked me questions, sought my opinion, took my side, showered me with praise.

In short, she was the loving parent figure I'd been searching for all my life.

Like I said, it doesn't take a genius to figure that one out.

My father's reaction to Elyse is a little harder to explain.

He'd been so dead set against having anyone invade his territory that I assumed it would take months for him to adapt to her presence, that his ingrained impulse to control everything and everyone around him wouldn't allow for any form of compromise, that I'd be lucky if Elyse didn't run screaming for the nearest exit before the first week was up. So I was shocked when my father's initial resistance to her not only dissipated with surprising speed but soon disappeared altogether.

While he occasionally tried to goad her into an argument—the same technique he'd used so successfully with my mother—Elyse simply would not rise to the bait. She ignored or laughed off his attempts to engage her in verbal combat—"Oh, Vic," she'd say. "You're so funny." That combined with her natural good looks and extreme competence was clearly more than enough to win him over.

And in the beginning, I couldn't have been more grateful. For my parents' sake.

For mine.

"It's amazing," I said to Harrison one night as I was crawling into bed. "Nothing fazes her. It's been barely three months and already she has the house running like a well-oiled machine."

Harrison said nothing. He was sitting in our king-size bed, surrounded by submissions for the latest assignment he'd given his creative writing class. Papers fanned out around him, covering the top of our billowy white duvet.

"My mother looks better than she has in ages," I continued, trying to scoot beneath the covers without disturbing his work.

"Careful," he warned without looking up.

"And my father," I continued. "It's like this ferocious lion has morphed into this harmless pussycat. It's unbelievable. I'm telling you, the woman is a magician. Harrison?" I said when he failed to respond.

"Hmm?"

"Have you heard anything I've said?"

"Your father's a pussycat; Elyse is a magician," he recited without enthusiasm.

"Well, that's pretty amazing, don't you think?"

"Amazing," he agreed, finally looking up from his papers. "Look. I know I've said this before, but I thought the whole point of hiring a housekeeper for your parents was so that you could spend less time worrying about them and more time taking care of your own family."

"The point of hiring a housekeeper was to help my father take care of my mother," I corrected. "And when haven't I given this family enough attention?"

"Really, Jodi? You want to get into this now? I have to have these assignments marked by morning."

I heard distant echoes of my parents' loud fights racing up the stairs toward my children's bedrooms. I pictured them cowering beneath their blankets at the sound of raised voices, their hands over their ears to block out the angry words. "Sorry," I said, pushing down my frustration and flopping back on my pillow with more force than I'd intended.

"Okay," Harrison said, gathering up his papers. "You've made your point. I'll go downstairs."

"I wasn't trying to make a point," I began. But he was already out of bed and out the door, his footsteps reverberating down the stairs.

I lay awake, reminded of the theory that, on a subconscious level, men marry their mothers, and women, their fathers. That we tend to repeat patterns from our childhoods, going with what's familiar, however unpleasant, hoping to rewrite history, desperate to find that elusive happy ending.

Had I done that?

Like my father, Harrison could be difficult and self-absorbed, but surely this was true of most successful men. I'd convinced myself that he was somehow entitled to these traits. Being difficult and self-absorbed were part and parcel of being creative.

Like my father, Harrison could be dismissive and superior, often wielding his easy command of language as a weapon. Surely that was part of his genius. And yes, like my father, Harrison enjoyed being coddled and admired and having the last word.

But then, who doesn't?

I had no way of knowing if I was anything like Harrison's mother as he'd always been loath to talk about her. I knew that she'd abandoned the family after her divorce from Harrison's father, moving across the country to pursue career opportunities, and that Harrison had spurned all subsequent attempts to reconnect and reconcile.

Watch the way a man treats his mother, a little voice whispered in my ear as I flipped off the overhead light and closed my eyes. *That's the way he'll treat his wife.*

Just another one of the voices I chose to ignore.

— THIRTEEN —

Enter Roger McAdams.

Handsome, successful, charming Roger McAdams. Early forties. Recently divorced, new to the city, and in the market for a place to live. He breezed into my life like a soft, warm wind.

But wait.

We're not there yet.

First comes Wren.

"Where's Harrison?" Tracy asked as we were sitting down to dinner one night—salmon, of course. The kids had already eaten and were upstairs playing video games before bed. It was mid-August. Harrison's course had two more weeks to go.

I poured my sister a glass of white wine. "He had a faculty meeting."

Tracy checked her watch. "Kind of late."

I checked my own watch. She was right. It was after eight o'clock. I poured myself a glass of the pleasant Chardonnay and took a sip, feeling the chilled liquid coat my throat like a salve. "He said the meeting might run long."

She shrugged. "I saw him today, you know."

I'd spoken to Harrison earlier, when he'd called to tell me about the unexpected meeting. "Really? He didn't mention seeing you."

"Probably because he didn't."

"Oh?" I asked, almost afraid to say more, although I wasn't sure why. Tracy's classes were in the same building on St. George as Harrison's. It wasn't surprising that they would occasionally run into each other.

"At Bar Mercurio," Tracy continued, naming a popular luncheon spot on Bloor Street, close to the university. "A group of us went there for lunch and he was outside on the patio. Place was packed, so we had to sit inside. Probably why he didn't see me."

"You should have gone over to say hello."

"No. I didn't want to interrupt him."

"I'm sure he wouldn't have minded."

"I don't know. He looked pretty busy."

"I take it he wasn't alone," I said, regretting my words the second they were out of my mouth.

"No," Tracy confirmed. "He was with this girl. They were pretty deep in conversation."

"Probably one of his students."

"Probably."

"Probably going over an assignment."

"Probably," Tracy said again, a word I was starting to dislike. "She was young," she continued, unprompted. "Pretty. Long brown hair. Big boobs."

I tried to block out the image of Wren that sprang immediately to mind. "What are you getting at?" I asked, taking another sip of my wine. This was Tracy's preferred operating procedure. She always played the innocent, coming at things obliquely, so that she could never be accused of deliberately trying to stir things up.

"Me? Nothing."

"You make it sound as if there was something going on."

"Really? I didn't mean to."

"I'm sure it was perfectly innocent," I told her.

"Did I say it wasn't?"

"You implied."

"I did no such thing."

"He has meetings with his students on a regular basis," I told her. "To go over their assignments, explain his notes, tell them where they can improve. That's part of his job."

"I know that," Tracy protested. "I've met with my instructor several times to discuss exactly what you just said."

"There you go," I said, feeling somewhat vindicated.

"Just not at lunch," she added.

"Shit," I said, finishing the wine in my glass and pouring another.

"My instructor says I have real talent," Tracy said, an obvious attempt to change the subject.

"Good for you."

"You're upset," Tracy said, realizing she might have gone too far. "Sorry. That wasn't my intention. Harrison would be a complete idiot to even think of cheating on you. Honestly. I'm sure the lunch was perfectly innocent," she continued, using my words, underlining how hollow they sounded. "I'm sure that Harrison will tell you all about it when he gets home."

He didn't.

"That must have been some meeting," I said when he finally pushed open the front door at almost ten o'clock. Tracy had left an hour earlier, and I was sitting at the dining room table, having finished off the last of the wine. A pleasant buzz had settled into the tops of my shoulders, brushing against my skin like a silk shawl.

"A bunch of us went out afterward for a bite to eat," he said. "Sorry. I guess I should have called."

"To Bar Mercurio?" I asked, emboldened by the alcohol in my system.

"What?"

"Did you go to Bar Mercurio?" I repeated.

"No. Actually, we went to the bar at the Four Seasons. Are you all right?"

"Fine."

"You seem a little . . . off. How much have you had to drink?"

I shrugged, glancing at the empty bottle. "Tracy was here for dinner."

He nodded, as if this explained everything.

"She said she saw you today."

Harrison's head tilted to one side, like an inquisitive puppy.

"At lunch," I said before he could ask. "At Bar Mercurio."

I watched his eyes digest this latest piece of information.

"Okay," he said. "I confess. I had lunch at Bar Mercurio."

"With one of your students?"

"With Wren Peterson, yes. To go over her last assignment. Yesterday I had lunch with Candace Fitzpatrick," he continued. "Did Tracy see me then, too?"

I felt the silk shawl slipping from my shoulders, leaving me exposed and unprotected.

"What is it exactly that Tracy thinks she saw?"

She saw you having lunch with a pretty, young girl with long brown hair and big boobs, I thought, but all I said was "She saw you having lunch at . . ."

". . . Bar Mercurio. Yes, I think we've established that. What else?"

"Just that your conversation seemed pretty intense," I offered.

"Which it was," he agreed. "Wren has dreams of being a writer, but frankly, that's never going to happen. And I think she's starting to realize that, and it hit her pretty hard. I was just trying to comfort her. I take it Tracy saw me reach out to pat her hand, and jumped to the wrong conclusion, as only Tracy can."

I silenced a gasp. My sister hadn't said anything about Harrison reaching for Wren's hand.

"And she just couldn't wait to rush over here and tell you all about it." Harrison ran an exasperated hand through his hair. "Just as you couldn't wait to jump to conclusions. Look, it's been a long night, and I'm exhausted. I'm going to bed."

I sat at the dining room table for the better part of an hour, the invisible silk shawl lying crumpled at my feet, before I pushed myself to my feet and went upstairs.

I washed my face and brushed my teeth, then crawled into bed beside my husband. "I'm sorry," I whispered, surrounding him with my arms and burying my face into his warm back.

But if he was awake, he gave no such sign. He left for the university the next day without so much as a "good morning."

Enter Roger McAdams.

—FOURTEEN—

"Excuse me," the voice said. "Jodi Bishop?"

I looked up from the contract I was perusing to see a handsome head—hazel eyes, light brown hair, patrician nose, full mouth—appear in the doorway to my office.

"Roger McAdams?"

"In the flesh," he said, approaching my desk and extending his hand. He was tall and slim, stylishly dressed in gray slacks and a navy linen sports jacket, his handshake firm, his gaze steady.

"Please," I said, motioning toward the two oak chairs in front of my desk, "have a seat."

"I appreciate your seeing me on such short notice."

I smiled. "How can I help you, Mr. McAdams?"

"Roger, please." He explained that he had relocated to Toronto from Detroit for a new job several months earlier and the time had come to move out of the tiny apartment he'd been renting and into a place of his own.

"What kind of place are we talking about? House? Condo?"

"Condo, definitely. I'm divorced, no kids. Not expecting a lot of visitors. But maybe two bedrooms, so I can use one as an office."

"Any particular area you're considering?"

"Well, I work on Bay Street. So preferably something downtown. Maybe overlooking the water."

"Condos on the water run pretty steep. What's your budget?"

"Flexible," he said. "Maybe you could show me a few places, so I could see what's available and for how much, and that way I could get a better feel for what my options are."

"Sounds reasonable," I said. *And vague,* I added silently, understanding that unless we were very lucky, the search for a suitable condo could take some time. "Why don't you look through our listings online and see if anything stands out. And meanwhile, I'll try to put together a good cross-section of what's available, and get back to you by the end of the day."

"Sounds perfect."

"Are there any times that work best for you, in terms of showings?"

"Well, evenings or weekends, I guess. If that works for you."

"Whatever works for you, works for me," I told him honestly, although I could already hear Harrison's objections to my schedule slamming against my ears.

He handed me a card with his name and cellphone number. "I look forward to hearing from you," he said as he was leaving.

I look forward to being heard, I thought, watching him go.

"So, what you're telling me is that you're going to be working all weekend," Harrison was saying as we were getting ready for bed.

"Not all weekend."

"No. Just mornings and afternoons."

"Not all morning," I said evenly. "Not all afternoon."

"Really?" he challenged. "How does that work, exactly? Break it down for me."

"I have showings between ten and twelve, and two and four on Saturday."

"And Sunday?"

"Sunday might not be necessary."

"But it could be," he said.

"It could be," I agreed.

"So, what you're saying is that I should be prepared to have the kids on my own all weekend."

"I'll be home for breakfast, lunch, and dinner," I said.

"And I get to entertain them all the hours in between."

"Is that really such a hardship? They're great kids."

"How would you know?"

"That's not fair. I spend as much time with them as you do."

"Really?" he scoffed. "In what universe? Face it, Jodi. Your husband and kids come third. Behind your parents and your career."

Normally, I would let such accusations slide. I'd learned from listening to my parents fight that trying to defend yourself only led to a greater escalation in accusations. But I was tired of hearing the same litany of complaints. "Not only is that not fair," I protested. "It's not true."

"Let me tell you what's true," Harrison countered. "The truth is that your work always takes precedence over mine. I'm always having to adapt my schedule to yours. You have no respect for my time or how hard I work."

I shook my head, mindful of our rising voices, of the children sleeping in their beds down the hall.

"You blithely go about your business, making appointments without even thinking to consult me. Evenings, weekends . . ."

"It's not like I have a choice."

"You always have a choice."

"I have to make myself available when it suits my clients' schedules."

"What about *my* schedule?"

"Your schedule is more flexible than mine."

"Only because I know how to prioritize."

"Somebody's got to make some money around here," I snapped, instantly regretting my words.

"Okay," he said. "Now we're getting to what's really going on here."

"I'm just trying to point out . . ."

". . . that you make more money than I do, so you get to call the shots."

"That's not what I said."

"'Somebody's got to make some money around here.' Were those not your exact words?"

"Yes, but I was just trying to point out that . . ."

"That you make the money, so you make the decisions."

"When have you ever not been involved in a single major decision?" I shouted.

"Could you lower your voice?" he said, suddenly lowering his. "You're going to wake up the kids."

It was all I could do to keep from screaming. "It's because of my income that we're able to afford this house and send the kids to daycare and day camp, giving you all day to write," I said, struggling to regain control, my voice low and as gravelly as an unpaved road.

"Which you obviously resent," he said.

"I don't resent it at all. What I *do* resent is your refusal to acknowledge how much I contribute."

"So you're doing all this for us? Is that what you're saying? You don't enjoy your job? You don't get any personal satisfaction out of it?"

"Of course I enjoy it. You're twisting everything I'm saying."

"It's because of you that we're able to afford our comfortable lifestyle. Isn't that what you said?"

"Yes, but . . ."

"I contribute nothing."

"I *definitely* did not say that."

"You didn't have to."

"You started this," I reminded him. "I wasn't the one complaining."

"No," he said. "It's never you, is it? You're blameless."

"I never said I was blameless. What the hell is going on here?" I cried in frustration. "I don't understand what's happening."

"Mommy!" a little voice called from the doorway.

I turned to see Daphne, clutching her stuffed bunny rabbit by one long droopy ear, her eyes shifting rapidly between Harrison and me. "Oh, sweetheart. I'm so sorry. Did we wake you up?"

Her eyes settled on Harrison. "You made Mommy cry!"

"It's okay, sweetheart," I told her. "Everything's okay."

"Nice work," I heard Harrison say as I led Daphne from the room.

—FIFTEEN—

"I was thinking of bringing the kids around for a swim on Saturday, if that's all right with you," I told my father. It was the day after my fight with Harrison, and I'd stopped by after work, ostensibly to check on my mother, but mostly because I was reluctant to go home and face my husband. I had no appetite for a repeat of last night's fiasco.

Hadn't I striven my entire life to avoid such a scene?

"No showings?" my father asked. We were sitting at the kitchen table, my father nursing a tall glass of ice-cold lemonade.

"Not this weekend." I'd called Roger McAdams first thing in the morning and told him a minor family emergency had come up and we'd either have to reschedule or I could recommend another agent. He said he hoped everything would work out, and that he was happy to wait another week.

He may have been sanguine about the delay, but I wasn't. Having to cancel my appointments to soothe my husband's wounded ego both saddened and enraged me.

Still, I felt I had no choice. It was either that or face days, possibly even weeks, of resentments and growing estrangement. If I could prove to Harrison that my family's needs came first simply by canceling my weekend appointments, then that's what I would do. Surely he would see the error of his ways and apologize for his unjust accusations.

Of course, I was wrong. Since when has appeasement ever worked?

"I would have thought that, with the market being so hot, you'd be run off your feet," my father said, sensing I was holding out on him, and never one to let things simply slide by.

"Well, I *did* just finalize an eight-million-dollar sale on a house in Forest Hill." I tugged at one of the silver-and-pearl hoop earrings I'd bought myself as a reward.

If I'd been expecting to be congratulated, I was quickly relieved of that notion. My father merely shrugged. "Piece of cake in this market," he said. "You probably should have held out for more."

"What's that I just heard?" Elyse asked, coming into the room, looking fresh and lovely in a floral-print skirt and a white off-the-shoulder blouse. "You sold a house for eight million dollars?" she asked me. "Congratulations. That's fantastic."

"It's no big deal," my father said.

"What are you talking about, Vic? Of course it's a big deal. Well done, Jodi! You should be very proud of yourself."

"Thank you," I said, bracing myself for my father's angry rebuke. Astoundingly, none was forthcoming.

"And what's this I see? You didn't offer your daughter a glass of lemonade?"

"That's all right," I demurred. "I'm not thirsty."

"Nonsense. I made it fresh this afternoon and it's not too sour, not too sweet. You must try some." She retrieved the pitcher from the fridge and poured me a glass. "Well?" she asked as I took a sip.

"Perfect," I said. "Exactly the right amount of tart."

"Just like the woman who made it," my father said, and Elyse laughed.

I pushed aside a vague feeling of unease. Was my father flirting? I wondered, then immediately dismissed the notion as absurd. The man was almost eighty, for God's sake. Although he'd been quite the womanizer in his day, I recalled, understanding even as a child that his philandering was the source of many of my parents' worst fights. "That's a lovely blouse," I told Elyse, trying to still the echo of their angry voices in my head.

"Isn't it?" she agreed. "Your father saw it in a store window and insisted I go have a look."

"I knew she had the perfect shoulders for it," my father said.

"And he was right," Elyse agreed.

"I always am," my father said.

"Oh, Vic," Elyse said with a laugh, turning back to me. "Can I get you something to eat? A piece of apple pie, perhaps?"

"She doesn't need pie," my father said before I could answer.

"Right again," I said, taking another sip of lemonade to avoid throwing the glass at his head.

"Jodi is planning to bring the kids over for a swim on Saturday," my father announced.

"How wonderful," Elyse said. "Would you like me to stay and look after them?"

"Oh, no," I said quickly. "Weekends are your time off."

"It's no bother. And I have no plans."

"It appears that Jodi has no plans, either," my father said pointedly.

"Honestly. It won't be necessary," I said. "But thank you for the offer." *What is it with the men in my life that I can never please either one of them?* I wondered, checking my watch. "I should probably head out. I'll just go upstairs and say hi to Mom."

"Tell her I'll be up in a few minutes to check on her," Elyse said as I was leaving the room.

"Will do." I turned to see Elyse's hand brush against the side of my father's arm as she reached for the pitcher of lemonade in the middle of the table. My earlier unease returned as I watched my father's eyes follow her to the fridge, his lips curling into a sly smile. I turned away before I could see anything else.

"Hi, Mom," I said, entering the bedroom and stopping at the foot of her bed. "How are you feeling today?"

She didn't answer, and for a minute, I thought she might be asleep. Then I saw her legs twitch beneath her blankets and her arms shoot toward me.

I hurried toward her, not wanting to pass on an unexpected embrace. "You're looking well," I lied as her arms dropped to her sides before I could fill them.

She angled her head toward me, her mouth twisting around a word I couldn't make out.

"What's that? I'm sorry. I didn't understand."

She repeated the sound. I still couldn't make it out.

"One more time." I moved my ear to just below her mouth.

"Earrings," she hissed, the word vibrating with impatience.

My hand reached for my ear. "Yes, I bought them a few days ago. I sold this house in Forest Hill for quite a lot of money, and so I treated myself to a little reward. You're the first person to notice them," I added happily. I'd been wearing them all week and Harrison hadn't said a thing. "Do you like them?"

"No," she said clearly.

I almost smiled. My mother's taste and mine had rarely aligned, and she'd never been one to mince words. It was strangely comforting to realize that some things never changed.

"Earrings," she said again.

I perched on the edge of the bed, eager to change the subject. "So, how are things going with Elyse? She taking good care of you? You like her?"

"Earrings," my mother persisted stubbornly.

I nodded, mindful that people suffering from dementia often become fixated on inconsequential things. Had she reached that stage? I reached for her hand, but she jerked it away. A spasm, I told myself, determined not to take it personally.

"Everything all right in here?" Elyse asked from the doorway.

"It seems that she doesn't care for my earrings," I answered.

"Really? I think they're quite lovely."

I leaned over to kiss my mother's forehead, but another spasm suddenly shook her and I ended up with a mouthful of her hair. "Bye, Mom," I whispered to the top of her head. "I'll see you soon." I moved quickly to where Elyse was standing. "I'm not sure she even knows who I am anymore," I whispered.

"She knows," Elyse said, laying a comforting hand on my arm. "And those really are beautiful earrings."

"Thank you."

"Earrings! Earrings!" I heard my mother shout as I left the room.

SIXTEEN

Elyse was waiting at the door with a plate of chocolate chip cookies when I arrived with the kids on Saturday. "Just one each," she warned as they reached for them. "I've prepared a very special lunch for you, and I don't want you ruining your appetite."

"Elyse, no," I protested. "You're not even supposed to be here. It's your day off."

"What's a day off?" asked Daphne.

"It means that she doesn't have to work," I said pointedly to Elyse.

"She's not working," Sam informed me. "She's going swimming with us. Aren't you, Elyse?"

"Just try to stop me."

"Can I have another cookie?" Daphne asked.

"Do you promise to eat all your lunch?"

"I promise."

"Okay, then. One more. What about you, Sam?"

"What's for lunch?" he asked, always the more cautious of my two children.

"How does fish heads and fiddlesticks sound?" Elyse asked.

"Ew! No!"

Daphne promptly dropped the cookie she was holding back onto the plate.

"All right, then," Elyse said with a smile. "How about peanut butter and jelly sandwiches and homemade blueberry popsicles? Sound better?"

"Much better," Sam said, stuffing another cookie into his mouth before Elyse could reconsider her offer. "Can we go for a ride in the elevator?" he asked as we entered the house.

"Why don't we save that for later?"

"Okay," Sam said without protest.

"You're so good with them," I marveled as we headed down the stairs to the lower level.

In a matter of minutes, the kids had discarded the clothes covering their swimsuits and were waiting at the side of the pool. "Come on, Elyse," Sam called. "Hurry up."

"Mommy, put on my water wings," Daphne urged.

"I'll do it. You just sit here and relax," Elyse told me, motioning me toward one of the chaise longues. "You're looking a little tired. Are you feeling all right?"

"I'm fine," I said, hearing the weariness in my voice.

"You don't sound too sure."

"It's been a rough week."

"But you had that big sale."

"It's not work. Work's going great." Unexpected tears suddenly filled my eyes.

"Oh, dear," Elyse said, her own eyes welling up in sympathy. "Home . . . not so much?"

"Not so much."

"Well, I won't pry," she said. "Just know that I'm here, if you ever want to talk about . . . anything."

"Elyse," Sam cried. "Come on. Hurry up!"

"Coming!"

"You really don't have to do this," I said as she pulled her shapeless mauve shift up over her head to reveal a well-toned body in a black one-piece bathing suit. *I should look half as good when I'm her age,* I thought, then wondered if anyone would notice. It had been weeks since Harrison and I had been intimate. He'd barely looked at me since our fight.

"Are you kidding me?" Elyse asked. "I've been looking forward to this all morning." She walked toward the pool, then stopped, staring back at the house. "Oh, look, kids," she said, waving toward my mother's bedroom window. "There's Grandpa."

"Where?"

"There. In the window. See?"

I craned my neck to glimpse my father standing by the window, looking down at us.

At Elyse.

I wasn't sure if I actually saw the wide grin on his face or if I only imagined it.

"Hi, Grandpa," Sam shouted, waving.

"Hi, Grandpa," Daphne echoed, jumping up and down.

My father acknowledged their greeting with a nod, then turned away.

"Your mother's been quite agitated this morning," Elyse confided. "Your father hasn't left her side."

"Can I ask you something?" I asked her, not sure exactly what question I had in mind.

"Of course." Elyse looked toward the pool where my children were waiting. "Give me two more minutes, kids. Then I'm all yours." She tilted her head, waiting for my question.

"It's about my father."

"Yes?"

"How is he treating you?"

"How is he treating me?" she repeated. "He's been lovely. Why? Is there a problem?"

"How lovely?" I pressed.

She looked confused. "I'm not sure I understand the question."

"My father," I began, then stopped, began again. "My father can be . . . complicated."

"Makes him that much more interesting," she said. "Most men are rather simple creatures, don't you think?"

"It's just that when he was younger . . ." I said, trying a different approach.

"Elyse!" Sam called.

"One second, sweetheart!" she called back. "Go on," she said to me. "When he was younger . . . ?"

"Well . . . he wasn't the most faithful of husbands."

She looked genuinely shocked. "Really? He seems so dedicated to your mother." She glanced toward my mother's bedroom window.

"Yes, he is, but . . ."

"But?"

"I'm just concerned that . . . well, he's still a relatively attractive man and he's always had a very healthy ego. He likes to . . . how can I say this?"

"Flirt?" Elyse said for me.

"Yes," I acknowledged. I chose my next words very carefully. "He's from a different generation. He doesn't understand that what was once considered acceptable behavior just *isn't* anymore, and I wouldn't want you to take offense." *Or quit,* I was thinking. "Like if he makes a suggestive remark or touches you in a way you consider inappropriate. You don't have to put up with it. You just have to tell him to cut it out . . ."

She laughed, her eyes sparkling. "Oh, Jodi. You can stop worrying. It takes a whole lot more than that to offend me. That's the problem with *your* generation, if you don't mind my saying. You're all so easily offended. Such a waste of energy."

"So . . . everything's okay?"

"Couldn't be better. And to be honest, I like to flirt a bit myself. It's fun." She winked. "Maybe you should give it a try."

Yeah, right, I thought, watching her slip the water wings onto my daughter's arms with the same ease with which she handled everything else.

I doubted that Harrison would be receptive to any attempt at flirting on my part. And the truth was that flirting wasn't exactly my strong suit. I'd always been too direct, too straightforward, to be a successful flirt, which usually involved an innate cunning I lacked.

I slipped off my cover-up and settled into the chaise longue, watching Elyse frolic in the water with my children.

And to be honest, she'd said, *I like to flirt a bit myself.* I confess that, at the time, I found her admission charming. Now I realize that it was one of the few honest things she ever said.

— SEVENTEEN —

Whenever I can't sleep, I compile lists of names.

I start with the letter *A* and work my way through the alphabet. *A* is for Anne; *B* is for Barbara; *C* is for Courtney. Down to *Z* is for Zelda. Then I start over again, using different names: *A* is for Amy; *B* is for Blythe; *C* is for Caroline. Down to *Z* is for Ziva.

Sometimes, I use only girls' names, sometimes boys'. Occasionally, I combine them. *E* is for Ellie; *F* is for Frank; *G* is for Gwynneth; *H* is for Hayden. This is a little easier than it used to be now that so many names apply to either sex.

Occasionally, I make it more difficult for myself. I try for five names a letter: R is for Renee, Rose, Ruth, Rhonda, and Rachael; *S* is for Shannon, Skylar, Susan, Sheila, and Samantha; *T* is for Tommy, Timothy, Travis, Tony, and Teddy.

Well, you get the idea.

At first, I'd be asleep within minutes, but as I grew accustomed to the game, I found it taking longer and longer to work. Certain letters, in particular, gave me great difficulty. There are only so many names that begin with *U*, *V*, *W*, and *Y*, and I defy anyone to come up with more than a couple of names for *Q*, *X*, and *Z*. Sometimes, trying to come up with new names is the very thing keeping me awake.

Still, I persist. Like most habits, it's a hard one to break.

And I've been doing it since I was a child.

It started as a way to block out the sound of my parents' fighting. "A is for Alison," I'd whisper, my hands pressed tightly against my ears to block out their angry voices. "B is for Bonnie. C is for Cathy."

"What are you mumbling about?" I remember Tracy asking one especially bad night. "Whatever it is," she continued, not waiting for my reply, "stop it. I'm trying to sleep."

This was followed by a loud thump. "What was that?" I asked her.

"What was what?"

"That noise. Didn't you hear it?"

"It's nothing. Go to sleep."

"I'm scared," I said, but I received only an exasperated sigh in response.

The angry voices bounded up the stairs, took root in the hallway. I climbed out of bed and approached the bedroom door, opening it a crack and peeking down the hall to where my parents stood.

"You're nothing but a bully," I watched my mother shout. "A bully and a liar."

"And you're a crazy bitch," my father shot back, his right arm lifting into the air.

"Go ahead," my mother dared. "Hit me again, you miserable bastard!"

Which was exactly what he did.

I gasped as she fell to the floor.

"For God's sake, Jodi. What are you doing?" Tracy demanded. "Shut the door and get back into bed."

"What are you doing?" another voice asked suddenly. Harrison.

What was happening? What was he doing in my childhood bedroom?

I opened my eyes, glancing toward the unfamiliar bedside clock, noting it was after midnight. What was happening? Where was I? "What?"

"Who are Alison and Bonnie?"

"What?" I asked again.

"You were talking in your sleep."

"I was?"

"Something about a bunch of women. Alison . . . Bonnie . . . somebody else."

"Oh," I said, my surroundings coming into clear focus as I came fully awake. "Oh, no. Sorry. It's just this thing I do when I can't sleep," I started to explain.

"You were definitely asleep," he interrupted, turning onto his side, away from me. His posture told me that he was no longer listening.

"Harrison?"

"What?"

"How long are you going to stay mad at me?" I'd canceled all my appointments to spend the weekend with him and the kids, and he'd spent all that time holed up with his computer. Not only that, but he was still giving me the silent treatment. I was starting to wonder if a knock-down, drag-out fight might be a preferable alternative.

Was that the reason for my disturbing dream?

And had I been dreaming . . . or remembering?

Had my father actually struck my mother?

"I'm not mad," Harrison said, flipping onto his back.

My heart felt a surge of hope. "No?"

"Just disappointed," he said.

The surge instantly died.

"I guess I shouldn't be surprised," he added. "It's like this every summer."

"What is?"

"You."

"Me?" I propped myself up on my elbow, stared through the darkness at his face, as if watching his lips move would help clarify what he was saying.

"I don't know what it is. Whether you feel left out or threatened . . ."

"Threatened? By what? What are you talking about?"

"I'm talking about how every summer, when it comes time to teach my course, you get . . ."

"I get what?"

"You change."

"I change . . . how? I don't understand."

"I know you don't," he said. "That's part of the problem."

"What is it that you think I do differently?" I pressed, genuinely curious.

"It's not so much what you do . . ."

"Then what?"

"You're just . . . different. I don't know. It's hard to explain. It's like we're suddenly in competition. You get extra busy at work, you're never around. When you *are* here, you're distracted . . ."

"Summer's my busiest time. You know that."

"You take off the second a client summons. You assume I'll drop whatever I'm doing to look after the kids," he continued, as if I hadn't spoken. "So, in addition to my teaching, I'm expected to be at their beck and call when I'm home, which you know is the time I need for writing. It's almost like you're trying to punish me."

"That's ridiculous. I'm not trying to punish you."

"It sure feels like it. What is it, Jodi? Are you jealous?"

"Jealous? Of what?"

"You tell me."

"I don't know what you're talking about," I said.

He sighed. "Look. Let's just drop it. Okay? It's late. We're tired. And we're not going to solve anything by going around in circles. There's just one more week of classes, and then my course will be over. You think you can tough it out for one more week?"

"I honestly don't have a problem . . ." I started, then stopped. He was right. We weren't going to solve anything by going around in circles. "Okay," I said. "I guess I can try scheduling my appointments so that I'm home more."

"That would be great," he said. "Oh, and I've been meaning to tell you. I've been asked to attend a writers' workshop this weekend in Prince Edward County."

"This weekend? Prince Edward County?" I repeated, although I'd heard him perfectly well. Prince Edward

County was prime cottage country, about a four-hour drive from Toronto. "When did this happen?"

"About a month ago. I kept meaning to mention it, but you were always in a mood, and it never seemed like the right time to bring it up."

"What kind of writers' workshop?" I asked, mostly to keep from asking, *What do you mean, I was always in a mood?*

"More or less an extension of what I've been doing all summer. Teach a few classes, give a few lectures, sit on a panel. I'll leave Friday afternoon, right after the closing luncheon. Be back late Sunday night."

"So, you accepted?"

"Is that a problem?"

"I guess not." I decided not to bother asking whether the kids and I could tag along, since it was obvious what the answer would be. "It would have been nice to have a little more notice, that's all."

"Now you know how it feels," he said, giving me a light peck on the forehead. "It's late," he said again, flopping over on his side, facing the far wall. "I have a very busy week ahead of me."

I lay there, my eyes wide open, my body vibrating with frustration, staring at the ceiling and praying for a sleep that never came. *A is for Adam,* I began silently. *B is for Bill . . . C is for Chandler . . . D is for Daniel . . . E is for Eric . . .*

—EIGHTEEN—

"It's Roger McAdams," the voice on the phone announced.

"Mr. McAdams," I said. "I was just about to call you."

"Perfect timing. And please, call me Roger."

"I've been compiling a list of properties that I think might be suitable . . ."

"Which is exactly why I called. I think I may have found something."

"Oh?"

"I got a tip from a co-worker about a condo at Harbourfront. Not on the market yet, but the owner is willing to let me have a look-see. Are you free to go over there around five this afternoon?"

Shit, I thought. Last night Harrison had accused me again of putting my job ahead of my family, of not being around enough for Sam and Daphne. And then he'd added a new wrinkle, asking if I was jealous, if I felt threatened. And however vague and unfair such statements had been, hadn't I promised to try scheduling my appointments so that I was more available to him and the kids?

Of course, that was before he sprang the news of his little weekend getaway to Prince Edward County.

Now you know how it feels, he'd said, a tad too smugly for my liking.

"Sure," I said to Roger McAdams. "What's the address? I'll meet you there."

He gave me the address. I hung up the phone and left a message for Harrison on his cell, telling him something had come up and I likely wouldn't be home before seven, and to start dinner without me.

Half an hour later, Harrison left me a message in return: "Why aren't I surprised?"

No surprise there, either.

Roger McAdams was waiting for me in the all-white marble lobby of the condominium building at Harbour-front. He was taller and better-looking than I remembered, and he seemed so genuinely pleased to see me that it was all I could do to keep from bursting into tears.

"Well, aren't you a sight for sore eyes," he said in greeting. "You look beautiful. Blue is definitely your color."

I brushed some invisible hairs away from my face in an effort to hide the blush I felt spreading across my cheeks. Was he flirting with me? I wondered. "Have you been waiting long?" I asked in return. As I've mentioned, flirting has never been my forte.

It's fun, I heard Elyse say. *Maybe you should give it a try.*

"Just got here," he said. "I really appreciate you being able to do this on such short notice."

"No problem," I lied, already anticipating the cold shoulder waiting for me at home.

"This way." He led me through the lushly furnished marble lobby to the bank of elevators to his right. "The condo is on the eighteenth floor, overlooking the water. I have the key."

"You heard about this place through a co-worker?" I asked on the ride up, even though I already knew the answer. But it was better than listening to the unexpectedly rapid beating of my heart.

What's the matter with you? I thought. *A man pays you a simple compliment and you go all weak in the knees?*

"Yes. It's her boyfriend's place. He proposed over the weekend, so she thinks they'll be in the market for something a little bigger. This is supposedly a two-bedroom, but technically it's really a one-bedroom and a den. Not sure what the distinction is."

"It means the room has no windows," I explained. "It would have to have windows for it to qualify as a bedroom."

He smiled. "You see. That's why I called you. I didn't know that."

The elevators opened onto the eighteenth floor.

"This way," he said, his hand on my bare elbow as he led me down the carpeted hall.

I felt a jolt of electricity as the palm of his hand connected with the flesh of my arm, and I confess to being disappointed when his arm returned to his side.

"Here we are," he said, stopping in front of a large double door and sliding the key into the lock. "Shall we?" He pushed open the door and we stepped into a beautiful apartment whose floor-to-ceiling windows offered a panoramic view of Lake Ontario that could only be described as breathtaking.

The apartment was impressive as well: a spacious, open-concept, living-dining-kitchen area, the kitchen boasting all the latest in high-end appliances and custom-built cabinets. The master bedroom down the hall was a nice size and came with its own en suite. Even the smaller, windowless room to the right of the front door felt airy and bright. There were hardwood floors throughout, a powder room, and a decent-size, south-facing terrace.

"It's lovely," I said as we walked through the unit. "Do you have any idea how much they're thinking of asking?"

"None," he said. "Do you?"

Actually I did. I'd spent the better part of the afternoon researching similar sales in the area, and this building in particular. "I'd say in the neighborhood of two and a half million dollars." I waited for a gasp that never came.

"Sounds reasonable," he said.

I tried not to let my surprise register on my face. Even though it was my job, it was hard for me to get my head around the ever-escalating, skyrocketing prices of the Toronto real estate market. The analysts kept predicting it wouldn't—couldn't possibly—continue, and yet every year, prices not only jumped, they soared.

I was also trying not to be impressed by the ease with which he'd accepted my evaluation, as if he'd expected as much. As if two and a half million dollars was no big deal. As if it was well within the price range he'd been considering.

Handsome, charming, and a man of means, I couldn't help thinking.

"So, what do we do now?" he asked when we'd completed our tour.

"I guess we wait till they make up their minds about selling. In the meantime, I can show you other condos in a similar price range. It's always a good idea to have options."

"Sounds good. This weekend?"

"This weekend?" I repeated.

"To look at condos?" he clarified.

I hesitated, knowing how Harrison would react, already hearing his all-too-familiar list of complaints. But then, Harrison wouldn't be around this weekend, I reminded myself. "This weekend is good," I said, wondering if I could impose on Elyse one last time.

"How about some dinner?" he asked.

"What?"

"Well, it's almost six o'clock. I know a nice little spot not too far from here . . ."

"Oh, no. Thank you, but I should really be getting home."

"Of course."

Home to a cold dinner and an even colder reception, I thought, reaching inside my purse for my phone. "Could you give me a minute?"

"Of course," he said again, moving toward the long expanse of windows to give me some privacy.

I called Harrison to tell him I'd finished earlier than expected and to wait dinner for me after all.

"We already ate," he said.

"Already? It's not even six o'clock."

"Kids were hungry. So was I."

I glanced toward where Roger McAdams stood, staring at the lake. "Well, maybe I'll just grab something on my way home."

"Suit yourself."

"Harrison . . ."

The line went dead in my hand.

"Thank you. I think I will." I returned the phone to my purse and then stood there, staring at the polished hardwood floor, debating what I should do. The smart option was to go straight home. The other option was standing by the windows, staring at the lake.

"Problems?" Roger asked, catching my gaze and walking back toward me.

Don't do it, a little voice warned as he drew near.

But it was already too late.

I smiled. "It seems that I'm free for dinner after all."

NINETEEN

"What should we toast?" Roger asked, clicking his wineglass against mine. We were sitting in a small, brightly lit Italian restaurant on King Street, having ordered dinner—pasta for me, grilled shrimp for him—about to partake of a bottle of Chianti.

"To finding you the condo of your dreams," I offered.

"I will definitely drink to that." He took a sip of his wine, then watched as I did the same. "So, what do you think?"

"About what?"

He laughed. "The wine. Do you like it?"

"It's wonderful," I said, feeling silly. Harrison never asked my opinion of the wine he selected. "Very smooth."

"Very smooth indeed." He leaned back in his chair. "So, tell me about Jodi Bishop."

"Not much to tell," I demurred. "What you see is pretty much what you get."

"Somehow I doubt that. You strike me as a woman with very deep thoughts."

I laughed, feeling flattered, and took another sip of my wine.

"What's funny?"

"Just that no one has ever accused me of having deep thoughts before."

His turn to laugh. "Sounds like no one has ever looked closely enough."

I took another, longer sip of my wine. *Is he flirting with me?* I wondered again. This was immediately followed by: *So, what if he is? A little flirting never hurt anyone.*

"Have you always wanted to sell real estate?" he asked.

"I don't think any little girl ever grows up dreaming to be a real estate agent," I said honestly.

"What *did* you grow up dreaming to be?"

"Initially, a dancer. Like my mother."

"What changed your mind?"

"My father," I said with a shrug. "He said I had absolutely no talent, and it would be a waste of everyone's time."

"He sounds lovely."

"Unfortunately, he was right." I shrugged again, this one bigger than the first. "Then, in college, I decided I wanted to study interior design."

"What stopped you?"

"My father," I said again. "He said I should concentrate my energy on something where I'd have a better chance at success, leave the more artsy, stylish pursuits to my more artsy, stylish sister."

He smiled. The smile said: *You are ineffably charming.*

Or maybe it was the wine that was telling me that.

Whatever it was, I was enjoying it.

Elyse was right: flirting *was* fun.

"What about you? Did you always want to be in . . . whatever it is that you do?" I asked, realizing I had no idea what that was, other than that he worked on Bay Street, which likely meant it involved finance.

"That would be wealth management," he said.

"Something every little boy dreams of."

A sly grin spread across his face. "Actually, when I was a kid, I wanted to be an astronaut."

"And what changed *your* mind?"

"The whole zero gravity thing," he said. "I absolutely loathe throwing up. Plus, I'm a little claustrophobic, so the idea of being stuck in a capsule orbiting the earth with no way out for months on end didn't exactly thrill."

"And managing other people's money does?"

"It does," he said. "More wine?"

I looked down at my glass, and was surprised to see that it was empty. "I probably shouldn't," I said as he poured more into my glass. "Okay, just a bit."

"So, okay. How did we get from interior design to real estate?" he asked.

"You really want to know?"

"I really do."

I told him about my father's company, how I'd started working there as his assistant one summer, and how after graduating university with a more or less useless general arts degree, I'd opted to get my real estate license, then joined my father's agency.

"Hoping to finally get Daddy's seal of approval," Roger stated more than asked.

I opened my mouth to respond, but no sound emerged. Was I really that transparent? So much for my deep thoughts.

"And do you enjoy selling real estate?"

"I'm good at it," I answered.

"Not quite what I asked."

I said nothing.

"What is it you like best about it?" he pressed.

I took another long sip of wine, feeling almost giddy. I wasn't used to anyone showing so much interest in what I did. Harrison had never questioned me with such intensity. Oh, he'd tried on occasion to feign curiosity in what I did, but I could tell by the glaze that overtook his eyes after a few minutes of shop talk that his heart wasn't in it. The fact was that my husband had never been terribly interested in my work. Our conversations, even when we first started dating, usually centered on *his* work, *his* thoughts, *his* opinions.

And for a long time, I'd been okay with that.

"What do I like best about what I do?" I repeated, wondering when that had changed. "Like I said, I think I just discovered something I was actually good at," I said simply.

"Don't do that," Roger said.

"Do what?"

"Underestimate yourself."

"I don't . . ."

"You do," he said. "You want to know what I think?"

"I'm not sure," I said honestly, more than a little taken aback.

"I think you'd be good at whatever you set your mind to."

"You haven't seen me dance," I said, hoping for a laugh. I was finding it increasingly disconcerting that a man I barely knew seemed to know me so well.

"How long have you been married?" he asked, his eyes glancing toward my wedding band.

At this point, I probably should have told him that we were venturing into increasingly uncomfortable territory, getting perhaps a little too personal, and we should stick to discussing real estate. Or the weather.

Something safe.

Instead I took another sip of wine and said, "Going on ten years. How long have you been divorced?"

"Four."

"And I seem to remember you saying you had no children."

"Correct. You?"

"Two. Sam is eight and Daphne is three."

"Great names."

"Great kids," I said.

"Never a doubt."

The waiter approached with our dinners, and I dug in gratefully, it being harder to talk with your mouth full. My mind was racing, my thoughts not so much deep as they were disconcerting. I watched him eat, wondering how his lips would feel on mine. I watched his fingers deftly and delicately remove the shell from a piece of shrimp and imagined those same fingers unbuttoning my blouse and sliding it off my shoulders. I watched him lick the sauce from his fork and felt his tongue trace the inside of my thigh.

I heard myself sigh.

"Something wrong?" he asked, looking up from his plate, unaware of my musings.

"No," I answered.

Only everything, I thought.

—TWENTY—

I didn't go straight home.

I stopped at my parents' house first, ostensibly to check on my mother, but really to give myself an excuse for why I was so late getting back. It was after eight o'clock, and Harrison would no doubt question what had taken me so long. This way I wouldn't have to lie. I already felt guilty enough, even though technically, I'd done nothing wrong.

It wasn't as if I'd been on a date or anything, I told myself.

I parked in the driveway and approached the front door. It was still light out, and would remain so till after eight. The house itself was dark, although that wasn't unusual. The lights were probably on toward the back. I checked my watch again, deciding it was too early for everyone to be asleep, then rang the buzzer and waited.

And waited.

"That's odd," I said to the empty street. "Where is everybody?"

The street had no response.

I rang the buzzer again, my mind filling with increasingly outrageous possibilities: My father and Elyse had taken my mother for a walk. Or a drive. Or maybe my mother had taken a turn for the worse and they were on their way to the hospital. Or maybe there'd been a gas leak the previous night and they'd all died in their sleep. Or maybe some lunatic had broken in and slaughtered them all.

I shook my head. My thoughts weren't so much deep as they were hysterical, I decided, ringing the buzzer a third time before remembering that I had a key.

I rifled through my purse until I found it. "Hello?" I called as I entered the main hall. "Anybody home?"

No answer.

"Hello?" I said again, louder this time. "Dad? Elyse? Anyone?"

Still no response.

I walked toward the stairs, listening for signs of activity, but heard nothing. "Dad?" I called as I mounted the stairs. "Elyse?"

I stopped in front of the closed door to my mother's bedroom, not sure what to do. Should I knock or just go in? What if she wasn't there? What if she was dead?

Enough with the what-ifs. "Just open the fucking door," I told myself.

I took a deep breath, twisted the doorknob, and pushed the door open.

The blackout shades were down and the room was in darkness. I debated flipping on the overhead light, then decided to give my eyes time to adjust to the dark. Slowly, I approached the bed.

I smelled her before I saw her.

She was lying on her side, and the steadiness of her breathing told me she was asleep. That she'd soiled herself was obvious from the unpleasant odor drifting up through the sheets. "Poor Mom," I whispered, gently patting the awkward rise of her hip.

Where is my father? Where is Elyse?

I tiptoed out of the room and ran down the hall to my father's bedroom. His door was open and I reached in and flipped on the light. But the room was empty. Had he and Elyse gone out and left my mother alone?

I hurried down the stairs to the main floor, quickly peeking into each room, finding no one.

"Dad?" I called, descending the stairs to the lower level. "Elyse?"

Unfamiliar voices wafted toward my ears.

"You killed his dog?!"

What the hell was happening?

"Who is this guy anyway? The boogeyman?"

I tiptoed down the hall.

"He's the guy you send to kill *the boogeyman!"*

I stopped in front of the door to the home theater, found myself staring at the wide-screen TV mounted on the wall. *John Wick!* I realized. An old movie starring Keanu Reeves. "Oh, my God!" I said, seeing my father and Elyse sitting side by side in the oversize leather chairs, a large bowl of popcorn on the armrest between them.

Elyse screamed at the sound of my voice and jumped from her seat, upending the bowl of popcorn and sending kernels flying in all directions.

"What the hell?" my father shouted as the sound of gunfire erupted from the screen. He immediately muted the sound and paused the action. "Jodi?! What are you doing here? How did you get in?"

"I used my key," I told him as Elyse turned on the overhead light. "I rang the buzzer but nobody heard me."

"So, you just walked in?"

"She was obviously worried," Elyse said, coming to my defense. "Are you all right, dear?"

"I don't understand," my father said, not so easily mollified. "What are you doing here?"

"I had a late showing in the area," I lied, "and I thought I'd drop in, see how Mom was doing."

"You should have called first."

"She's soiled herself," I said, as if one thought followed naturally on the other.

"Oh, my goodness," Elyse said quickly. "She was perfectly fine less than an hour ago. I changed her diaper and made sure she was asleep before we came downstairs. I'll go right up and get her taken care of."

"You'll do no such thing," my father said, his hand reaching for Elyse's arm to stop her. "This is hardly the first time this has happened. And waking your mother up," he said to me, "disturbing her now, will only upset her. Best to let sleeping dogs lie."

I wasn't sure what alarmed me more, picturing my helpless, once-elegant mother lying in her own waste till morning, or my father comparing her to a sleeping dog.

My face must have registered my horror, for Elyse was quick to respond. "Your father didn't mean that the way it sounded," she assured me. "I'll go upstairs and get her changed. She's had her sleeping pill, so I'm pretty sure I can do it without waking her up."

"Thank you," I whispered as she exited the room.

My father and I stared at each other in silence.

"I guess I should be going," I said finally.

"Call first next time," he said instead of goodbye.

—TWENTY-ONE—

I spent the next half hour driving aimlessly around, trying to wrap my head around my father's seeming indifference to my mother's plight. I told myself that after years of playing nursemaid, it was only natural that he'd become somewhat inured to, even resentful of, her condition, and that in order to effectively care for her, he'd had to distance himself emotionally.

Not that he'd ever been the warmest, most sympathetic of men. And their relationship, perhaps understandably, had deteriorated along with her condition. It was pretty obvious that they hadn't had any kind of sexual relationship in years, so it was only natural that he would enjoy the company of an attractive woman whose job it was to make him comfortable.

He just seemed a little too comfortable for my liking.

I told myself that I was being petty and judgmental. What was wrong with my father and Elyse watching a movie together?

Surely it was every bit as innocent as my dinner with Roger McAdams.

"Oh, God," I said, pulling into my driveway and laying my head against the steering wheel.

I'm not sure what I'd been expecting when I arrived home, probably a continuation of the silent treatment I'd been getting from my husband for days, or maybe a rebuke for coming home so late. But when I walked through our front door at just after nine o'clock, there were no complaints from Harrison about his having had to feed the children and put them to bed. On the contrary, he seemed genuinely happy to see me. "How'd it go?" he asked.

I told him about going to check out the condo at Harbourfront and then dropping in to see my mother. I left out the part about having dinner with Roger McAdams in between.

Best to let sleeping dogs lie, I heard my father say.

A fresh wave of guilt swept over me.

"I'm sorry I've been such a jackass the last few weeks," Harrison surprised me by saying, compounding my guilt.

"I'm sorry I was so late getting home," I whispered.

Which was when he grabbed me, his hands seemingly everywhere at once, inside my blouse, under my skirt, ultimately tugging my panties down over my hips, unzipping his fly.

"The kids . . ."

"Asleep," he said, pushing into me.

We made love with an urgency that took my breath away, standing up against the wall, my skirt balled around my waist, his jeans around his knees, as he thrust repeatedly into me.

Had he missed me these past weeks as much as I'd been missing him, I couldn't help wondering, or was there something else at play here? Had Harrison sensed there was more to tonight than I was letting on?

He pulled out, giving my backside a playful slap. "I'm going to take a shower."

I watched him bound up the stairs, then wobbled on unsteady legs into the living room, where I sank into one of the chairs, my happiness sinking under the weight of my guilt. I should never have had dinner with Roger McAdams. Flirting might be fun for other people, but it was definitely not for me. I had a husband who loved me, I told myself. Never again would I do anything to jeopardize that.

Which was when I heard the beep of an incoming message and noticed Harrison's cellphone on the coffee table.

I'm not sure what made me pick it up, or what made me flip open the phone's protective case and glance at the message. Of course, all I could access without my husband's passcode was the first line, but that was more than enough: *Can't wait for the weekend* . . . the message began.

The message was from @songbird. It didn't take a psychic to figure out that @songbird was Wren.

I'm not sure how long I sat there, my body shaking, my legs unable to move. So it was Wren, and not me, who'd aroused Harrison's unexpected and sudden passion. Clearly, my husband couldn't wait for the weekend, either.

"Hey," he called, coming halfway down the stairs, wrapped in the navy-and-gold terry cloth bathrobe I'd given him last Christmas. "Aren't you coming up?" He stopped. "Jodi? Is everything all right?"

I held out his phone. "You have a message."

He padded into the living room on bare feet, and took the phone from my hand, barely glancing at the screen. "You opened it," he said, more acknowledgment than accusation.

"I did it without thinking," I said, hoping to avoid a confrontation while organizing my thoughts.

He nodded. "You read it."

"I didn't mean to."

"And now, you think . . . what exactly?"

"I'm not sure what to think. Suppose you tell me."

"Tell you what?"

"What's going on," I said, praying for a logical explanation, one I could accept without having to twist my common sense into too many knots.

"There's nothing going on."

"'*Can't wait for the weekend*'?" I challenged. "Sounds like plenty going on to me."

"Would you like me to explain?"

"Can you?"

"Yes. But you're not going to like it."

"I'm pretty sure of that," I agreed.

"Not for the reasons you think," Harrison said. "But because you're going to feel like an idiot."

I waited, said nothing. *Won't be the first time,* I thought.

He shook his head. "Okay. Here's the story." Deep breath, another shake of his head. "Wren approached me at the beginning of the summer, said her parents have a cottage in Prince Edward County, and every year, they hold a literary event where they have an author come speak, hold seminars, et cetera. Apparently, they'd had a local author lined up but he'd had to cancel. Normally they wouldn't think of asking someone of my stature, especially on such short notice, yada, yada, yada, but would I consider doing it? The pay was a thousand dollars. I said to let me think about it. And the more I thought about it, the more I thought it was a good idea, so I said okay."

"Why didn't you tell me that it was Wren who'd arranged it?"

"I didn't think it was important."

"Not important," I repeated.

"Okay. I knew how you'd react."

"Which was?"

"Exactly how you're reacting."

I nodded. "I take it that Wren will be there?"

"Of course she will. Her parents have a cottage there. What are you implying, Jodi? You think I'm having an affair?"

"Are you?"

"Of course not! For one thing, it's unethical, and could get me fired. She's my student, for God's sake. And for another thing, I'm a married man who happens to love his wife. And I thought that she loved me!"

"I *do* love you."

"You just don't trust me."

"I *do* trust you."

"Really? Because it sure doesn't feel like it."

"What am I supposed to think when I see a message like that?" I asked him, feeling every bit the idiot he'd warned me about.

"I don't know. I guess that's the problem with snooping."

"I wasn't snooping."

"Weren't you?" He ran an impatient hand through his damp hair. "Look. Think whatever the hell you want. Believe me; don't believe me. It's up to you. All I know is that if the situation were reversed, I wouldn't be jumping to conclusions before I knew all the facts. I would trust you." One last shake of his head. "Way to ruin a nice night," he said, turning on his heel and disappearing up the stairs.

TWENTY-TWO

I have no excuse for what happened next.

That being said, I'll try anyway.

It started with Tracy.

"So, hypothetically, would you want someone to tell you if your husband was having an affair?" she asked, the supposedly hypothetical question clearly one that she'd been mulling over all evening.

It was Friday night and we were sitting across from each other at my parents' dining room table, Tracy sipping her second cup of espresso, me finishing off a second piece of the peach pie Elyse had baked for dessert. Our mother was upstairs in her bed. Our father had excused himself moments earlier to check on Sam and Daphne, who were watching cartoons downstairs. Elyse was in the kitchen, tidying up and singing softly to herself.

I'd phoned that morning to ask if I could impose on her generosity one last time and bring the kids over for a few hours the next afternoon so I could meet with a client, explaining that Harrison was out of town for the weekend. She'd said yes immediately, then invited me and the kids over for dinner. "I'll ask Tracy, too," she'd said. "I think it's good for your father to have his daughters and grandchildren around as much as possible. And I know your mother will be so happy to see you all again."

I don't know why I didn't find it odd that it was Elyse who'd issued the invitation, and not my father. Or that she would do so without first checking with him. I guess that it felt so seamless that I didn't think to question it. Elyse was the one cooking dinner, after all, and she obviously had my parents' best interests at heart.

We spent some time at my mother's bedside when we first arrived, but she was alternatively unresponsive or overly agitated, and we all breathed a sigh of relief when Elyse summoned us downstairs for dinner.

"So?" Tracy asked, returning her espresso cup to its tiny saucer. "Would you?"

"Would I what?"

"Would you want someone to tell you if they knew your husband was having an affair?"

"What are you getting at?" I asked bluntly, in no mood for Tracy's "hypotheticals." "You're suggesting that Harrison is having an affair?"

"Look. I'm not trying to upset you . . ."

"What *are* you trying to do?"

"Just that, if it were me, I'd want someone to tell me. I'd want to know . . ."

"What is it you *think* you know, Tracy?"

She looked toward the kitchen, then lowered her voice. "I saw him this afternoon after the closing luncheon. With that girl. The one I saw him with before."

"She's his student, for God's sake."

"I know that."

"So . . . what?" I asked, picturing Harrison slamming into me against the wall of our living room. "Did you catch them in some sort of compromising position?"

"Not exactly."

"What *exactly*?" I repeated, looking around the table for something to throw at her head.

"He was putting her overnight bag into the trunk of his car."

I dug my fingernails into the palm of my hand, trying not to let my shock register on my face.

"Then she climbed into the front seat next to him and they drove off. They were laughing and they didn't see me," she added, lowering her voice another notch.

It took me a few seconds to formulate a response. "Her parents have a cottage in Prince Edward County," I said, repeating what Harrison had told me. "She's the one who arranged for Harrison to be the guest speaker at this weekend's event. It's only natural that they'd drive there together," I added for good measure, angry that Harrison had chosen to omit that little detail from his account.

Then I remembered that I'd neglected to mention my dinner with Roger McAdams.

"What are you girls whispering about in here?" Elyse asked, returning to the dining room to clear the rest of the dishes. "No, you sit," she directed as I rose from my chair to help her. "Finish discussing whatever it is that has you looking so serious."

"I was just asking Jodi what she thought about this idea I have for a story," Tracy improvised.

"So, you're serious about writing, are you?" Elyse asked.

"I might be. My instructor says I'm a natural."

"Well, if you ever want someone to read anything you've written, I'd be thrilled to offer my two cents," Elyse volunteered. She reached across the table for Tracy's empty espresso cup.

The color instantly drained from Tracy's face.

"Did you see that?" she asked as soon as Elyse left the room.

"See what?"

"She's wearing Mom's watch."

"What are you talking about?"

"I'm talking about the fact she's wearing Mom's watch. The Cartier with the red alligator strap."

I glanced toward the kitchen. "You're sure?" I asked, in no mood for more of Tracy's misperceptions.

"Of course I'm sure. I used to love that watch. When Mom stopped wearing it, I asked if I could have it, and she joked that she'd leave it to me in her will."

"There must be dozens of watches like that."

"How many housekeepers do you know who own Cartier watches?"

"It's probably a knockoff."

"You think?"

"Ask her."

"Ask me what?" Elyse said, returning to the room.

"Your watch . . ." Tracy began.

Elyse glanced at her wrist. "It's your mother's," she said without hesitation. "My watch stopped working and I had to take it in to be repaired, and your father insisted

I wear this one in the meantime. I hope you don't mind."

"Of course not," I answered for both of us.

"I'll take it off," Elyse said, absorbing the look on Tracy's face, her fingers moving quickly to undo the strap.

"No," Tracy said. "It's fine. Honestly. Leave it." She rose from her seat. "I should really get going. Thank you so much for dinner. It was delicious." She moved toward the front door. "Bye, everyone," she called toward the stairs. "Talk soon," she added in my direction.

"I'm so sorry," Elyse said when she was gone. "I think she was more upset than she let on."

"She'll be fine," I assured her, pushing my chair away from the table. "We should probably get a move on as well. Kids!" I called out. "Time to go home."

"Aw. Do we have to?" Sam whined as he and his sister reached the front hall, my father following a few steps behind.

"You'll be back tomorrow afternoon for a swim," I reminded them.

"I have an idea," Elyse said. "Why don't we make it a sleepover? We'll swim, then make popcorn and watch movies. They can sleep in your old bedroom. How does that sound?"

"Yay!" Sam shouted, his cry echoed by his sister.

"What?" I said. "No! That's way too much to ask."

"You didn't," Elyse said. "It was my idea."

I glanced toward my father, waiting for him to erupt in protest. "Dad?" I asked when he didn't. "Is that all right? It won't be too much for you?"

"I think we can manage," he snapped. "I'm not an invalid."

I winced, thinking of my mother lying upstairs in her bed, a prisoner of her own body. The word "invalid" danced around my brain. *Invalid. In-valid. No longer valid.*

Elyse leaned toward me, as if my thoughts were printed on my forehead. "Don't worry about us," she whispered. "Look after yourself for a change. You look like you could use a bit of a break."

"Can we come for a sleepover, Mom?" Sam asked.

"Can we?" Daphne repeated. "Can we, Mommy? Can we?"

"I guess so," I answered. "As long as you're sure . . ."

"We're sure," Elyse said, smiling toward my father.

I marveled at her certainty, the effortless way she took control. If only my mother had handled things—handled my father—as well, I thought. "Well, okay, then. If you're absolutely sure . . ."

"Yay!"

"Yay!"

I thanked Elyse for dinner and even hugged her good-bye. "You're the best," I told her.

God, I was such a fool!

—TWENTY-THREE—

I called Harrison as soon as the kids were settled in bed. I got his voicemail, so I left a message. "Just checking in," I said, as pleasantly as my voice would allow. "Call me when you get the chance."

He didn't return my call until the next morning. "Sorry," he offered by way of apology. "It was pretty late by the time I checked in. Then I had to meet with the organizers and grab a bite to eat. By the time I got back to the motel, it was after eleven. I figured you'd probably be asleep."

"How was the drive?" I asked, deciding not to tell him that I hadn't slept more than a couple of hours all night, that images of him and Wren had kept me tossing and turning until morning.

"Long," he said. "Uneventful."

That was it.

I waited, but there was no mention of Wren.

"What about Wren?" I asked finally.

I felt him tense even before the constriction in his voice confirmed it. "What about her?"

"Have you seen her?"

"Of course I've seen her. Are we really doing this again?" he asked.

He was right. Now was definitely not the time to have this discussion, especially since it was exactly the kind of confrontation I grew up listening to, the kind I'd spent most of my life desperate to avoid. Because it never ended well. I knew that. "Tracy saw the two of you drive off together," I said anyway.

There was a second of silence. "So?" he said.

"So?"

"I don't understand the problem, Jodi," Harrison said. "I told you that Wren's parents have a cottage here, and that I'd be giving her a ride up."

"You said that her parents have a cottage there," I corrected. "You didn't say anything about giving her a ride."

"I most certainly did. I can't help it if you only hear what you want to hear."

"That's not true. What does it even mean?"

"It means that you don't listen. You *think* you do, but you don't. And you're not the most rational person on earth when you're upset."

Was it possible he was right? That I didn't listen? That I was being irrational? I wondered, replaying our earlier argument in my head. Had he really told me that he and Wren would be driving to Prince Edward County together?

"Look. I really don't have time for this nonsense. I have to go."

"Harrison," I began. But even before I heard the click on the other end of the line, I knew he was gone.

Less than an hour later, Roger McAdams called. "Are we still on for this afternoon?" he asked.

"Absolutely," I said.

What can I say?

Roger was attractive, funny, sophisticated, and interesting. He was also *interested*. In me. In what I thought. In what I had to say. He listened; he laughed at my jokes; he told me I was beautiful. He made me *feel* beautiful.

We toured half a dozen waterfront condos, and when he asked me out for dinner afterward, I didn't hesitate. This time, the restaurant was dimly lit and romantic. We shared a bottle of expensive Shiraz. We talked until midnight.

Then we checked into the King Edward Hotel.

Like I said earlier, I have no excuse for what happened. Yes, I was more than a little drunk. Yes, I was upset about Harrison. Yes, I was feeling vulnerable and insecure. And yes, the kids were at my parents' and I had the night all to myself. I convinced myself that the stars had all aligned and the universe was giving me its permission, that fate itself was urging me on.

Roger was as wonderful and considerate a lover as I'd imagined him to be. We made love several times over the course of the night, each time better than the time before. I felt reckless; I felt wanted; I felt appreciated; I felt *seen*.

It was only as I was drifting off to sleep that I felt guilt.

It hit me like a sucker punch to the gut, and it was probably only the alcohol in my system that allowed me to get any sleep at all.

I woke up early the next morning, my body all but vibrating with the guilt of what I'd done, my head heavy with a regret worse than any hangover I'd ever experienced. I glanced over at Roger, still sleeping soundly beside me. *What have I done?* Even if Harrison was being a total ass, even if he *was* having an affair—and I had no real proof that he was—did that justify my jumping into bed with a man I barely knew? How many times had I told my children that two wrongs don't make a right?

I climbed out of bed and headed for the shower. I knew that no amount of soap could wash away the stench of my betrayal. *I cheated on my husband. I'm an unfaithful wife. If there is a hell, I will burn in it.* My whole body shook. *What in God's name have I done?*

Roger was just opening his eyes when I came out of the bathroom, wrapped in a towel, my hair soaking wet. "Hi, beautiful," he said.

I smiled, then promptly burst into tears.

"Oh, no. No," he said, jumping out of bed and surrounding me with his arms. "No. Please don't cry. No, don't be sad."

I shook my head, unable to speak.

He led me back to the bed, and sank down beside me. "What's happening, Jodi? Tell me what's going on."

"I just feel so bad," I managed to spit out between sobs. "You probably won't believe me, but I've never done anything like this before."

"Why wouldn't I believe you?" he asked earnestly.

"Oh, God," I wailed. "You're such a sweet man. And I'm so awful."

"You aren't awful. Who says you're awful?"

"I do! I'm a married woman. I'm supposed to be faithful. I'm not supposed to be waking up in hotel rooms next to men who aren't my husband."

"From everything you told me, your husband's not exactly a paragon of virtue," he said. "Not to mention, he's a damn fool."

"He's not . . ." I started, then stopped, trying to remember exactly what I'd told Roger about my situation. Probably more than I should have, I thought. "It still doesn't justify my being here with you." I took a deep breath, felt my exhalation shudder into the air between us.

We sat in silence for several seconds.

"You know that this can't ever happen again."

"I know," he said. Then, gently taking my hand, "Are you hungry? Would you like some breakfast?"

"Yes," I said, trying unsuccessfully to hold back a renewed onslaught of tears.

He smiled. "What would you like? I'll order room service."

"Coffee, orange juice, French toast?" I asked, tears streaming down my cheeks. *Have I no shame?*

"Sounds perfect," he said, placing the order, then returning to my side, kissing me gently on the forehead.

"We should get dressed," I said.

He nodded.

We didn't move.

"I'll find someone else at the agency to help you look for a condo," I said after several more moments had passed.

"Is that really necessary?"

"I think so, yes."

"Okay," he said. "But if you change your mind . . . about anything . . ."

"I won't."

"But if you do . . ." he said. He left the rest of the sentence unfinished.

TWENTY-FOUR

"What's wrong?" Elyse asked as soon as she opened the door and saw my face.

"Nothing." I forced a smile.

"You're a terrible liar," she said, ushering me inside the house.

"Mommy!" yelled Daphne, running up from downstairs into my arms.

"We had the best time," Sam said, joining his sister. "We swam and watched movies . . ."

". . . and had popcorn," Daphne interjected.

"And potato chips."

"And Elyse made us chocolate chip pancakes for breakfast."

"Wow. Sounds wonderful."

"What can I get for you?" Elyse asked.

"Oh, no, nothing. Thank you. I ate before I came over." I pictured Roger and me sitting side by side on the bed, silently eating our French toast. It seemed that nothing, not even an adulterous affair, could put a damper on my appetite. "We really should get out of your hair."

"Aw," whined Sam. "Elyse said we could go for a swim this morning."

"I'm so sorry," Elyse apologized. "I didn't realize you'd come for them so early."

"Please, Mommy. Can't we go swimming?"

"Do you have appointments?" Sam asked warily, sounding disconcertingly like his father.

"No, no appointments."

"So, can we go swimming?"

"Sure," I agreed. "Why not?"

Elyse swiveled toward my children. "Well, then, why don't you two go downstairs and put on your bathing suits? They should be dry by now. And you," she said, turning back to me as they scurried off, "why don't you go join your father out by the pool while I make us a fresh pot of coffee?"

"My mother . . . ?"

"She had a bit of a rough night," Elyse said. "I just got her settled before you arrived. She's sleeping now. But you can look in on her, if you'd like."

I nodded and went upstairs, brushing aside the uncomfortable realization that Elyse had just given me permission to see my own mother.

My mother was indeed asleep, and I sighed with relief that the only thing I smelled was lavender. "Sleep well," I whispered, laying a gentle hand on her hip, not sure who I was feeling sorrier for in that moment—her or me. I seriously doubted I'd ever have a good night's sleep again.

My father put down his Sunday *New York Times* as I stepped outside and walked toward him. His eyes narrowed as they looked me up and down, as if searching for any wayward pounds I might have added to my frame since Friday. Or maybe he was doing no such thing. Perhaps that was just my guilt assigning him nefarious motives that didn't exist.

"Hi, Daddy," I said in greeting.

"No clients today?" he asked in return.

"No. Harrison is out of town and I can't keep imposing on Elyse to look after the kids."

"Probably a good idea," he said brusquely. "You hired her to look after your mother, not your children." He returned to his paper before I could even begin to formulate a response.

"Mommy!" Daphne cried, freshly changed into her pink-flowered bathing suit, running toward me and grabbing me around the knees. "Are you going to come swim with us?"

"Oh, sweetie. I didn't bring my bathing suit."

"I have an old one I haven't worn in years," Elyse offered, approaching with a tray containing a freshly brewed pot of coffee, some mugs, and a selection of homemade muffins. "I'm sure it would fit."

I was about to refuse when I heard my father mutter, "I doubt it," his voice just loud enough to be heard.

I reminded myself that last night a man had looked down at my naked body and told me I was beautiful. "Well, okay," I said. "I guess I can try it on . . ."

"Please, Mommy. Please."

"I'll go lay it on my bed for you," Elyse said.

"Take the muffins with you," my father directed. He didn't have to add the corollary *Jodi doesn't need any* for me to hear it.

Elyse ignored him and went back into the house.

Would that I could ignore him so easily, I thought as I sank into a nearby chaise, fighting back tears. Daphne promptly jumped into my lap. "What did you do last night, Mommy?" she asked.

A lump lodged in my throat and I had to clear it several times to dislodge it.

"You don't have a cold, I hope," my father said before I could speak.

"No, Daddy. I don't have a cold."

"The last thing any of us needs is a cold," he said.

"I don't have a cold."

"Did you miss us?" Daphne asked as her brother raced toward the pool.

I pictured Roger and me entwined in each other's arms. "I sure did," I said as my son jumped into the deep end, his splash coating the provocative image. It dispersed into hundreds of tiny pixels, then evaporated.

"For God's sake, Samuel!" my father bellowed, glaring in my direction. "They don't act like this when you're not here."

Somebody, shoot me, I thought, turning away from him at the sound of the patio door opening. Gratefully, I watched Elyse step outside.

"Bathing suit's on the bed," she said.

"Thank you."

Daphne ran for her water wings.

"No running," I heard my father instruct sternly as I went inside the house, the tears I'd been holding at bay building behind my eyes.

"What did you expect?" I asked myself out loud as I entered Elyse's room. When had my father been anything but a withholding, controlling son of a bitch? Elyse might have been able to "handle" him, to soften some of his harder edges, but there were limits to what even she could do. "You should be used to it by now," I said, lifting Elyse's old navy-and-white bathing suit into my hands. *Please let it fit,* I prayed.

Miraculously, it did, although I needed to see it in a full-length mirror to be sure. No way was I going to expose myself to my father's potential ridicule. I marched toward the closet and opened it, staring at my image in the long mirror on the inside of the door, surprised by how well the suit flattered me. There were no unsightly bulges, no crepe-y overhangs of flesh. "You don't look bad at all," I told myself.

Which is when I saw it.

An emerald-green silk shirt belonging to my mother.

Of course it was possible that Elyse had one just like it, I told myself, examining the blouse more closely. But after viewing it from all angles, I became convinced it was my mother's blouse. What was it doing in Elyse's closet?

Granted, my mother hadn't worn it in years, and she clearly had no use for it now. Still, I doubted my mother would have parted with it. Had my father loaned it to Elyse, just as he'd loaned her my mother's Cartier watch? Or had he given it to her outright? And if so, wasn't it a little premature for him to be giving away my mother's things?

The other possibility was even more unsettling: that Elyse had seen the blouse, liked it, and simply helped herself, assuming no one would be the wiser.

Either way, would I find more of my mother's belongings in Elyse's room?

My hand rifled through the remaining hangers, but found nothing familiar. I breathed a sigh of relief, assuring myself that there was undoubtedly a logical explanation for the presence of the blouse, and that it was probably best not to even broach the subject with either Elyse or my father. I didn't want an angry lecture from him, and I didn't want to chance alienating her over something that would likely prove to be no big deal. Wasn't she taking wonderful care of my mother? Didn't my father look better than he had in years? Wasn't Elyse the housekeeper of my dreams? Hadn't she gone overboard to help me out, refusing repeatedly to be reimbursed? Did it really matter if she'd helped herself to one of my mother's old blouses?

And, of course, I was hoping to avoid a confrontation. God knows, I'd had enough of those lately.

My life was complicated enough.

So I'm not sure what prompted me toward the dresser across from her bed, or what propelled me to sift through each drawer, what made me remove the coral-colored jewelry box I found hidden underneath a bunch of scarves at the back of the bottom one, what pushed me to open it and peek inside.

I saw the simple Timex watch immediately, and recognized it as the one Elyse had been wearing the first time we met. I checked the time against my own watch, my eyes following the tiny second hand as it ticked off the next two minutes.

It was working perfectly.

Which meant that Elyse's explanation of taking her watch in to be repaired was a lie. Unless, of course, she'd picked it up yesterday.

Which was possible, I tried telling myself.

How then to explain the magnificent sapphire-and-diamond earrings that I discovered next?

"Dear God," I said aloud, recognizing them immediately as the earrings that my father had given my mother on their thirtieth wedding anniversary. I knew that there was no way my mother would ever have parted with them.

Earrings! I heard her shout, the word slamming against my brain like an unpleasant echo. *Earrings! Earrings!*

I'd assumed she'd been referring to the newly purchased ones I'd been wearing, but had she been trying to tell me something else entirely? Had she been trying to say that Elyse had stolen hers?

I sank to the bed, the earrings feeling like hot coals in the palm of my hand.

I heard footsteps, followed by a gentle knock on the door. "Jodi," Elyse called. "Everything all right in there?"

I quickly buried the earrings inside the folds of my dress. I needed time to figure out the meaning of my discovery, time to decide what to do about it. "Everything's fine," I told her. "I'll be right out."

—TWENTY-FIVE—

Maybe I should have fired her right then and there.

But hindsight, as they say, is twenty-twenty, and it's easy to see now all the mistakes I made then. But at the time, I was just so unhappy and confused about my own life, and I desperately wanted there to be a plausible explanation for the presence of my mother's earrings in Elyse's jewelry box.

But instead of telling my father or confronting Elyse directly, I simply secreted the earrings inside my purse, making the conscious—and cowardly—decision to remain silent. At least for the time being. Until I had time to figure things out, to decide my next move.

I spent the rest of the morning cavorting in the pool with my children. We even stayed for lunch.

Before we left, I went upstairs to see my mother, hoping she might be able to allay my suspicions and provide me with some much-needed answers, but she was still sleeping. "Does she usually sleep this much?" I asked as we were leaving.

"More and more lately," Elyse said. "It's hard, I know. But try to see it as a blessing. This way she's not in pain."

"Are you giving her more sedatives than usual?" I asked.

"Just what the doctor prescribed," my father said. There was no mistaking the testiness in his voice. He'd never taken well to being questioned.

"When was the last time he saw her?"

"We spoke just this week," my father said, not quite answering the question.

"And?"

"Jodi," he said, my name reverberating with rebuke. "Your mother has a terminal illness. At best, she has another six months. There's not much that can be done at this point, other than to make her as comfortable as possible."

I nodded, tears filling my eyes.

"Oh, you poor dear," Elyse said, taking me in her arms and hugging me close.

I wondered if she would feel so warmly disposed toward me when she discovered that the earrings were missing, and when that would be. Would she spend hours frantically searching for them, or would she know instantly that I had found them and taken them?

What would she do then?

"Don't cry, Mom," Sam said, interrupting my thoughts.

"What's terminal?" Daphne asked.

"It means Grandma isn't going to get better," I explained softly.

My son was less delicate. "It means she's going to die," he said.

"Are *you* going to die, Mommy?" Daphne asked from the backseat on the ride home.

"No, sweetheart," I answered. "Not for a very long time."

"I don't want you to die."

"I won't. Please don't worry."

I'm worried enough for all of us, I thought.

Harrison didn't get home that night until almost midnight.

I'd tried waiting up for him, but ultimately I'd fallen asleep in front of the TV in the family room at around ten. I woke up and turned it off when I heard his car pull into the garage.

Seconds later, the front door opened and he stepped inside. "How was it?" I asked as he walked toward the stairs.

He jumped. "Shit! You scared me."

"Sorry."

"What are you doing, sitting there in the dark?"

"I was waiting for you," I started to explain, but he was already halfway up the stairs.

"There was a lot of traffic," he said, throwing the words over his shoulder like a handful of salt. "It was stop and start the whole way home." He came to an abrupt halt at the top of the stairs. "And just so you know, I was alone. Wren stayed at the cottage with her parents. Who are lovely people, by the way."

"I'm sure they are."

"They put on one hell of an event."

"I'm glad. Look. I'm sorry about our misunderstanding," I began, following him to our bedroom.

"The misunderstanding," he repeated, as if the word was new to him.

"I honestly don't remember you telling me you'd be giving Wren a lift. It doesn't matter," I said before he could interject. "The point is that I wasn't trying to accuse you of anything, and I'm sorry."

"Me, too," he said, although from his tone it was clear that we were apologizing for different things. Clearly, as far as he was concerned, he'd done nothing wrong. *I* was sorry for my behavior, and *he* was sorry for my behavior. So maybe we were apologizing for the same thing after all.

"So, how was it?" I asked again.

He started to undress. "Great. By all accounts, I was a huge hit."

"I'm not surprised." I turned away, remembering how just last night I'd watched another man undress.

I'd even helped.

"How many people?" I asked, banishing the unwanted image with a shake of my head.

"Well, it varied, of course, depending on the venue," Harrison said, warming to his subject. "There were at least two hundred people at Saturday night's event."

"That's terrific."

"Even better, they all bought books. I was up half the night signing them."

And the other half? I wondered. "That's so great," I said.

He disappeared into the bathroom. I undressed and climbed into bed, part of me hoping we'd make love, the other part praying that we wouldn't. Would Harrison be able to tell that I'd been with another man?

Would he care?

"So, what did you do while I was gone?" he asked as he reentered the room, turning off the overhead light and crawling beneath the covers.

I'd be wrestling all night with whether or not to confess my infidelity and beg his forgiveness. For my lack of trust, my lapse in judgment, my weakness, my stupidity. Yes, there were reasons why I'd been unfaithful, but none of those reasons mattered.

All that mattered were facts.

And the fact was that it wasn't my husband who'd been unfaithful. It was me.

I knew that forgiveness had never come easily for Harrison. And I knew that if I confessed my affair, my marriage would be over.

I couldn't take that risk.

"Not much," I said. "Took the kids swimming, watched a movie, had pizza for dinner." Not a complete lie. Still, a long way from the truth.

"I'm sure they enjoyed that." He gave me a quick peck on the cheek, then laid his head on the pillow next to mine.

"I'm worried that Elyse might be stealing from my mother," I said to his closed eyes. I told him of finding my mother's blouse and earrings in Elyse's room.

"Have you told your father your concerns?" Harrison asked, one eye opening.

"No."

"Don't you think you should?"

I nodded. Suddenly, it seemed so clear. "Thank you."

"Anytime. Now, get some sleep." He flipped onto his other side. "Good night, hon. See you in the morning."

"I love you," I whispered, waiting for him to say it back.

I fell asleep waiting.

TWENTY-SIX

I drove to my parents' house first thing the next morning.

I parked in their driveway, checking my watch as I climbed out of the car. It was just after eight o'clock, but my father had always been an early riser, and I was pretty sure he'd be up. I'd tell him that I had some confidential, work-related issues to discuss with him before heading into the office, and hope for a few minutes alone in which to confide my concerns about Elyse.

I rang the bell, and waited, my eyes scanning the street, noticing that some of the trees were starting to change color. Already? I marveled. September was closing in, and fall was hovering, making its presence known. Soon it would be Halloween, and then Christmas, I thought, picturing the street with its elaborate, constantly shifting array of holiday decorations, watching the year disappear before it had even begun. Next week, Sam would be starting third grade and Daphne would be entering junior kindergarten.

Soon they'd be heading off to college, I thought, laughing at how quickly my mind could vault from the present reality into the realm of the absurd. Was that what I'd done with Elyse? Had I jumped to a bunch of ill-conceived conclusions? Would there be a perfectly logical explanation for everything?

"Guess I'm about to find out," I said, about to ring the bell again when I remembered my key. "Hello?" I called as I entered the front hall. Was it possible my father was still asleep? "Dad? Hello?" I remembered the last time I'd entered the house unannounced, the displeasure on my father's face when I'd discovered him and Elyse watching a movie while my mother lay sleeping upstairs in her own waste. *Call first next time,* he'd instructed angrily.

"I should have called," I said to the empty hall. But phoning first would have tipped them off to the possibility that something was wrong, and my intention had been to surprise them. "Dad?" I called again. "Elyse?"

It was then that I heard it, a low moan that seemed to be emanating from the walls themselves. The moan sank to the floor, slithering along the hardwood planks to where I stood. It wrapped itself around my ankles, then coiled around my thighs and torso until it reached my chest, squeezing the air from my lungs even as it filled my head.

My eyes shot to the stairway. I saw what appeared to be a bundle of clothing lying on the floor near my mother's bedroom. At first I assumed that it must be a pile of dirty laundry Elyse had left there. I told myself that Elyse and my father were undoubtedly in with my mother right now, Elyse changing her bedsheets while my father fed her breakfast.

But then it moved.

And moaned.

And I knew.

"Mom?" I shouted, racing up the stairs. "Oh, my God! Mom!"

She was lying on the floor, halfway between the elevator and the stairs. Her whole body was shaking, her face contorted by a combination of pain and rage. "Tracy," she cried, grabbing my hand as I reached for her, her nails digging into my flesh.

"It's Jodi, Mom," I corrected gently, recognizing this was not the time for hurt feelings. "What happened?" My eyes shot toward the bedrooms at the end of the hall as I tried unsuccessfully to lift her up. But it was impossible. She was like a dead weight in my arms. "How did you get here? Where's Dad?"

"I've been calling him for hours," my mother said, each word a struggle to get out. "He doesn't answer. I got out of bed. I fell."

"I don't understand. Where is he?" I laid her back down, struggled to my feet.

"Don't leave me."

"I'll be right back," I said, hurling myself toward my father's closed bedroom door. "Dad!" I shouted, opening it and flipping on the overhead light.

The room was empty.

His bed hadn't been slept in.

What does it mean? I wondered, already knowing it could mean only one thing. "Oh, God," I said, returning to my mother's side.

"He's with her," my mother said. This time there was no mistaking her words, no struggle for clarity on either her part or mine.

"Oh, God," I said again.

Which was when I heard the footsteps racing up the stairs from the bottom floor.

"What the hell is going on here?" my father yelled as he wrestled with his bathrobe, trying to throw it over his T-shirt and boxer shorts. His feet were bare, his hair an unruly mass. He reached the front hall, and stopped, staring up at my mother and me on the floor above his head.

"What is it, Vic?" Elyse asked, coming into view behind him. She was wearing a long blue negligee, her bare toes peeking out from beneath its silk folds. Her mouth opened when she saw me, but no sound emerged.

"What are you doing here?" my father demanded.

"What am I doing here?" I repeated. "I think the more urgent question is what the hell are you doing down there?"

"You have no business just barging in," he said, ignoring my question. On the offensive, as always.

"I didn't barge in," I said as he took the stairs two at a time, Elyse right behind.

"For God's sake, Audrey," my father said to my mother, his arms reaching for hers. "What do you think you're doing, my love?"

My love? I thought. *My love?!*

You were just caught red-handed with another woman. Are you really going to pretend that didn't happen?

"My poor dear," Elyse echoed, coming around to take my mother's other arm, effectively pushing me aside.

I watched the two of them lift my mother to her feet and half walk, half carry her back to her room. They succeeded in getting her back into bed, arranging her pillows and making her comfortable, neither remotely self-conscious about their state of undress.

"Are you hungry, dear?" Elyse asked. "Can I make you a smoothie?"

"Didn't the doctor say she wasn't supposed to have dairy?" I said as Elyse headed down the stairs.

"It's one of the few pleasures she has left," my father stated, taking my elbow and ushering me from the room. "Are you so cruel as to deny her that?"

"Me?" I responded, scarcely able to believe my ears. "I'm the one who's cruel?! You're sleeping with the housekeeper and you're trying to turn this back on me?!"

"What I do is none of your business."

"Maybe not. But my mother's welfare certainly is."

"Your mother is being very well looked after."

"Is she? I found her on the floor, for God's sake!"

"You're not being fair."

"Really? You're sleeping with the *help* right under my mother's nose and I'm the one who's not being fair?" I asked, purposely using the word he'd used only months ago.

"I'm a man," he said evenly. "I have certain needs."

"Oh, please," I said dismissively. "You're almost eighty, for God's sake."

"Okay. So I'm an *old* man," he said, suddenly looking very old indeed. "That doesn't mean I've ceased to be human. That I don't relish the feel of a woman in my arms, that I don't enjoy being held or caressed."

I squirmed at the unwanted image of Elyse caressing my father.

"It's been years since your mother and I have had any kind of relationship, physical or otherwise," he continued, unprompted. "I'd almost forgotten what it was like to have a normal conversation . . ."

"Is that what you were doing while my mother was lying on the floor?" I asked, unwilling to feel sorry for him or let him off the hook so easily. "Having a conversation?"

"It's easy to be judgmental," he said. "Can you not find it in your heart to be even a little forgiving? A little understanding? Are you so pure? So without blemish?"

Oh, God, I thought. Could I really be so contemptuous of my father after what *I'd* done? *Let he who is without sin . . .*

"You need to fire her," I said. "Give her whatever she wants in the way of severance, but—"

"I'm not firing her," he interrupted, his previous anger returning to his voice.

I reached inside my purse, removed my mother's earrings. "I found these in Elyse's room, in her jewelry box," I told him. "She's been stealing from you."

He took the earrings from my hand. The silence that ensued was all but deafening. "What were you doing, going through her things?"

"You're missing the point here, Dad."

Another interminable pause. "Elyse isn't stealing."

I waited, too afraid to ask what he meant.

"I gave her these earrings," he said finally.

"You gave her Mom's earrings?"

"She was straightening up the drawers, and she found them and remarked how beautiful they were, and

I thought, why not let her have them? Your mother clearly has no use for them anymore."

"You had no right," I said, straining to keep my outrage at bay.

"I had *every* right."

"These earrings are very valuable, Dad. You don't think Tracy or I might have liked to have them?"

"So, that's what this is really about," he said, shaking his head. "Money."

"No, that's not what this is about," I argued, silently marveling at my father's ability to turn things around, to put me on the defensive. "I'm just saying—"

"I'm no longer interested in what you're saying," he said. "You, of all people, should be very grateful for Elyse, after all she's done for you. She is not a thief. And I'm not firing her. End of discussion."

I heard the elevator beginning its slow ascent.

"One more thing," he said as the elevator doors opened and Elyse emerged with a tray containing my mother's smoothie and two pieces of toast. "I'd like the key to my house back."

"Dad . . ."

He held out his hand. "I don't want any more surprise visits."

Reluctantly, I dropped the key into his waiting palm. "I'll just say goodbye to Mom."

"Make it quick," he said. "Your visits upset her."

I reentered my mother's bedroom, stood for several seconds at the side of her bed, tears building behind my eyes.

"Tracy?" she asked.

"No, Mom. It's me, Jodi." My tears broke free and started streaming down my cheeks. "Goodbye, Mom," I said finally, patting her hand. "I'll see you soon." I walked from the room, down the stairs and out the door.

The next time I saw my mother, she was dead.

TWENTY-SEVEN

Not that I didn't try to see her.

But between the time of my last visit and her death just over two months later, I was rebuked at every turn.

In the beginning, I decided it would be best to give my father some space, to let the dust settle, allow cooler heads to prevail. Surely he would come to understand why I'd been so upset, that I only had my mother's—and his—best interests at heart.

"What did you expect?" Tracy asked when I told her what had happened, as if she'd suspected what was going on all along. "The man hasn't had sex in years, and Elyse looks pretty good for a woman her age. Finally, he's getting laid. Can you blame him?"

It was only after I told her that he'd given Elyse Mom's sapphire-and-diamond earrings that she grew indignant.

"I knew right from the start she was trouble," she said. "So, what do we do now?"

"I'm not sure there's anything we *can* do."

"You never should have hired her."

"Thank you. That's very helpful."

"The next time you go over there," Tracy said, ignoring my sarcasm, "you should just take off with the rest of Mom's jewelry."

"You're suggesting that I steal it?"

"Well, it doesn't look as if Dad's just going to give it to you. And it wouldn't be stealing exactly. I mean, it's supposed to be ours eventually anyway."

I have to admit that I'd been thinking the same thing. Not that any of the jewelry, other than a few select pieces, most notably the sapphire-and-diamond earrings, was especially valuable. It was more the idea that these pieces, whatever their worth, should go to us, her daughters, and not the outsider who was bedding our father.

But every time I called my parents' house to say I was thinking of stopping by, I was told to think again.

"Now isn't a good time," my father would tell me. "Your mother is having a nap."

"She had a rough night," Elyse would say. "Best not to disturb her."

"Try again tomorrow."

"Try again next week."

What I tried was a different approach. "The kids would love to come by this weekend for a swim," I suggested.

"We've closed the pool," my father informed me.

"So early?"

"No earlier than usual," he said, although it was only mid-September and he'd always kept the pool open at least another month.

"Give them time," Harrison advised. "You've obviously ruffled their feathers. You have a way of doing that," he added with a smile. The smile did nothing to disguise the remark's inherent criticism. I believe the expression is "kidding on the square," a remark that allows you to be mean without owning it. "But they'll come around," he added before I could react.

They didn't.

The more time passed, the more things deteriorated. Harrison went back to his writing schedule and resumed his usual complaints regarding my work and the kids; I tried not to think about Roger McAdams, who, I was told by another agent in my office, had temporarily abandoned his search for a condo. I wondered if that had anything to do with me, and fought the daily urge to contact him. September became October.

And then one day, out of the blue, Elyse phoned. "Your father is going out for a while this morning," she said, "and I was thinking that you might like to stop by for a visit while he's away."

"I'd like that," I told her before she could rethink her offer.

"Come in one hour."

Exactly an hour later, I pulled into their driveway. Elyse was waiting at the front door. Her hair had been freshly styled, as if she'd just come from having it done, and she was wearing formfitting leather pants and an expensive-looking white silk shirt. Not exactly the uniform of someone whose job it was to cook and clean. More the look of the well-heeled lady of the house, I thought, wondering if the look was deliberate, if she was sending me some sort of message. Best to keep such thoughts to myself, I decided. No point in ruffling any more feathers.

You have a way of doing that, I heard Harrison say.

"Thank you for calling," I said instead.

Elyse ushered me inside the front hall. "I was hoping we could clear the air."

"Sounds good." I realized that, in spite of everything, I'd missed her. "I'll just go upstairs and say hello to my mother."

"She's not here," Elyse said as I started for the stairs.

"What?"

"Your father took her for a ride to see the changing of the leaves."

What? "Oh. I just assumed . . ."

"Why don't we go into the kitchen? I've made a fresh pot of coffee and there's some leftover apple pie."

I followed her into the kitchen and sat down at the table, trying to grasp what was happening. I'd assumed that she'd invited me over to see my mother, but clearly that assumption had been incorrect.

"I hate this estrangement between you and your father," she began, "and I can't help feeling at least partly responsible. It was never my intention to cause any problems, and I'm so, so sorry."

I nodded, not sure how to respond. "I'm sorry, too," I said finally, realizing this was true.

"You have absolutely nothing to be sorry about," she insisted. "It must have been such a shock when you realized that your father and I . . . well, you know. Please believe that it was never planned. It just kind of happened. Your father's been so lonely, and to be frank, so have I—"

"I *do* understand," I interrupted, not wanting to hear the details, and straining to be magnanimous. "It's just that . . ."

"You don't have to explain." She poured me a cup of coffee, adding the correct amount of cream and sugar before sliding it across the table and lowering herself into the nearest chair. "And then finding her earrings . . ."

"I didn't mean to snoop. Just that I saw my mother's blouse hanging in your closet and I . . ."

"Oh, my goodness," Elyse interjected. "Well, no wonder you assumed I was stealing. No, I saw that blouse lying crumpled on the floor of your mother's closet and brought it downstairs to iron it. I just hadn't had a chance to take it back upstairs yet. Oh, you poor thing. That explains everything."

I sipped at my coffee, not sure where we went from here. Understanding why something happened was one thing. Allowing it to continue was another. And there was no way that Elyse could continue looking after my mother while sleeping with my father.

"I realize that I can't keep working here," she said, as if privy to my deepest thoughts. "I've already started packing up my things."

I nodded. "Does my father know?"

"Not yet."

"I don't know what to say except that I'm sorry. I wish it didn't have to be this way."

"I know, and I understand. I really do." Elyse pushed herself slowly to her feet. She walked to the sink and opened the cupboard directly below, reaching inside and retrieving a large see-through baggie, laying it on the table in front of me. It contained my mother's jewelry. "You should have this," she said. "For safekeeping. In case the next housekeeper isn't quite so honest.

Everything's there, including the Cartier watch and the sapphire-and-diamond earrings. There's no way I could keep them. They belong with you."

"Thank you," I whispered, dropping the baggie into my purse and pushing myself to my feet. "You know that my father will be furious."

"Initially. But he'll get over it. He's a tough man, your father."

"Yes, he is."

We stood there for a while in silence. I realized I was holding back tears. "What will you tell him?"

"Don't you worry about that," she said, enfolding me in her arms and giving me a final hug. "Just leave it to me. I'll think of something."

—TWENTY-EIGHT—

The police arrived at dinnertime.

We were just sitting down to a Kraft dinner of macaroni and cheese—"Really, Jodi?" Harrison had remarked. "You shouldn't have gone to so much trouble."—when we heard the patrol car pull into our driveway. "Who the hell is that?" my husband asked, as if the unexpected intrusion was somehow my fault. "Your sister, no doubt," he said, answering his own question.

"It's the police," I told him, looking out our front window as I walked toward the door.

"The police?" he repeated, following after me, Sam and Daphne behind him. "What are they doing here? Kids, go back to the table," he directed.

"Are they going to arrest you, Daddy?" Sam asked.

"Of course not. They've obviously got the wrong house."

They had the right house.

"Jodi Bishop?" the older of the two officers standing on my doorstep asked.

"Yes?"

"I'm Officer Stankowski, and this is Officer Lewis," he said, introducing his younger partner, who was as dark-skinned as Officer Stankowski was pale. "May we come in?"

My first thought was that there'd been an accident, that my father and mother had been seriously injured—or worse—while out for their morning drive to view nature's changing colors. My father had never been the world's best driver. He was a bully *on* the road as well as off, rarely yielding the right of way. Coupled with his love of speed, it was a recipe for disaster, although he often boasted of never having received so much as a speeding ticket in his more than sixty years of driving. Had his luck run out? "Has there been an accident?"

"No," Officer Lewis responded. "No accident. May we come in?"

"What seems to be the problem?" Harrison asked as we backed up to allow the men entry.

Officer Stankowski looked toward the dining room, where Sam and Daphne sat, wide-eyed and watching. "Hello, there," he said, waving in their direction.

"Are you going to arrest us?" Sam asked.

"Have you done something wrong?"

"No," Sam said, although his tone indicated he wasn't entirely sure.

"What about you, young lady?" Officer Lewis asked. "You look like trouble to me."

"I'm not trouble," Daphne protested. "I'm a cupcake of cuteness."

Both officers laughed. "You certainly are."

"She won't eat her vegetables," Sam offered.

"Okay, kids. That's enough. Finish your food and go upstairs," Harrison directed, ushering the policemen into the living room. "What's this about?"

The officers declined the invitation to sit down. "Sorry to disturb you at dinnertime, but we've received a complaint," Officer Stankowski said.

"A complaint?" I looked from the officers to my husband and back again. "What kind of complaint?" Had I "ruffled the feathers" of any of our neighbors? "About what? From whom?"

"Are you acquainted with a Mr. Victor Dundas?" Officer Lewis asked, checking his notes.

"Yes. He's my father. You said there wasn't an accident. Is he all right?"

"He's fine."

"I don't understand."

"He says that you were over there this morning. Is that true?"

"Yes."

"Do you mind telling us what happened?"

"What do you mean, what happened? Nothing happened. I went to see my mother—she has Parkinson's—but it turned out that my father had taken her for a drive, so I talked to the housekeeper for a little while. We had coffee, and I left."

"You didn't take anything with you when you left?"

"Excuse me?"

"According to your father, you absconded with all of your mother's jewelry."

"I absconded . . . ? *What?!*" I said, incapable of saying anything more. *My father actually called the police and accused me of stealing?!*

"Your father isn't interested in pressing charges," Officer Lewis explained quickly. "He just wants the jewelry back. He asked us to come over and talk to you as a courtesy."

"I did not steal that jewelry!"

"Do you have it?" one of the officers asked.

I was so shocked that I could no longer discern who was speaking and who wasn't. I felt dizzy and light-headed, the macaroni and cheese in my stomach in danger of coming back up. "It's upstairs," I muttered. "But I didn't steal it. Elyse gave it to me."

"That would be the housekeeper, Elyse Woodley?"

"Yes. My father had given her a pair of my mother's earrings and she didn't feel right about accepting them. She said I should take my mother's jewelry home. For safekeeping. She had everything in a baggie, all ready to go. Talk to her," I urged. "She'll tell you."

"We have talked to her."

"So, then, you know . . ."

"She confirms your father's story."

"*What?* No! What do you mean, she confirms . . ."

"She says that you dropped over unexpectedly, demanding to see your mother . . ."

"No, that's not true. She called *me*, invited me over."

"Why would she do that when your parents weren't there?"

"She said that she wanted to clear the air . . ."

"Clear the air?"

"There were some issues," I said, loath to reveal the details.

"You were upset that your father had gifted her a pair of your mother's earrings," Officer Lewis stated.

"Among other things, yes."

"You accused her of sleeping with your father."

"She *is* sleeping with my father!" I sputtered. "But I didn't accuse her of anything this morning. In fact, she's the one who brought it up. She apologized, said she understood that she'd have to leave, that she'd already started packing, and that I should have the jewelry."

"For safekeeping."

"Yes."

"According to Elyse Woodley," Officer Stankowski said, reading from his notes, "you dropped over unexpectedly and accused her of sleeping with your father. She tried to calm things down by offering you coffee and a piece of pie, which you accepted but then excused yourself to use the washroom. She then went into the kitchen to put the coffee on, and a few minutes later, she heard the front door close. She assumed you'd had a change of heart and left. It wasn't until your father came home and she told him about your visit that they discovered your mother's jewelry was missing."

I shook my head. "She's lying!"

"Your father believes her."

"My father is getting laid for the first time in years," I said, hearing my sister's voice, and noting the shocked look on both officers' faces at my outburst.

"Please, officers," Harrison said. "My wife is understandably upset at these ridiculous accusations."

"She's setting me up," I marveled.

"For what?" Officer Lewis asked.

"Why would she do that?" asked Officer Stankowski.

I had to admit that I didn't know. "I just know that she's lying."

"Look, Mrs. Bishop," Officer Lewis said. "Like we said, your father has no interest in pressing charges. He just wants the jewelry back."

I shook my head, as if trying to shake meaning into what I was hearing. To say I felt numb would be wrong. Numb implies a lack of feeling, a lack of pain. Instead it felt as if someone was reaching inside me and ripping out my internal organs, one by one. What I felt was gutted. "Fine," I said. "I'll take it back first thing in the morning."

"Your father would like it returned this evening."

"This evening," I repeated. "Sure. Why not? I'll do it as soon as I get the kids settled."

"He said you should just ring the bell, then leave the bag on the doorstep."

"Are you kidding me?"

"Look," Officer Stankowski said. "I'm sure this is all a big misunderstanding, and that in a day or two, you'll be able to talk this over calmly and work everything out."

I nodded, understanding there was no point in doing anything else. I thanked the officers for their concern and even commended them on their sensitivity. I watched them pull out of our driveway and disappear down the street.

"Do you believe that?" I asked Harrison.

"You hired her," he said.

—TWENTY-NINE—

In the end, it was Tracy who called to inform me of our mother's death.

It was a cold Monday morning in early November. The kids were in school. Harrison was upstairs working on a presentation he was set to give at the Whistler Writers Festival in British Columbia at the end of the week. I was about to leave for the office when the landline rang and my sister announced, "Dad just called. Mom died."

"What?" I remember shouting into the phone. "No! No! Don't tell me that!"

"There's more," she said. "Don't move. Don't do anything. I'll be there in five minutes."

"What's all the screaming about?" Harrison asked, coming down the stairs as I replaced the receiver and sank into the family room sofa.

"My mother died."

He took a moment to digest this information. "I'm sorry, sweetheart," he said, sitting down beside me and surrounding me with his arms. "But you had to know this was coming," he said, as I cried against his shoulder.

I nodded into his gray sweater, the soft cashmere tickling my nose. How could I explain that, while it was true that my mother had been an increasingly sick woman for most of the decade, it still came as a shock to realize she was gone? She'd hung on far longer than anyone had expected, outlived everyone's expectations. I guess I'd just assumed we still had lots of time.

I was also overwhelmed with guilt. I hadn't seen or spoken to her in more than two months.

I hadn't seen or spoken to my father, either—not since he'd sent the police to my door, when he'd chosen to believe Elyse over me. Which I guess explained why he'd called my sister with the news, and not me. Somehow, no matter what Tracy did or (mostly) didn't do, she managed to avoid the pitfalls I was always tripping over.

"It's better this way, honey," Harrison said. "At least she's not suffering anymore."

"I know."

"Be thankful for that."

I nodded, biting my tongue to keep from saying, *Be thankful my mother is dead?*

I knew Harrison meant well, that he was simply spouting what people often say in times like these, that his words were meant to comfort, not inflame. Maybe it was unfair to expect more than clichés from a writer of his supposed insight and sensitivity.

At least he hadn't told me that she was in a better place.

Maybe I was just being selfish. But the fact that my mother was no longer suffering provided me with scant comfort. She was dead. I would never hear her tell me that she was proud of me, that I was a good mother, a good daughter. I would never hear her say "I love you."

The buzzer sounded.

Harrison walked to the front door, then stepped aside as my sister burst through.

"Good," she said when she saw me. "You're sitting down."

I fought back a mounting sense of dread. Tracy had always been prone to theatrics, and she was nothing if not dramatic. Still, this was a little over-the-top, even for her. "What's going on? Is Dad all right?"

"He's fine. It's Mom."

"I don't understand. You said she was dead."

"She *is* dead. But she didn't . . . she didn't just . . . die."

"What are you talking about?"

Tracy took a deep breath, her eyes shooting between Harrison and me.

"Tracy, for God's sake . . ."

"It wasn't the Parkinson's."

"What do you mean, it wasn't the Parkinson's?"

"Well, I guess it was partly the Parkinson's . . ."

"Tracy!"

"She fell down the stairs."

"*What?*"

"She fell down the fucking stairs."

"I don't understand," I sputtered, trying to make sense of what Tracy was saying. Surely I'd heard her incorrectly. "How could she fall down the stairs? How is that even possible?"

Tracy perched on the edge of the sofa, took my hands in hers. "All I know is what Dad told me, and he was pretty upset, to say the least. Apparently, he and Elyse were in the kitchen having breakfast when they heard this loud crash. They ran into the hall and found Mom at the bottom of the stairs. Dad thinks she must have gotten out of bed and somehow made it to the landing, and then tripped or something. Anyway, she fell down the stairs and broke her neck."

"Holy shit," Harrison exclaimed.

"They called an ambulance. Dad said that it got there within minutes, but the paramedics told him she was dead, that she'd died instantly."

"Where is she now?"

"They took her body to the morgue."

My thoughts returned to the last time I'd seen my mother, lying in a crumpled heap in the upstairs hallway. Had she gotten tired of crying out for attention and tried to make it to the elevator on her own, then tripped over her own useless feet? I shook my head, trying to rid my mind of the image of my mother somersaulting down a flight of stairs.

"Dad's a mess," Tracy said.

"We should go over there."

"No," she said. "He doesn't want that. He said he has too much to do, that he has to phone the cemetery, make the funeral arrangements, put the notice of her death in the papers, all that shit."

"We can help."

"He doesn't want our help."

"You mean, he doesn't want *my* help."

Tracy shrugged. "He's in shock, Jodi. He'll come around."

"Can we go to the morgue? Can we see her?"

"Are you kidding? You want to see her?" Tracy looked as if she was about to be sick.

"I don't think that's a good idea," Harrison said.

Tracy breathed an audible sigh of relief.

"So, what do we do?" I asked, feeling as helpless as I could ever remember. My mother was dead. My father wanted nothing to do with me. I was essentially an orphan.

"I don't think there's anything we *can* do," Tracy said. "We just have to wait, see what Dad wants. At least Elyse is there to look after him."

"I'll bet she is."

"Would *you* rather do it?" Tracy asked.

I had to admit she had a point.

"Did he give you any indication when the funeral might be?" Harrison asked.

Poor Harrison, I thought, knowing what he was thinking. This couldn't have happened at a more inconvenient time for him. He'd been so excited to receive the invitation to the writers' festival in Whistler, and was scheduled to fly to Vancouver on Wednesday, returning to Toronto on Sunday. In addition to his own presentation, he'd been asked to interview one of his favorite authors, and he'd been busy rereading the man's books for weeks, making copious notes. Unless the funeral were to take place next week—and there was no reason why it should—he'd have to notify the festival, cancel his appearances, disappoint the organizers and his publishers, not to mention his fans . . .

Tracy shook her head. "No idea. Sooner than later, I would think."

"What a mess," I said.

"That it is," Harrison agreed.

Tracy scooted closer beside me, surrounding me with her arms and hugging me close. I laid my head against her shoulder, felt the bones of her clavicle against my cheek. And then, each of us lost in thoughts of our own, nobody said anything.

THIRTY

The funeral was on Friday.

It was a small affair, maybe fifteen people. Most of my parents' friends had either died or fallen by the wayside over the course of the last ten years. A few of my friends and a couple of elderly business colleagues of my father's showed up to pay their respects, as well as a handful of people who looked vaguely familiar, but whom I couldn't quite place.

"Who's that?" Tracy pointed with her chin toward several well-dressed women at the back of the small chapel.

"They work in my office," I told her, nodding gratefully in their direction. I'd called the receptionist to say that I wouldn't be in that week, and she'd clearly spread the word.

I'd made the decision not to take the kids out of school for the funeral, deciding that they were too young and it was too cold to make them stand beside an open grave watching my mother's coffin being lowered into the ground and covered with earth. They hadn't really known her all that well. She'd been bedridden for most of Sam's life and virtually all of Daphne's. The truth was that she'd been a scary-enough presence for them when she was alive, and I saw no need to subject them to further discomfort.

"Is Grandma in heaven?" Sam had questioned when told of her death.

I debated telling him that I didn't really believe in heaven before deciding that I didn't necessarily have to believe everything I told him, and simply answered, "Yes."

Daphne looked suitably perplexed. "Is she standing up or sitting down?" she'd asked.

This time I answered honestly. "I hope she's standing straight and tall."

"Me, too," said Daphne.

My husband, after some discussion and much equivocating, had opted to attend the writers' festival in Whistler after all. "What good will I be doing here?" he'd asked. "I'll just be disappointing a lot of people who have worked very hard to organize this festival, which they already had to delay a month because of scheduling conflicts, and this will only create more chaos. Besides, the time to pay respects is when people are alive," he'd added, trying a different tack. "But I'll stay, if that's what you want."

"I could really use your support," I'd told him.

"Then, of course, I'll stay."

He went.

"You're sure you're okay with this?" he'd asked as he was waiting for the cab to take him to the airport.

"I'm sure," I lied, tired of going around in circles until we ended up where he wanted to be.

There was no point in insisting he stay or trying to shame him into not going. Harrison had never had a good relationship with his mother. He'd cut her out of his life without so much as a second thought. He couldn't possibly understand what I was going through.

How could he, I wondered, *when I don't understand it myself?*

"Wish me luck," he said with a smile, kissing me on the nose as he headed out the door. "Try not to ruffle any feathers."

"Good luck," I replied dutifully.

To nobody's surprise, my father didn't consult anyone about the service. He'd informed my sister of the location and time—the Mount Pleasant Cemetery on Friday at eleven A.M.—and she'd relayed the details, such as they were, to me. According to my mother's wishes, there was to be no eulogy, no flowers, no speeches of any kind. A viewing, a few prayers, the burial.

Of course, Elyse was there, resplendent in a royal blue winter coat, standing a discreet distance from my father just inside the chapel doors. It was the first time I was seeing them since they'd accused me of stealing my mother's jewelry. "Jodi . . . Tracy," Elyse said as we entered the chapel, smiling at me with a warmth that almost took my breath away. "How are you girls holding up?"

"We're doing okay," Tracy answered.

"You look beautiful," she said. "Both of you."

"Thank you." Tracy smiled, running her manicured fingers along the lapel of her down-and-lace black jacket. "It's Valentino."

"Nordstrom Rack," I said, pointedly, of my own brown wool coat. I glanced toward my father, but he was talking to a former colleague and pretending he hadn't seen us come in.

"Where's Harrison?" Elyse asked, checking the empty space behind me.

Are we really doing this? I wondered. *Are we just going to carry on as if nothing happened?* "He had to go out of town," I answered, deciding a funeral was no place to air our grievances, and that if she could pretend, then so could I. At least for now.

"Well, he didn't *have* to," Tracy corrected.

"He's one of the keynote speakers at a writers' festival in Whistler," I explained, embellishing Harrison's role to make his absence more palatable. "It was arranged months ago, and it's already been delayed. He couldn't just cancel at the last minute."

"He certainly could," Tracy insisted. "I think you're a little more important than some writers' festival."

"What good would it . . . ?" I started to ask, then stopped. Why was I defending him? Tracy was right.

"Your mother is over there," Elyse said, as if she were alive and well. She motioned toward the front of the chapel where my mother's open casket was situated. "Your mother picked out the casket herself some years ago. It's walnut. Not too elaborate. Very tasteful, don't you think? Just like she was."

I said nothing.

"She looks lovely," Elyse continued. "I think you'll be very pleased with what the cosmetician accomplished. Why don't you have a look."

"What? Oh, God, no," Tracy exclaimed. "I couldn't."

"I'll go," I said, walking toward the casket, as much to get away from Elyse as to view the cosmetician's handiwork.

My mother lay on a cushion of white satin, her eyes closed, her hands folded neatly on her chest. I was startled to realize that Elyse was right—she *did* look lovely. There were no bruises, no evidence of her calamitous tumble down the stairs. Her face, while a touch too made-up, showed no sign of the pain that had tormented her for years. Her body, relieved of its spasms and deformities, stretched to its full length and clad in a high-necked, white dress, betrayed none of the horrors she'd endured over the past decade.

"She looks so peaceful, doesn't she?" Elyse said, coming up behind me.

"Please don't tell me she's in a better place," I said, feeling my hands form fists at my sides and wondering what the hell Elyse was up to.

"God, no," she said. "I hate when people say that. It makes me want to smack them over the head."

I almost smiled. "What do you want, Elyse?"

"To explain."

I continued staring down at my mother, concentrating on the straight line of her lips, half expecting her to start gasping for air at this woman's audacity. "Can you?"

"I'd like to try."

I swiveled toward her. "Then, by all means. Knock yourself out."

She glanced over her shoulder to where my father and Tracy were engaged in what appeared to be earnest conversation. "I lied to your father," she admitted. "And to the police."

I shrugged, not sure what to say. Whatever I'd been expecting, it wasn't this.

"Your parents had come home from their drive, and your mother was very agitated. It took a while to get her into bed and settled down. She was going on about her earrings. Your father was getting frustrated. You know how he can get."

I nodded, knowing only too well how he could get.

"So, he went into the drawer where she kept her jewelry, and he realized that everything was missing, and he just . . . exploded. I'd never seen him like that. It was quite terrifying, really. He demanded an explanation, and I was afraid to tell him what I'd done, that I'd taken it upon myself to give it all to you . . ."

"So, you told him that *I'd* taken it instead?"

"I'm so, so sorry," she said. "I honestly planned to tell him the truth once he calmed down, but before I knew it, he'd called the police, and then, well, things just went from bad to worse."

"It's been weeks," I reminded her. "Surely you've had plenty of opportunities . . ."

"Yes, and I've tried to tell him the truth so many times. Just that . . ."

"Just that what?"

"He's still so angry. I told him that I was sure you just took the jewelry for safekeeping, that those earrings should always have gone to you, but he won't listen. He actually ordered me never to bring it up again. And the more time went on, the more difficult it became to tell him the truth. And I felt that, under the circumstances, I just couldn't up and quit. And then your mother had that terrible fall, and well . . . here we are."

"Here we are," I repeated without inflection, my head spinning, my body numb.

Stephanie Pickering, our firm's top-selling agent, approached, and Elyse quickly excused herself to return to my father's side. "I'm so sorry for your loss," she said, patting her stiff blond bouffant.

"Thank you."

Her hand moved from her hair to my arm, her red lips forming an exaggerated pout. "She's in a better place."

THIRTY-ONE

"Come back to the house," my father instructed as we were leaving the burial site, the first words he'd spoken to me since "jewelrygate," as Tracy had taken to calling it. "There are some things we need to discuss."

I knew from experience that when my father said there were things that needed to be discussed, it meant only that there were things he wanted to say. His idea of a discussion was that he talked and everybody else listened. And obeyed.

"Sounds ominous," I whispered to Tracy as we walked down the winding road to where we'd parked our cars.

"Look on the bright side," she said. "At least he's talking to you."

I'd suggested driving to the cemetery together, but Tracy had been adamant about taking her own car in case she needed to make a quick getaway. "Funerals aren't exactly my thing," she'd said.

"I don't think funerals are anybody's thing," I countered.

"You'd be surprised," she told me, in all seriousness. "Some people *love* funerals. Serial killers, for example, they show up at them all the time."

I laughed in spite of myself. Comments like that were one of the reasons why, despite her self-absorption, I dearly loved my sister. "I'll be sure to keep an eye out."

Mount Pleasant Cemetery, occupying miles of prime real estate in the very heart of the city, is one of the largest cemeteries in Canada. A daunting maze of greenery, where tombstones dot the land like flowers, and mausoleums rise from the earth like mini-skyscrapers, its sprawling grounds are popular with both pedestrians and cyclists, even in winter.

"Busy place," I told Tracy, dodging a group of joggers running along the side of the road toward us.

"People are just dying to get in," she said.

Ten minutes later, I followed her car onto Scarth Road, parking behind her at the end of the street and walking beside her toward our parents' house. "What do you suppose Dad wants to tell us?"

Tracy shrugged, but there was something about the shrug that announced she already knew.

"Tracy?" I prodded. "Do you know something that I don't?"

"What did Elyse say to you in the chapel?" she asked in return.

I wasn't sure if the two questions were connected or if she was just trying to change the subject. I told her of Elyse's apology, her attempt at an explanation.

"You believe her?"

"I don't know. I'd like to." The truth was that I *desperately* wanted to believe Elyse. I told myself that her explanation was plausible. And it was somehow easier to believe ill of my father than it was to believe ill of her. Elyse had never been anything but kind to me, whereas my father . . . well, let's just say that kindness had never been high on his list of priorities.

Our father had arrived home minutes before we did, and he was waiting for us at the front door as we approached. Elyse was in the kitchen, he told us, preparing coffee and sandwiches for lunch.

"Just coffee for me," Tracy said.

"I tried to tell her that you only 'grazed' during the day," my father said with something approaching pride. "Don't worry," he continued. "I'm sure Jodi will eat whatever you don't."

And we're off, I thought, removing my coat and carrying it into the living room, holding it on my lap to hide whatever unsightly bulges might be lurking as I lowered myself into one of the three olive-green sofas grouped around the large stone fireplace. A mammoth limestone coffee table occupied the space in the middle of the sofas. A large, multicolored Persian rug lay at our feet.

Tracy perched at the edge of the sofa across from me, as if she was prepared to take off at the first hint of trouble. Our father remained standing.

"I wanted to discuss your mother's will," he said without preamble.

I looked at Tracy; she looked at the rug.

"Basically, your mother left everything to me," he began. "But Elyse has brought it to my attention that there are a few items your mother would likely have wanted you girls to have, and after much deliberation, I think Elyse is right." He took a deep breath, his arm extending toward the mantel over the fireplace, returning with a small velvet box. "I initially gave these earrings to Elyse as a token of my gratitude for taking such good care of your mother, but she has convinced me that this was a mistake and that you should have them," he said, looking at me.

I felt a flush of gratitude, understanding that this was as close to an apology as I was likely to receive from my father, "sorry" not being a normal part of his vocabulary. I shifted forward in my seat just as his gaze shifted from me to my sister.

"Tracy," he said, "these are for you." He held the box out for Tracy to take.

"Thank you," Tracy said, taking the box from his hands and glancing only briefly at the sapphire-and-diamond earrings inside. She carefully avoided looking at me.

I fell back against the sofa's well-stuffed cushions, my cheeks burning with a combination of embarrassment and rage.

"And Jodi," our father continued, handing me an oblong cardboard box, "these are for you."

The box contained a single strand of large pearls that I knew to be fake. "Why buy the real thing," my mother had once asked, "when nobody can tell the difference?"

I felt quite sure that my father knew the difference.

"What do you think he plans to do with the rest of Mom's jewelry?" Tracy asked me, dropping the earrings into her purse and crossing over to my sofa as soon as our father left the room to see what was keeping Elyse.

"Ask *him*," I said curtly.

"You're mad," she said.

"Why would I be mad?"

"Because he gave *me* the earrings."

"I don't give a shit about the earrings," I said honestly.

"Then why are you mad?"

"I'm mad because you knew this was going down and you didn't warn me."

"Because he pretty much ordered me not to."

"What else did he tell you?"

Tracy looked back at the rug. "Nothing."

"Tracy . . ."

"You're not going to like it."

"Tracy!"

"Okay. He said that Elyse said I should have them because I was . . . well . . . you know . . . Mom's favorite."

"Elyse said that?" *So much for telling me that those earrings should always have gone to me. So much for her apology.* "What the hell kind of game is she playing?"

"What do you mean?"

"She's trying to turn us against each other," I said, answering my own question, the realization hitting me like a slap in the face.

"What are you talking about? Why would she do that?"

"Because she thinks it works to her advantage if we're not a united front."

"A united front against what?"

"Her and Dad."

Tracy looked confused. "I'm not sure I understand."

"Divide and conquer," I told her.

"Divide and conquer," she repeated, as if I were speaking a foreign language.

"Tracy," Elyse called from the kitchen. "Could you give me a hand with the coffee, dear?"

Tracy was instantly on her feet. "Really, Jodi. Don't you think you're being a bit paranoid?"

Divide, I repeated silently as she left the room.

And conquer.

THIRTY-TWO

I phoned Harrison in Whistler as soon as I got home, desperately needing to talk to him about what had gone down. Was I overreacting, letting my imagination get the better of me?

Really, Jodi, I heard my sister say. *Don't you think you're being a bit paranoid?*

"Hey, babe," he said, sounding rushed. "Can I call you later? I'm supposed to be having breakfast with some of the other writers, and I'm already running late."

I checked my watch. It was twelve-thirty, which meant that it was nine-thirty on the West Coast. "I guess. It's just that—"

"Everything go okay today?" he interrupted.

"The funeral was fine. It was afterward . . . at my dad's. Tracy says I'm being paranoid, but . . . Hello? Harrison? Are you there?"

"Listen, honey. I want to hear all about it, I really do, but I've gotta run. Can we talk later? Is that okay?"

"Sure," I said, even though it wasn't. "Love you," I added, but he was already gone.

I replaced the receiver and walked around the main floor of the house, straightening things that didn't need straightening, emptying the dishwasher, putting on the TV and zipping through several dozen channels before turning it off again, searching for tiny superheroes and errant pieces of Lego under the sofa, trying to occupy my time before I had to pick up the kids.

My cellphone rang. "Harrison?" I asked, answering without checking the caller ID, thinking that my husband must have thought better of his casual dismissal and decided the other writers could wait a few more minutes while he listened to his wife.

"Not Harrison," the familiar voice said into my ear.

My body suddenly vibrated with girlish tingles. "Roger?"

"Am I catching you at a bad time? You're obviously expecting a call from your husband."

"No. I just spoke to him, actually. He's in Whistler. At a writers' festival. Is everything all right? The agent I spoke to about you said you'd stopped looking for a condo . . ."

"That's not why I'm calling."

"Okay," I said, not sure what else to say.

"I've actually been wanting to call for weeks now. Well, since the last time I saw you, if I'm being honest." He gave a small chuckle. "But I decided it was probably better if I didn't."

"What changed your mind?"

"I saw the notice of your mother's death in the paper," he said. "And I saw that the funeral was today. I thought I'd call and see how you're holding up."

"That's very kind. Thank you."

"So . . . how are you doing?"

"Okay, I guess."

"You guess?"

"To be honest, not all that great."

"You want to talk about it?" he asked.

Yes! I shouted silently. "Not really," I said aloud.

"Okay." Then, "There's another reason I'm calling."

I waited, too afraid to ask what it was.

"I'm leaving Toronto."

"What?"

"I'm being transferred back to Detroit."

"Oh." I felt my eyes well up with tears.

"Yeah. So I guess it's a good thing that we didn't find that condo."

"When are you leaving?"

"The end of next week."

"So soon," I said.

"Any chance of seeing you before I go?"

I took a deep breath, then checked my watch. I had almost three hours before I had to get the kids from school. "What are you doing right now?"

Ten minutes later, he was at my door.

"Hi," he said as I ushered him inside and closed the door behind him. "You look beautiful. As always."

"I don't. But thank you."

"You do. And you're welcome."

"Would you like anything to drink?"

"Nothing, thank you."

What now? I wondered, thinking that I never should have invited him over. He looked too damn good. And he was here. *Here.* Where Harrison should have been.

It was all I could do to keep from throwing myself into his arms. Instead, I led him into the family room at the back of the house, motioning for him to sit down. He sat at one end of the sofa; I sat on the other, afraid to get too close. My heart was beating so loudly, I was certain he could hear it.

"So, tell me what's been going on," he said.

That's all it took.

In the next second, I was pouring my heart out, relating the grisly details of my mother's death, the fiasco regarding her jewelry, my subsequent estrangement from my father, his decision to give my mother's earrings to Tracy, my worries regarding Elyse.

It felt so good to let it all out. It felt even better to know that someone was listening.

"You really think she's consciously trying to drive a wedge between you and your sister?" Roger asked.

"You think I'm being paranoid," I acknowledged.

"On the contrary," he surprised me by saying. "I think you should trust your instincts. If your instincts are telling you that this woman is trying to drive a wedge between you and your sister, then you're probably right. Do you have any idea why she'd want to do that?"

I told him that my father and Elyse had been sleeping together for months, and that I suspected she was interested in being more than a housekeeper.

"You think she wants to marry your father?"

"You think I'm crazy?" I asked in return.

"Makes perfect sense to me."

Again, I fought the urge to fling myself across the sofa into his embrace. "So, what do I do?" I asked instead.

"Not a whole lot you *can* do, other than keep the lines of communication open."

"My father isn't the easiest person in the world to communicate with."

"No, I get that. If you don't mind my saying, he sounds like one miserable son of a bitch."

"He certainly can be."

"So maybe they deserve each other."

I smiled through the tears that were suddenly filling my eyes.

"That being said," Roger continued, his hand extending toward my face, his fingers gently wiping away the tears now sliding down my cheeks, "*you* definitely deserve better."

I nodded. "Unfortunately, we don't get to choose our parents."

"I'm not talking about your father."

"What *are* you talking about?" I asked, although I already knew what he was going to say.

"Why isn't your husband here? What's he doing at some writers' festival on the other side of the country? Your mother just died, for God's sake. You're in obvious pain. He should be here for you."

"You're here," I said, my hand reaching for his.

This time I made no attempt to hold myself back.

THIRTY-THREE

How do I describe the next few months?

Frustrating? Exhilarating? Mundane? Terrifying?

In truth, they were all those things, sometimes separately, sometimes in combination, occasionally even all at once.

I lived those first weeks after Harrison got back from Whistler in constant fear of being found out, that I would say or do something that would betray me, much as I'd betrayed my vows, and that Harrison would somehow instinctively sense I'd been unfaithful.

He'd come home from the West Coast energized and full of ideas. "Honestly, babe," he told me repeatedly in the days immediately following his return, "it was the best thing I could have done. Meeting with those other writers, talking through shit, listening to their speeches, hearing their insights, learning from their mistakes, just being around them . . . it was mind-blowing."

"Sounds amazing," I said, trapped in the guilt of my own rather mind-blowing experience. *What's the matter with me?* I berated myself constantly. *Have I no self-control? Does my husband's selfishness justify my jumping into bed with the first man who offers me a sympathetic ear?*

As with the previous time Roger and I had been together, I'd regretted my actions almost immediately, and breathed a deep sigh of relief that he was heading back to Detroit and I would likely never see him again.

"You know that you can call me anytime," he'd said as he was leaving.

"I won't," I told him. "I can't."

"I know," he said, kissing me, tenderly, one last time. "Take care of yourself."

I'd watched him walk toward his waiting Uber, determined to recommit myself to my marriage. I told myself that whatever problems Harrison and I had could be worked through. All that was needed was a little patience and a good deal of fresh resolve. We had to learn to talk about our issues without assigning blame. We had to "keep the lines of communication open," as Roger had said in reference to my father.

Intellectually, I understood that you can never change another person, that to try means to be constantly frustrated, that the only person you can change is yourself. So I determined to do just that. I would be the best wife, the best mother, the best listener, the best lover. Whatever my husband wanted, I would try my damnedest to provide. I would be supportive, not critical. I would think before speaking. I would carefully consider my responses, refuse to take offense, to argue, to overreact. I would take great pains not to "ruffle any feathers."

To this end, I cut back on my weekend appointments, made sure I was home for dinner every night, and gave Harrison frequent massages to ease his aching back, sore from long hours spent hunched over his computer, at long last putting the finishing touches on his new book.

Happily, Harrison seemed to have reached the same conclusions as I had during his brief time away. Perhaps determined to atone for leaving me on my own to cope with both my mother's death and its unpleasant aftermath, he was attentive, caring, and thoughtful. He stopped complaining about my work schedule, was helpful around the house, playful with the kids, and openly affectionate with me.

Our marriage seemed back on track, and I determined that I would never do anything to derail it again.

As for my father, I followed Roger's advice and called weekly, determined to keep those lines of communication from shutting down. These conversations were short and often frustrating—we rarely discussed anything other than the real estate market or the weather—but I persevered.

More often than not, it was Elyse who answered the phone, and she was always friendly and eager to chat. In keeping with my newfound resolve regarding Harrison, I went out of my way to be courteous, to not take offense, to not jump to unwarranted conclusions, to keep my so-called "paranoia" at bay.

Rather than fight Elyse—a fight I would surely lose—I determined to "kill her with kindness." I decided that any woman who could put up with my father deserved the benefit of the doubt, and I resolved to cut her some slack.

The truth was that, whatever ulterior motives Elyse might have had, she made my life easier.

And, at that moment, I desperately needed my life to be easier.

I knew from Tracy that Elyse had moved upstairs and was now openly sharing my father's bed. How long, I wondered, before the two of them moved across the hall into the master suite?

Part of me was appalled. My mother had just died, for God's sake. Wasn't it a little early for my father to be playing house with another woman? But part of me also recognized that my father wasn't getting any younger and that, surely, he was entitled to whatever happiness he could find.

"She's actually pretty cool," Tracy said to me one night as we sat in the family room of my house, finishing off a bottle of red wine and admiring my newly decorated Christmas tree. It was almost eleven o'clock. The kids were asleep. Harrison had excused himself an hour earlier to go watch TV in the bedroom. Outside, a light snow was falling.

Maybe it was the lateness of the hour. Or the holiday atmosphere. Or the wine. Whatever the reason, I was finally starting to unwind, to feel more relaxed about life in general, more optimistic about the future.

A mistake.

What's that old expression? If you want to make God laugh, tell him your plans?

Not quite on the money but close enough.

"Did you know that Elyse used to be an actress?" Tracy asked.

"An actress? Really?"

"A long time ago. When she lived in L.A. She was in a few episodes of *The Young and the Restless*, and she almost got a lead role in some big blockbuster, but she wouldn't sleep with the director, so . . ."

"You two seem to have gotten pretty tight," I remarked.

Tracy shrugged. "Jealous?"

I laughed. Then I realized she was serious. "No. Of course not."

"You're sure?"

"Why on earth would I be jealous?"

"I don't know." Another shrug. "Elyse said you might be."

I felt my jaw clench. "Elyse says I'm jealous? Of what?"

Tracy glanced at the tree she'd helped decorate, then down at the floor. "Of me."

"Why would I be jealous of you?"

"I don't know. I guess in general. You know."

"I *don't* know. You'll have to be more specific."

"I guess because I'm thinner and have more style and everything," Tracy said. At least she had the good grace to look embarrassed.

"Are you kidding me? That's ridiculous."

"Is it?"

"What else did Elyse say?"

"She said I should think about becoming an actress, maybe moving to L.A. She thinks I'd get lots of work."

"Please tell me you're not seriously considering this."

"Maybe I am. Why shouldn't I?"

Out went my newfound resolve to think before speaking. And the truth is that I was too damn pissed to bother tempering my response. This wasn't the first time I'd been falsely accused of being jealous, and it rankled. "Isn't it a little late in the game to be thinking of taking on Hollywood?" I asked, the question an answer in itself.

"What's that supposed to mean?"

"Just that you're over forty, and Hollywood is notoriously unkind to women as they age . . ."

"That's changing," Tracy insisted, her face flushing pink with anger. "And besides, I look way younger. Elyse says I could easily pass for late twenties. Why do you always put me down?"

"I don't put you down."

"Yes, you do. You do it all the time. People have noticed."

"By 'people,' I take it you mean Elyse? She says I put you down?" I realized I was clutching my wineglass so tightly, I was in danger of snapping off its stem. I quickly deposited it on the floor by my feet.

"Not in so many words," Tracy said.

"What words exactly?"

"I don't know, *exactly*."

"Approximately, then."

"She just said that she's noticed that you talk down to me a lot, that you don't take me seriously."

"I see."

"I don't think you do."

"Just what is it that I'm supposed to take seriously?" I demanded. "You're all over the place, Tracy. Last month you wanted to be a writer. The month before that, it was a model, and the month before that, a dance instructor. Now you're talking about moving to Hollywood . . ."

"Yeah, and you're jealous because you're stuck here with two kids and a husband who . . ." She stopped.

"Who what?"

Tracy pushed herself off the sofa. "Nothing. I should go."

"Yes, you should."

She carried her empty wineglass to the kitchen sink, then marched to the front door. "Don't bother getting up," she said without looking back. "I'll show myself out."

"Goddamn it!" I shouted, jumping to my feet as the door closed behind her.

"What's going on down there?" Harrison called from the top of the stairs.

I glanced at my feet, realizing that, in the commotion, I'd knocked over my wineglass. "I spilled my wine," I told him, watching the dark red liquid as it spread across the sisal rug like blood.

THIRTY-FOUR

I have to admit that, until I had children of my own, I never really enjoyed Christmas.

Maybe it's because I never got the chance to believe in Santa Claus, Tracy having robbed me of that fantasy when I was four years old. She'd heard some of the older kids talking about it at school and couldn't wait to share the news with me. "Santa doesn't exist," she said, flat out. "It's Mommy and Daddy who fill our stockings and leave the presents under the tree."

I immediately ran crying to our mother, begging her to say it wasn't so. "Thank God," she said instead. "At least we don't have to carry on with that ridiculous charade anymore."

After that, the whole thing seemed more an obligation than a celebration. We dutifully hung our stockings on the mantel in the living room on Christmas Eve, only to find them filled with leftover chocolates and oranges from the fridge on Christmas morning. We feigned surprise at the gifts we received, Tracy having already uncovered their hiding places and opened each box weeks before. Even as a child, I could tell that her presents were nicer, certainly more expensive-looking, than mine. Our father considered toys frivolous, so we rarely got any, and never Barbie dolls, which was what I always asked the fake Santa in the mall for anyway.

Just in case everyone was wrong about him.

As I got older, I tried to overcompensate by buying Tracy and our parents the nicest presents I could afford. A pathetic attempt to gain their approval, I knew even then. It never worked. The things I picked out—one memorable year, a sweater for Tracy, a silk scarf for my mother, a vest for my dad—always came up short.

"It's not really me."

"I've never really liked these colors."

"Since when have I worn vests?"

It was the same thing every year, more or less.

Less joy.

More anxiety.

The closer to Christmas it got, the less joy I felt, the deeper my anxiety grew. It wasn't until after Tracy and I had moved out and our parents abandoned the early morning ritual that I started to breathe easier. We were still expected home for Christmas dinner—dry, overcooked turkey with all the requisite trimmings—but we were no longer encouraged to bring gifts, although my mother always seemed somewhat put out not to receive any.

Things changed after Harrison and I had children of our own. Christmas finally became a joyous event, filled with presents and laughter. Plenty of video games under the tree. Dozens of superheroes and Super Mario plushies, even the occasional Barbie doll.

At first, we were still obliged to show up at my parents' house for Christmas dinner, but as my mother's condition deteriorated, this fell by the wayside. I tried inviting them to our house instead, but they always refused. Tracy might or might not decide to show up at the last minute to celebrate with us, depending on whatever other invitations she'd received. That was fine with me. Tracy was Tracy, and contrary to what she seemed to think, I had no problems accepting her for who she was. Yes, she could be infuriatingly self-involved, and yes, she could be shallow and insensitive, but she could also be sweet and funny. Whatever she was, she was always, unapologetically, herself.

Which was one of the reasons I loved her.

And why I missed her when we were on the outs. As we were for much of that first holiday season after our mother's death.

That year, Christmas came and went with little fanfare. I invited my father over for dinner, but as expected, he declined. As did Tracy. "Thank you, but I have plans," she said. I found out later that she'd had dinner with our father and Elyse.

It hurt, but I stuck to my earlier resolve and refused to take offense. I would not let Elyse divide us.

Besides, there were other things happening.

Harrison finally finished the novel he'd been working on for the better part of the last five years. "It's done," he announced, coming down the stairs, his hands sagging with the weight of his manuscript.

"That's so wonderful," I said. "Congratulations!"

"I think it may be the best thing I've ever done."

"That's so exciting. I'm so happy for you. Can I read it?"

He hesitated. "On one condition."

"What's that?"

"That you're completely honest with me. If you think it's good, tell me. If you think it stinks, you have to tell me that, too."

"I'm sure I'll love it."

"You have to promise you'll tell me the truth. You're no good to me if you don't."

"Okay. I promise."

He handed over all six hundred pages of the freshly printed manuscript.

"It's still warm," I said, laughing with excitement.

"Hot off the presses," he said. "Can you read it today?"

"Today? The whole thing? I thought we were taking the kids tobogganing in High Park . . ."

"*I'll* take them to the park and then to McDonald's for dinner. You read. I want to email a copy to my editor as soon as the holidays are over, and this way, if you have any problems or suggestions, I'll have time to make adjustments."

"What possible suggestions could I have?"

"Well, hopefully, none. But in case I've made any egregious errors in spelling or grammar . . ."

"I'll be sure to tell you." I kissed him, so flattered by his trust that I almost cried. "I know I'm going to love it."

I hated it.

Where Harrison's first book had been short, pithy, and beautifully constructed, this book was long, self-indulgent, and unnecessarily obtuse. It was both overblown and underdeveloped. He never used one word when he could use ten. After three hundred pages, I gave up, and burst into tears.

What could I possibly say to Harrison?

It was dark when he brought the kids home. They were rosy-cheeked and exhausted, so there was no problem convincing them to get ready for bed. "Well?" Harrison asked after they were settled. "How far did you get? What did you think?"

His face fell the minute I hesitated.

"It's probably just me," I began.

"What's just you?" A slight edge crept into his voice.

"It feels a little long . . ."

"You think it's too long," he said.

"There's a lot of repetition . . ."

"A lot of repetition." He nodded. "Tell me, what exactly would you cut?"

"I'm not claiming—"

"To know what you're talking about," he interrupted.

"It just feels a bit wordy . . ."

"Wordy," he repeated, making the word sound vaguely obscene.

"Look. I'm not trying to hurt you. I'm as disappointed as you are. I was hoping to love it. I *expected* to love it. But you asked me to be honest. You said I was no good to you if I wasn't."

"That was because I assumed you knew how to read a manuscript."

Whoa, I thought, understanding that no good would come of trying to press my point. "Hey. It's just my opinion. I could be completely wrong."

"Really? Are you *ever* wrong?"

I ignored the sarcasm. *What's the matter with me?* I wondered. *I should know that writers in general, and Harrison in particular, are notoriously thin-skinned, that as much as they might say they want an honest critique of their work, all they really want is praise. They just want to be loved. Isn't that true of all of us?* "Maybe you should ask someone else to read it."

"Maybe I will." He gathered up the pages from the family room sofa. Then he marched up the stairs without another word.

"Fuck," I whispered as our bedroom door slammed behind him. Would I never learn?

The New Year arrived, and with it my usual slate of resolutions. Once again, I resolved to be more under-standing and supportive, to be patient, to think twice before speaking, to be the best wife, the best mother, the best sister, the best daughter. But unlike previous years where I always fell short, I resolved that this year would be different. This would be the year it all came together. This year, I would succeed.

You hear that sound?

It's God, laughing.

—THIRTY-FIVE—

That February was one of the coldest months on record. Both outdoors and inside my house. Not a lot of snow; plenty of ice.

Harrison still hadn't really forgiven me for not liking his manuscript, even after his editor also complained about its length. Not that he confided any of this to me until I asked about the publisher's response. "She feels it needs a bit more work," he admitted reluctantly.

"What kind of work?"

He hesitated. "She feels it's a little long. She wants me to make some cuts."

"Oh."

"Go ahead," Harrison said. "Say it."

"Say what?"

"Say 'I told you so.' I know you're dying to say it."

"That's not true."

He shrugged. The shrug said he didn't believe me.

"Did she say when they plan to publish it?"

"No. She said that they'll wait till they have the finished product in hand before making that decision."

I nodded, knowing that the publication date had already been pushed back numerous times because the book wasn't ready. I also knew that Harrison wouldn't receive the next installment of his advance until the manuscript had been accepted. Which meant that our income would depend solely on what I earned for the foreseeable future. Which meant that this was not the best time to cut back on my schedule.

After a relatively quiet few months—December and January were traditionally a slow time for house sales—the market was starting to heat up again. I couldn't afford—*we* couldn't afford—to slack off now.

Harrison wasn't happy about it, but then Harrison wasn't happy about much these days, especially where I was concerned. Although, interestingly enough, our sex life had never been better. What it might have lacked in tenderness, it more than made up for in frequency.

I was happy to take what I could get.

I told myself that once he'd finally finished with that damn book, the tenderness would return. The success and acclaim he'd had with his first book, while initially validating and rewarding, had come to feel like an albatross around his neck, weighing him down, holding him back. If he could just get that second book out of the way, no doubt that weight would be lifted. He could lay claim to being a legitimate author, and not simply a flash in the pan, the literary equivalent of music's one-hit wonder.

I tried to imagine what it was like for him, the anxiety and frustration he lived with on a daily basis, in much the same way as I'd tried to picture what it had been like for my mother. The difference, of course, was that Harrison had chosen his path, while my mother had not.

Yet, somehow, I'd managed to fail them both.

As for Tracy and me, we were barely speaking. I'd called to wish her a happy New Year, and she'd wished me the same, but after that, unless I reached out, there was little contact. I'd invite her for dinner; she'd respectfully decline. I'd ask what she was up to; she'd say she was busy, working out with a new personal trainer, exploring the possibility of starting her own blog, taking acting classes and looking for an agent.

Valentine's Day came and went. The only two valentines I got were handmade cards from my children. *To the greatest Mommy in the world!* Sam's card read; *I Love My Mommy!* said Daphne's. Both were accompanied by surprisingly similar-looking drawings of a round-faced, curly-haired woman with stick-like arms and legs, and a wide-eyed expression that could be viewed as either joyful or deranged. I kept both cards on my office desk as a reminder that there were at least two people in my life who loved me unconditionally.

"Knock, knock," a voice said, followed by a gentle rapping on my office door.

I returned the cards to their previous positions as Stephanie Pickering popped her stiffly coiffed helmet of blond hair inside the room.

"Can I talk to you a minute?"

I motioned for her to take a seat. "Everything okay?"

Stephanie perched at the edge of the chair across from my desk and leaned forward, her impressive cleavage peeking out from the top of her white silk shirt. She crossed one slim leg over the other and smiled, revealing a row of perfect white veneers. It was a smile that graced ads on benches all over the city. I shuddered to think of how many times she'd heard some man drunkenly boast that he'd sat on her face. "How's your father doing?" she asked.

"He's good," I said, although I hadn't talked to him in days, and hadn't seen him in weeks.

"Still living over on Scarth Road?"

"Yes."

"Managing okay since your mom passed?"

I nodded, though I've always hated the term "passed." As if she'd done well on an exam. "Seems to be."

"That's great," she said. "How old is he anyway?"

"Almost eighty."

"Wow. That's a lot of house for one person, especially someone that age."

"I agree."

"Don't you think he'd be better off in a condo?"

"Absolutely."

"Or a retirement community. Upscale, of course."

"Of course."

"So . . . ?"

"So?" I repeated, although I knew full well where she was going with this. Realtors are among the most unsubtle people on earth.

"So," she said, "I have a buyer, someone willing to pay big bucks."

"How much are we talking about?"

The figure she quoted took my breath away. "Wow."

"You think he might consider it?"

"I honestly don't know. You'd have to ask him."

"I was hoping you'd do that."

"I'm not sure that's a good idea . . ."

"Just feel him out. If he's at all interested, I'll do the rest."

I lifted my hands in the air in a gesture that told her I'd do my best, while simultaneously warning her not to get her hopes up.

"Great," she said, pushing herself to her feet, wobbling only slightly on her four-inch Louboutins. "The sooner, the better, of course."

"Of course."

"You'll keep me posted?"

"I will."

What the hell, I decided, hearing the click of Stephanie's heels as they retreated down the hall. *What do I have to lose?*

Now that my mother was dead, there was no real reason for my father to stay in that mausoleum. And this could be just the excuse needed to get rid of Elyse.

Hell, the worst that can happen is that he'll say no.

So I picked up the phone and called him, listening as it rang four times. I imagined that it took three rings for the person on the other end to get to the landline in the kitchen and check out the caller ID, and the fourth to decide whether or not to answer it. I felt almost flattered when the call was picked up.

"Jodi, hello," Elyse said in greeting. "How nice to hear from you."

"How's it going?" I asked.

"Very well. And you?"

"Good. I was wond—"

"Those darling children?"

"Great. I was wondering if—"

"Harrison?"

"Fine. Busy with his book."

"Such an awesome talent."

"Yes. Is my father around?" I managed to get out before she could interrupt me again.

"He is, dear, but he's a little busy at the moment."

"I need to talk to him about something. Do you think I could drop over in, say, an hour or so?"

There was a moment of hesitation. "Is there a problem?"

"No. No problem. I just need to talk to him. It won't take long."

"Can you give me some idea what this is about?"

"It's really none of your concern," I told her, bristling at the need to justify my wanting to visit my own father.

"Of course," she said quickly, perhaps aware she'd overstepped. "I was just trying to make things easier for everyone."

"Not your job," I said. "See you in an hour."

I hung up before she could object.

THIRTY-SIX

I arrived at the house exactly sixty-six minutes later.

"Late, as usual," my father said, opening the door as I walked up the front path.

Every muscle in my body tightened. "I didn't realize we were punching a time clock." *Not even in the door and already on the defensive,* I thought, leaning forward to kiss my father's cheek.

He accepted the kiss without any effort to return it. "Come in. Come in. You're letting all the cold air inside."

"It's a cold one, all right," I said, hugging my coat around me as I crossed the threshold. "Guess we should be grateful there's no snow."

"Is that why you insisted on coming over, why you were so rude to Elyse? To give me the weather report?"

"It's called small talk, Dad. And I didn't mean to be rude to Elyse."

"She inquired as to the reason for your visit and you told her to mind her own business."

"I told her that it was none of her concern," I corrected, knowing I was splitting hairs.

"You made her cry."

I made her cry? "That wasn't my intention."

"She's simply trying to protect me."

"From *me?* I'm your daughter, for God's sake. I shouldn't have to clear my visits with the housekeeper."

"Why *are* you here?" my father asked.

So much for small talk. "Do you think we could sit down, let me take off my coat?"

He turned toward the living room without answering. I followed after him, leaving my coat on as I sank into one of the sofas, aware of his critical gaze. My father remained standing, arms crossed, waiting for me to speak.

"You remember Stephanie Pickering," I began.

"Of course I remember her. I hired her. One of the best decisions I ever made. A superlative agent. Brings in top dollar every time. Works her ass off."

I tried not to hear the unspoken addendum, *and you don't.*

"How is she? Still as gorgeous as ever?"

"She is," I agreed.

"Great legs," my father continued. "Keeps herself in wonderful shape."

I gathered my coat tighter around me. "Yes, she does."

"Be sure to give her my regards."

"I'll do that. Anyway, she . . ." I heard footsteps and turned to see Elyse approaching.

"Hello, Jodi," she said. "You're looking well. Sorry to interrupt the two of you, but I was wondering if I could make you a cup of coffee or whip up some hot chocolate. It's so bitter out there."

Not as bitter as in here, I thought. "Please don't go to any trouble on my behalf."

"It's no trouble," she said. "It's my *job*, after all." She smiled. "Can I hang up your coat?"

"That's okay. I can just keep it here." I patted the seat cushion beside me.

"Whatever you like." Elyse looked from me to my father. "Sorry again for the interruption. I'll let you get on with it."

"Hang on a sec," my father said before she could leave the room. "Jodi, I believe you owe Elyse an apology."

"I beg your pardon?"

"Oh, Vic," Elyse protested. "That's really not necessary."

"It most certainly is."

"Your daughter was absolutely right. Whatever she's here to discuss with you is none of my concern. I had no right to ask."

"There will be no discussion about anything until Jodi apologizes," my father insisted.

Wow, I thought, torn between indignation at my father's pigheadedness and admiration for Elyse's skill at manipulation. Part of me wanted to get up and leave; the other part of me wanted to stick around and see what would happen next.

"I'm sorry if you thought I was being rude," I began, removing my coat and placing it on the seat beside me.

"What the hell kind of apology is that?" my father groused. "Don't be sorry about what *she thought*. Be sorry for what *you did*."

"I'm sorry if I was rude," I said immediately, managing

to sound reasonably sincere. I was getting pretty good at recognizing lost causes.

"Apology accepted," Elyse said. "Now, let me get you that hot chocolate."

"No hot chocolate," my father said. "She doesn't need the calories. Let's just proceed, shall we?"

I took a deep breath, trying not to cry as I waited for Elyse to leave the room. Only when she was gone and I was sure I could speak without bursting into tears did I continue. "Anyway," I began, as if there'd been no interruption, "Stephanie came into my office earlier today and asked if you might be interested in selling the house. Apparently, she has a potential buyer . . ."

My father's sneer was almost audible. "And you fell for that?"

"What do you mean?"

"There is no client! You should know that. Don't tell me you've never tried that shit yourself. No wonder she's always beating you in commissions earned."

"I don't think she was fishing. I honestly think she has somebody interested in buying the house."

"Please. It's the oldest trick in the book. You plant a seed in a person's mind, get them to consider selling when the idea never occurred to them. But now that the seed's been planted, the homeowner is seeing dollar signs and is suddenly *very* interested in selling."

"So, are you?"

"Interested in selling? Don't be ridiculous."

I quoted him the price the clients were willing to pay. "It's a damn good offer," I told him.

"Rule number one: there is no offer until it's on paper. Something else you should have learned by now."

"So, if they submit an offer in writing," I said, ignoring the insult, "you'd be willing to look at it."

"Not a chance."

"Why not, for God's sake?"

"I've lived here for almost fifty years. This is my home, and I have no intention of leaving. End of story."

"You bought this house when you were a young man with a growing family. Things have changed. You're almost eighty. Mom is dead. And this is way too much house for one person to look after. You *know* that."

"I have Elyse," he said stubbornly.

"Who isn't exactly a spring chicken. How much longer do you think she'll be able to look after everything? What happens if she quits?"

"Suppose you let me worry about that."

"You shouldn't have to worry at all. You could sell the house, make a huge profit, buy a condo or move into a first-class retirement community. You wouldn't need a housekeeper . . ."

"Aha!" he said. "So that's what this is about, getting rid of Elyse."

"I just meant—"

"I know what you meant. Thank you for dropping by." He turned and walked toward the front hall.

I sat for several seconds without moving before gathering up my coat and scrambling to my feet. "What do you want me to tell Stephanie?" I asked when I reached the front door.

"Tell her whatever the hell you'd like," he said, opening the door before I had the chance to put on my coat. He swiveled toward the kitchen, where Elyse stood, watching and waiting. "I'll have that hot chocolate now," he told her.

"Coming right up," she said with a smile. "Nice seeing you again, Jodi. If you wouldn't mind closing the door after you . . ."

I nodded. What else could I do? I tossed my coat over my shoulders and stepped out into the cold. I closed the door after me.

THIRTY-SEVEN

"You really didn't have anything better to wear?" Tracy asked me, literally turning up her nose at the oversize white T-shirt and wrinkly black shorts I had on.

It was early March and we were in the locker room of the boutique gym she'd joined at the start of the year, waiting to begin our joint session with Jeremy, her new personal trainer, who she claimed was "the best trainer ever." I'd been so surprised when she called that morning and invited me to accompany her, even offering to drive over and pick me up, that I'd said yes without fully thinking it through. The sad truth was that I hadn't exercised in years so, aside from being out of shape, I was somewhat limited in my choice of wardrobe.

"They sell workout stuff here, you know," she said. "You could buy something more fashionable and . . . you know . . . flattering."

I glanced at the sleek, black one-piece jumpsuit she was wearing, thinking that she looked like a picture in a magazine. Her long blond hair was pulled into a high ponytail and her makeup had been expertly applied. "I thought we were here to work up a sweat."

"We are," she said. "But we don't have to look like shit doing it. Not that you look like shit," she added quickly.

"I look like shit," I acknowledged.

"No. You just look a little tired, that's all. Are you okay?"

"I'm fine. Just . . . busy."

"You do too much. You work too hard. Frankly, I was a little surprised you found the time to do this."

Frankly, so was I. But the kids were in school, I didn't have any appointments booked, and my clothes were starting to feel a little tight. So, when Tracy surprised me with the invitation to join her at the gym, I agreed without hesitation.

"There's time before our session, if you want to try something on," she said, checking her watch.

It was our mother's Cartier, the one with the red alligator strap.

"When did that happen?" I asked, trying not to look too shocked as I nodded with my chin toward it.

"What? Oh, this. Yeah. I don't know. Last month, maybe. Elyse convinced Dad I should have it. You should be nicer to them, Jodi," she advised. "That way you'll get stuff, too."

"I'm always nice," I said. "Besides, I have my fake pearls. What more could I want?"

She laughed. "Next time they give me anything, I'll give it to you. I promise," she said.

"That's really not necessary."

"When was the last time you spoke to them anyway?" she asked.

I was surprised. I was the one usually asking that question. "It's been a few weeks," I admitted. My initial desire to keep open those lines of communication had taken a definite hit since being tossed unceremoniously out into the cold. There were only so many times you could bang your head against a brick wall without doing yourself serious harm. I'd decided that a break was necessary for my well-being. "You?"

"I called them a few times last week and left messages, but they didn't get back to me. There's this dress I saw at Holt's but it's molto expensive, and I thought I better clear it with Dad first, seeing as I've already exceeded my clothing allowance for this month."

"You have a clothing allowance?" I asked.

"You don't?" she asked in return. "Anyway," she continued before I could answer, "I was thinking of stopping by the house after our session, and I was really hoping you'd come with me."

"I don't think that's such a great idea."

"Please. I don't want to go alone."

"Why not? It looks as if you've been going over there on your own a lot lately." Once again, I nodded toward the Cartier watch on her wrist.

"Yeah," she acknowledged. "But they're kind of starting to freak me out."

"What do you mean?"

"The way they look at each other, like they're about

to eat each other up. Ew! You don't think they actually do that, do you?"

"Do what?"

"You know. Oral."

"Oh, God."

She shuddered. "I mean, so gross! Right?"

I had to laugh. While Tracy might not actually be able to pass for late twenties, despite Elyse's assurances, she had no trouble sounding it. "Is that why you invited me here today?"

Tracy looked genuinely offended. "No, of course not." She paused for half a second. "Well, maybe that's part of it. I mean, think about it, Jodi. Old people sex! Ew! And this way you get to put in an appearance at Casa Dundas and show you still care, we can say hello, I can describe how gorgeous the dress is, and how for sure somebody else will snap it up before next month if I don't buy it now, and that it'll be perfect for auditions and everything, and Dad'll grouse a bit, but then he'll say okay, and then we can leave because, you know, you aren't exactly his favorite person these days . . ."

"When have I ever been his favorite person?" I asked.

"Pretty please? I'll owe you big-time."

"Let me think about it."

"Don't think too hard," she advised. "Besides, I'm driving. Remember? You don't have a whole lot of choice."

A tall, good-looking young man in hot pink shorts and a matching sleeveless T-shirt that showcased his impressive biceps approached. "Ladies?" he said. "I'm ready for you now."

—

"Oh, God," I moaned as Tracy pulled her sports car into our father's driveway and turned off the engine. "I don't think I can do this."

"I promise we'll be in and out in two minutes."

"No. You don't understand," I told her. "I literally can't move. Every muscle in my body is screaming. I think I might actually be dying."

Tracy laughed. "You're just not used to exercising."

"I can't believe you do this every day."

"It gets easier the more you do it. But I gotta tell you, you were pretty good for someone who never works out. I could tell that Jeremy was impressed. So was I."

"Really?"

"Really. You gotta start giving yourself more credit. Now, let's get that not-such-a-bad-looking ass out of the car and get this over with." She scooted around the car and opened my door, extending her hand to help me out.

"We probably should have called first," I said, mindful of my father's earlier admonition.

"I did," she told me. "Three times. Nobody picked up. Oh, God," she said, "you don't think they're . . . you know . . . doing it, do you?"

"Guess we're about to find out."

I followed Tracy to the front door, amazed at how gracefully she moved, even all bundled up against the cold. "Here goes nothing," she said, ringing the bell, then ringing it again two more times when nobody answered.

I straightened my shoulders inside my winter coat. "Try knocking."

Tracy knocked. Still nothing.

"They must have gone out."

"Check the garage," she instructed.

I crossed to the side of the house and stood on my toes to peek through one of the two small windows near the top of the wooden door. "Car's here," I told her. "Maybe they went for a walk."

"Are you kidding me? It's freezing out."

"So, maybe they went to the movies."

"Dad hates movies."

"Dad's tastes have changed," I said, recalling him and Elyse in the home theater watching *John Wick*.

Tracy knelt down to peer through the mail slot. "House looks empty," she said. "Dad? Elyse? Hello? Anybody home?"

"Guess we should get going," I said, more relieved than I cared to admit.

"And miss this golden opportunity to have a look around?"

"What are you talking about?"

She reached into her purse, held up a familiar-looking object.

"You have a key?"

"Dad may have confiscated yours, but he forgot all about mine."

"You're suggesting we go inside?"

"Do you think we should?" she asked, as if this was somehow my idea. "You know, in case something's wrong."

"I don't know. What if they come back while we're inside?"

"I'll say I was worried when no one answered my calls, and we went inside to check. They can't blame me for being worried."

No, I thought. *They'll blame me.*

"Come on," she urged. "We'll take a quick look around, make sure everything's where it should be, and then leave. No one will ever know we were here."

"Famous last words," I muttered, backing toward her car.

But it was already too late. Tracy's key was twisting in the lock. The door was opening.

And the burglar alarm was going off.

THIRTY-EIGHT

"Shit!" I shouted, glancing up and down the street.

"Don't worry," Tracy said. "I know the code." She pressed in a series of numbers, and the alarm went mercifully silent. "It's the same one they've had since forever," she explained to the surprised look on my face. "My birthday. Now get in here and shut the door. We don't have a lot of time."

"What exactly are we planning to do?"

"Like I said, have a look around. Come on." She moved quickly to the stairs. "We haven't been up here since Mom died."

I was about to object when I realized I was at least as curious as Tracy was. We went directly to the master bedroom, and I confess to being relieved to find it essentially the same as when our mother was alive. The only difference was that the bed she'd once occupied had been stripped of its linens, its billowy white comforter now folded neatly at the bottom of the bare mattress.

Tracy moved immediately to the dresser, rifling expertly through each drawer. "Nothing. Dad must have moved the rest of her jewelry."

Not so with her clothes, which were still hanging neatly in the closet, the high-heeled shoes she hadn't worn in years lying in rows along the closet floor.

"God, look at all this stuff," Tracy said. "There are some real classics here. Versace, Dior. Oh, my God. A Chanel suit! Remember when Mom used to wear it? Amazing! It's got to be, like, twenty years old. I can't believe it's still in style." She held the pink skirt and matching jacket against her body. "What do you think?"

I shrugged, glancing nervously around.

"I'm gonna try it on."

"What? No!"

"It'll just take two seconds." Tracy promptly threw off her winter jacket and stepped out of the warm slacks she'd put on over her exercise leotard. "What do you think?" she asked, pulling the skirt up over her slim hips. "How does it look? It fits perfect, right?"

"Like it was made for you," I said as she adjusted the jacket's shoulders.

"It does, doesn't it?" She ran into the en suite bathroom to get a look at herself in the mirror over the sink. "I love it. I'm taking it."

I recalled the visit I'd had from the police when Dad noticed the missing jewelry. "I'm not sure that's such a good idea."

"Don't be silly. Mom would want me to have it, and Dad will never know. Come on. There must be something here for you."

"Nothing that would fit."

"Maybe a blouse," she offered. "A blouse would probably fit."

"Is there a green silk shirt?" I was thinking of the blouse I'd found in Elyse's closet, the one she claimed she was ironing and hadn't had a chance to return.

"You're strangely specific," Tracy said, milling through the rest of the hangers. Suddenly, she stopped. "What was that?"

"What was what?"

"I thought I heard something."

"Like what?"

"Like a car."

My eyes shot toward the front of the house. "Are you kidding me?"

"Go check."

I didn't have to be asked twice. I raced down the hall to the bedroom Tracy and I once shared, ducking down before I reached the window, then slowly peeking my head up over the bottom of the frame.

But the street was empty, and the only car I saw was Tracy's.

"Nothing," I said, returning to the master bedroom.

"Thank God. I almost had a heart attack. Look at this," she said, holding up a pair of black dress pants. "Can you believe it? They're Saint Laurent."

I smiled, picturing our mother in those pants, remembering when she was healthy enough to wear them. "Please don't try them on," I said. But it was already too late. The Chanel skirt lay on the floor. The Saint Laurent pants were halfway up her hips.

"If only she had any Victoria Beckham."

"Tracy, enough! We have to get out of here."

"Oh, all right. I don't see anything else that I want anyway." She grabbed her winter jacket and the clothes she was taking, but instead of heading for the stairs, she crossed directly across the hall into our father's room.

"Tracy, for God's sake . . ."

"I told you that Elyse was sleeping up here now," she said, ignoring my warning as she tossed the clothes she was holding on to my father's bed and opened the closet. "Just a quick peek. The jewelry's got to be somewhere. Oh, my God. Look! A green silk shirt! What are you—clairvoyant or something?"

"It was Mom's," I said, feeling vaguely ill at the sight of Elyse's clothes hanging next to my father's.

"And now it looks like it's Elyse's," Tracy said. "Can't very well take *that* without her knowing. And the rest of this stuff's a little old lady-ish, even for you. No offense meant."

"None taken. Now can we please leave?"

"Just a minute." She crossed to the dresser and opened its top drawer. "Oh, my God."

"What is it?"

"I think I'm gonna be sick!"

"Why? What's in there?"

Tracy spun toward me. In her hands was a black lace corset, complete with dangling garters.

"Wow," I said. Then again, when no other words would come. "Wow."

"That's not all. I'm pretty sure I saw a pair of black fishnet stockings."

"Don't tell me that."

"Who do you think wears them?" Tracy asked. "Elyse or Dad?"

And suddenly we were both doubled over, shrieking with laughter. Great belly laughs that traveled from the bottoms of our feet to the tops of our heads.

"Oh, God. For sure I'm going to be sick," she hollered between hoots.

"I don't think I can stand up straight," I cried, my arms around my waist as I tried pushing myself back into an upright position. I couldn't remember the last time I'd laughed so hard. I was literally gasping for air.

It was between gasps that I heard it.

"Ssh!" I said, the laughter freezing in my throat.

"What?"

"I heard a car door slam."

"Are you sure? You were wrong last time."

"I'm sure." I didn't bother reminding her that she was the one who thought she'd heard something before. "What do we do?"

Tracy grabbed her jacket from the bed and put it on, stuffing the clothes she'd taken inside it. "Wait," she said, although I hadn't moved. "It can't be them. Dad's car's in the garage, remember?"

"Right."

"Unless they took a cab," she said.

"Shit."

"Go look."

Again, I raced toward the bedroom at the front of the house. This time, Tracy was right behind me.

"Shit," she said, her chin on my shoulder as we stared out the window at the street below.

A taxi was indeed sitting in front of the house, its rear passenger door open. A man was bent over, helping the remaining passenger out of the car. We couldn't see his face.

And then he straightened up. And turned around. And looked directly up at our bedroom window.

Immediately, Tracy and I ducked to the floor.

"Was it Dad? Did he see us?"

"I don't know," I said, answering both questions at once.

"Shit. He's gonna be so pissed. You and your dumb ideas."

"Are you kidding me?"

"Okay, okay. *Our* dumb idea. It doesn't matter. What matters is what we do now. Do you think we have time to make it out the back way?"

Another door slammed shut. Seconds later, we heard the taxi drive off down the street.

"It's too late," I said, standing up straight, resigning myself to my fate. I was already in our father's bad books. How much worse could it get?

I should have known.

It can always get worse.

THIRTY-NINE

It wasn't our father.

Tracy and I stood at the window, staring down at the street below, our bodies numb with relief.

"Who the hell are they?" she asked of the elderly man and woman standing in front of our house.

"I have no idea."

"Are they coming here?"

"I don't think so. No," I said, watching the man take the woman's elbow and lead her toward the house next door.

"Whew! That was a close one."

"Too close. An omen. It's time to leave."

"Oh, come on," Tracy said. "Two more minutes. We've come this far. I just want to find Mom's rings. Her engagement ring is over four carats. And that diamond eternity band. Please tell me they weren't buried with Mom."

I pictured our mother lying in her coffin, her bare hands folded neatly across her chest. "There were no rings."

"Thank God for that. They must be worth a small fortune, and they're not doing anybody any good tucked away in some drawer."

"Why don't you just ask Dad if you can have them?"

"I can't do that."

"Why not?" I asked, as she took a cursory glance inside the bedroom closet before crossing the hall to our father's office.

"I don't want him to think I'm greedy."

"You'd rather he thinks you're a thief?"

"He won't think that."

No, I realized, entering our father's office, already anticipating another visit from the police. *He'll find a way to blame me.*

Despite my father having been retired for the better part of the decade, the room was much as it had always been. An oversize oak desk faced the window, its surface home to a computer, a landline, and a crystal table lamp with an oblong black shade. A massive brown leather chair sat in front of the desk, the chair matching the cracked leather sofa on the opposite wall. A Persian rug similar to the one in the living room covered the hardwood floor. One wall was lined with built-in bookcases and file drawers. The room was masculine and somewhat forbidding, rather like the man himself.

Tracy moved immediately to the file drawers, opening and closing each one in turn. "Nothing," she said when she was through.

"Can we get out of here now?"

"Let's split up. I'll take the main floor. You check the rest."

"No," I told her. "You're on your own. I'm leaving, with or without you." I promptly exited the room.

"Oh, okay. You're no fun," she grumbled, following me down the stairs and resetting the alarm before we left. "Is the coast clear?"

I looked up and down the street. "Not a soul in sight."

"Where do you suppose they are?"

I shook my head. "Beats me."

We found out four days later.

It was Sunday afternoon and I was supervising an open house in Leaside. It was a sunny day, the air crisp and clean, and there was a surprisingly large turnout of prospective buyers, considering that the house was listed at over three million dollars and it needed a new roof.

My cellphone rang as I was answering a young couple's questions about monthly maintenance costs. Caller ID informed me it was Harrison, likely phoning to remind me of my promise to be home no later than five o'clock—he was having dinner with a writer friend from out of town—and it was getting dangerously close to that now. "If you'll excuse me a minute," I said to the prospective buyers. "Harrison," I said as another four people walked through the front door. "I swear I'm doing my best to get out of here, but people keep coming—"

"Your father called," he interrupted.

"He did? When? Where is he?"

"He just called. He's home, I guess."

"Is he all right?"

"He sounded fine. He wants you to call him."

I didn't like the sound of that. My father rarely phoned me, and when he did, it was usually to tell me something I didn't want to hear. "Did he say why?"

"No. Just that it was important."

"What did you tell him?"

"That you were working, and I'd pass along the message."

"Okay, thanks."

"Jodi . . ."

"Yah?"

"Remember, you promised to be home by five."

"I'm trying."

"I'm counting on you."

"Shit," I whispered, returning my phone to my pocket when it rang again. "Tracy," I answered. "What's going on?"

"Dad just called."

"I know. He called the house. What's going on?" I asked again.

"He wants to see us."

"When?"

"Now."

"Now? I can't now! I'm working, and then I promised Harrison I'd be home for the kids . . ."

"It sounds pretty urgent. Do you think he knows?"

"Knows what?"

"That we were there," Tracy whispered, as if our father were within earshot. "That we went through his things."

"How could he possibly know that?"

"I don't know. Maybe the neighbors saw us. Or that old couple from the taxi . . ."

"I can't imagine. Dad didn't give you any hint?"

"He just said that he needed to see us right away, that it was really important."

"What did you tell him?"

"I said I'd call you and get back to him."

"So, he just disappears for a week," I sputtered in frustration, "doesn't tell anybody where he's going, and then expects us to drop everything . . ."

"Wait," Tracy said. "Who does that sound like? Oh, yeah. Dad! So, what time do I tell him we'll be there?"

"Shit," I said, forcing a smile toward the waiting couple, not sure whose wrath I preferred incurring, my father's or Harrison's. "Tell him we'll be there in one hour."

"See you then," she said.

"This isn't the way to McDonald's," Sam said from the backseat as we pulled onto Scarth Road. "You said we were going to McDonald's."

"I want McDonald's," Daphne whined.

"We *are* going to McDonald's," I assured them. "We just have to stop at Grandpa's first. We won't be long. I promise."

How many promises have I made today? How many have I broken?

Harrison had been as angry as I'd feared when I arrived home at almost five-thirty. He was already in his coat, his waiting car parked on the street, when I pulled into our driveway. "I don't want to hear it," he said, even before I had a chance to open my mouth. I watched him run down the walkway to his car, wondering what the hell I was going to do now.

"Okay, kids. Get your coats on. We're going to McDonald's," I heard myself say.

"Yay!" they cried in unison.

At least I'm still capable of making somebody happy, I thought, deciding that this might work to my advantage after all. My father was less likely to yell and carry on with Sam and Daphne present.

Why had he summoned us anyway? Had Elyse quit, leaving him high and dry? Had he had a change of heart regarding selling the house? Had a nosy neighbor informed on me and Tracy?

Whatever it was, we'd know shortly.

"Okay," I said, pulling into the driveway and turning off the engine just as Tracy's car pulled up behind me. "Everybody out."

FORTY

"Here goes nothing," Tracy said as I leaned in to ring the bell.

"We're going to McDonald's," Daphne told her.

"Lucky you," Tracy said, and seemed to mean it. Normally, the mere suggestion of a Big Mac was enough to activate Tracy's gag reflex. Clearly she was as nervous about this meeting as I was. "You're really sure he has no idea we were here this week?" she whispered.

"*You're* the one who talked to him," I reminded her. "Did he sound angry?"

"He always sounds angry."

"More than usual?"

"Hard to tell."

"Guess we're about to find out," I said as the door opened.

Our father stood on the other side, looking very dapper in a pair of black pants and matching black turtle-neck sweater. "Well, well," he said, smiling toward Sam and Daphne. "What a nice surprise. Who have we here?"

"I'm Daphne!"

He crouched down on one knee. "Daphne, huh? Do I know you?" He looked up at me and winked.

"Did he just wink?" Tracy whispered in my ear.

"You're my grandpa, silly," Daphne told him.

"I am?"

"You're *my* grandpa, too," said Sam.

"And who might you be?"

"I'm Samuel Bishop."

"Samuel Bishop . . . Samuel Bishop. The name is vaguely familiar."

"I'm your grandson."

"Well, in that case," my father said, "I guess you'd better come in." He ushered them inside.

"We're going to McDonald's," Daphne informed him. "I'm going to have Chicken McNuggets and fries."

"I'm going to have a Big Mac and fries," Sam said.

"Nothing like McDonald's fries," my father agreed. "Come in. Come in." He motioned Tracy and me inside and closed the door.

"Do you think he's had a stroke?" Tracy muttered.

"Can we ride in the elevator?" Daphne asked.

"Do you remember how to operate it?"

"I do!" said Sam. "You just press the button."

"There you go," my father said. "Take your coats off first."

"Where do we put them?" Sam called over his shoulder, his coat already dangling from one arm.

"Just drop them on the floor."

"Did he just tell them to drop their coats on the floor?" Tracy asked. "Who is this man? Oh, my God. Do you think he has a brain tumor?"

I confess to being as confused as my sister. Whatever I'd been expecting, it wasn't this. At the very least, I thought our father would be irritated at the unexpected appearance of his grandchildren. He'd never been what one would describe as a doting grandfather, preferring the *idea* of grandchildren to their actual presence. "Dad," I said, "are you feeling okay?"

"Of course. Never better. Why do you ask?"

"Well, it's been a while since anyone's heard from you, and then you suddenly call and say it's important that we come over immediately . . ."

"We were starting to worry," Tracy interjected.

"Well, I'm sorry if I worried you, sweetheart," he said. "That was not my intention. Let's go into the living room, shall we?"

I glanced toward the elevator carrying my children as it made its painfully slow ascent to the second floor before following my father into the living room and removing my coat. A fire had already been lit, giving the room a warmth it generally lacked.

"Where's Elyse?" Tracy asked, looking around the room as she discarded her coat to reveal a stunning red cashmere sweater-dress. "Did she finally take a day off?"

"Not exactly."

"Did she quit?"

"Not exactly."

"Did you fire her?" I asked, trying not to sound overly hopeful as I lowered myself to the sofa beside Tracy, our coats occupying the space between us.

"Not exactly," our father said yet again. The glint in his eyes told me he was enjoying himself immensely.

"So, what's going on?" I asked, in no mood for his games.

"I prefer to wait until Elyse is here to share the news."

I didn't like the sound of that.

"I don't think I like the sound of that," Tracy whispered.

"So, where is she?" I asked.

"Still unpacking. She'll be down in a minute."

"Can you at least tell us where you were?" I said.

He looked toward the hall. "I guess I can do that."

We waited.

"Niagara Falls," he said.

"You went to Niagara Falls?" I repeated. "In March?"

"That's right."

"Who goes to Niagara Falls in the middle of winter?" Tracy asked.

"I guess I do," our father said.

"With Elyse," I said.

"With Elyse."

"Did you go to the casinos?" Tracy asked, and then more hopefully, "Did you win?"

"You might say that."

"How much?" she pressed.

"Oh, maybe a few hundred dollars. But that's not the point."

"The point being . . ." I said.

"I won something much more valuable than money."

Tracy and I exchanged worried glances. Our father had always been the exact opposite of sentimental. To him, the only thing more valuable than money was *more* money.

There are only a handful of reasons why people visit Niagara Falls. One, of course, is to view the falls, one of the true wonders of the world, and weather permitting, take a boat ride under the falls on the *Maid of the Mist*; another is to gamble and see the shows; a third is to visit MarineLand and other surrounding tourist attractions.

There is only one other reason people go to Niagara Falls: to honeymoon.

"You got married," I said.

"No, he did not," Tracy exclaimed. "Daddy, you did not get married! Did you?"

Our father's face broke into a huge grin as he extended his arms toward the living room entrance, and Elyse all but danced into the room. She was wearing a lilac-colored suit and a dazzling smile. On the ring finger of her right hand was a diamond sparkler of at least four carats; on the ring finger of her left was a diamond eternity band.

"Tracy, Jodi," our father said, grabbing Elyse around the waist and spinning her around. "Say hello to my beautiful bride."

FORTY-ONE

"Are those Mom's rings?" Tracy whispered.

"Looks like it," I replied, careful not to move my lips.

"I think I'm going to throw up."

"This must be quite the shock," Elyse acknowledged.

I nodded, but the truth was that I really wasn't all that surprised. At least a small part of me had suspected this was where their relationship was headed. I just hadn't expected it to happen so quickly. It was barely four months since my mother's death.

Not that I was one to stand on ceremony, to demand an obligatory one-year period of mourning, even though most experts on grieving advise waiting a year before making any major decisions. But my father had been stuck in place for so many years that I could hardly begrudge him his need to move on, or deny him his right to be happy. Still, couldn't he and Elyse just have continued on as they'd been doing? Why get married? Why the secrecy? And why the big rush?

"Do you think she's pregnant?" Tracy deadpanned, as if privy to my thoughts.

"I'm sure you have questions," Elyse said. "I just want you girls to know how much I love your father, and how I'm going to do everything in my power to be the wife he deserves."

"I appreciate that," I said, striving to be magnanimous. "I'm just not sure I understand."

"What's not to understand?" our father asked. "I asked Elyse to marry me; she said yes; we took the train to Niagara Falls last week and got married."

Elyse laughed. "I know it sounds silly, but ever since I was a little girl, I've dreamed of honeymooning in Niagara Falls. And, well, it seems that your father is a man who makes dreams come true."

"Now for sure I'm going to throw up," Tracy mumbled into my shoulder.

"But why the secrecy?" I asked. "Why didn't you tell us?"

"Well, it was all rather spur of the moment," Elyse began.

"You had to make arrangements; you had to get a marriage license—"

"Do you want the truth?" my father interrupted, his smile threatening to disappear. "*This*, what's happening now, is why we didn't tell you. We knew how you'd react, that you'd disapprove, that you'd try to talk us out of it . . ."

"Now, Vic," Elyse said, laying a gentle hand on his arm. "You're being a little harsh. The girls are in shock. And they're understandably hurt . . ."

"Hurt? Why would they be hurt?"

"They feel left out," she answered, as if she had any clue as to how we felt. "I don't know. Maybe we *should* have waited, had a proper wedding . . ."

"We *had* a proper wedding."

"To which we weren't invited," I said.

"Would you have come if you had been?"

Probably not, I thought. "I don't know," I said.

"*I* know," my father said, his mouth a sneer. "Anyway, what's done is done. Elyse and I are married now, and I expect you to treat my wife accordingly."

"Now, Vic," Elyse said again.

I smiled, wondering how long it would take my father to tire of that particular phrase.

"You'll have to give your daughters some time to adjust. I was hired to be your housekeeper, not your wife. It's going to take some getting used to." She turned her attention back to Tracy and me. "Any more questions?"

"Ask him if they have a prenup," Tracy urged me under her breath.

"Are those my mother's rings?" I asked instead.

Elyse looked from her hands to the floor. "I didn't want your father wasting money on new rings when these are so beautiful."

"We're going to have them reset," my father added. "Make them more to Elyse's taste."

"She must be dynamite in bed," Tracy whispered.

"What's that?" our father asked. "You have something you'd like to say, Tracy? Unlike your sister, you've been very quiet up till now."

Tracy took a deep breath, then rose to her feet. "Just that an announcement like this calls for a toast. Where's the champagne?"

"What a wonderful idea," Elyse said, clapping her hands.

"I'll go get a bottle," my father said, quickly exiting the room.

"I'll get the glasses," Elyse added, following after him, "and some cheese and crackers."

"Are you kidding me?" I said, spinning toward Tracy as soon as they were gone. "What was that all about?"

"What was what about?"

"'An announcement like this calls for a toast'?"

"What was I supposed to say?"

"How about what you really think?"

"What good would that do? As Dad so eloquently pointed out, what's done is done. And what's that expression? You catch more flies with honey than with . . . whatever."

"Vinegar."

"What?"

"You catch more flies with honey than with vinegar," I told her.

"My point exactly."

"You threw me under the bus."

"I did no such thing."

"You made it seem as if I'm the only one who has a problem with this marriage."

"I just didn't see the point in antagonizing Dad any more than you already had."

"Thank you. That's just lovely."

"What's lovely?" Elyse said, reentering the room, carrying a tray containing four delicate glass flutes and a plate of cheese and crackers.

"You are," Tracy said. "That's a beautiful suit."

"Isn't it? Your father bought it for me. He has such exquisite taste."

"Who has exquisite taste?" our father asked, striding purposefully into the room with a large bottle of Dom Pérignon.

"You do, of course," Elyse said with a laugh. "Tracy was just admiring the suit you bought me."

"Of course Tracy would notice," our father said. "Where do you think she got her sense of style?"

"Don't forget about Jodi," Elyse said, offering me her most pitiful smile. "That's a very attractive pantsuit you're wearing, dear."

I glanced down at my black wool pantsuit and white cotton blouse, my go-to outfit when conducting an open house. "Well, I just came from work. And it's not as if I knew we'd be celebrating—"

The loud popping of the champagne cork interrupted my explanation, for which I was more than grateful. Since when did I have to account for what I wore? Just because Tracy always dressed as if she was half-expecting an invitation to the Met Gala didn't mean I had to.

My father poured the champagne into the flutes and gave one to each of us. "To my beautiful bride," he said, raising his glass.

We each followed suit. "Welcome to the family," Tracy said.

"Thank you, sweetheart," Elyse said. "I just want you girls to know that I've always been terribly envious of women with daughters. I always wanted one of my own, and now I have two, and I couldn't be prouder or more grateful! Not that I'm trying to take your mother's place.

Not that I ever could," she qualified. "But I want both of you to know that you can always count on me, that I'm here for you, should you ever need me. For anything. At any time."

"I'll drink to that," Tracy said.

I downed what was left in my glass, watching Elyse as she cupped her flute in both hands and raised it to her mouth, my mother's diamonds reflecting off the flute's surface to shine directly in my eyes.

FORTY-TWO

"Can you imagine?" I groused at Harrison, pacing back and forth in front of our bed. "She actually said that she wasn't trying to take our mother's place! As if we were teenagers. As if we weren't grown women, over forty, for God's sake. As if . . ."

". . . As if you still lived at home," Harrison said, repeating my harangue back to me. "I know, Jodi. You've been saying the same thing for the past half hour. You must be exhausted. I know I am."

"I'm just so damn mad. And Tracy . . . Tracy . . ."

"Just sat there and smiled . . . threw you under the bus . . . welcomed Elyse into the family . . . butter wouldn't melt in her mouth. Have I left anything out?"

"She's the one who ransacked our parents' house, for fuck's sake, looking for those damn rings, and then when they show up on Elyse's fingers, does she say a goddamn thing?"

"She does not," Harrison said.

"She says bugger-all."

"In fairness," he offered. "What could she say?"

"How about, 'Gee, Dad. Maybe Jodi and I would have liked those rings. Maybe you could buy Elyse a ring of her own.' No. She leaves it up to me to be the bad guy. So, as usual, I end up sounding like this spoiled, selfish ingrate and she ends up smelling like a rose."

"I think you're mixing your metaphors, sweetheart."

"Seriously?" I ranted. "My father marries a fucking gold digger, and you're complaining because I'm mixing my metaphors?"

"Sorry, hon," he said. "I'm a writer, remember?"

"Well, can you kick Hemingway to the curb for a few minutes and just be my husband?"

"Sorry. I was just trying to lighten the mood."

"Forget it. Can't be done."

"Obviously." He patted the pillows beside him. "Look. It's after midnight. This isn't getting us anywhere. Can we at least try to get some sleep and I promise we'll discuss it in the morning."

"Sure thing," I said, bouncing down hard on the bed before burrowing under the covers and staring up at the ceiling. I wasn't used to Harrison being so damn supportive and it was starting to get on my nerves. "Are you sleeping?" I asked after the passage of several minutes.

"Trying to."

"I don't think I can."

"Maybe if you stop talking . . ."

"I haven't even asked you about your evening," I said, realizing this was true. Harrison had come home over an hour ago, and I'd been ranting and raving about my father, Elyse, and Tracy the entire time.

"That's quite all right."

"So, how was it?"

He laughed. "Not nearly as eventful as yours."

"How was . . . whatever his name is?"

"John Geller," Harrison said, still chuckling. "He's fine. Has a new book coming out this spring."

"Really? What's it about?"

"Jodi . . ."

"I'm sorry. I'm just too upset to sleep."

"Okay. But I have a lot to do tomorrow, so maybe you could go downstairs and watch TV or something."

"You want to have sex?" I suggested instead.

"Now? Really? Maybe if you'd asked me an hour ago . . ."

"It's just that, you know, I'm the one who pushed for my dad to hire her."

"Jodi . . ."

"And she seemed so perfect. She came with these glowing references . . ." I stopped abruptly.

"What?" he asked.

"Her references."

"What about them?"

"What if they were fake?"

"Didn't you check them before you hired her?"

"Yes."

"And?"

"They were fantastic."

"Okay. I'm going to sleep now."

"I'm going to call them again." I threw the covers off, scrambling to get out of bed.

"What? Jodi, it's after midnight."

"Oh. Right. Okay, then. First thing tomorrow." I walked toward the bedroom door.

"So, where are you going?"

"To find her reference letter."

"Now? Can't it wait?"

"No. I don't want to waste time tomorrow searching for it."

"Okay. Do what you want. Just try not to wake me when you come back up."

"Fine," I said, leaving the room and padding down the stairs on my bare feet.

I flipped on the light in the kitchen, proceeding to the drawer where I kept miscellaneous items, and upending its entire contents across the dining room table. I spent the next hour unfolding each piece of stray paper, most of which contained nothing but unaccompanied phone numbers, and most of which I ended up tossing in the bin for recycling. There were also at least a half dozen old menus from Pizza Nova as well as some from several Japanese restaurants and the New Yorker Deli, places I couldn't even remember visiting. These were mixed in among instruction booklets for how to operate various appliances, including an espresso maker I'd thrown out years ago. "Lovely," I said, about to give up my search when I saw it—the single piece of lavender notepaper that was Elyse's list of references.

"Jodi," Harrison called quietly from the bottom of the stairs.

I jumped. "Shit. You scared me."

"You're scaring *me*," he countered. "It's after two o'clock."

"It is? I guess I lost track of the time."

"Did you find it?"

"Yes."

"Then come to bed."

I pushed myself to my feet, followed him wordlessly up the stairs and into bed, snuggling in beside him.

"Has it occurred to you," Harrison asked as I was drifting off, "that Elyse might be exactly who she says she is? That she's a great housekeeper who came to work for your father and they just happened to fall in love? That there was no nefarious plot to insinuate herself into your father's life and cut you and your sister out?"

I thought about all that had happened since Elyse had come into our lives—how my initial infatuation had been replaced by doubt and eroded by lies. Was it possible I was wrong? That I'd been too quick to see things that weren't there, assume motives that didn't exist? Was it possible that Elyse genuinely loved my father? "It's possible, I guess," I had to concede.

"Good. Now get some sleep," Harrison said.

"But I don't think so."

Harrison groaned, covering his head with his pillow to discourage any further attempts at conversation.

I flipped onto my side, began my silent recitation: *A is for Annie; B is for Bernard; C is for Corinne; D is for Derek.*

I shuddered. "E is for Elyse," I said out loud.

—FORTY-THREE—

Tracy called me first thing that morning. "So, what are we going to do?"

Seriously? I wondered. I knew the question she was really asking was *What are* you *going to do?* "I don't know about you," I answered, tired from lack of sleep and in no mood to deal with her. "But I'm going to drive the kids to school and then head to the office." I decided not to tell her about my plans to recheck Elyse's references. "I'll talk to you later," I said, hanging up before she could protest.

As soon as I got to the office, I closed the door, sat down at my desk, my coat still on, and pulled the lavender piece of paper listing Elyse's references from my purse. There were only two contacts: Ken Billings, whose father had died of cancer the previous year, and the Robertsons, Susan and Jack, the daughter and son-in-law of Elyse's former neighbor, Alice Kernohan. I'd spoken to both Ken and Susan before and received references that were nothing short of ecstatic. There was no reason to suspect I'd hear anything different this time around.

Still . . .

I took a deep breath and called Ken Billings. The call was answered almost immediately. "I'm sorry," announced a familiar recording. "The number you have reached is no longer in service. Please check the number and try your call again."

Okay, I thought. Maybe I dialed the wrong number. I hung up and dialed the number again.

"I'm sorry. The number you have reached . . ."

Okay. So, Ken Billings got a new number. It was possible.

I tried the number for Jack and Susan Robertson.

"I'm sorry. The number you have reached is no longer in service."

What the hell was going on?

While it was conceivable that one of Elyse's references had changed their number, it seemed highly unlikely that both had.

What did it mean?

According to Elyse's reference letter, she'd served as a housekeeper/caregiver for two years to a Mr. Thomas Billings, who'd lived with his son and his family at 1163 Old Forest Hill Road up until his death. Before that she'd been employed by the Robertsons to care for Susan's mother, Alice Kernohan, Elyse's onetime neighbor, in an apartment building at Yonge and St. Clair.

I picked up my phone, pressed in the extension for our receptionist. "Hey, Vicki," I told her. "Listen. Something's come up and I have to be out of the office for a few hours. Can you see if you can reschedule my ten o'clock? Thanks."

Then I stuffed the lavender piece of paper back in my purse and left the office.

Lower Forest Hill Village is, along with Rosedale and the Bridle Path, one of Toronto's toniest neighborhoods, its wide, tree-lined streets filled with gorgeous, multimillion-dollar homes. It lies right in the heart of the city and is only a short drive from my office, so it took me only minutes to get there.

"Now what?" I said as I pulled my car to a stop in front of the old stone house that was 1163 Old Forest Hill Road, watching my breath fog the windshield. *Now you get out of the car, go knock on the door, and find out what the hell is going on.*

Of course, the Billings family might have moved, in which case my amateur sleuthing would be all for naught, but what the hell, I was here already, I reasoned, ringing the bell.

The front door opened just as I was about to give up and return to my car. "Can I help you?" a woman asked.

"I'm sorry to bother you," I said to the uniformed housekeeper before realizing I had no follow-up question. Some detective I was!

"Who is it, Mary?" a woman called from inside the house.

"My name is Jodi Bishop," I called back. "I was just wondering if I could ask you a few questions."

"We only vote Conservative," the woman responded, coming into view. She was mid-fifties, with jet-black hair and elegant cheekbones.

"I'm not a pollster," I said. "And I'm not selling any-thing," I added before the housekeeper could close the door in my face. "Are you Mrs. Billings?"

"Yes?"

"I tried to phone but I was told the number had been disconnected."

"That's strange. We've had the same number for more than twenty years," Mrs. Billings replied. "What number were you calling?"

I pulled out the lavender piece of paper and showed her the number.

She shook her head. "Elyse Woodley, huh?" she scoffed, reading the name at the top of the page.

"You know her," I stated more than asked.

"I certainly do. She used to work here. Don't tell me she had the nerve to give my name as a reference."

"Your husband's name, yes."

"You're thinking of hiring her?"

"Actually, we already have. Last spring."

"And yet, here you are, checking up on her. Things not going so well?"

"There are a few red flags," I said.

"I'll bet there are. Let me guess. Everything started out swimmingly. You thought you'd died and gone to heaven. Then little things started happening. Small things went missing. Then more expensive items. Stories didn't quite add up. She got a tad too friendly with, I'm guessing . . . your father?"

I nodded, unable to speak.

"With us, it was my father-in-law. She actually talked him into putting her in his will without our knowledge.

Walked away with fifty thousand dollars, and we couldn't do a damn thing about it. Stay away from that one, if you know what's good for you."

Too late, I thought. "Thank you for your time," I managed to spit out before hurrying down the walkway to my car.

"Shit! Shit! Shit!" I swore, banging my hand against the steering wheel. *What the hell am I supposed to do now?*

I drove directly to the apartment building on St. Clair, just east of Yonge Street where, according to Elyse, she'd help care for her elderly neighbor, Alice Kernohan.

"Oh, yes, Mrs. Kernohan," the balding building manager said with a smile that emphasized the substantial gap between his two front teeth. "I remember her. Lovely woman."

"She doesn't live here anymore?"

"No. Her daughter moved her into a home a few years ago. She couldn't really manage on her own anymore."

"I understood that she had someone looking after her. A neighbor in the next unit?"

The frown on the building manager's round face told me I wasn't going to like what I was about to hear. "Elyse Woodley. Yes. A real piece of work, that one."

"What makes you say that?"

"Well, I don't like to tell tales out of school . . ."

"Please," I urged. "She's applied for a job, and she gave the daughter's name as a reference."

The building manager laughed. "I can't imagine in my wildest dreams Susan ever giving her one."

"Why is that?"

"Well, from what I understand, Mrs. Woodley ingratiated herself with poor Mrs. Kernohan, made herself virtually indispensable, and then proceeded to rob her blind. Nothing the family could prove, of course. She even talked Mrs. Kernohan into giving her a sizable amount of money. Family was furious. She actually had the nerve to give Mrs. Robertson's name as a reference?"

I nodded, feeling sick to my stomach. "Thank you for your time."

"You won't tell her I said anything, will you?" the building manager asked timidly.

"No, of course not."

"Thank you. Like I said, she's a real piece of work. I hate to think what she might be capable of."

FORTY-FOUR

I called Tracy as soon as I got back to my office, and told her what I'd discovered about Elyse.

"I don't understand," she said. "Why on earth would she give these people as references, knowing that's how they felt?"

"Well, she clearly didn't expect me to pay them a personal visit."

"Didn't you check them out before you hired her?"

"I *phoned* them. She obviously gave me fake numbers. God only knows who I spoke to."

"She has an accomplice," Tracy whispered dramatically.

Oh, God, I thought. Was it possible? What were we dealing with here?

"She actually walked away with fifty thousand dollars?"

"And now she's hit the jackpot," I conceded.

"So, what are we going to do?"

I felt almost pitifully grateful that Tracy had included herself in finding a solution to the problem I'd created. "I don't know. Any suggestions?"

"Call Dad's lawyer," she said.

"Old Mr. Miller? He's got to be Dad's age. Is he still practicing?"

"I have no idea. Call him and find out."

"And say . . . what?"

"Tell him what's going on. Ask him what our options are. Legally speaking."

"I'm not sure we have any."

"Which is why you have to call him. You don't want Elyse walking away with our inheritance!"

"It's Dad we should be concerned about here," I reminded her.

"I don't think we have to worry about Dad. He's having the time of his life."

"At the moment, maybe. Who knows how long that's going to last now that they're married."

"Oh, my God," Tracy said.

"What?"

"You don't think she'd do anything to speed things along, do you?"

"Like what?"

"Like poison his food or push him down the stairs or . . . Oh, my God!" she said again.

"What?"

"You don't think she . . . ?"

"*What?*"

The silence that followed was so long, I thought we might have been disconnected. "No. It's too crazy."

"What's too crazy?"

Another long silence. "You don't think she could have had anything to do with Mom's death, do you?"

"No way," I insisted, as much to reassure myself as my sister. In truth, the thought had occurred to me more than once, but I'd always been too afraid to voice it out loud. "Dad was with her at the time, remember? They were having breakfast in the kitchen when they heard Mom fall."

"Unless they weren't."

Another long silence, this time from my end of the line. "What are you saying? You're seriously suggesting that Elyse may have murdered Mom? And that . . . what? . . . Dad is covering it up to protect her?"

"Not necessarily. I mean, he *might* be trying to protect her, but not because he thinks she killed her. Maybe he has no idea what really happened. Maybe he and Elyse were just in different parts of the house when he heard Mom fall, and he has no idea Elyse had anything to do with it."

"You really think that's possible?"

I hate to think what she might be capable of, I heard the building manager say.

"Do you?" Tracy asked.

"I think we should give old Mr. Miller a call."

The offices of Miller, Ferguson, and Miller were located on the twenty-seventh floor of the giant white office tower that is First Canadian Place, in the heart of downtown Toronto.

I'd called Ronald Miller as soon as I got off the line with Tracy, and was able to get an appointment for three the next afternoon. I picked Tracy up at the gym, relieved when she only spent a few minutes grumbling about having had to cut short her session with Jeremy. "We were lucky to get this appointment," I told her on the drive down. "He had a cancellation, or we would have had to wait another week."

Tracy looked unimpressed. She pulled down the passenger seat visor to arrange her long hair into a high ponytail, then expertly applied a fresh coat of mascara to her lashes and gloss to her lips with a surprisingly steady hand, considering the number of potholes in the road.

I parked in the underground garage and we took the elevator up to the twenty-seventh floor.

"We're here to see Ronald Miller," Tracy announced as we approached the sweeping black marble counter in the large reception area. Two well-dressed, immaculately coiffed women—one about thirty, the other perhaps two decades older—sat at opposite ends of the counter, smiling at us expectantly. One was blond, the other blonder. Both were wearing identical shades of beige. I wondered if this was deliberate, if they made a conscious effort to coordinate their outfits.

"We have a three o'clock appointment," I explained. "I'm Jodi Bishop. This is my sister, Tracy Dundas."

"Yes, Ms. Bishop. I have you right here," the older, blonder of the two women said. "You were very lucky. We got that cancellation two minutes before you called. Mr. Miller is just finishing up with a client. If you'll have a seat"—she motioned toward a grouping of four red leather chairs beneath an imposing oil painting of a prairie landscape—"he'll be with you shortly."

"Thank you."

"What did I tell you? We'll probably have to sit here forever. I could have finished my session with Jeremy." Tracy picked up several newspapers from a nearby black-lacquered coffee table, then immediately tossed them back. "God, the *Financial Post* and the business section of *The Globe*. Does anybody actually read these things? Would it kill them to have a copy of *People*?"

In fact, we waited less than five minutes before being ushered into the inner labyrinth of small offices and smaller cubicles reserved for support staff, until we reached the large corner office belonging to Ronald Miller.

"Ladies," said the skinny, boyish-looking man behind the impressive oak desk, motioning us toward the two navy blue chairs stationed in front of it. "Please, have a seat."

"He doesn't look almost eighty," Tracy whispered.

"Is there a problem?" the lawyer asked, sitting down behind the desk.

"Just that we were expecting someone much older," I said.

He laughed. "You're thinking of my father, whose name is also Ronald. I'm afraid he retired some years ago."

"Oh." Tracy and I exchanged worried glances. "Our dad was one of his clients."

"Your dad was . . . ?"

"*Is*, actually. He's still very much alive. Victor Dundas. He founded Dundas Real Estate."

"Victor! Of course. Lovely man. Great agency. My wife and I used them when we bought our house. The agent's name was Sharon . . . Stephanie . . ."

"Stephanie Pickering."

"Yes. Right. Pickering. Terrific agent. Could sell coals to Newcastle, or whatever that expression is. She still with the agency?"

"Our top earner," I said.

He nodded, as if he were truly impressed. "It's been a while since I've seen your father. I take it he's well."

"Very well."

"He got married again," Tracy said, clearly impatient with the prolonged small talk. "We think she's a gold digger, and we want to know how we can protect our inheritance."

"Well," I qualified quickly, watching the smile fade from Ronald Miller's face, "we really just want to find out what our options are."

"Ladies," the lawyer said, holding up the palms of both hands. "I sympathize. I really do. But I'm afraid I have to stop you right there."

"Oh, we're just getting started," Tracy said.

"Which is why I have to stop you," he said. "This is what we call a classic conflict of interest."

"What's that supposed to mean?" Tracy asked.

"It means that your father is still a client of this firm and I'm not at liberty to discuss his business . . ."

"This isn't about his business," Tracy corrected. "It's personal."

"I'm afraid that it would be unethical for me to discuss your father's business, personal or otherwise, with anyone without his expressed consent or written permission."

"Fat chance of that," Tracy scoffed.

"Exactly," the lawyer agreed. He rose to his feet, indicating the meeting was over.

"Is there someone else at the firm we could talk to?" Tracy asked.

"I'm sorry, no. It would still be a conflict . . ."

". . . of interest. Yes, we get it." Tracy turned and marched from the room without so much as a backward glance.

"It was nice meeting you," Ronald Miller said, extending his hand across the desk toward me. "Good luck."

"Thank you," I said. "Looks like we're going to need it."

FORTY-FIVE

"Can you believe the nerve of that guy?" Tracy complained loudly as we were leaving the reception area. "As if he couldn't take two seconds to hear us out," she was still complaining in the elevator on the way down to the parking garage. "It's not like we don't have Dad's best interests at heart. I have half a mind to report him to the bar," she said as we were pulling out of the lot.

"He had no choice," I told her for what felt like the hundredth time. "His hands were tied."

"Bullshit." She pulled down the visor, examined her reflection in the small mirror. "So, what are we gonna do now?" she asked, snapping the visor back into position.

"Beats me," I said honestly. "Find another lawyer, I guess."

"*I* know what we're gonna do," she said as we headed north up University Avenue.

"What's that?"

"We're going shopping. Turn right on Bloor."

"What?"

"Turn right. We're going to Holt's."

"What?" I said again. "You can't be serious."

"I'm buying that dress I told you about. And something for you, too, assuming they have anything nice in your size."

I didn't know whether to feel grateful, insulted, or both. "This is ridiculous. You can't just . . ."

"I can't? Watch me. Do a U-y and pull up right in front. The valets will park the car."

"Tracy . . ."

"Come on. Don't be such a goody-goody. Dad owes us."

"He doesn't," I began, stopping my objection at the same time I stopped the car. *What the hell?* I reasoned, handing the car keys to the waiting valet and following Tracy inside the upscale department store. *When's the last time anybody bought me anything?*

We made our way through the counters selling brand-name cosmetics to the escalator in the center of the three-story store, getting off at the second floor, where most of the designer labels were located, many in little boutique-like areas of their own.

"This way," Tracy directed, removing her coat as she led me toward a rack displaying the latest in Victoria Beckham. "Here it is," she said, looking around. "We'll have to get a salesperson to unlock the hanger." She pulled the calf-length, copper-colored dress toward her. "What do you think?" she asked. "Of course, it looks better without the hanger. Where is everyone?" She looked around. "Excuse me," she called to a middle-aged woman with an old-fashioned bouffant of red hair. "Is Zack in today? Zack's who I usually deal with," she told me.

"It's his day off," the woman said. "Can I help you with anything?"

"I'd like to try this on," Tracy told her, "but I want Zack to get credit for the sale," she instructed. "He's the one I usually deal with, and he'd be really pissed if I let anyone else sell me anything."

"Of course," the woman said, although her tight smile indicated otherwise. She used her key to free the dress from its hanger. "No problem."

"We'll just look around for a bit, see if there's anything for my sister. I'm an extra-small. You're, like, what—a medium?" she asked me, wrinkling her nose, as if the word itself was distasteful.

"I'll start a dressing room for you," the saleswoman said, lifting the dress from Tracy's hands.

"Thank you," I said when Tracy failed to.

"So, you see anything you like?"

"Pretty hard not to," I admitted, focusing on a lovely camel-colored skirt. "This is beautiful, and I could wear it to work. Oh, my God!"

"What's the matter?"

"It's three thousand dollars!"

"Yes? So? It's Alexander McQueen."

"I don't care who it is. Who spends three thousand dollars on a skirt?"

"Lots of people," Tracy said. "And now, so do you."

"I can't. No way."

"Oh, come on. My treat, remember? Or Dad's treat. Whatever. You can at least try it on. Don't worry. It looks kind of small. It probably won't fit." She signaled for the saleswoman. "She's gonna try this on. And this, too," she said, pulling at a gorgeous brown silk shirt and holding it up against me. "Perfect. You will be the best-dressed Realtor in town. Give that witch Stephanie Pickering a run for her money."

I wasn't sure what surprised me more—that I was agreeing to try on the ridiculously overpriced skirt and blouse or that Tracy had actually been paying attention to the conversation in the lawyer's office and remembered Stephanie's name.

"See anything else you like?" Tracy asked me.

"I think this is plenty."

"In that case, follow me."

Tracy led me toward the dressing rooms, where our clothes were already hanging up and waiting. "Holler when you're ready," Tracy said as we disappeared inside our respective cubicles.

I stood for several seconds in the mirrorless cubbyhole, debating whether to bother trying the clothes on. There was no way I was actually going to let Tracy buy them, no matter whose money she'd be spending. Still, I have to admit that I was curious as to how the skirt and blouse would look. And what harm could it do to try them on?

"How are you doing in there?" Tracy called after several minutes.

"Not quite ready." I removed my coat and unzipped my blue wool dress, letting both fall to the floor. Seconds later, I was pushing my arms into the sleeves of the brown silk shirt and doing up its faux pearl buttons—which I decided would look great with my faux pearl necklace— then stepping into the camel-colored skirt, pleased beyond reason when it zipped up without even a hint of difficulty. "Okay, I'm ready," I announced, eager to see myself in a mirror.

"Wow!" Tracy exclaimed as I emerged. "You look fantastic."

I spun toward the mirror at the end of the narrow hall, amazed at what I saw. Tracy was right. I *did* look fantastic.

"What about me?" she asked, twirling around. "How do *I* look?"

"Beautiful, as always."

Tracy beamed. "Isn't this the most gorgeous dress you've ever seen?"

"It is," I agreed.

"We'll take everything," Tracy told the saleswoman.

"No," I demurred. "I can't."

"Yes, you most certainly can," Tracy insisted, handing over her credit card. "You don't treat yourself nearly enough, and you deserve nice things."

I was both flattered and touched by the unexpected compliment. "Thank you."

"I'll put this through and meet you back at the counter when you're ready," the saleswoman said.

"Well, I don't know about you," Tracy said. "But I'm feeling a whole lot better than I did an hour ago."

I laughed. The truth was that I was feeling pretty good myself.

We got dressed in our street clothes and approached the counter where the saleswoman was ringing up the sale.

"Is there a problem?" Tracy asked after a wait of several minutes.

"I'm afraid your card has been declined," the woman said, barely managing to suppress a smile.

"That's impossible. I shop here all the time."

"I've tried to put it through several times."

"Try again."

"Certainly."

"I'm probably just over my limit," Tracy said when the card was declined again. "What about just the dress?"

I almost laughed.

"Let's give it a try," the saleswoman said.

"Sorry," Tracy said to me. "I didn't realize you had such expensive taste."

"No problem." Half of me was disappointed, the other half relieved. Neither half was surprised.

"I'm so sorry," the saleswoman said, handing Tracy back her card. "It's still not going through. Do you have another card we could use?"

"No, I don't have another card. This is the only card I've ever needed. There must be some mistake."

"Perhaps you should take it up with the bank."

"Perhaps you should go fuck yourself," Tracy said.

"Tracy," I said, pulling her away from the counter. "It's not her fault."

"Really? Whose fault is it?"

The question hung, unanswered, in the air between us.

FORTY-SIX

"Where are you going?" Tracy demanded as I headed west along Bloor toward Avenue Road. It was almost five o'clock and getting dark. A light rain was starting to fall.

"I'm taking you home."

"No way. We're going to Dad's. We're straightening this out right now."

"I'm not sure that's a very good idea."

"I'm not asking your permission."

"It's my car," I reminded her. "I'm the one driving."

"Fine. Drive me to Dad's. You don't have to come inside, if you're too much of a coward."

"I'm not a . . . Fine. I'll drive you to Dad's."

Ten minutes later, I pulled up in front of our father's house. "Here you are."

She reached for the door handle, then didn't move. "You're really not coming in with me?"

"I'm really not."

"Please?"

"No."

"You're not going to tell him about Elyse? That she lied about her references?"

"Not till we know where we stand legally. Not till we have a plan."

"Okay," she conceded. "We'll just deal with the credit card issue."

"Okay," I agreed.

Again, she didn't move. "So, are you coming with me or not?"

"Tracy . . ."

"You don't have to say a thing. I promise I'll do all the talking. Just be there for, you know, support."

I sighed. We both knew that it was just a matter of time before I gave in. "What are you going to say?" I said, stalling. "You should have some idea what you're going to tell Dad before we go inside."

"A plan, right? Like you said before." Tracy thought for a few seconds. "Okay. I'll tell him the truth, that I went to use my credit card at Holt's, like I always do, and it was declined. Then I'll ask him if he could please look into it. How's that?"

I sighed again. "I guess that's okay."

"Thank you. You're the best."

"You're doing all the talking," I reminded her as she exited the car.

She was ringing the bell as I came up behind her.

Seconds later, Elyse opened the door. "Tracy! Jodi! This is a surprise." She made no move to usher us inside.

"Can we come in?" Tracy asked.

"Is something wrong?"

"We need to talk to our father."

Elyse glanced over her shoulder. "He's having a little nap right now. Is there something I can help you with?"

"No. We really need to speak to Dad."

"And I'd really hate to disturb him."

"It's important."

"So is his sleep. Are you sure this can't wait?"

"Let's go," I whispered.

"Elyse, what's happening out there?" our father called from inside.

"Daddy, hi!" Tracy shouted. "It's Jodi and me."

Elyse moved out of the way as our father came into view. "I tried to tell them you were having a little snooze, but . . ."

"What's this about?" our father asked.

"Can we come in? It's raining out here."

"We're having dinner shortly . . ."

Tracy checked the Cartier watch on her wrist. "Now? It's not even five o'clock."

"Eating early helps your father's digestion," Elyse explained.

"We won't be long," Tracy said.

"Well, then, where are our manners?" Elyse asked, stepping out of our way. "Please, come in. Why don't you go into the living room while I check on dinner."

We followed our father into the living room.

"I thought you said this wouldn't take long," he said as I was about to take off my coat.

I perched at the edge of the sofa, kept my coat on.

"Well?" he said.

"Well," Tracy began, choosing to remain standing. "The funniest thing just happened." She looked to me for confirmation.

I nodded and said nothing.

"We were at Holt's," she continued. "Jodi tried on this fabulous Alexander McQueen, and she didn't have the money to pay for it, so I offered to put it on my card."

My mouth fell open, but no sound emerged.

"Anyway, the long and short of it is that the card was declined. I tried to tell the saleswoman that there must be some sort of mistake, that I've never had a problem before, but she told me to talk to the bank. I thought I'd talk to you instead, because clearly someone got their wires crossed . . ."

"No wires were crossed," our father said.

"I'm sorry?"

"I canceled the card."

"What?"

"I canceled the card," he repeated, although we'd all heard him loud and clear.

"Why would you do that?" Tracy sputtered.

"Now, don't go getting all upset," our father said. "It's for your own good."

"My own good?" Tracy argued. "Says who? What the hell is happening?"

"Elyse and I have been discussing this for some time, and she feels I'm doing you no favors by continuing to treat you as a dependent, that I'm—what was the word she used?—*infantilizing* you . . ."

"Infantil . . . what the fuck?"

"She feels . . ."

"I don't give a fuck what she feels."

"We *both* feel . . . that you're a bright, accomplished woman, and that there's no reason I should still be paying all your bills."

"How else am I going to afford anything?"

"By getting a job like everybody else," our father said. "Like Jodi."

Oh, God, I thought. Much as I appreciated that for once I was being compared favorably to my sister, this was definitely not the time or the circumstances in which to do it.

"Doing what? Selling real estate? I'd rather die."

"What you choose to do is up to you," our father said. "I'm quite confident that you will be successful at whatever career path you choose."

"I'm forty-five fucking years old!" Tracy cried. "It's a little late to be talking career paths, don't you think?"

"Be that as it may," our father continued calmly, "we're confident you can do it."

"What about my rent? My phone? My cable?"

"Relax," our father said. "We're not cutting you off completely, and certainly not all at once. I'll continue covering the bulk of your expenses for the next year. I'm sure that by then you'll have found something."

"And if I haven't?"

"Elyse and I have every confidence that you will."

"Elyse is a fucking con artist!" Tracy shouted, spinning toward me. "For God's sake, Jodi. Tell him what you found out."

Oh, God, I thought as Elyse entered the room. *I knew I should have gone straight home.*

"What's all the yelling about in here?" she asked.

"Go on, Jodi," Tracy urged. "Tell Dad all about his blushing bride."

Elyse walked to the nearest sofa and sat down. "Yes, Jodi," she said, leaning back against the cushions and crossing one leg over the other. "By all means, let's hear what you have to say."

FORTY-SEVEN

"I really didn't want to get into this right now," I started, then stopped. I was trapped, and I knew it. We *all* knew it. Why I hadn't seen this coming was beyond me.

"Well?" my father said.

"Please understand that we were just concerned about your welfare . . ."

"She checked your references," Tracy said to Elyse.

"I assumed you'd done that some time ago," Elyse said to me, seemingly unconcerned.

"As I recall, you said they were impeccable," my father said.

"They were. Whoever I spoke to at the time was exceedingly complimentary."

"Am I missing something?" he asked.

"Just that when Jodi called those numbers again, they'd been disconnected," Tracy said, her eyes urging me to continue.

Our father frowned. "Why would you call them again?"

"We were worried about you, Dad. Mom just died;

you ran off to Niagara Falls and got married without telling us . . ."

"Do you even have a prenup?" Tracy asked.

"Ah," our father said. "So that's what this is about. It has nothing to do with my welfare."

"We worried that you were being taken advantage of . . ."

"Please," our father scoffed. "This is all about money. *My* money. Which is mine to do with as I damn well please."

"Nobody is disputing that," I argued. "But try to see it from our perspective. Our mother just died—"

"So you said," our father interrupted. "Hardly a surprise. She'd been dying for years."

I clutched the arm of the sofa, trying not to be overwhelmed by his apparent callousness.

"Do you know how hard that was for me?" he continued. "Are you so coldhearted as to deny me a little happiness after all I've been through, the years I spent looking after her?"

"It's not that we don't want you to be happy," I countered. "It's just that it's all happened so fast, and we were naturally concerned, so I rechecked Elyse's references, and found that the phone numbers she'd given me were no longer in service . . ."

"So? People move. They change phone numbers."

"So, she went to see them," Tracy said, clearly trying to speed things along. "Tell him what you found out."

"I spoke to Mrs. Billings," I began, watching Elyse's face closely for her reaction. But if she felt any apprehension about what I was about to say, she did a great job hiding it.

"Oh, yes," Elyse said. "How is Angela? Still dyeing her hair that horrible shade of black?"

"I'm afraid she didn't have many nice things to say about you."

"Frankly, I'm surprised she had any," Elyse admitted. "She wasn't my biggest fan."

"And yet you gave her name as a reference."

"I gave her *husband's* name as a reference," she corrected. "I'm afraid that Mrs. Billings and I never really got along. Poor Mr. Billings was terrified of her. He used to tell me the most awful stories, how cruel she was to him when no one was around, how his son was too weak to stand up to his wife. He said that he felt I was the only person in the world who truly cared about him, and told me that he intended to leave me a little something in his will. Of course, the family had an absolute fit when they found out. I'm sure she told you all about it. I also assume you went to see old Mrs. Kernohan," she surprised me by saying.

"I did."

"And? How is the dear thing?"

"Apparently, her daughter moved her into a home a few years ago."

"You spoke to her?"

"I spoke to the building manager," I said before remembering that he'd asked me not to identify him.

"Mr. Harris? That horrid little man? He cornered me in the elevator one day, tried to kiss me. It was awful.

That dreadful space between his teeth where food always gathered. I actually had to kick him to get him off me. Can't imagine what he told you."

"He said you conned Mrs. Kernohan into giving you a sizable amount of money . . ."

"If you consider five thousand dollars a sizable amount," Elyse said. "And I hardly conned her. I'd asked her for a loan, but she insisted it was a gift. Such a lovely woman."

"Anything else?" my father asked, his voice registering his impatience.

"No," I admitted. "That's about it." It seemed Elyse had an answer for everything.

"Then you've said your piece and you can be on your way."

"Dad . . ." I began.

"We're finished here." He turned, started walking from the room.

"Vic, wait," Elyse said. "We can't just leave things like this."

"Consider them left."

"But I feel terrible about what's happened."

"You have nothing to feel terrible about. You've done absolutely nothing wrong."

"I know that. But I hate being a source of friction between you and your daughters."

"You aren't," he told her. "This is on them."

"I'm sure they thought they were only looking out for you."

"I don't need looking out for."

"Everybody needs looking out for," Elyse said. "Come on, darling. Try to see it from their side. If I can understand their concern, surely you can at least try. Jodi hired me to be your housekeeper, not your wife. Their mother's death, our sudden marriage, well, it's a lot to take in. And they're understandably hurt that they weren't included in our plans. But they'll get over it, and so will you. You're their father, and they worry about you. Please, can't we all just try to get along?"

"Oh, she's good," Tracy whispered.

Our father pushed his shoulders back, took a series of long, deep breaths. "There will be no more checking up on Elyse, no more interfering in my life, no more 'looking out for me,' " he said. "Am I making myself clear?"

"Very," Tracy said.

"As a bell," I added.

"And no more visits to lawyers," he said, a sly grin pulling at the sides of his mouth.

Tracy gasped.

"You knew about that," I acknowledged.

"Thought you'd gotten away with that one, did you?" he asked, a twinkle in his eye underlining his delight at putting one over on us. "No such luck. Ronald Miller called me shortly after you left his office, told me he felt I should know about your little visit. He declined to discuss the specifics, of course, but I think I can guess. There are to be no more such visits. Are we understood?"

"Understood," Tracy said.

I nodded.

"Understood?" our father said again, this time directly to me.

"Understood," I obliged him by saying.
"Good. Then you can be on your way."
We watched him stride from the room.
"I'll show you out," Elyse said.

FORTY-EIGHT

"That went well," Tracy deadpanned as we were fastening our safety belts. "What are we going to do now?"

I shook my head, backing out of the driveway and turning onto Scarth Road. "I have no idea."

"You don't think he's serious, do you? I mean, about cutting me off in a year. He can't do that. Can he?"

"I don't know."

"We'll sue."

"On what grounds?"

"On the basis that it's cruel and unusual punishment."

"I don't think that applies in this case," I told her, not sure if she was serious.

"Well, there must be something we can do. He's been covering my expenses, like, forever. You can't just cut somebody off like that after all these years. He's set a precedent, right?"

"I guess so."

"Damn right it's so. We have to find a lawyer. A good one. Not like that stupid Ronald Miller."

"Good lawyers are expensive. And you no longer have a credit card," I reminded her.

"But you do."

"I also have a family to support. I can't afford to take Dad on."

"Oh, come on. You'll get it back once this is all sorted out."

"Which could take years. And in the meantime, we'll have totally alienated Dad. You could kiss that inheritance of yours goodbye."

"Assuming there'll be anything left."

I shrugged.

"So, what are you saying?" she asked.

"That it might be easier if you were to just find a job."

"Are you kidding me?"

"As a gesture of good faith. It would at least show Dad that you're trying. And maybe in a year's time, he'll have come to his senses and Elyse will be gone."

"Don't kid yourself. That bitch isn't going anywhere. *Shit!*" Tracy shouted at nothing in particular. "Where are you going?" she asked, staring through the darkness at the deserted street.

"I'm taking you home."

"I'm too upset to go home. I'm coming to your place. We'll order sushi."

"I don't feel like sushi."

"Sure you do. Come on. Don't give me a hard time. You know you're going to give in eventually."

I nodded, understanding that there was no point in arguing. She was right. Why prolong the misery?

—

"So, what do you think I should do, Harrison?" Tracy asked as we were finishing off the last of our sushi. She'd spent most of dinner rehashing and bemoaning the events of the afternoon. Sam and Daphne had long ago grown bored of the conversation and excused themselves to go upstairs to watch TV.

Harrison gave me a look that said he'd had about as much of my sister as any human being could possibly take for one night. "You may just have to do as Jodi suggested, bite the bullet, and get a job."

"Thanks a lot. You're a big help."

"You could write that bestseller you talked about doing last summer. I mean, you *did* take that course. Correct me if I'm wrong, but I believe your exact words were '*How hard can it be to write a novel?*'"

Harrison's sarcasm was lost on my sister. "Yeah, maybe," she said as Harrison rolled his eyes to the ceiling. "Speaking of which, how's your latest opus coming along?"

"Signed, sealed, and delivered," Harrison said.

"What? When did this happen?" I asked, trying not to feel slighted that I was just finding out about this now.

"Put the final touches on it last week."

"Why didn't you tell me?"

"I wanted to wait till I heard back from my editor."

"And did you?"

"This afternoon." He paused for suitable dramatic effect. "She loves it. It just needs a few more minor edits."

Thank God, I thought. "That's wonderful," I said. "Do they know when they'll be publishing it?"

"Sometime next year."

"Not till then?" Tracy asked.

"Well, the process takes time," Harrison explained. "They have to do the copyediting, choose a layout, design a cover—"

"When do you get your money?" Tracy interrupted.

Harrison hesitated, clearly uncomfortable with the turn the conversation had taken. "I get some now and some when the book is released."

"Like, how much? If you don't mind my asking."

"I *do* mind, actually."

"Oh, come on."

Harrison pushed his chair back from the dining room table, carrying his empty dinner plate into the kitchen before heading toward the stairs. "I'm going to check on the kids."

"So, how much is he getting?" Tracy asked as soon as he was gone.

"I'm not sure," I said. "It's been so long since he signed the contract, I forget the amount." Which was true. Harrison had signed the contract for his second novel as soon as his first book was released. He'd received a quarter of his advance upon signing, with the second installment due upon the acceptance of the manuscript, and the third and fourth installments due upon publication of the hardcover and mass market editions. Since the book had taken him so long to complete, it meant he'd essentially spent the last decade working for less than minimum wage. The checks he'd eventually be getting would do more for his self-esteem than our bank balance.

"So, have you read it?" Tracy asked.

"I read an earlier draft."

"And?"

"It was great," I lied.

"Well, that's good," she said. "I mean, the money will come in handy, you know, if we have to sue."

Good God, I thought. "I should take you home," I said.

It was almost ten o'clock when I climbed into bed beside Harrison.

"Sorry about tonight," I apologized.

"Not your fault."

"She was just so upset."

"She'll come out on top," Harrison said, putting his arm around me and drawing me close. "She always does."

"I guess."

"Look. I'm sorry if I've been a little . . . difficult lately."

"It's okay."

"I've just been so preoccupied with this damn book. And I was so pissed off that you were right about it—it *was* way too wordy."

I laughed, luxuriating in the warmth of his embrace. "I'm just thrilled that everyone's happy with it now."

"Me, too."

The phone rang.

"If it's Tracy, don't answer it."

"It's my father," I said, stretching to read the caller ID. "Oh, God. You don't think something's happened, do you?"

"I think you better find out."

I lifted the receiver gingerly to my ear. "Dad?"

"It's Elyse," the voice said.

"My father . . . ?"

"He's fine," Elyse said with a laugh. "I'm so sorry. I didn't mean to scare you. I didn't realize it was so late. I probably should have waited till morning to call."

"What's up?" I asked.

"I just wanted you to know that I meant what I said this afternoon. I really want all of us to get along, to put this unfortunate episode behind us and be a family."

"Sounds good," I agreed. What else could I say? The truth was that, deep down, I wanted the same thing.

"So I was thinking that we should have a little party, to celebrate. It would be your father and me, you and Harrison and Tracy, and I could invite a few of the neighbors and some of your father's friends, maybe even some of his former business associates . . ."

"That sounds like an awful lot of trouble."

"I was thinking of Saturday night," she continued, as if I hadn't spoken. "Would that work for you?"

"Sure. I guess I can find a sitter . . ."

"Wonderful. Saturday night at seven. I look forward to seeing you then."

"Saturday at seven," I repeated.

"What's happening Saturday at seven?" Harrison asked as I replaced the receiver.

"Apparently, we're going to a party." I scooted down in the bed, felt my husband's hands on my breasts, his lips on the side of my neck.

"Don't look now," Harrison said, "but the party's already started."

—FORTY-NINE—

We arrived at my father's house shortly after seven that Saturday night.

"You're late," my father said in greeting.

I looked past him toward the interior of the house. As far as I could see, no one else was there. "Where is everyone?"

"You're the first to arrive," he said. "Doesn't make you any less late."

"Can we go home yet?" Harrison whispered as Elyse approached.

"Jodi! Harrison! Welcome. Let me take your coats."

"They know where the closet is," my father said.

"Allow me," Harrison said, helping me off with my coat, then moving quickly toward the hall closet.

"How lovely you look," Elyse told me. "Is that a new dress?"

"No. I've had it a while."

"Well, turquoise is certainly your color. And Harrison," she said, watching as he hung up our coats, "looks so handsome all in black. Very much the distinguished author." She smiled at my father. "What do you think of Vic's new jacket?"

"Very nice," I remarked of the blue-and-black-brocade sports jacket he wouldn't have been caught dead wearing when my mother was alive. "And you've done something different with your hair," I said to him.

"I suggested he try parting it on the left," Elyse said, "and I think it suits him much better, don't you? So much more youthful. Don't you agree?"

"He looks very dapper," I said, astounded by my father's continuing silence. When had he ever allowed anyone else to speak for him? "And you look lovely," I said to Elyse.

She gave a girlish giggle that was as out of character as my father's silence, and fluffed out the sides of her floor-length chiffon skirt. "Your father thought I should buy something special to mark the occasion. He says it's our 'coming-out party.'"

I forced a smile onto my lips.

"Everything okay?" Harrison whispered, returning to my side.

I relaxed my mouth, recalling the increasingly frozen expression on my mother's face as her Parkinson's progressed. What would she make of tonight? I wondered.

"Why don't you go into the living room and help yourself to some champagne and hors d'oeuvres?" Elyse suggested. "It seems that I made enough food for an army."

"Don't overdo it on the hors d'oeuvres," my father advised, giving me a not-too-subtle once-over.

"Nonsense, Vic," Elyse admonished, giving him a playful slap on the arm. "You help yourself to as many as you want," she said to me.

The doorbell rang.

I turned around to see Stephanie Pickering sweep through the front door, every blond hair perfectly in place, imposing bosom on full display in her low-cut, cherry-red satin dress, as she allowed her black mink coat to slip from her shoulders into the waiting arms of her hapless husband, whose name I could never recall.

"Stephanie," I heard my father say, his voice blasting good cheer. "How wonderful to see you. You're looking spectacular, as always. I believe you met Elyse at the funeral."

"So nice to see you again," Stephanie enthused.

"Stephanie has been our top agent for more than a decade," he continued, as if he still ran the agency. "No one else even comes close."

"Yes, thank you for that," I whispered, leaving the hallway before I could hear more. "I could use that glass of champagne," I told Harrison.

"You and me both," he said as the doorbell rang again.

By seven-thirty, the living room was full of people, most of whom I recognized as either neighbors or real estate agents. My sister had yet to put in an appearance.

"Pretty good crowd," Harrison remarked as Ronald Miller and his wife entered the room. I watched as my father introduced them to Elyse and she, in turn, introduced them to the other guests.

"Oh, God," I whispered as they approached.

"Jodi," Elyse said. "I believe you've met Ronald Miller."

"Yes. Nice to see you again," Ronald Miller replied stiffly. "This is my wife, Rachael."

"My husband, Harrison."

"Harrison is a famous writer," Elyse said.

"Oh?"

"Surely you've heard of Harrison Bishop. He wrote *Comes the Dreamer*. Wonderful, wonderful book."

"Really? I'll have to read it. Perhaps you could send me a copy."

"Perhaps you could buy one," I said pointedly.

Ronald and Rachael Miller smiled and promptly moved on.

"What a nerve!" Elyse exclaimed. "Do you get that often?"

"Often enough," Harrison said. "You'd be surprised at the things people say to writers. There's this apocryphal story about the writer W.O. Mitchell," he continued without prompting. "He was apparently cornered at a party by a surgeon who informed him that when he retired, he was going to become a writer, to which Mitchell replied, 'Isn't that interesting? When *I* retire, I'm going to become a surgeon.'"

Elyse laughed, long and loud. "What a wonderful story! You must tell it to everyone." She looked around. "I think we're all here."

"What about *your* friends?" I asked.

"Your father is all the friend I need. Although I do have a surprise for you later." She made a point of checking her watch—a new gold Cartier. "Where's Tracy? Is she not coming?"

As if on cue, the doorbell rang, and seconds later, Tracy swept into the room, wearing jeans, shiny knee-high black vinyl boots, and a red sweatshirt that read *Underestimate Me. That'll Be Fun.*

"Oh, my God," Elyse exclaimed, arms extended toward my sister. "Aren't you the most adorable thing!"

"Not exactly the response I was going for," Tracy muttered when she reached my side.

"This house is spectacular, Vic," I heard Stephanie Pickering tell my father. "You know you're sitting on a gold mine here, don't you?"

"Would you like Jodi to show you around?" my father said, offering up my services without so much as a nod in my direction.

"I would love that," Stephanie said. "You don't mind, do you, Jodi?"

"Not at all," I said. Truthfully, I was more than happy to get away from all the good cheer. Did nobody remember that my mother had been dead only a few months? Was I the only one who thought it was a little early to be celebrating my father's hasty remarriage?

"What a magnificent staircase," Stephanie proclaimed as we reentered the front hall.

I pictured my mother lying at the bottom of it.

Is it possible that she'd had a little help getting there? I found myself wondering as I led Stephanie through the house.

"Elyse seems like such a lovely woman," Stephanie ventured at one point.

"Yes, she does."

"She seems to genuinely adore your father."

"Yes, she does," I said again.

"It's nice to see him so happy."

"Yes, it is."

Thankfully, she took the hint, and made no further attempts at conversation.

"Well, what did you think?" my father asked when we returned.

"Like I said, Vic. You're sitting on a gold mine. If you ever want to sell . . ."

"I know where to find you," my father said.

The doorbell rang.

"Oh, wonderful," Elyse exclaimed. "My surprise has arrived!" She ran from the room.

"What's that about?" Tracy asked.

"Beats me."

Elyse was back seconds later. She stood at the entrance to the living room, the smile on her face stretching from ear to ear. "Ladies and gentlemen, I'd like you to meet my son, Andrew."

She held out her arms, and a tall, handsome man walked into the frame.

Enter Roger McAdams.

—FIFTY—

How do I describe my reaction at seeing my erstwhile lover standing next to my father's new wife, to hear her introduce the man I knew as Roger McAdams as her son, Andrew?

To say I was shocked would be a gross understatement. To say I was stunned would be only marginally more accurate. To say I thought my head was about to explode would be edging closer to the truth, although even that overwrought, overworked expression fails to capture the enormity of the feelings, not to mention the confusion, that I was experiencing.

I felt dizzy, faint, light-headed, sick to my stomach, as if I'd stepped into an alternate reality, and there was no way of returning to the one I'd always known. I simply couldn't process what my ears were hearing, what my eyes were seeing.

This can't be happening, I thought. My mind was playing cruel tricks, my lingering guilt over my brief affair making me imagine things that weren't there. I actually entertained the idea that I might be having a stroke. *I have to be mistaken.*

Except I wasn't. And I knew it.

What does it mean?

"Wow," Tracy said, her words propelling me back into my body. "I didn't even know she had a son. Did you?"

I watched Elyse introduce the man I knew as Roger to my father, saw the two men shake hands and exchange pleasantries.

What's happening?

"Did you?" Tracy asked again.

"Did I what?"

Tracy rolled her eyes. "Did you know she had a son?"

"Yes," I mumbled, remembering that Elyse had mentioned a son named Andrew who lived in Los Angeles during our first meeting.

"How come you never told me?"

"What?"

"What do you mean, what? What's the matter with you?" Tracy asked.

"What?" I said again.

"Are you all right? You're acting really weird."

"Jodi?" Harrison asked. "Is everything okay?"

"Of course." I tried to smile, but stopped when I felt my lips start to tremble. "Sorry. I got a little dizzy there for a second. Probably too much champagne."

"You always were a cheap drunk," Harrison said, giving my waist an affectionate squeeze. "Does this mean I might get lucky tonight?"

Oh, God, I thought. *Why do you have to be so sweet all of a sudden?* I felt another stab of guilt. The past month had seen a definite improvement in our marriage. Harrison had been more attentive, less critical, more loving, than he had been in a long time. I was fairly certain that we'd made love more in the last four weeks than in the last four months combined. I assumed it was because he was feeling less stressed, more confident, about his manuscript, his career, his future. But maybe he'd felt the invisible presence of another man hovering, maybe he'd sensed he was losing me.

I confess that there were times I'd found thoughts of Roger filling my head, but I'd worked hard to keep them at bay, refusing to let them linger. There was so much more going on in my life, more urgent things to deal with. The fact that Roger hadn't even tried to contact me had made it a little easier. While I told myself that this was admirable—he was keeping the promise he made to me, trying not to complicate my life—I confess to being a little hurt. I was always half-expecting him to phone, to see him pop his head inside my office door.

And now, here he was.

Except he wasn't Roger.

He was Andrew.

Elyse's son.

Which meant . . . what?

My mind was racing, one question banging up against another, their answers no less confusing. Could this be a coincidence? No, impossible. An accident? That made no sense whatsoever.

Except nothing made any sense.

I tried to focus, to recall the exact circumstances of my meetings with the man I knew as Roger. He'd come into my office, ostensibly new in town, in a new job, recently divorced, and looking for a condo by the water. *Was any of that true?* We'd spent several afternoons together, had dinner twice, exchanged confidences, made love on two separate occasions, once in a hotel room, once in my own house, my own bed.

At the time, I was extremely vulnerable, and Roger was just so sympathetic and easy to talk to. He knew exactly the right things to say, but even more important, he *listened*.

He cared. Or seemed to.

Much as Elyse had, I realized, with a start.

"What's the matter?" Tracy asked.

"Nothing. Why?"

"You gave a little gasp."

"I did?" *Shit*.

"Something going on with you?"

"Just surprised," I told her.

"No kidding."

Had it been a setup from the start? Had Elyse merely feigned interest in me, lent a sympathetic ear, pretended to be my friend, to gain information and therefore the upper hand? Had she passed this information on to her son to make it easier for him to successfully seduce me?

Why? To what end?

Was Roger really her son? Was his name really Andrew? What game were they playing?

And perhaps the most important question of all—what happens next?

"He's quite nice-looking," Tracy remarked, once again jolting me out of my head. "Do you think he's single?"

"No," I answered quickly, recalling the little information about him that Elyse had given me. "He has a wife in Los Angeles."

"What else do you know about him?"

"That's about it," I lied.

The truth was that I knew nothing.

"Here they come," Tracy said. "Brace yourself."

In the next second, Elyse and Roger were standing in front of us. "Jodi, Tracy, Harrison," she began, smiling at each of us in turn. "I'd like you to meet my son, Andrew."

"Nice to meet you, Andrew," Harrison dutifully replied, shaking his hand.

"I didn't know Elyse had a son," Tracy said.

"I'm sure I must have mentioned it." Elyse looked to me for confirmation.

"I believe you did." I strained to keep my voice steady as I looked Roger in the eye. "You're from Los Angeles?"

"Up until about six months ago," he replied. "I got divorced, got transferred to Detroit. But I really love Toronto, and I'm thinking seriously of relocating."

Dear God.

"What is it that you do?" Harrison asked.

"Wealth management."

"I think I like the sound of that," Tracy said with a laugh.

"Tracy, is it?" Roger asked.

"That's right."

"With an *i* or a *y*?"

"A *y*."

"Love your sweatshirt, Tracy with a *y*. I'll be sure not to underestimate you."

"Smart man," Tracy said.

He swiveled toward me. "And Jodi, correct?"

I bit down hard on my lower lip. "With an *i*," I said before he had a chance to ask. It took all my self-restraint to keep from slapping him across his handsome face. "Andrew, is it?"

He nodded.

"Why do I think you look more like a 'Roger'?"

He smiled. "I have no idea. But you can call me Roger, if you prefer. I've always liked that name."

"Come," Elyse urged, taking him by the elbow and moving him toward the other guests.

"What an odd thing to say," Tracy said to me. "He looks like a Roger? Who on earth looks like a Roger?"

I shrugged. What else could I do?

"What do you think this means?" Tracy asked, her gaze following him around the room.

"I have no idea."

"For us, I mean," she clarified.

"I know what you mean. I still have no idea."

"We have to get back in Dad's good graces."

"Why? What are you talking about?"

"Think about it," she said. "If Dad dies, Elyse could inherit the bulk, if not all, of his estate, which means that when she dies, her son could walk away with everything. And we, my dear sister, end up with nothing."

"I think you're getting a little ahead of yourselves, ladies," Harrison said.

"Better ahead than behind," Tracy told him. "Right, Jodi?"

I nodded. But the truth was that being ahead or behind only mattered when you knew where you were. And as I'd already told my sister several times, I had no idea.

FIFTY-ONE

The evening went from bad to worse.

At approximately eight-thirty, Elyse announced that dinner was ready, and told everyone to help themselves to the buffet she'd set up on the dining room table. There were a variety of salads and several large platters of homemade lasagna, as well as generous helpings of shrimp and poached salmon.

The thought of food made me sick, so I remained in the living room while the others lined up with their plates.

"You're not eating anything?" a voice asked from behind me.

"Not hungry," I said, eyes staring resolutely ahead.

"My mother's a wonderful cook. You really should eat something."

"You should go fuck yourself," I said.

He laughed. "I'd rather fuck you," he whispered, brushing past me on his way to the dining room.

"Oh, God." I felt my knees go weak and my legs about to collapse under me.

"Are you okay?" Tracy asked moments later, returning to the living room with a single, large piece of salmon on her plate. "You look kind of sick." She inched away from me. "You're not coming down with anything, are you?"

"Too much champagne," I said, as I'd said earlier.

"Then you should probably eat something," Harrison said, joining us, his plate filled to overflowing. "Say what you will about Elyse, she knows her way around a kitchen."

"She knows her way around, period," Tracy said. "Her son's kind of cute, though. What do you think—I marry him, and collect no matter what."

I felt another flash of nausea. "I'd stay away from him," I warned. "He looks like trouble."

"I like trouble," Tracy countered.

"Excuse me," I said. "I need to use the washroom."

I quickly made my way to the powder room under the stairs to the right of the elevator. The door was closed, so I knocked.

"One minute," Stephanie Pickering responded, her voice as distinctive as her helmet of blond hair and impressive cleavage. She emerged a few seconds later. "Lovely evening," she said when she saw me. "Did you try the lasagna? Best I've ever tasted."

"I'll have to try some."

She leaned in toward me. "Work on your father a bit, will you?" she urged. "He's not getting any younger, and Elyse confided to me that the house is getting a bit much for her to handle."

"Elyse said that the house is too much for her to handle?"

Stephanie brought her fingers to her lips. "Don't say anything. She told me in confidence. And they're really sitting on a gold mine here."

A gold mine that Elyse, a gold digger if ever there was one, couldn't wait to get her hands on, I thought, as I entered the powder room and locked the door after me. I lowered the lid on the toilet and sat down, trying to clear my head.

I knew that according to Ontario law, without a pre-nup, the house was now deemed the marital home and considered communal property and thus half the house already belonged to Elyse. If my father could be per-suaded to sell it, that meant Elyse would have access to all that cash, and could potentially walk away with everything.

It wasn't that I begrudged Elyse what was rightfully hers. If she were to stay with my father for the rest of his life, be it two more years, or five, or ten, or even more, and take care of him, make him happy, then more power to her. She deserved whatever she could get.

But I knew that this wasn't the case. And I feared that my father was at risk, that he could actually be in danger.

"Oh, God," I cried into my hands, not sure what Roger's being here meant. I knew only two things for sure: one was that I needed answers; the other was that I had no idea how to get them.

I stayed in the powder room until I felt I could carry on a conversation without bursting into tears. Then I flushed the toilet, in case someone was waiting on the other side, and opened the door.

Rachael Miller was standing there. "Are you all right?" she asked, her face a mask of concern that barely hid the rebuke in her voice. "You were in there a very long time."

"I'm fine. Sorry," I muttered, returning to the living room where my husband was regaling the guests with his story about W.O. Mitchell's encounter with the surgeon. I approached Roger from behind. "We need to talk," I whispered.

"When and where?" he asked.

"The kitchen," I told him. "Now."

"After you."

I walked from the room. He followed seconds later.

"Your husband's quite the storyteller," he remarked.

"He's not the only one." We stood facing each other by the side of the kitchen counter. "Tell me what the hell is going on," I directed. "Who are you?"

"You know who I am."

"I thought I did. But the man I knew was named Roger."

"Yeah. Sorry about that. It's Andrew."

"So, you really *are* Elyse's son?"

"I really am."

I shook my head, trying to digest the implications of what he was saying. "Why the pretense? I don't get it."

"I think you do."

"I don't."

"You're a smart girl," he said. "I'm sure you'll figure it out eventually."

"On the contrary, I'm every bit the idiot you took me for. I need it spelled out. What kind of game are you playing?"

He smiled. "No game."

"Really, what would you call coming to my office and pretending to be someone you're not? Getting me to show you condos, taking me to dinner . . ."

"To bed," he whispered, leaning toward my ear.

I looked toward the hall, in case someone might be coming. "Why?" I asked simply.

"Why not?"

"Not an answer."

"Okay, then. Call it an insurance policy."

"Insurance policy against what?"

"Against unwarranted interference in my mother's life."

"Meaning?"

"Meaning that as long as you stay out of her way, everything will be fine."

"Stay out of her way?" I repeated.

"My mother will continue to make your father a very happy man for as long as she's able to tolerate his rather autocratic ways. Well, I certainly don't have to tell *you* what he's like . . ."

"And?"

"And you and your lovely sister will do nothing to upset that. You won't bad-mouth her or question her decisions. You won't go seeking any more unsolicited legal advice. You won't interfere with her plans. You will be agreeable and supportive and, well, just as sweet as I know you can be."

"And if I'm not?"

"Let me show you something." He pulled his phone from the pocket of his navy blazer and stretched it toward me.

I stared at its small screen, saw a picture of me sleeping soundly in a bed I didn't recognize. The picture morphed into a video, and I watched as the camera panned a room I now recognized as the room I'd shared with Roger at the King Eddy Hotel. The camera moved slowly from my clothes, thrown over a nearby chair, to the mirror on the back of the bathroom door, my lover's naked body on prominent display in the full-length glass.

"Oh, God," I moaned.

"I know," he said. "Not my best angle. On the bright side, *you* look very content. A good orgasm does wonders for a woman's complexion, don't you think?"

"You bastard!"

"I think we can do without the name-calling. Andrew's good enough. And don't worry. I have no intention of showing this to anyone, especially your husband who, I assume, wouldn't be too thrilled with that post-orgasmic glow."

"So, this whole thing was a setup? You used me . . ."

"I prefer to think we used each other. Any more questions?"

"Elyse's references . . . ?"

"Both me. Different voices, throwaway phones. Pretty amateur stuff. But it's easy to fool people when they want to be fooled."

My head was spinning. *Is this all* my *fault?* "So, what happens now?"

He smiled. "Now we make like good little stepbrother and sister, and rejoin the party. What do you say, sis?"

"I say go to hell."

The smile disappeared. "You first."

Don't worry, I thought as I rejoined the others. I'm already there.

FIFTY-TWO

"You'll never guess what just happened," Tracy said as we were leaving the party.

"What just happened?" I asked as a gust of cold night air slapped across my cheeks on the way to our respective cars.

"He said he'd like to see me again."

"Who did?" I questioned, although the sinking feeling in my gut told me that I already knew the answer.

"Andrew, of course." She giggled. "I knew he was interested. I could tell from the way he kept looking at me."

"Please tell me that you said no."

"Why would I do that?"

I stopped in the middle of the road. "Because he's Elyse's son. Because I don't trust him."

"You don't have to trust him," she said. "*I'm* the one he wants to see again."

"You shouldn't trust him, either."

"Why shouldn't I?"

"Because I think he's bad news."

"Based on what?"

"Based on the fact that he's Elyse's son," I repeated. *Based on the fact that the man you know as Andrew is the same man I knew as Roger when I slept with him a few months back, and now he's using that to blackmail me into not interfering with his mother's plans, whatever the hell they might be.* "I just think you should be careful, that's all."

"Be careful of what?"

"I don't know," I lied. "I just don't want you to get hurt."

"Since when do you care about that?"

"What are you talking about? I've always cared about that."

"Really? I don't remember you objecting when I dated that asshole Mark Webster."

"Who?"

"Exactly!" she proclaimed.

"Ladies," my husband interjected from somewhere beside us. "It's late, it's freezing, and we're going to get run over, standing here arguing in the middle of the road. Surely you can debate this in the morning."

"Debate's over," Tracy declared. "I win."

I swallowed my outrage. "When is this date happening?"

"Not for a while. He has to get back to Detroit, and he's not sure when he'll be back."

Thank God, I thought. It gave me some time to try to figure out my options.

Assuming, of course, that I had any.

—

I doubt I slept more than a couple of hours that night. I kept replaying the party in my head, from the moment Elyse introduced Roger as her son, Andrew, to the moment he showed me the incriminating video of my postcoital slumber, to Tracy's startling revelation that he'd expressed an interest in seeing her again, and that she fully intended to go along.

Mixed in with those moments were the ones I'd spent with Roger, at the restaurants, in the various condos I was showing him, in bed at the King Edward Hotel, in the bed I was lying in right now, next to my sleeping husband. "Oh, God," I groaned, flipping onto my stomach and trying to smother the unrelenting series of images with my pillow.

How could I have been so stupid? To jeopardize my marriage, my family, my principles, all because I was feeling a little neglected, because I was unreasonably jealous of a woman half my age, because I let my unfounded suspicions get the better of me. What was the matter with me?

When I did manage to fall asleep, I descended into a jangle of pixelated nightmares, horrifying images of face-shifting monsters who pursued me through dark, icy, windswept streets, only to break up into hundreds of tiny shards and change shapes again when I worked up the courage to confront them.

You're dreaming if you think I'm going to stay with you after what you've done, I heard my husband say, his voice infiltrating my nightmares to jolt me awake. *I'm leaving and I'm taking the kids with me. You'll never see them again.*

"What?" I shouted, jerking up in bed, my eyes searching for his in the dark.

"It's okay," he was saying, his face suddenly looming over mine. "You were having a bad dream. Take deep breaths. Try to calm down. Your yelling is going to wake up the kids."

"I was dreaming?"

"Sounded like one hell of a nightmare."

"I was yelling?"

"Screaming is more like it. Who's Roger?"

"What?"

"You kept yelling to *watch out for Roger!* "

Shit. "I don't know anyone named Roger," I told him. Not exactly a lie. The man I knew as Roger didn't exist.

"Try to get some sleep," Harrison urged, pulling me back down.

I felt my head crease the pillow, but I knew I wouldn't sleep. How could I when my subconscious could betray me at the first unguarded moment?

So, I lay there, wrapped in my husband's arms, the husband I'd so carelessly betrayed, and tried to think of other things: the kids, my job, the appointments I had lined up for the week ahead.

But try as I might, my thoughts kept circling relentlessly back to tonight's party, to Elyse's knowing smile as she introduced us to her son, to her son's warning not to interfere with whatever his mother might be planning, to Tracy's careless decision to court disaster by seeing the man again.

I couldn't even talk to her about my reasons for objecting so strenuously to her seeing him. If she couldn't grasp the folly in dating the son of a clearly predatory woman, how could I confide in her about my affair? Not that I didn't trust Tracy to keep a secret, although the truth was that I *didn't* trust her entirely in that regard. Not that she would willfully betray me. More that she would somehow let it slip. Tracy was careless, and she'd never been what one would call discreet. She tended to talk first and think later, and I just couldn't risk it.

Elyse understood this, and she used it, as she used everything, to her advantage. Divide and conquer had always been part of her plan. Now, with her son's help, she was taking things a step further. By threatening to romance my sister, Roger—as I still thought of him—was ensuring my silence, my compliance. How could I discuss anything with Tracy without being certain that she wouldn't reveal it to Roger?

But, if I'm being honest, it was more than that. Telling Tracy about my affair would mean revealing myself to be as careless as she was. More so. My sister wasn't in a committed relationship; she didn't have children; she didn't consider herself to be more grounded, more self-aware, more responsible.

How could I have been so gullible, so trusting, so *wrong*?

Who was I to try telling her what to do?

My life might be a churning, cloudy mess, but one fact was now painfully clear: I was in this alone.

FIFTY-THREE

A famous poet once christened April "the cruellest month." As I recall from my university courses in English literature, April was considered cruel because, unlike winter, which had "kept us warm" by "covering the earth in forgetful snow," April's thaw not only laid bare the dormant rot below, it unearthed a fresh hope—of renewal, of change, of brighter days ahead—that was ultimately doomed to disappoint.

In my case, it was less a question of unrealized hopes than it was overwhelming regret for what I had done, the constant fear of my ill-advised affair being exposed, the pervasive dread that things were about to get worse.

So, despite my concerns for my father's welfare, I chose the coward's way out and decided that the best thing for me to do was to lie low, to keep my thoughts and reservations to myself, and not to rock the boat in any way. What difference did it make if Elyse was only after my father's money, if she ultimately inherited everything, if Tracy and I received nothing? It was our father's money and he was entitled to do whatever he wished with it. As long as he was happy, I reasoned, who were we to interfere?

My mother will continue to make your father a very happy man for as long as she's able to tolerate his rather autocratic ways, my former lover had said.

And when those *rather autocratic ways* were no longer tolerable, I found myself wondering, uncomfortably aware of the implicit threat those words carried—what happened then?

My thoughts drifted back to Tracy's earlier speculation that Elyse had played a part in our mother's death, that her fatal tumble down the stairs might not have been an accident at all.

Was it possible?

Was our father in danger now as well?

And if so, was there anything I could do about it?

These questions occupied my every waking hour, kept me tossing and turning each night. Still, I continued to keep these thoughts to myself. I consoled myself with the knowledge that my marriage was back on track, my relationship with my sister, while strained, was relatively stable—helped no doubt by Roger/Andrew's continued absence—and even my relationship with my father, while decidedly chilly, had settled into a cordial formality. I called weekly; we spoke briefly; Elyse continued to tolerate his *rather autocratic ways*.

Don't go looking for trouble, I told myself, mindful of the Alcoholics Anonymous prayer: *God grant me the serenity to accept the things I cannot change, the courage to change the things I can, and the wisdom to know the difference.*

This was one of the things I couldn't change.

At least that's what I continued telling myself throughout that most cruel of months.

And then it was May.

It had been almost a year since that first fateful meeting with Elyse. So much had changed. My mother was dead. I was an adulteress. The woman I'd hired as a housekeeper was now, quite literally, the keeper of the house.

"Knock, knock," I heard a voice say, accompanied by a tapping of knuckles on my open office door.

I looked up to see Stephanie Pickering, resplendent in a tomato-red blazer, white silk shirt, and black pants.

"Someone's deep in thought," she said. "I've been standing here for five minutes."

"Sorry," I apologized, motioning her inside. "What's up?"

"I just wanted to thank you," she said, pulling out one of the chairs in front of my desk and sitting down, crossing one leg over the other to reveal a pair of bright red Louboutins with skinny, sky-high heels.

"For what?"

"I just got a call from your father. It seems they're interested in selling the house after all."

"What?"

"You look surprised."

"What?" I said again, my go-to question whenever I didn't know what else to say.

"Sorry. I just assumed you had something to do with his change of heart, that you must have said something to convince him . . ."

"I'm sorry," I apologized again. "My father told you he's considering selling the house?"

"Asked me if that client I had was still interested. Of course, I had to tell him that ship had unfortunately sailed, but that I was quite certain I'd have another buyer for him in no time. I'm going over there this afternoon to have another look-around, and I'm taking a few of the other agents with me, so we can come up with the best price. Oh, dear," she added. "I can see you're upset."

I shook my head, not sure what I was.

"I hope you're not angry that he reached out to me," she said before I could formulate a response. "I'm sure it's because he thought it best to have a non–family member handle the sale, that it was less likely to cause friction."

Since when had my father ever cared about causing less friction? I wondered. My father loved friction. He thrived on it.

"Of course, you're more than welcome to tag along this afternoon, if you'd like."

I could think of few things I'd like less. "No, that's okay. I think you can handle everything on your own."

"Great." She rose to her feet. "Jodi," she began, then stopped, her eyes circling the room, as if searching for just the right words. "Just so there's no misunderstanding . . ."

"This is *your* sale," I said, finishing the sentence for her.

"Thank you for being so understanding."

I smiled. What else could I do?

FIFTY-FOUR

By the end of the week, Stephanie had come back to my father and Elyse with a suggested asking price of five and a half million dollars, and they had agreed to sell.

"I'm sending someone in to draw up the floor plans next week, and hoping I can get Max Prescott to do a home inspection as soon as possible," she told me, dropping by my office as I was getting ready to meet with clients.

"So when are you planning to list the house?" I asked, trying to sound as if my father had already informed me of his decision and this was old news.

"Probably not for another month. We'll see what the home inspection turns up. You never know what unexpected issues can arise with these old houses," she said, as if I were new to the business. "I've suggested that they do a few repairs to the exterior of the house, make it more welcoming, not quite so . . ."

"Spooky?" I volunteered, using my son's adjective.

"Exactly," she said. "How old's the roof anyway? Do you have any idea how long it's been since they replaced it?"

"None," I said truthfully, wondering why, as the firm's reputedly top agent, she hadn't asked my father this question herself.

"If we need to install a new roof, that could delay things. But we'll cross our fingers and hope for the best."

Too late for that, I thought, crossing my fingers nonetheless.

As soon as she was gone, I called my father.

Elyse answered. "Jodi," she said. "I assume you've heard we've decided to sell."

"I have."

"I hope you aren't too upset. I really think it's the right decision. It's time. And it's a good price."

"It's a good price," I agreed. "Can I speak to my father?"

"I'm afraid he's a little busy right now."

"I can wait."

"I wouldn't. He's in the shower, and he could be a while. The man loves his showers. I'll be sure to tell him that you called."

"You do that." I shook my head as I replaced the receiver, amazed at the woman's ability to carry on as if everything was normal between us. As if she hadn't arranged for her son to seduce me, relying on information I'd been stupid enough to give her, feelings I'd been reckless enough to confide. As if she weren't essentially blackmailing me into silence, forcing me to accept what seemed increasingly clear: she was the one in charge.

I sat at my desk for several more minutes, trying to rid my mind of all such unpleasant thoughts, before realizing that if I didn't leave immediately, I would be late for my appointment. I was taking a married couple to their second viewing of a house in Moore Park. It was a relatively ordinary-looking three-bedroom, two-bathroom house on a dead-end street in a quiet neighborhood. The sellers were asking way too much for the place, given the amount of repairs the house required. Nonetheless, offers were being submitted on the weekend, and there were multiple buyers interested, so the odds were that the house would go for considerably more than asking, despite its condition.

My clients—Joel and Joanna Rowe, early forties, both lawyers—were parked in front of the house when I pulled into the driveway. "Have you been waiting long?" I asked as we met at the large double doors.

"Just a few minutes," Joel Rowe replied.

I used my key to open the lock and we stepped inside the front foyer.

"It's smaller than I remember," his wife said as we walked through the downstairs.

I waited in the outdated kitchen while they toured the upstairs.

"We'd like to submit an offer," Joanna Rowe said when they were done. "How much would you recommend?"

"Well, there are already four other registered bidders," I reminded them, "which means that the house will go for over-asking. It's just a question of how much over you're willing to go."

"How much would you advise?"

I looked around the uninspired space, the walls that needed painting, the hardwood floors that needed refinishing, the kitchen that needed to be totally redone. "It's whatever you're comfortable with," I said. "My guess is that the house will likely sell for at least fifty thousand dollars above the list price. Putting in anything lower than that will just be a waste of everyone's time and energy." *Mostly mine,* I thought, but didn't say. I'd lost track of the number of times during the last year that I'd spent hours drawing up contracts and submitting offers, only to see the house go to a higher bidder.

"Okay," Joel Rowe said. "Offer them seventy-five thousand above listing, all cash and an early closing."

"Sounds good," I told them. "I'll get started on the offer right away."

"Do you think we have a chance?" Joanna asked.

"I think you have a chance," I told them, although the truth was that these things were impossible to predict. "Can I ask you something?" I heard myself say.

Joel and Joanna Rowe looked at me expectantly. "Certainly," Joanna said.

"It's a legal issue. It has nothing to do with this house."

The two lawyers exchanged worried glances. "Okay," they responded together, the wariness in their voices evident.

I hesitated. Hadn't Roger warned me against seeking legal advice? Although how would he ever know? And it wasn't as if I'd gone looking, I told myself. Fate had dropped these lawyers into my lap, and I'd be a fool not to take advantage of the opportunity being presented. "Well, a friend of mine . . ." *Really?* I thought. *You're really pretending this is happening to a friend?* "Her father recently remarried, and his new wife is clearly only after his money, and now she's urging him to sell the family house, and my friend was just wondering if there's anything she can do to stop him—" I broke off. "There's nothing she can do," I said, acknowledging the looks on both their faces.

"Well, you understand that neither of us is an expert in family law," Joel began. "I'm in mergers and acquisitions and Joanna specializes in corporate—"

"I take it that your friend has no financial stake in the house?" Joanna asked, interrupting.

"That's right."

"Then unless she can prove her father is incompetent to manage his affairs . . ." she said. "Is he? Incompetent?"

"No. Not really." *Not yet,* I thought.

"I know a little about this because something similar happened to a client of mine," Joanna continued. "Her mother died, and her father remarried this woman half his age, and when he died a few years later, the new wife walked away with everything. My client took the wife to court, and they eventually settled, but it was for a fraction of what his estate was worth, and after she paid the lawyers, she ended up with almost nothing. Believe me, it wasn't worth the aggravation. Tell your friend to do herself a favor, write it off, and forget about it."

Her husband nodded. "Good advice," he said.

"I'll tell her. Thank you."

We walked to the door.

"Your friend's father's house," Joanna said, stopping, "should we have a look at it?"

FIFTY-FIVE

"Elyse, hi," I said into the phone the following week, determined to keep the lines of communication open. "I was wondering if I could bring the kids over for a swim this afternoon. They haven't seen their grandfather in a while and—"

"I'm so sorry," Elyse interrupted. "It's really not a good time. As you know, we're having some work done on the house and there are workers everywhere."

"How about tomorrow, then? Surely the workers won't be there on Sunday."

"I'm afraid tomorrow won't work, either. We're so busy, and the truth is, what with everything that needs to be done around here, we haven't even bothered turning on the pool heater."

"Well, how about we just drop over to say hello?"

"It's really not a good time."

"Just when *would* be a good time?" I pressed.

"Maybe next weekend. I'll ask your father."

"Why don't *I* ask him?"

"Certainly. He's napping right now, but I'll tell him you called."

The line went dead in my hands.

The same scenario was repeated throughout the following weeks. Every time I called, my father was either napping, in the bathroom, or otherwise engaged; I left messages that he either ignored or wasn't aware of; he made no attempt to contact either me or my sister; he showed no interest in his grandchildren.

"Did Grandpa die?" Daphne asked me one Saturday afternoon.

Her innocent question propelled me into action. I called Tracy. "I'm going over there," I told her. "Want to meet me?"

"Think I'll pass," Tracy said. "No point going where you aren't wanted."

She was right, and frankly, I'm not sure why I was being so insistent. My father and I had never been close. He'd always been ornery and unpleasant. I was always failing him in some way.

Maybe that's why I was so determined not to fail him now.

"You're leaving me with the kids?" Harrison asked when I told him of my plans.

"I really need to check on my father. I won't be long."

"You're starting with this shit already?" he said, his irritation catching me off guard. "I don't know why I'm even surprised," he continued. "Happens every June. I have twelve assignments to read and evaluate before my course starts next month. How am I supposed to get any work done with two kids running around the house, screaming?"

"I'll take the kids," I said, deciding not to argue.

Harrison waved as we pulled onto the street. Another man I was always disappointing.

"Is this the right house?" Sam asked, as we parked in my father's driveway. "It looks different."

He was right. The brick had been recently sandblasted, the front windows replaced, and the wood around them given a fresh coat of white paint.

I knew from Stephanie that the home inspection had turned up only a few minor issues and that new floor plans were in the process of being drawn up, so the house would likely be on the market by the end of the month.

"Can we go swimming?" Daphne asked as we exited the car.

"We didn't bring our bathing suits," Sam reminded his sister.

"Okay, kids," I told them. "Remember what I told you?"

"After we say hi to Grandpa," Daphne said, "ask Elyse if we can have some milk and cookies."

"Perfect." I hoped that would give me the chance to talk to my father alone.

I rang the bell and we waited. No one came to the door. "Looks like no one's home," I said after the passing of several minutes.

"There's someone in the window!" Sam exclaimed, one skinny arm extending toward an upstairs bedroom.

My eyes followed my son's arm to the upstairs window. There was no one there.

"You're sure you saw someone?" I asked.

"Pretty sure."

I rang the bell again. And then again.

No one came.

We walked around to the side of the house, but the high wooden fence surrounding the pool was locked.

"Maybe they went for a walk," Sam offered.

"I'm tired of waiting," Daphne whined.

"Me, too," said Sam.

"Me, three," I agreed, grateful when my children laughed at the old joke as if it were something I'd made up on the spot. Grabbing my cellphone from my purse, I called the house.

No one answered.

"Dad," I said, leaving a message, "It's really important that I speak to you." I returned the phone to my purse and guided my children back to the car. As I backed out of the driveway, I thought I saw something move in the upstairs window. But when I stopped the car and squinted to get a better look, I saw nothing.

The phone rang as we were sitting down to dinner.

"Work or your sister," Harrison remarked, the unpleasant edge to his voice a holdover from earlier in the day. "Who else calls at dinnertime? What is this stuff we're eating anyway?" he continued, one sentence disappearing into the next.

"Beef stew," I said, walking toward the kitchen. "I thought you liked my stew."

"And I thought we were cutting back on red meat."

"Don't eat the meat, then," I said.

"Great dinner," he sneered. "Potatoes and vegetables."

I sighed and picked up the receiver. "Hello?"

"Jodi," the man's voice said.

"Dad?"

"I got your message. What's so damn urgent?"

"Nothing urgent," I said. "We just haven't spoken in a while. I was getting concerned."

"Nothing to be concerned about. We're very busy, that's all."

"Too busy to see your grandchildren? Too busy to call?"

"I'm calling now, aren't I?"

"Are you all right?"

"Why wouldn't I be?"

"How's everything going?" I asked, trying a different tack.

"Everything is proceeding on schedule. Stephanie is a real ball of fire. No grass growing under *her* feet."

"Glad to hear it," I said, ignoring the inference that implied grass was definitely sprouting under mine.

"She tells me that you missed out on a sale in Moore Park by a bid of only five thousand dollars."

"Well, you never know how much someone else is going to bid," I said wearily.

"Is there anything else?" my father asked. "I should get going."

"Where are you going?"

"Elyse will be looking for me. She gets anxious when she can't find me."

"I don't understand. Where are you?"

"In the bathroom. She wouldn't like it if she found out I was talking to you."

"What do you mean, she wouldn't like it? What about what *you* like? Dad? Dad?"

But my questions went unanswered, and by the time I hung up and returned to the dining room, Harrison had already left the table, leaving most of his stew untouched, and my dinner was cold.

FIFTY-SIX

Ronald Miller phoned the following week.

Since my father's lawyer had informed Tracy and me that it was a conflict of interest for him to discuss our father's business with us, I was more than surprised to hear from him.

"What can I do for you, Mr. Miller?" I asked.

"Look," he began, clearing his throat. "I shouldn't be speaking to you, and if you tell anyone I called, I'll deny it. I mean it," he continued before I could protest. "You can't discuss this call with anyone, not your husband, not your sister, and especially not your father. I'm taking a huge risk here. I could be disbarred if anyone found out."

"I won't say anything," I assured him, my interest piqued, my senses on full alert.

"I need your word."

"You have it. What's going on?"

"It's about your father."

"I assumed as much."

"I'm worried about him."

Welcome to the club, I thought. "What's happened?"

Another loud clearing of his throat. "Your father and his wife came to see me several weeks ago about giving Elyse power of attorney over his finances should he become unable to manage his own affairs."

"I see."

"That, in itself, isn't overly troubling. Lots of couples have that arrangement. But . . ."

"But?"

"He also directed me to make some rather significant changes to his will."

"What kind of changes?"

"I really can't go into details."

I took this to mean that he was leaving everything to Elyse. "I'm not sure I understand why you're telling me this," I said honestly.

"I'm not sure, either," he agreed.

"Then why are you?"

"Because I got the distinct feeling that your father was . . . how can I say this?" He stopped, as if searching for the perfect words. "Not being coerced exactly . . ."

"You're saying he was being forced?"

"No. Not forced. Just . . . he seemed confused and . . . uncomfortable."

"Confused and uncomfortable?" It wasn't like my father to be confused about anything. And uncomfortable was what he made everyone else.

"Frankly, I'm not sure he was fully aware what was going on. He looked tired, haggard even. To tell you the truth, I barely recognized him, with all the weight he's lost."

"He's lost weight?"

"You haven't noticed?"

"W-well, maybe a few pounds," I stuttered, not wanting to admit how long it had been since I'd seen my father.

"Plus, there was this vagueness in his eyes I found more than a little troubling. Just not the man I'm used to dealing with. Albeit, he'll be eighty in another week . . ."

Eighty, I repeated silently. Was it possible?

"At any rate, I advised him to think things over again before making such drastic changes, and I could tell that that advice didn't sit well with the new Mrs. Dundas."

I said nothing, waiting for him to continue.

"And then yesterday I received a letter from your father," the lawyer continued, "informing me that my services were no longer required, and asking me to forward his files to another firm. It's not a very reputable firm, to say the least—they're known for taking shortcuts and being somewhat less than ethical—and in light of the things you told me, plus my own recent observations and misgivings, I felt it was my duty to inform you of these developments."

"Did you forward the files?"

"I had no choice."

"Do *I*?"

"You could go to the police, I suppose. Not that they'll be able to do anything. But at least you'll get your concerns on the record. Just in case . . ."

He left the sentence dangling, but we both understood what came next.

In case something should happen to your father.

"I'll think about it," I told the lawyer, even though I knew that going to the police was out of the question. If they launched any kind of investigation, Elyse would surely find out, and my affair with her son would be revealed. I couldn't take that chance.

"Do you think he's in danger?" I asked.

"Of being taken to the cleaners, definitely. Of anything more than that, I certainly hope not. At any rate, I think I've said quite enough. Remember," he added before hanging up. "We never had this conversation."

The phone rang at midnight. I groped for it in the dark.

"What the hell?" Harrison mumbled beside me.

"Hello?"

"Tracy?" the voice said.

"Dad?" I asked.

"Tracy," he said again.

"No, Dad. It's Jodi," I said, too tired to be offended. "What's wrong?"

"Jodi?"

"Yes, Dad. It's Jodi. What's happening?"

"What's going on?" Harrison muttered beside me.

"What do you want?" my father asked.

"Dad, *you* called *me*."

"I called *you*?"

"Well, you thought you were calling Tracy."

"I did?"

"Is everything all right? Do you need me to come over?"

"What are you talking about?" Harrison grumbled. "It's after midnight! You're not going anywhere."

"Where's Elyse?" I asked my father.

"Your mother is in bed, asleep."

"Dad, Mom is dead," I reminded him as gently as I could.

"Vic," I heard Elyse call out. "Vic? Where are you? What are you doing in the closet, for God's sake? Who are you talking to? Hello? Who is this?" she said into the phone.

"It's Jodi. What's happening?"

"Go back to bed, darling," I heard her tell my father. "That's right, sweetheart. I'll be right there."

"What's happening?" I asked again.

"It's nothing," Elyse said calmly. "Your father sometimes gets confused when he takes a sleeping pill, that's all."

"Since when does he take sleeping pills?"

"Since he sometimes has trouble sleeping."

"He's always been against taking unnecessary drugs," I argued.

"Sometimes these things are necessary," she said.

"For whom?" I asked.

"Elyse!" I heard my father call out.

"Coming, darling. Everything's fine, Jodi. I'm sorry he disturbed you. Now get some sleep. Everything's fine," she repeated before hanging up.

Everything's fine, I repeated silently, lying back down. *Everything's fine. Everything's fine.*

Elyse called first thing the following morning.

"I just wanted to apologize for last night," she said. "I'm sure that your father didn't mean to alarm you."

"Can I talk to him?"

"He's still sleeping. Obviously, he had a rather rough night."

"We all did."

"These things happen when you get older," she said, an almost audible smile in her voice. "Speaking of which, it's your father's eightieth birthday next Saturday, and I was hoping you could all come for dinner."

"Sounds lovely," I said, the exact opposite of what I was thinking. Still, such invitations were rare these days, and it would give me an opportunity to see my father, observe his behavior firsthand, maybe even give me a chance to talk to him alone.

"Lovely," she said, using my word. "I'll call Tracy. Six o'clock?"

"Sounds good."

"We'll look forward to seeing you then."

FIFTY-SEVEN

"God, what am I going to do about this hair?" I wailed, looking in the bathroom mirror, watching my husband shake his head behind me in the reflection.

"What's the matter with it?" he asked.

"It looks awful."

"It looks the same way it always does."

I didn't know whether to laugh or cry, so I did a combination of both.

"I don't know what you're so upset about," Harrison said. "You look fine."

"*Fine* isn't exactly the response I was hoping for."

"It's just a family dinner, for heaven's sake. I don't recall you getting this worked up over my annual barbecue."

I walked out of the bathroom, sank down on the bed. Here we go again, I thought. Harrison was still upset because he'd had to postpone his barbecue for a week because of my father's birthday. I'd wondered which of this year's crop of students he was trying to impress, but dismissed such thoughts as unnecessary and even unkind. Besides, I had bigger things to worry about. Much as I'd tried to convince myself that tonight's dinner was "just a family dinner," I suspected that it was really a pretext for whatever bomb Elyse was about to hurl at me next. I pulled at my hair. The least I could do was look good when she dropped it.

The last thing I needed were more comments about how tired and pale I looked. Since my hair was one of the few things in my life that I felt I had any control over, it was where I chose to concentrate my energy. If I could just get my hair to behave, then maybe I could magically get the rest of my life to follow suit.

"Mommy!" Daphne cried, running into the room. She was wearing a pink party dress and she looked as delicious as always. "Are you ready yet?"

"Almost," I told her. "I just need to fix my hair."

"What's wrong with it?"

"There's nothing wrong with it," Harrison answered, scooping Daphne into his arms. "Where's your brother?"

"Watching YouTube."

"Great," Harrison said, shaking his head at me in dismay as the phone in his side pocket pinged with an incoming text. He promptly lowered Daphne to the floor. "Go get Sam. Tell him to get off YouTube, we're leaving in two minutes."

Daphne was halfway out of the room when she stopped and ran back to where I sat perched at the edge of the bed, her head tilting from side to side as she examined my wayward locks. Slowly, she lifted her hands to my hair, brushing several strands away from my face, tucking several more behind my ears, then stepping back to examine her handiwork. "Beautiful," she pronounced. "Go look."

I walked back into the bathroom and stared at my reflection. While "beautiful" was perhaps too strong a word, I had to admit that whatever she'd done was a definite improvement. "Thanks, doll," I said, watching her little face beam.

"Sammy!" I heard her call as she ran from the room. "Daddy says to get off YouTube. We're leaving in two minutes."

I smoothed out the skirt of my blue-and-white-striped dress and adjusted my gold hoop earrings, deciding this was as good as it was going to get. "Okay," I said, glancing at Harrison as he finished typing in a text of his own before returning his cell to the side pocket of his black pants. "Who was that?"

"Not important," he said.

I decided not to pursue it. "How do I look?"

"Fine."

Again, not exactly the response I'd been hoping for.

"You ready?" he asked.

I nodded.

"Then let's get this show on the road."

We were stopped at a red light when Harrison's phone pinged with another incoming text. He quickly withdrew the phone from his pocket, glanced at the message and then dropped the phone to his seat. Seconds later, it pinged again.

"Who keeps messaging?" I asked, ignoring the little voice in my head telling me to be quiet.

"It's nothing."

"It's obviously something."

As if sensing trouble, the kids began arguing in the backseat.

"Sam, Daphne, keep it down!" Harrison snapped.

"Daddy's trying to drive," I added as the light turned green. "Is there a problem?" I asked as he resumed driving.

"Okay. Look. I don't want you to get upset . . ."

"Why would I get upset? Is this something to do with my father?"

He shook his head impatiently. "Why does everything have to be about you?"

"Sorry. I didn't mean . . . What *is* it about? Why would I be upset?"

"I've been asked to organize a series of seminars at the end of August—"

"That's great," I interrupted.

". . . in Prince Edward County."

"Prince Edward County?" I repeated, desperately trying not to see the name *Wren* that was suddenly flashing in bold letters across my brain, or to picture her lovely face framed by her perfect hair. "But you did that last year."

"This is different," Harrison explained. "Apparently I was such a hit that they decided to enlarge the program, expand it into a weeklong series of lectures and events. They asked me to design the whole thing, gave me pretty much free rein to do whatever I want, bring in whomever I choose."

"Sounds very ambitious."

"It is."

"But isn't it a little late to be trying to organize all that now?"

There was a moment's pause. "Actually, it's been in the works for a while."

"What do you mean, for a while? For how long?"

Harrison hesitated. "Since last fall, pretty much."

"Since last fall? And you're just telling me about this now?"

"I wanted to tell you earlier, but with everything that's been going on in your life, it just never felt like the right time."

"You're saying it's my fault you didn't tell me?"

"I'm not saying it's anybody's fault," he argued. "It's just the way it is. God, why do you always have to make everything somebody's fault?"

"I don't always . . ." I stopped, aware of the sudden silence in the backseat, mindful of the old adage about little pitchers having big ears. "I take it that Wren is somehow involved in this . . . what would you call it?" I ventured, lowering my voice.

"I call it a huge opportunity," Harrison replied. "And yes, she's been helping out. Which is another reason I didn't say anything to you before. You've always been so paranoid about Wren."

"I'm not paranoid."

"What's paranoid?" Sam questioned from the backseat.

"What's Wren?" Daphne asked.

"Mommy and I are having a discussion," Harrison said. "This doesn't concern you."

"Are you fighting?" Daphne asked.

"You don't like when *we* fight," Sam added.

"We're not fighting," Harrison and I replied together, our voices overlapping.

"So, it's Wren who's been texting?" I asked after several seconds had passed and the kids had returned to their own squabbles.

"Okay, yes. It was Wren," Harrison replied between tightly clenched teeth. "She was excited because one of the writers I suggested we contact just emailed that he'd be happy to take part. It's quite a coup, everyone is thrilled, and she wanted to let me know."

I absorbed this latest tidbit with a nod of my head. "You said this is happening at the end of August?"

"The last week, yes."

"And you'd be gone the whole week?"

"Obviously."

"I assume Wren will be there as well?" I asked as calmly as I could.

A noticeable stiffening of his shoulders, a narrowing of his eyes. "Of course."

I forced a smile as he turned onto Scarth Road. "A week in Prince Edward County actually sounds pretty nice," I offered. "Maybe the kids and I could join you. We could rent a cottage for the week, make it a family vacation. We haven't had one in a while. I could do some investigating, see what's available . . ."

"I'm not sure that's a good idea."

"Why not?"

"I'll be very busy."

"I'm sure we'll find lots to do."

"I just don't think it's a good idea to combine business and pleasure. Someone inevitably ends up feeling short-changed."

"I don't see how we'd be in the way."

"Okay," he said testily. "Let me think about it." He turned in to my father's driveway and shut off the car's engine. "Well, kids, here we are."

"Yay!" they cried in unison.

"I get to push the elevator button first," Sam said, already halfway out the door before Daphne could undo her seatbelt.

"We'll discuss this later," Harrison told me.

I took a deep breath. *Can't wait,* I thought.

FIFTY-EIGHT

"You're late," my father said.

"Happy birthday, Dad," I said in return, trying not to notice how gaunt he looked, and experiencing a moment of relief at the familiar greeting. I leaned in to kiss his dry, hollow cheek, feeling several days' growth of unfamiliar stubble. My father had always been so fastidious about his appearance. "My God, how much weight have you lost?"

"Only a few pounds," Elyse said, joining us in the front hall, looking very chic in black silk palazzo pants and matching satin shirt. "It looks like more because he didn't shave today, said not shaving was his birthday present to himself." She turned her attention to my children. "And how are my little angels?"

"Mommy and Daddy were fighting," Daphne told her.

"They were?"

"That's enough, Daphne," cautioned Harrison. "We weren't fighting."

"They were having a discussion," Sam explained.

"Ah, yes," Elyse said knowingly. "A discussion."

I handed my father the gift we'd bought him.

"It's a book," Sam announced.

"So I suspected," my father said, not bothering to unwrap it.

"Your new one?" Elyse asked Harrison.

"No. That won't be out for a while yet."

"So exciting. May I ask what it's called?"

"*Maroon Sky.*"

"Ooh. Sounds very intriguing."

"I thought it was *Dark Sky*," I said.

"I thought this was better. More evocative."

"I agree," I said, hearing footsteps approaching from the living room. I turned to see my sister. She was wearing a short, black leather skirt and a see-through leopard-print blouse over a black lace bra, a pair of spotless white sneakers on her shapely, bare legs.

"What's going on out here?" Tracy asked.

"I didn't realize you were here already," I told her. "I didn't see your car."

"That's because someone picked me up."

Her smile told me that I didn't have to ask who that someone was.

"You remember my son, Andrew," Elyse said as my former lover entered the front hall.

He was wearing a light blue shirt and a pair of navy pants, and while he looked as handsome as ever, I felt a wave of revulsion so powerful at the sight of him that I almost lost my balance. "Harrison . . . Jodi," he said. "Nice to see you again. And these gorgeous children must be Sam and Daphne."

"I'm Daphne!" my daughter proclaimed.

Andrew—the man I knew as Roger no longer existed—knelt to her level. "Very pleased to meet you, Daphne. I love your dress. Is pink your favorite color?"

"I like pink, then yellow, then purple."

"Those are great colors."

"I like blue and green," Sam said, not to be outdone.

"Excellent choices." Andrew pushed himself back to his full height.

"Andrew got in this afternoon," Tracy said.

"Couldn't very well miss Vic's eightieth birthday party now, could I?"

"Staying long?" Harrison asked.

"Just overnight. Unless, of course, I'm needed here."

I turned away, recognizing his answer for the implicit threat it was.

"Let's eat," my father said. "I'm starving. I haven't had anything to eat all day."

"Why haven't you eaten?" I asked.

"Of course you've eaten, darling. You had poached eggs on toast for breakfast and a lovely tuna salad for lunch. He's forgotten," Elyse said with a laugh.

"It's not like my father to be forgetful," I said, looking to him for confirmation.

"I haven't forgotten anything," my father said. "I'm starving and I want to eat."

"Now, Vic . . ."

"Don't 'Now, Vic' me."

I smiled. *Now, that's the man I know.*

"Then, by all means," Elyse said, her own smile freezing on her lips, "let's eat."

—

I don't know how I made it through the evening without exploding or breaking down. My world was collapsing, all the familiar signposts disappearing. First, there was my father, a normally strong, proud, and stubborn man. While on the surface he remained as ornery as ever, there was something missing. It was more than just the weight he'd lost. Ronald Miller was right: his eyes were vacant. I was reminded of that old black-and-white movie where people were replaced by aliens, physically alike in every respect, but missing the emotions that made them human, that made them who they were.

My father was no longer who he was.

The man who normally took great pains with his appearance, always smooth-shaven and nattily attired, now appeared slovenly and unkempt. Dried-in stains dotted his wrinkled trousers. He'd lost at least ten pounds, appeared tired, and most alarming of all, seemed confused and forgetful.

Yes, he was eighty, but in today's world, that was no longer especially old. And his behavior—timid, meek, even subservient, despite his welcome snap at Elyse—was in sharp contrast to his behavior of even a few months back. As pleased as I was to see some of his more unpleasant bluster disappear, I was alarmed as well.

Then there was Elyse, a woman who now occupied my mother's place at the table as well as in her bed. If I were to peel away the sweet smile and glossy veneer, would I find a woman or a serpent?

And her son, Andrew, a chameleon I once knew as Roger, whom I'd had to sit across the table from all night, watching him cozy up to my sister. I saw him look at her the way he once looked at me, as if charmed by her very existence. And Tracy, uncharacteristically quiet, hanging on his every word, as if utterly smitten.

And lastly, there was Harrison. He'd been keeping things from me for months. When had he been planning to tell me about Prince Edward County? What else was he hiding from me?

Who were these people? I wondered.

"What's going on with you?" Tracy asked as we were leaving.

"What do you mean?"

"I mean, you haven't been yourself all night."

I laughed.

It was either that or cry.

—FIFTY-NINE—

It was after midnight the following night when the landline beside my bed rang.

I groped for the phone in the dark, trying to answer it before it could wake Harrison. Instead, I knocked it off its receiver and had to feel around for it on the floor for several seconds before finally locating it half under the bed. "Hello?" I whispered, hearing nothing but ragged breathing on the other end. "Dad?"

Silence.

"Dad? Is that you?"

Seconds later, the silence was replaced by a busy signal.

Maybe it wasn't my father, I told myself. Maybe it was just an obscene caller. Did people still do that? I wondered. Were obscene calls even a thing anymore?

"Great," I said, sitting there in the dark, wondering what, if anything, I should—or could—do. "Harrison," I said, turning toward him, amazed he could have slept through all the commotion.

He wasn't there.

"Harrison?" I flipped on the bedside lamp and looked toward the en suite bathroom. But its door was open and the light was off. Was he with Sam or Daphne? I wondered, pushing off the bed and padding into the hallway on bare feet.

But a quick glance into their rooms revealed that the kids were both in their beds, sleeping soundly.

"Harrison?" I called again, wondering if he'd gone to the kitchen for a midnight snack. Elyse had insisted we take home what remained of my father's birthday cake, and there was still some left. Maybe Harrison had decided to finish it off. And maybe I'd go join him, apologize for my part in our continuing coolness, assure him that I'd make his annual barbecue something extra special this year to make up for his having had to postpone it.

It was at that moment I realized that the door to his office, a door he normally kept open, was closed. A sliver of light emanated from beneath it. Ignoring the little voice in my head telling me to go back to bed, I crossed the hall and opened the door.

Harrison was sitting at his computer in his bathrobe, and he jumped when he saw me. "For God's sake, Jodi!" he cried. "What are you doing?"

"What are *you* doing?" I countered, watching him quickly click out of whatever file he'd been accessing as I walked toward him.

His computer screen immediately filled with the image of the cover of *Comes the Dreamer* that was his screensaver. "I couldn't sleep, so I thought I'd do some work on the latest round of revisions for my new book."

"I thought they were already done."

"They're never done," he said wearily. "What are you doing up?"

"You didn't hear the phone?" I asked in return.

"Someone called?"

I filled him in on the details.

"You think it was your father," he stated.

"Don't you?"

He shrugged. "I'm too tired to think."

But not too tired to be on your computer, I thought, though I refrained from voicing this out loud.

Harrison gave a little half smile, got up from his chair, and turned off the light. "Come on. Let's get you back into bed."

I let him lead me from his office and back to our room, relieved when he crawled into bed beside me, his body folding around the curve of my backside, his arm draping lazily across my hip.

Ten minutes later, the steady sound of his breathing told me he was asleep.

Ten minutes after that, I gently extricated myself from his casual embrace, got out of bed, and returned to his office.

I left the door open and the overhead light off. There was enough light from the street coming through the window, so I had no trouble finding his desk or activating his sleeping computer. The cover of *Comes the Dreamer* quickly popped into view. I wasn't sure exactly what I was looking for, but instinct guided me toward the icon of a stamp that symbolized Harrison's email on the toolbar at the bottom of the screen. I clicked on it, and seconds later, his inbox revealed a long series of recent correspondence, some from his editor, some from various stores, some from charities seeking donations, some from enamored fans.

Most from one enamored fan in particular.

I gasped as her name reached out to grab me by the throat.

Wren Peterson
Re: Missing you!
Dear Harrison. Counting the days till we're together. Every day feels like an eternity. Can't wait for the summer to be over so we . . .

Wren Peterson
Re: Congratulations!
Dear Harrison. Congratulations on getting Gregory Marcus to be one of our guest speakers. Everyone is so thrilled and it's all be . . .

Wren Peterson
Re: You're the best!
Dear Harrison. Last night was beyond wonderful. I loved meeting your friend John. Looking forward to many more such get-togeth . . .

Wren Peterson
Re: Maroon Sky!
Dear Harrison. Sooo thrilled you love my suggestion
to change the title of your new book to Maroon Sky.
I loved the book so much . . .

"Oh, God," I moaned, glancing toward the office door, half wishing that Harrison would appear so that he could provide me with an explanation I could somehow persuade myself was true, that Wren was simply a delusional young woman who'd created a fantasy world wherein the two of them were lovers, that he was playing along with these delusions only until the summer was over and his obligations to the festival he was helping to organize ended . . .

And then I saw it:

Wren Peterson
Re: Photos from Whistler!
Dear Harrison. Thought you'd get a kick out of
some of these pictures from our magical trip. You
look handsome, as always . . .

I clicked on the email so I could view it in its entirety.

"Dear God," I whispered, as half a dozen photographs of my husband and his former student filled the screen, the magnificent mountain scenery that was Whistler serving as backdrop.

Here they were, arms around each other's waists, waiting in line for a cable car ride. There they were, hiking along one of Whistler's many nature trails. Here they were, enjoying breakfast in bed.

"Oh, God. Oh, God. Oh, God."

Yet shocked as I was by these selfies, I admit I wasn't entirely surprised. A part of me had suspected—no, a part of me had *known*—about their affair all along. The only question left to me now was what I intended to do about it.

— SIXTY —

I wish I could report that I stormed into our bedroom and confronted Harrison, pushing him out of bed, then onto the street. But of course, I did no such thing.

Instead I sat there in the dark until the computer went into automatic sleep mode and the screen went black. I immediately pressed the bar on the keypad that reawakened it, once again coming face-to-face with the undeniable proof of my husband's betrayal. I continued sitting there, staring at the horrifying images of my husband and his young lover until the computer drifted back to sleep, whereupon I wakened it yet again.

And again.

And again.

I like to think that I was contemplating my options, but the truth is that I'm not sure I was thinking anything at all. I was too numb to think clearly, too devastated to be angry, too tired to be much of anything.

Strangely enough, a part of me was also relieved.

Harrison had made me feel as if our problems were all *my* fault—*Why do you always have to make everything*

somebody's fault? he'd had the nerve to chastise me—and
while I was certainly willing to accept part of the blame for
our marital issues, these emails proved the fault didn't rest
entirely, or even mostly, on my shoulders. I wasn't crazy. I
wasn't paranoid. I wasn't seeing things that weren't there.
I wasn't overreacting to a threat that didn't exist. My concerns were real, my suspicions justified, my instincts sound.

My husband was having an affair with a former student, an affair that had been going on for months. He'd
taken her to Whistler just days after my mother's death,
cavorting with his lover under the guise of fulfilling
his obligations, knowing how much I could have used his
support at home. He'd taken her to meet an old writing
buddy and had actually had the nerve to be incensed
when I was half an hour late getting home so he could
leave. Who knew how many times they'd met up over the
last few months or how many people knew of their
affair? These emails confirmed that Harrison had been
lying to me for the better part of the past year, and possibly even longer than that.

My mind took a quick journey down memory lane,
conjuring up a series of the nubile young women who'd
taken his course over the past five years, women I'd welcomed into my home for his annual barbecue. How
many of these girls had he seduced with his charm and
celebrity? I doubted that Wren was Harrison's first affair.
If I dived into his emails from years past, how many
more incriminating posts would I uncover?

I shook my head, deciding there was no need to tor-
ture myself further. I had all the evidence I needed to
prove my husband was a liar and a cheat.

Just like my father, I realized, a startled cry escaping my throat.

The cry bounced off the walls and echoed down the hall. My eyes shot toward the office door. Had I wakened Harrison? I held my breath, relieved when the ensuing silence confirmed he was still asleep.

"I married my father," I whispered to the indifferent walls, aware that at least part of my reluctance to storm into our bedroom and confront my husband was because I had no desire to become my mother. How many nights had I lain in my bed, listening to their furious fights, my mother's angry accusations, my father's dishonest denials? The last thing I wanted was to subject my own children to that same trauma. I couldn't bear the thought of them trembling in their beds, their hands covering their ears in a failed effort to dull the sound of our fury, all the while praying desperately for the fighting to end.

How could I have been so stupid as to fall into the same sordid trap?

At least my mother hadn't gone down without a fight, I realized, as thoughts of my mother led inexorably to thoughts of the woman who'd replaced her. What would Elyse do now, if she were me? I wondered.

And then I knew.

I felt her invisible hand grab mine and guide it toward the keyboard. Within minutes, I had clicked on each incriminating email that Wren had sent and forwarded copies to my own computer, feeling an unfamiliar rush of euphoria with each telltale whoosh. *For insurance,* I heard Elyse say.

Wait a minute, I heard Tracy chime in. *What about me?*

Which was when I started at the beginning again, and erased each and every one of Wren's messages. I left all the other messages—the stores, the charities, his publishers—intact.

When I was done, I exited my husband's email, watching the screen go blank as the computer drifted back to sleep. Then I stood up, making sure Harrison's chair was in roughly the same position as before I sat down, and tiptoed from the room.

I tried imagining my husband's reaction when he realized Wren's emails were missing. What would he do? What *could* he do? Would he risk confronting me? What could he say without giving himself away?

I was strangely calm when I reentered my bedroom. Slowly, I approached the bed and stared down at Harrison, his mouth semi-parted in sleep, a slight whistle emanating from somewhere deep inside his throat. Had he felt any guilt at all? I wondered. God knows I'd raked myself over the coals over my own infidelity, an infidelity I recognized had been fueled by a combination of Harrison's indifference and Elyse's manipulations.

I shook such self-serving rationalizations aside, recognizing that while I could provide good reasons for my behavior, I couldn't excuse it altogether. I was an adult. I was responsible for my own actions. Ultimately, I couldn't blame anyone else for the things I'd done.

So maybe that was another reason I didn't confront Harrison that night. I don't know. I only know that I was confused, disappointed, and exhausted. The time for confrontation would come soon enough, I decided, pulling back the covers and crawling into bed beside my husband. Immediately, I felt the warmth of his body as he snuggled up against me. "Where'd you go?" he mumbled, sleepily.

"Bathroom," I said.

"Hmm," he said, accepting the lie as easily as I'd accepted his.

Underestimate me, I thought, recalling Tracy's sweatshirt as his arm settled across the rise of my hip. *That'll be fun.*

I called Tracy as soon as I got to my office the next morning.

"Is Andrew there?" I said instead of hello.

"Good morning to you, too."

"Is he?"

"What? No. He went back to Detroit yesterday. Why? What's going on?"

"Tell me the truth," I said. "Have you slept with him?"

"I don't understand . . ."

"Just answer the question."

"Well, it's really none of your business, Mother Teresa, but the answer is no," she said.

"Don't," I warned.

"Why not?"

I took a deep breath. "Because I already did."

"What?"

"I slept with him."

"You slept with who?"

"With Andrew."

"Get out of here. You did not."

"Except I knew him as Roger."

"Are you okay? You're starting to scare me."

"He came to my office months ago, introduced himself as Roger McAdams, said he was looking to buy a condo. And I slept with him. Twice."

"Go on," she said warily.

"It's a long story."

"Which I can't wait to hear."

"Can you meet me later?"

"Wouldn't miss it. When and where?"

"One o'clock. I'll pick you up."

"I'll be waiting."

SIXTY-ONE

"Holy shit!" Tracy said when I finished laying out all the sordid details of my tryst with Roger.

"Exactly."

We were parked on a quiet side street not far from her apartment.

"I have to admit I'm impressed."

"Yes, they're very clever," I agreed.

"Not with Elyse and whatever the hell his name is. With you!"

"Me?"

"I didn't know you had it in you."

"I cheated on my husband!"

"Which he totally deserved."

"Why do you say that?" I asked.

She shook her head.

"What do you know? Tell me."

She hesitated. "You have to promise not to get mad at me."

"Tracy . . ."

"Okay. Okay. Remember when I asked you if, hypothetically, you'd want someone to tell you if your husband was having an affair . . ."

I nodded.

"He was having an affair."

"Go on," I said, as she'd said on the phone earlier.

"With one of his students. More than one, according to the university gossip mill. He's kind of famous for it, actually. I heard all about it when I was taking that course last summer. I tried to tell you, but you got so defensive . . ."

I nodded, remembering.

"It was never my intention to hurt you."

"I know. I also know that Harrison was—*is*—having an affair."

Which was when I told her about going through Harrison's emails, finding the evidence of his infidelity, and then erasing Wren's emails after forwarding them to my computer.

Tracy fell back against her seat. "Wow. Now I'm really impressed."

"Don't be."

"Are you kidding me? You're my hero!"

I gave a small chuckle.

"So, what are you going to do?"

"About Harrison? Nothing. At least not yet. Not till we've sorted out what to do about Elyse."

"What *can* we do?"

"Well, the one good thing about discovering that my husband is a lying son of a bitch is that Elyse no longer has anything to hold over my head. I no longer care if Harrison finds out about Roger. In fact, I think I'll enjoy watching the look on his face when he sees those pictures of me as much I will seeing his reaction to those missing emails."

"Look at you, discovering your inner cunt," Tracy said.

This time I laughed out loud. "I'll take that as a compliment."

"Meant as one."

I started the car's engine and pulled onto the street.

"Where are we going?" she asked.

"Forty College Street."

"What's there?"

"Police headquarters."

The main branch of the Toronto Police Service is a twelve-story, postmodern, brown-brick-and-glass building in the heart of the city. Tracy and I approached the long reception counter in the middle of the bright, spacious lobby. "I'm Jodi Bishop and this is my sister Tracy Dundas," I told the uniformed officer behind the counter. "We're here to see Officers Stankowski and Lewis. I called earlier."

The officer directed us to the bank of glass elevators to our right. Officers Stankowski and Lewis were waiting for us in interview room 710.

"Mrs. Bishop," Officer Stankowski said. "Nice to see you again. Please have a seat." He motioned us toward a beige leather sofa across from two similarly upholstered chairs. "How can we help you?"

"We understand that you specifically requested to speak to us," Officer Lewis said, leaning against the unimpressive desk in front of the large window overlooking a tree-filled inner courtyard.

"Yes. We need some advice, and since you're already somewhat familiar with the family dynamics—"

"I assume we're talking about the incident with your father some months back, when he accused you of stealing your mother's jewelry," Officer Lewis interrupted, making a show of reviewing his notes, something I was quite sure both officers had already done.

"My sister and I are very concerned about our father's welfare," I said, ignoring the reference to the supposed theft of the jewelry.

The officers sat down in the chairs across from us. Officer Stankowski took out his notepad, his ballpoint pen poised to capture anything he considered worth jotting down. "What are your concerns?" he asked.

"We're concerned that he could be in danger," I began.

"We think he married a gold digger and that she might be planning to do him harm," Tracy clarified.

"A gold digger," Officer Lewis repeated.

"What kind of harm?" Officer Stankowski asked.

"His housekeeper," I explained, answering the easier of the two questions. "You met her."

"Oh, yes. Charming woman, as I recall."

"She gives that impression, yes," I agreed.

"You think otherwise?"

"We think she's after our father's money."

"That may very well be true," the officer conceded. "But, unfortunately, that's not a crime."

"We think she might be drugging him." I told the officers about my father's strange phone calls and Elyse's rather suspect explanations.

"Sleeping pills have been known to cause unpredictable reactions in the elderly," Officer Stankowski said. "My grandmother fell and broke her hip because she got disoriented after taking what's considered to be a very mild and safe sedative."

"We think Elyse murdered our mother," Tracy said, clearly not interested in the officer's relatives.

That got their attention.

That Elyse might have been responsible for our mother's death was a theory Tracy had voiced before, one I'd tried to convince myself was a product of her overactive imagination. Hadn't our father always insisted that he and Elyse had been having breakfast together at the time of our mother's fall?

"That's a pretty serious accusation," Officer Lewis said. "Do you have any evidence to back it up?"

Tracy quickly elaborated on the circumstances of our mother's death.

"But you don't think it was an accident," the officer stated when she was through.

"We think she might have had help," Tracy said. "That she might have been pushed."

Do we? I wondered, noting the look of skepticism that passed between the two policemen, a look that told me they were no longer taking our concerns—or us—very seriously.

"Again, do you have any evidence . . . ?"

"No, but . . ."

"Do you have any evidence *at all* that your father is in danger?"

"No," Tracy said again. "But . . ."

"He's lost a lot of weight," I offered. "He's confused. He looks disheveled. He was always so fastidious about his appearance—"

"Does your father share your suspicions about his wife?" Officer Lewis broke in to ask.

"Not that we know of," I admitted.

"Has he voiced to you that he's afraid for his safety?"

"No. But when he phoned, I could tell . . ."

"Tell what? Has he told you that he fears for his life?"

"No, but . . ."

"Look. We understand your concern. We really do," Officer Stankowski said, "but his wife's explanation for your father's behavior makes perfect sense, and unless your father makes a complaint, our hands are tied."

"So . . . what?" I asked. "Can't you at least go over there, check things out for yourselves?"

"We have no grounds," Officer Lewis said. "We just can't go barging in on private citizens . . ."

"Look. If you're asking my advice," Officer Stankowski offered, somewhat reluctantly, "I would say to keep in regular contact with your father, maybe even drop over unexpectedly from time to time. If Elyse refuses to let you see your dad, then you have grounds for us to interfere. Other than that . . ."

". . . our hands are tied," I said, finishing the sentence for him.

"I'm afraid so."

Tracy and I rose to our feet.

"Thank you for seeing us," I said.

Tracy walked toward the door, then stopped. "If something happens to our father," she said, "don't say we didn't warn you."

SIXTY-TWO

"Well, that was a colossal waste of time," Tracy said as we returned to my car.

"At least we got our concerns on the record," I told her.

"I guess." We climbed into the front seat. "Can I ask you something?" she asked as we secured our seatbelts.

"Can I stop you?"

She smiled. "What was he like?"

"What was who like?" I asked, although I already knew who and what she was referring to.

"Andrew . . . Roger . . . whatever you want to call him. What was he like . . . you know . . . in bed?"

I groaned, pulled out onto the street, heading north up Bay Street.

"He was good, wasn't he?"

"Very good," I admitted.

"I knew it. The stinkers are always great in bed."

"Can I ask *you* something?" I asked in return.

"Can I stop you?" she replied, with a laugh.

"Why didn't *you*?"

"Why didn't I what?"

"Why didn't *you* sleep with him?"

"Are you kidding me?" Tracy answered. "Sleep with Elyse's son? I may be shallow, but I'm not stupid. You think I couldn't sense there was something fishy about that whole scenario? I knew he was just using me to keep tabs on us, using that considerable charm to get whatever information he could out of me. Basically, the same thing I was trying to do with him."

"Really? You seemed so enamored."

"Told you I'm a great actress."

I laughed. "So, *did* you find out anything useful?"

"Nothing I didn't already know from googling him."

"You googled him?"

"You didn't?"

I groaned. How stupid *was* I? "So, he really does live in Detroit and work for some big wealth management company?"

"Apparently. But who knows?" she mused. "The whole thing could be a setup. People have been known to create fake accounts." She looked around. "Where are you going now?"

"To Dad's."

"What? Why?"

"Remember Officer Stankowski's advice about dropping in unexpectedly? If Elyse denies us access . . ."

"Then we can involve the police."

"It's worth a shot," I told her.

"Definitely worth a shot," she agreed.

—

Elyse was outside conferring with one of the men working on the exterior of the house when I pulled into the driveway. She was wearing a T-shirt and a pair of Bermuda shorts that skimmed the tops of her knees. The man was wearing a bright yellow hard hat; Elyse, a wide-brimmed straw bonnet.

"Jodi . . . Tracy," she said, cupping her hand over her eyes as she walked toward us. "To what do we owe this unexpected treat?"

Really? I wondered as Tracy and I exited the car. *How long were we going to play this game?*

"We're here to see our father," Tracy said.

"Oh, I'm so sorry. He's having a little nap right now."

Tracy checked her watch. "It's three o'clock."

"Which is when he usually takes his nap."

"He always said that afternoon naps were for sissies," I told her.

"Well, your father is certainly no sissy." Elyse smiled. "Nor is he as young as he used to be."

"Yes. He seems to have aged rather rapidly since you got married."

The smile disappeared from Elyse's face. "Is there a message I can give him?"

"We can wait till he wakes up," I said.

"That could be a while."

"Are you denying us access to our father?" Tracy asked.

Elyse's eyes opened wide, as if an alarm had sounded silently in her head at Tracy's use of words. She paused, the smile returning to her lips, although it failed to reach her eyes. "Of course not. Why on earth would I do that?"

"You tell us," Tracy said.

"I doubt I could tell you girls anything." Elyse's left arm motioned toward the front door. "After you."

Our father was lying on his side on top of the new ivory-colored, quilted bedspread covering the king-size bed, facing toward the back window, snoring softly.

"Vic, darling," Elyse all but cooed as we entered the room. "Wake up, sweetheart. Look who's here."

Our father stirred. "Huh?"

"Your daughters are here to see you, darling."

He sat up, turned toward us, his gaunt face a mask of confusion. "Who's that?" he asked, watery eyes moving warily between Tracy and me.

"It's Tracy and me, Dad," I told him. "Don't you recognize us?"

"Of course he recognizes you," Elyse said for him. "He's still half-asleep."

"Of course I recognize you," our father parroted. "What do you want?"

"We were in the neighborhood," I began.

"And we thought we'd stop in to say hello," Tracy added. "See how you were doing."

"I'm doing just fine. Or I *was*, till you woke me up."

"I tried to tell them," Elyse said.

"Do you mind if we have a few minutes alone with our father?" I asked.

"I'm afraid I *do* mind," Elyse said. "As you can see, your father doesn't respond well to surprise visits."

"Dad?"

"You heard Elyse. You're being very rude."

"Excuse me," one of the workers called from downstairs. "Mrs. Dundas? Could I speak to you for a second?"

Elyse hesitated.

"Go ahead," I told her. "We aren't going anywhere."

"I'll only be a second," Elyse told our father. "Don't do anything to upset your father," she said, her eyes boring into mine, issuing a silent warning.

"What's happening, Dad?" I asked the second she was gone.

"I don't understand."

"Did you call my house last night?"

"Did I?" His eyes searched the room, as if struggling to remember.

We were wasting precious time. Elyse would be back any second. I had no choice but to dive right in. "I understand Elyse took you to see a new lawyer, that she's pestering you to change your will and give her power of attorney."

"What?!" Tracy asked. "Where did you hear that?"

I waved her questions aside. "Dad, listen to me. It's important that you find a way to delay signing anything . . ."

"Why would I do that?" he asked, running an agitated hand through his uncombed hair, his eyes fighting to focus. "What are you trying to tell me?"

"We think Elyse might be drugging you, that you might be in danger," I told him as I heard Elyse's footsteps bound up the stairs. "We need you to call the police."

"The police?!"

"Everything all right in here?" Elyse asked, entering the room, eyes ricocheting between my father, Tracy, and me.

"Right as rain," Tracy said.

"Glad to hear it," Elyse said. "Now, if you don't mind, I think it's time for you girls to leave and let your father get some rest."

"What do *you* think, Dad?" I asked.

He looked from Tracy to me to Elyse, then back to me. "I think you should leave," he said.

SIXTY-THREE

"What's this about a new lawyer?" Tracy demanded as we climbed back into my car.

"Wait," I told her, backing out of the driveway, wanting to put as much distance as I could between us and the house before I said anything, at the same time trying to figure out how I could reveal what I knew without betraying Ronald Miller's confidence. "Look," I told my sister when we were several blocks away. "It's not important how I know. The important thing is *that* I know."

"You know for a fact that Elyse took Dad to see a new lawyer, that she's pressuring him to give her power of attorney and to change his will?"

"Yes."

She paused, absorbing the news. "Does Elyse know you know?"

"Not unless Dad tells her."

"Do you think he will?"

"I have no idea. I'm not sure how much of anything we said in there got through to him."

"Do you think he'll call the police?"

I shrugged.

"Can I ask you something else?"

"Can I stop you?" I asked, and we both smiled.

"Why are you so concerned about what happens to Dad? I mean, I know why *I'm* doing this. It's because I'm a selfish, spoiled brat and I don't want Elyse getting her hands on my inheritance. But I don't think it's about the money with you. So, what is it?"

"I don't understand the question," I told her honestly. "I'm concerned about Dad. He's my father and I love him."

"Why?"

"Why what?"

She twisted her body toward me, her brow wrinkling in confusion. "What's to love?"

Her question caught me off guard. "Seriously?"

"Seriously. What do you love about him? Other than you're *supposed* to love your father. When was the last time he said anything even remotely nice to you?" she continued when I failed to come up with a response.

I didn't have to give her question more than a second's thought. The truth was that I could sit here all day and not be able to remember the last time my father had paid me any sort of compliment. "I admit that he doesn't make it easy, but . . ."

"He's a miserable, self-centered son of a bitch."

"He took good care of Mom all those years," I offered, wondering why I was taking such pains to defend him. "He stopped working so he could be home to look after her . . ."

"Are you kidding me? He loved it. Her condition gave him total control. The last few years, Mom was more his prisoner than his wife."

"That's not fair."

"Who says the truth has to be fair?"

I had no answer for that.

"Do you miss her?" Tracy asked.

"I miss the *idea* of her," I answered honestly. "What about you?"

She shrugged. "Not really."

"She adored *you*," I reminded her.

"Only because when she looked at me, she saw herself. Dad's the same. You're looking at the sum of their worst parts."

I shook my head. "You're nothing like either one of them."

She smiled. "I'm not so sure about that."

I reached over to grab her hand. "I am."

I dropped Tracy off at her apartment, then stopped by my office to check on the day's transactions, although it wasn't necessary. I could have easily done this by phone. But the truth was that I was in no hurry to get home. Harrison would have picked up the kids from camp by now. He would have checked his emails.

"What are you going to do about Harrison?" Tracy had asked me, as if sensing my indecision, as I pulled to a stop in front of her building.

"I don't know," I was forced to admit. "What would *you* do?"

"Me? Probably cut off his you-know-what and feed it to the pigeons in the park."

"Lovely. Thank you for that."

"My pleasure," she said, exiting the car. "Call me if you need help holding him down."

I could hear Harrison yelling even before I reached our front door.

"Hello? Harrison? What's all the yelling about?" I asked, entering the foyer and approaching the stairs.

"I didn't do anything!" I heard my son cry out from somewhere above me.

"Don't lie to me!" Harrison shouted.

"What's going on, sweetie?" I asked, as Sam came running down the stairs, all but flying into my arms, his beautiful face awash in tears.

"I didn't do anything."

Harrison appeared at the landing, his face flushed with anger. "The hell you didn't."

"Mommy!" Daphne cried, pushing past her father to join her brother and me at the bottom of the stairs.

"What's going on?" I asked again.

"Stay out of this," Harrison warned. "And stop coddling them. Sam, get away from your mother."

In response, Sam hugged me even tighter.

"I didn't do it," he cried into the folds of my skirt.

"Do what?"

"Daddy says that Sammy broke his computer," Daphne said.

My breath froze in my chest. "What do you mean, he broke your computer?"

"The little shit erased half my emails," Harrison fumed.

I felt my whole body tremble. It hadn't occurred to me that Harrison might blame Sam for what I'd done.

"How many times have I told these kids my office is out-of-bounds, that they're never to go near my computer?"

"We didn't!" Sam shook his head with such ferocity that his tears sprayed into the air like errant drops of rain. "I swear."

"Stop," I told Harrison as he descended the steps. "Just calm down."

"Don't tell me to calm down."

"Then tell me why you think Sam had anything to do with your missing emails?"

"Who else could it be?"

"We were playing in my room," Sam said. "We never went into your office."

"We were in Sam's room," Daphne repeated.

"Stop lying for your brother," Harrison warned.

"We're not lying," Sam insisted. "Please, Mommy. We're not lying."

"It's okay, sweetheart."

"It's not okay!" Harrison snapped. "Don't tell him it's okay."

"I didn't touch Daddy's computer," Sam insisted.

"I know, sweetheart."

"Stop defending him," Harrison ordered.

"He didn't touch your fucking computer!" I shouted. "He didn't erase your fucking emails!"

Daphne gasped. "Mommy said a bad word!"

"How the hell would you know that?" Harrison demanded.

I pushed my shoulders back, stared my husband right in the eyes. "Because I did!"

— SIXTY-FOUR —

Never have three little words felt so good to utter. "Go to hell!" doesn't come close. Not even "I love you" provides the same level of pure satisfaction, the sheer sense of release I experienced in that moment. *Because I did!* bounced off the walls and filled the house.

They say that confession is good for the soul.

They're only partly right.

In this case, it was also good for my heart, my self-respect, my very *sense* of self.

"What?!" Harrison's face went from red to white, his eyes widening in disbelief as he reflected on the ramifications of what I'd just said.

"I erased your fucking emails," I said, louder this time, partly to make absolutely certain that Harrison had heard me correctly, but mostly because I just loved saying it. I turned toward Sam and Daphne, their collective gasps frozen on their open mouths. "Kids, why don't you go play in the backyard for a while?"

"Are you and Daddy going to have another discussion?" Daphne asked.

"Yes, sweetheart. I believe we are."

"Come on, Daphne," Sam urged, grabbing his sister's arm and leading her quickly through the kitchen toward the back door.

My eyes remained locked on my husband's as we waited until we heard the door close.

"You erased my emails," Harrison said, as if still processing what this meant.

"Your *fucking* emails. Yes, I most certainly did."

"I don't understand."

"I think you do."

"You broke into my computer?"

"Well, I didn't exactly break in. It was just sleeping. All I had to do was wake it up."

"When? Why?"

"Last night. After we went back to bed. Something just didn't feel right, so I waited till you fell asleep, then went back to your office to check things out."

"You had no right."

"Really? You're going to make this about me?"

"*You're* the one who broke into my email."

"*You're* the one having an affair!"

"Look. I don't know what you think you saw . . ."

"Oh, I don't *think* anything. I *know* what I saw, what I read. *Dear Harrison . . . counting the days till we're together again . . . You're the best . . . Last night was beyond wonderful . . . Loved meeting your friend John.* And the pictures from your *magical* trip to Whistler. Correct me if I'm wrong, but I believe that magical trip was just after my mother died. So inconsiderate of her to almost ruin your plans by dying," I continued, unable to stop myself at this point, even if I'd tried. "I especially liked the picture of you and Wren enjoying breakfast in bed. She really knows how to take a great selfie, how to get those angles just right. I can never manage to take a good one . . ."

"Okay, okay," Harrison said. "You've made your point."

"How long has this been going on?" I asked.

"I really don't want to get into it."

"Oh, trust me, you're already in it. How long?"

He exhaled, long and loud. "Since Prince Edward County."

"You've been sleeping together since then?"

"I tried to break it off . . . we stopped seeing each other for a while . . ."

Probably around the time our lovemaking became more frequent and intense, I realized.

"But she was so persistent . . ."

"I see. This is all *her* doing."

"That's not what I said."

"Really? Because it kind of sounded like that's what you said."

"Why do you always have to twist everything? Maybe if you'd been a little more understanding, a little less critical . . ."

"Oh, so now it's *my* fault?"

"I think you have to accept at least part of the responsibility."

"For *your* affair? I don't think so."

"Try to see it from my perspective for just a minute,

will you? You make the money, so you make the decisions. You make the money, so your career is more
important than mine. You make the money, so your
schedule takes precedence over mine. Meanwhile, I make
the meals, I look after the kids . . ."

"That's ridiculous. I make as many meals as you do;
I'm just as involved with the kids—"

"You have no appreciation for what it's like to stare
at a blank computer for hours on end," he interrupted,
"trying to create something worthwhile, to live up to
people's expectations."

"You obviously lived up to Wren's quite nicely."

"She made me feel like a man again, instead of a fucking housekeeper. And, yes, I confess to enjoying feeling
wanted and appreciated for a change. Is that so wrong?"

"I have always wanted and appreciated you."

"Really? Maybe if you'd spent half the time trying to
please me as you do trying to please your father . . ."

"That's a load of crap and you know it."

"Do I?" he asked. "Where were you this afternoon?
I know you weren't at the office because I called there to
tell you I was running late and ask if you could pick up
the kids at camp, and they told me you'd left around one.
Where were you? No, don't tell me. Let me guess. You
went to see Daddy."

"Your sordid little affair has nothing to do with me or
my father."

"I'm right, though, aren't I?" He shook his head. "If
you only devoted half the energy to me, to our family, as
you do to . . ."

Oh, fuck! Here we go again. "This isn't about me," I said, cutting short the familiar round of complaints. "It's about you and the fact that you've been having an affair, with one of your students no less, since last summer. It's about the fact that you're a liar and a cheat and an all-around fucking jackass."

He shook his head. "Does it make you feel better to call me names?"

"It does, actually," I admitted. "Yes."

We stood staring daggers at each other for what felt like an eternity.

"So, where does that leave us?" he asked finally.

"I don't know."

The back door opened. "Can we come in now?" Sam asked. "It's starting to rain."

I looked toward the front window, saw a barrage of large drops slam against the glass. Nature imitating the thoughts of man, I thought. *Pathetic fallacy,* if I remembered my English classes correctly. *Pathetic* was right. "Of course you can come in," I told my son.

"Are you and Daddy finished with your discussion?" Daphne asked.

"We're finished," I told her, wondering if this was true of our marriage as well.

"Can we watch TV?"

"Sure. Go watch in Mommy's room. Okay?"

"*Mommy's* room?" Harrison asked as the kids disappeared up the stairs.

"I think it's best if you sleep down here until we get everything sorted out," I told him.

He nodded. "Does it make any difference if I tell you that I don't love her, that I'll end it once and for all?"

Does it? "I don't know," I said, thinking of my own affair. *Do I have any right to sit in judgment?* "I don't know."

SIXTY-FIVE

Not much changed during the next two weeks. I kept busy working. Harrison was busy teaching. We alternated driving the kids to and from camp. We ate dinner together every evening. We took great pains to be civil, rarely addressing each other directly. Harrison was still sleeping on the couch.

Tracy and I took turns dropping by our father's house without prior notice, although such visits quickly lost the element of surprise. We'd pull into the driveway to find Elyse waiting at the door, and our father either sleeping, just waking up, or about to lie down. Elyse never left his side, making her the proverbial thorn in ours.

Our father was, by turns, silent, confused, sullen, and most alarming of all, docile. He had moments of lucidity, but they were increasingly few and far between. Had anything I'd said gotten through to him at all?

"When was the last time you saw a doctor?" I asked him during one such visit.

"Your father had a complete physical just last month,"

Elyse answered. "He got a clean bill of health. The doctor said that he's in excellent shape for a man his age."

"Really? Dr. Abramson said everything was okay?"

My father said nothing. The blank look in his eyes said he had no idea.

"Your father is seeing Bryce Carter now," Elyse said.

"Who the hell is Bryce Carter?"

"He's *my* doctor. We saw no point in seeing two different people and having to make two separate trips."

I struggled to digest this latest piece of information. "But you've been going to Dr. Abramson for years," I told my father. "He knows your background, your history. I'm not sure that switching doctors at this stage is such a good idea."

"Nobody asked you," he replied testily.

"But—"

"End of discussion."

Elyse smiled. "You needn't worry so much, Jodi. Your father is all grown up and quite capable of making his own decisions."

"This seems to be more *your* decision than his."

"Nonsense. Vic is very much his own man. Aren't you, darling?"

"Damn right."

Even in his diminished state, it was obvious that my father hated his authority being questioned. It was also obvious that Elyse knew just how to play him.

"Now, don't go getting yourself all agitated," she told him. "I'm sure that Jodi means well. I think you should probably go now," she whispered between barely parted lips. In the next minute, she was leading me to the door. "But, of course, feel free to stop by anytime."

As soon as I got home, mindful of Tracy's earlier chiding, I googled Dr. Bryce Carter.

Amazingly, there were two Bryce Carters in the Toronto area. One was a chartered accountant, which ruled him out. The other was a self-described "wellness practitioner." Not exactly a medical doctor, I thought, deciding that regardless, there was no point challenging Elyse on the subject. Instead, I made a note of it in the journal I'd started keeping. Would this qualify as evidence? I wondered.

Evidence of what?

A few days later, I was at the office when the receptionist poked her head in my door. "Sorry to bother you," she began. "But there's a man calling, demanding to speak to you. He won't give his name, but he's very insistent. I didn't know whether to put him through."

"Put him through," I directed, lifting the phone gingerly to my ear.

I recognized the sound of my father's ragged breathing immediately. "Dad, is that you? What's wrong?"

"You have to do something," he whispered.

"Do something about what?"

"She's insisting I sign the papers. She says that if I don't sign them, she'll leave me. I'll be all alone."

"You won't be alone. You have Tracy. You have me. We'll find another housekeeper."

"She says if I don't sign them, she'll leave," he repeated, as if I hadn't spoken.

"Then let her leave!"

"I can't do that. She'll . . . Oh, no. She's coming. I have to go."

"What do you mean? She'll . . . what? Dad? Dad? Where are you?"

"She's coming. I have to go."

"Dad, wait! Call the police. Dad . . . Dad!"

I hung on to the line until a dial tone replaced the silence.

"Was that your father?" the receptionist asked seconds later, popping back into view. "I didn't recognize his voice."

I don't recognize my father, I thought, but didn't say.

"Should we call the police?" Tracy asked when I told her of the call.

"And say what? They're just going to tell us that this is a domestic issue and that unless Dad calls to report he's being physically abused, there's nothing they can do."

I called the police anyway. They said that it was a domestic issue and that unless my father called to report he was being physically abused, there was nothing they could do.

I made a note of my father's phone call in my journal. More evidence, although I was starting to worry that by the time anyone expressed any interest in such evidence, it would be too late.

Too late for what?

Was I really worried that Elyse was going to harm my father?

This is what I knew: She was intent on him changing his will, no doubt making her the sole beneficiary. And once the house was sold and the deal finalized, she'd collect the cash from that as well. I had little doubt that she'd been medicating my father for months, giving him sedatives and God only knows what other drugs to make him sleepy and easy to control.

What else was she capable of?

Would my father meet the same kind of unfortunate accident as my mother? Would I drop over for one of my surprise visits to find his broken body at the bottom of the stairs? *He was groggy from all the sleeping pills he'd taken,* I could hear Elyse sob to the police. *I warned him so many times to be careful, not to take so many, but he was so stubborn.*

Would they be interested in my evidence then?

I shook my head in dismay. Even if they were, I understood that evidence wasn't proof.

There was still a little something known as reasonable doubt, and there was absolutely *no* doubt in my mind that Elyse would get away with everything.

Including murder.

Had she already?

One down, one to go.

"Knock, knock," a voice said from the doorway. I turned to see Stephanie, resplendent in a neon yellow jumpsuit, a grin stretching from one side of her unnaturally taut face to the other.

A picture formed in my mind of her lips suddenly snapping back into place, like an elastic band, causing her top row of perfect veneers to spew from her mouth like so many Chiclets, and I smiled.

"I have great news," she said.

I waited, the smile freezing on my lips.

She threw her hands up in the air, as if she were sprinkling fistfuls of confetti. "I sold the house!"

SIXTY-SIX

"What do you mean, she sold the house?" Tracy asked me when I called to tell her the news. "I thought it wasn't quite ready yet."

"She got what they call a bully offer."

"What the hell is that?"

"It's when someone makes an offer peremptorily, before other offers can come in."

"Can they do that?"

"They can, and they did. Full asking price. Closing is in thirty days."

"Thirty days? Isn't that kind of fast?"

"Very. But apparently, the buyers have young kids, and they want to be in the house before school starts in the fall."

"Shit."

"Exactly."

"What do we do now?"

I shook my head, wondering how many times we'd asked each other that question over the past months, how many times we'd given the same answer. "I have no idea."

"We can't let her get away with this."

"I don't see how we can stop her."

"You have to talk to Dad."

I couldn't help noticing the change in pronouns. "It won't do any good. You know I've tried."

"Try again."

I tried again.

"I hear congratulations are in order," I told Elyse when she answered the phone.

"Yes," she agreed. "Isn't it wonderful? Apparently, the buyers have had their eye on the house for some time, and . . . well, they made us an offer that we couldn't refuse." She laughed.

"Can I speak to my father?"

"Oh, I'm so sorry. He's resting now. The excitement of the sale . . ."

"Really, Elyse?" I said, in no mood for her games. "You're going to make me surprise you with another visit?"

"Just a minute," she said, all traces of warmth vanishing from her voice. "I'll see if I can get him before he settles down."

"You do that."

"Vic, darling," I heard her call. "Jodi's on the phone, sweetheart. She wants to congratulate you on selling the house."

Two minutes later, I heard him shuffling toward the phone.

"Dad?" I asked when I heard him breathing.

"Yes." His obvious impatience caused the single word to vibrate.

"How are you feeling?"

"Tired."

"Tell her you were just about to lie down," Elyse directed.

"I was just about to lie down."

"Stephanie tells me you sold the house."

"We sold the house," he said.

"Are you sure you want to do that?"

"What do you mean?"

"Are you sure you want to sell the house?"

"Of course you're sure," Elyse told him.

"Of course I'm sure," my father said.

"It's happening awfully fast. Are you sure you've thought this through?"

"You're not questioning your father's judgment, are you?" Elyse asked.

"Just that a thirty-day closing doesn't give you a lot of time to find another place," I offered before my father could take offense.

"Actually," Elyse said. "We may have already found something. A lovely condo on the water. My son—I'm sure you remember Andrew. I know he thinks so highly of you—he stayed in this lovely Airbnb during one of his earlier visits, and he says that the owners might be interested in selling. Failing that," she continued, her smug smile evident through the phone wires, "I'm sure Stephanie will be able to find us something suitable."

"Dad . . ."

"I'm afraid he's gone back to bed. Careful on those stairs, darling," she called out. "Honestly, I don't know what I'm going to do about that man. He's not very steady on his feet these days, and he simply refuses to take the elevator."

"I'm warning you, Elyse," I told her. "If anything happens to my father . . ."

"Goodbye, Jodi. Have a lovely evening."

My phone rang at just after two o'clock that morning.

I was in the middle of an unpleasant dream wherein I was in a dark closet hiding from a serial killer when the cellphone in my pocket rang, giving away my position. It took three rings for me to realize that the sound wasn't emanating from my nightmare but the landline beside my bed. "Hello? Dad?" I said, answering the phone before it could ring again.

"Who's this?" my father asked.

"It's Jodi, Dad. What's wrong?"

"Why are you calling?"

"I didn't call, Dad. You phoned me."

"I did?"

"Yes, Dad. Where are you? Where is Elyse?"

"Elyse is asleep. Why are you phoning?"

"I didn't . . . Are you okay, Dad?"

"I don't want to sell the house."

"Then don't," I said, coming fully awake. "The closing's not for another month. Tell Stephanie you've changed your mind."

"Stephanie?" he asked, as if he didn't know who she was.

"It's okay. I'll tell her."

"You'll tell her?"

"First thing tomorrow. Dad?" I asked, hearing the line go dead. "Shit," I said, plopping down on the side of the bed, letting the phone drop from my hand.

"Jodi?" a voice whispered from the hallway.

I turned toward the sound, saw Harrison standing in the doorway.

"What's going on?" he asked.

"Nothing. It's okay."

"It's not okay," he said, advancing into the room. He was wearing the bottom half of a pair of old pajamas, his chest bare, his hair tousled. "Was that your father? I thought I heard you say 'Dad.'"

I nodded. "Sorry if the phone woke you up."

"I wasn't asleep. The couch isn't the most comfortable . . ." He approached the bed and returned the receiver to its carriage. "Do you want to talk about it?"

"No," I said, a rush of tears cascading down my cheeks. What was there to say?

He sank down on the bed beside me. "What can I do?"

"Nothing. There's nothing anybody can do."

"I can hold you," he said, reaching for me. "If you let me . . ."

I'm embarrassed to admit that at that moment, my husband's arms around me was what I wanted more than anything in the world.

I let him.

SIXTY-SEVEN

The final phone call came ten days later.

It was just after eleven o'clock, and Harrison and I were getting ready for bed. Yes, we were back to sleeping in the same bed, although we had yet to make love. Harrison hadn't tried to do more than just hold me, and truthfully, I wasn't sure what I would do if he did.

My feelings for him were all over the map: I hated him; I loved him; I wanted him gone; I wanted him inside me; he was a liar and a cheat; he was the father of my children.

It was that fact that gave me the most pause.

Did I really want to deprive my children of the father they loved? A father who, despite his many faults, truly loved them, and despite his grumblings, had always been there for them?

Unlike *my* father.

Did my father love me? I wondered constantly. Had he *ever* loved me?

Try as I might, and I've racked my brain trying to recall a single instance when he might have uttered those

words, I'm forced to admit that I can't remember any.
"Use your words," I used to tell my children. My father
used a lot of words. "I love you" was simply not a part
of his vocabulary.

Had I ever told my father that I loved *him*? Maybe
once, long ago, probably expecting—hoping—I'd hear it
back. *Did* I love him? Tracy had asked me that, and
I hadn't been able to come up with a response that satis-
fied either of us. Certainly, I *wanted* to love my father.
More likely, I felt an *obligation* to love him. He'd given
me life after all, and had been a fierce presence in that life
for more than forty years. The least I owed him, now that
he was reduced to a mere shadow of his former self, was
my loyalty. Whether I loved him or not, whether he loved
me or not, I considered it my duty to protect him.

"Shit," I muttered when the phone rang that night.
"Here we go again."

It had been over a week since my father's last call, over
a week since my last "surprise" visit to his home.

"You don't have to answer it," Harrison said, although
we both knew that option was out of the question.

I took a deep breath and picked up the receiver. "Dad?"

"Help me!" my father cried.

"Oh, God. What's happening?"

"You have to help me."

"Where's Elyse?"

"She was so angry. She . . . she threatened . . ."

"She threatened you? Please, Dad. Call nine-one-one!"

"No! Not the police!"

"Dad, listen to me . . ."

"You have to come over. I'm begging you!"

"Okay. Okay," I told him. "I'll be right there."

"Hurry!"

"You can't be serious," Harrison said as I dropped the phone and ran to the closet. "You can't actually be thinking of going over there at this hour."

"I have to. He's desperate."

"Then call the police."

"And say what?" I asked, pulling a pair of jeans over my nightshirt.

"Anything!" Harrison responded.

I nodded, grabbing my purse and racing for the stairs. "I don't have time. *You* call them."

"For God's sake, be careful," he called after me.

The drive to my father's house was pretty much a blur. I sped the whole way, half hoping that a cop would spot me careening through the streets, pull me over, and insist on accompanying me to my father's house to check out my story.

And discover what?

A belligerent and confused old man with no memory of having called his daughter, let alone pleading for her help?

A seemingly concerned and caring wife apologizing for her husband's erratic behavior and his daughter's unfortunate overreaction?

In any event, no one stopped me. I pulled into my father's driveway, and jumped out of the car, hurrying toward the front door, wondering what the hell I was walking into.

The house was in darkness. I rang the doorbell repeatedly, then knocked—loud and hard—when nobody answered.

In frustration, I kicked at the door, and to my shock, it fell open.

"Dad?" I called, stepping gingerly into the front hall, the sound of my breathing bouncing off the walls. "Dad, where are you?"

I heard moaning coming from the stairway and reached for the switch on the wall next to the door, flipping on the overhead light.

The first thing I saw was the body at the bottom of the stairs.

"Oh, my God!" I cried, thinking immediately of my mother, and deciding that this must be another one of the crazy dreams I'd been having lately. This couldn't happen twice, I assured myself. *This can't be happening at all.*

The moaning grew louder, a low wail that filled every inch of the wide hall. My eyes warily followed the sound to the top of the landing.

My father was sitting on the floor at the top of the stairs, clinging to the railing, his pajama-clad body folded in on itself, his eyes staring blankly into space.

I moved forward, pushing one reluctant foot in front of the other, as if I were wading through a heavy syrup. *This isn't happening. Wake up, damn it! Wake up!*

"Is she dead?" my father asked as I knelt beside the body.

I knew even before my fingers reached out to feel for the pulse in Elyse's outstretched arm that she was gone. Her head was twisted horribly to one side, her neck obviously broken, her open eyes seeing only death.

"How . . . what . . . ?" I began, unable to complete a thought, let alone a sentence.

"Is she dead?" my father repeated.

"Yes," I heard myself say, my eyes shooting toward his. "Are you all right?"

"I had no choice," my father was muttering as I mounted the stairs. "She gave me no choice."

I sat down beside him, surrounded him with my arms, hugged him tightly to my side, feeling his bony frame beneath the soft cotton of his pajamas.

"Why are you here?" he asked suddenly. "Where's Tracy?"

I was too tired, too numb, to be offended. "You called *me*, Dad."

"I did?"

"What the hell happened?"

He shook his head, as if trying to make sense of my question. "She was taking too long to die," he said finally.

"What?"

"She should have died years ago," he continued. "But she kept hanging on, refusing to give in."

"What are you talking about?"

"I looked after her all those years. Elyse said I deserved a bit of happiness."

Now I was the one struggling to make sense of what he was saying, what I was hearing. "I don't understand. Are you talking about Mom?"

"Tracy?"

"No, Dad. It's Jodi. Are you saying that Elyse had something to do with Mom's death? That you've been protecting her all this time? That . . . that she killed Mom?"

"She's been putting drugs in my food," he said, snapping back into the present. "I told her I was on to her, that I knew she was just after my money. I told her to get out. She got so angry. She said she'd go to the police, tell them . . ."

I felt my entire body start to tremble. "Tell them . . . what?"

"That it was me! That I was the one who dragged Audrey out of bed and carried her to the stairs, as if I could have managed it alone . . ."

My arms fell from around my father's torso to hang limply at my sides. My head was spinning, my mind incapable of absorbing the words I was hearing. "You're saying that the two of you . . ."

"What kind of life did your mother have?" he demanded angrily. "What kind of life did *I* have?"

My mind shook with distant echoes. I heard my parents screaming at each other down the upstairs hall—*Go ahead! Hit me again, you miserable bastard!*—felt the thud of my mother's body hitting the floor after he struck her a second time.

"No!" I said, trying to convince myself that my father wasn't in his right mind, that he was confused by all the drugs Elyse had been feeding him, that he had no idea what he was saying.

But try as I might to deny it, deep down I knew the truth: that my father was more than capable of such violence, that with Elyse's help, he had callously tossed my mother down a flight of stairs when he tired of playing nursemaid, that he'd pushed Elyse to her death when he tired of her manipulations and she threatened to go to the police.

"Oh, God," I cried, as the sound of police sirens drew near.

"What are you crying about?" my father demanded angrily as car doors slammed outside, and police came bursting through the front door. "Where's Tracy?"

—SIXTY-EIGHT—

"Wow," I said, looking around the crowded bookstore. "Standing room only. Impressive."

"Pretty amazing," Tracy agreed.

"There must be over a hundred people here."

"It's a good book."

"It is," I agreed.

"Are you okay?" she asked. "You look a little nervous."

"Just excited," I told her. "I'm fine."

And I was.

Almost two years have passed since the events of that July night. Two years of confusion and tears and change, some major, some momentous.

My father is dead, having succumbed to the ravages of pancreatic cancer five months ago. Even though some might say that he got what he deserved, I'm not sure I would wish that particular fate on anyone. He might have preferred a helpful push down a flight of stairs to the slow, painful exit he endured.

Before he went into hospice care at Princess Margaret Cancer Centre, he'd been living in a nursing home, the powers that be having declined to lay charges in the death of my mother, referencing his obviously confused mental state and a lack of any real evidence. As for Elyse, my father claimed to have acted in self-defense—insisting that *she* was the one who'd attacked *him*—and indeed, all the "evidence" I'd been collecting over the past months seemed to support that claim, as did my earlier visit to police headquarters. Combined with my father's age and suspect competence, it was decided that there would be little point in trying to prosecute him.

I'm not so sure I agree with that decision.

Old, yes. Confused, maybe. Incompetent, never.

They called me from the hospital the day he died to inform me that he likely wouldn't last the night, and I went down and sat beside his bed. Tracy declined to accompany me, citing her well-known aversion to hospitals. I was neither surprised nor disappointed. I'm still not entirely sure why *I* bothered going.

Except, of course, despite everything, the man was still my father.

So, maybe it was to give him one last chance to be one, to see him acknowledge my presence with a smile, to hear him say my name.

Jodi.

Of course he didn't.

And again, I was neither disappointed nor surprised.

I still feel the occasional stab of guilt. I'm the one who brought Elyse into our lives, after all. Maybe if I hadn't, things would have turned out very differently. My mother and Elyse might still be alive. My father wouldn't be a murderer.

The day after he died, I quit my job at Dundas Real Estate. Our father's will left Tracy and me financially independent, allowing me to take some much-needed time for myself, to decide what I really wanted to do. Which, it didn't take me long to discover, involved going back to school to become an interior designer. Classes start in the fall. In the meantime, I've happily accepted my sister's invitation to accompany her on a monthlong tour of Europe.

The kids will be spending the summer with their father in Prince Edward County. Yes, we're divorced. The final nail in the coffin that contained our marriage was his reluctance to abandon his plans regarding Prince Edward County that summer. One moment of hesitation was all it took to convince me that our marriage was over and done. *Maroon Sky* was released last spring and was a modest critical and commercial success. Hopefully, it won't be another decade before his next novel. But hey, it's no longer my concern. He's living with Wren now, and she's welcome to him.

I know. It took me long enough.

As for Roger McAdams, aka Andrew Woodley, we tried contacting him after Elyse's death, but he was nowhere to be found under either name. He simply vanished, along with his profile on Facebook, and nobody has heard from him since. Was he really Elyse's son? Her accomplice? Maybe even her lover?

Who knows?

Who cares?

He's gone.

"See anyone you know?" Tracy asked, surveying the ever-increasing crowd.

My eyes scanned the room. "Not a soul," I said gratefully, checking my watch. "Almost seven o'clock."

A representative from the publishing house approached my sister. "Are you ready?" she asked.

Tracy swiveled toward me. She was wearing a gorgeous blush-pink cotton shirtdress from Victoria Beckham that she had recently purchased for this event. "How do I look?"

"Like the best-dressed, bestselling author in town," I told her honestly.

"You look pretty stylish yourself," she said.

I was wearing the blue Chanel suit that she'd bought me when sales of her novel started going through the roof. "Thanks to you."

"Told you what happened had all the elements of a good mystery novel," Tracy said as the host of the event approached the podium and leaned into the mic.

"Ladies and gentlemen," she announced, looking over the large crowd, "it's so gratifying to see so many of you here tonight. We feel extremely privileged to have Tracy Dundas here to read from her bestselling novel, *The Housekeeper*, before she embarks on her sold-out European tour. And great news—she tells me she's almost finished her next novel."

There was a spontaneous burst of applause from the audience.

"Of course, Tracy will be signing autographs afterward, and we'll be handing out pieces of paper on which to write your names, should you want your copy personalized. And now, without further delay, please welcome the author of the number one *New York Times* bestseller, *The Housekeeper* . . . Tracy Dundas."

"Knock 'em dead," I said.

She stopped, spun around, and grabbed my hands. "I love you, you know," she said.

"I know," I said gratefully. "I love you, too."

ACKNOWLEDGMENTS

Unbelievably, *The Housekeeper* is my thirtieth novel. I hadn't intended to write another book so soon after *Cul-de-sac*, but then along came the pandemic. With traveling and normal socializing no longer options, I found myself with nothing to do. Initially, this was okay, as I had too much anxiety and too little focus to do much of anything. I could barely read a book, let alone write one. But as the months wore on, an idea started forming, and *The Housekeeper* is the result. And because there were no interruptions, I was able to finish the book in under five months. It just poured out of me! Would that all books were so easy!

What hasn't changed since the pandemic is the long list of people to thank for their contributions in bringing this book to life, starting with my first readers: Larry Mirkin, Beverley Slopen, and Robin Stone. Once again, their critiques were beyond valuable. Thanks to my fabulous agent at WME, Tracy Fisher, and her assistant, Sam Birmingham, for their tireless work on my behalf. A big thank-you to my editor, Anne Speyer, for her sharp eye and kind words, and to the rest of the production crew at Ballantine: Jesse Shuman, Jennifer Hershey, Kim Hovey, Kara Welsh, Derek Walls, Dennis Ambrose, Steve Messina, Courtney Mocklow, and Emma Thomasch. Thank you also to everyone at Doubleday Canada: Kristin Cochrane, Val Gow, Kaitlin Smith, Robin Thomas, Christina Vecchiato, Maria Golikova, Martha Leonard, and my gracious Canadian editor, Amy Black. I also want to thank my publishers and translators in various countries throughout the world for the terrific job they do in translating and promoting my books. Long may our association continue.

A very special thank-you to my family and friends, especially my ever-supportive husband of forty-eight years as of January 11, 2022. I don't think it's always easy being married to me, and I thank you for sticking it out and for being the smartest and most honorable man I've ever known.

Thank you to my gorgeous daughters, Shannon and Annie, for being the really wonderful young women they've turned out to be. (It's Shannon who does such a bang-up job with my social media.) And a shout-out to the men in their lives—Annie's husband, Courtney, and Shannon's boyfriend, Eric (whom she met while out for a walk during the early days of the pandemic and has been with ever since). And of course, to the two most precious grandchildren that ever lived, Hayden and Skylar, my very own "cupcakes of cuteness," for bringing such joy into my life as well as helping me to create believable youngsters for my books.

Thank you to my sister-in-law, Bessie, who provided me with much-needed information as to what's involved in the buying and selling of real estate in Toronto. Hopefully, I got everything right. If not, the fault is mine, not hers.

Thank you to my sister, Renee, with whom I've gone for hours-long walks almost daily during this prolonged COVID nightmare. I look forward to continuing these walks even after things—fingers crossed—return to normal.

Thank you to Corinne Assayag, the woman who designed and oversees my website. We've been together a very long time now, and while we live on different coasts and don't get to see each other much, her continuing support means the world to me.

And to my very own housekeeper, Mary, who keeps me fed and my condo clean. Thank God you're back!

@ Warren Seyffert

JOY FIELDING is the *New York Times* bestselling author of *Cul-de-sac*, *All the Wrong Places*, *The Bad Daughter*, *She's Not There*, *Someone Is Watching*, *Charley's Web*, *Heartstopper*, *Mad River Road*, *See Jane Run*, and other acclaimed novels. She divides her time between Toronto, Ontario, and Palm Beach, Florida.

joyfielding.com
Twitter: @joyfielding
Instagram: @fieldingjoy
Find Joy Fielding on Facebook